Michelle Smart's love when she was a baby a in her cot. A voracious found her love of romance established when she stumbled across her first Mills & Boon book at the age of twelve. She's been reading them—and writing them—ever since. Michelle lives in Northamptonshire, England, with her husband and two young Smarties.

Lorraine Hall is a part-time hermit and full-time writer. She was born with an old soul and her head in the clouds—which, it turns out, is the perfect combination for spending her days creating thunderous alpha heroes and the fierce, determined heroines who win their hearts. She lives in a potentially haunted house with her soulmate and a rumbustious band of hermits in training. When she's not writing romance, she's reading it.

Also by Michelle Smart

Resisting the Bossy Billionaire
Spaniard's Shock Heirs

The Diamond Club collection

Heir Ultimatum

Greek Rivals miniseries

Forgotten Greek Proposal

Also by Lorraine Hall

A Wedding Between Enemies
Pregnant, Stolen, Wed

Work Wives to Billionaires' Wives collection

The Bride Wore Revenge

Discover more at millsandboon.co.uk.

CRAVE ME

MICHELLE SMART

LORRAINE HALL

MILLS & BOON

All rights reserved including the right of reproduction in whole or in part in any form. This edition is published by arrangement with Harlequin Enterprises ULC.

This is a work of fiction. Names, characters, places, locations and incidents are purely fictional and bear no relationship to any real life individuals, living or dead, or to any actual places, business establishments, locations, events or incidents. Any resemblance is entirely coincidental.

Without limiting the author's and publisher's exclusive rights, any unauthorised use of this publication to train generative artificial intelligence (AI) technologies is expressly prohibited. HarperCollins also exercise their rights under Article 4(3) of the Digital Single Market Directive 2019/790 and expressly reserve this publication from the text and data mining exception.

® and TM are trademarks owned and used by the trademark owner and/or its licensee. Trademarks marked with ® are registered with the United Kingdom Patent Office and/or the Office for Harmonisation in the Internal Market and in other countries.

First published in Great Britain 2025
by Mills & Boon, an imprint of HarperCollins*Publishers* Ltd,
1 London Bridge Street, London, SE1 9GF

www.harpercollins.co.uk

HarperCollins*Publishers*, Macken House, 39/40 Mayor Street Upper, Dublin 1, D01 C9W8, Ireland

Crave Me © 2025 Harlequin Enterprises ULC

His Pregnant Enemy Bride © 2025 Michelle Smart

Unwrapping His Forbidden Assistant © 2025 Lorraine Hall

ISBN: 978-0-263-34479-0

09/25

This book contains FSC™ certified paper
and other controlled sources to ensure responsible forest management.

For more information visit www.harpercollins.co.uk/green.

Printed and Bound in the UK using 100% Renewable Electricity
at CPI Group (UK) Ltd, Croydon, CR0 4YY

HIS PREGNANT ENEMY BRIDE

MICHELLE SMART

MILLS & BOON

CHAPTER ONE

LYDIA ANTONIADIS PEERED intently through the binoculars she'd borrowed from a deckhand, watching the supply boat heading in the direction of Kos. She'd caught a fleeting glance at a figure slipping below deck, which in itself was not in the least strange, but what was strange was that the figure bore a strong resemblance to Lucie Burton. But it couldn't be Lucie because Lucie was marrying Lydia's brother the next day on Sephone and so definitely wouldn't be sailing away from the island. It must have been a trick of the mind. After all, the distance between the yacht Lydia stood on the sundeck of and the supply boat was immense.

Definitely a mind trick, she assured herself again before training the binoculars on Sephone itself. The island's gorgeous multiple-domed villa was gleaming under the rising sun, and she slowly scanned the faces in its front grounds. The only ones she recognised were the household staff, which wasn't really surprising considering it was barely nine a.m. They all looked stressed, which wasn't surprising either considering hundreds of people were about to descend on the island for the wedding. Most would be there before nightfall.

Draining her glass of water, she looked out again over

the Aegean. More vessels had appeared since she'd become distracted by the figure on the supply boat.

'You're up early, *baba*.'

Lydia flinched but didn't drop the binoculars. 'I didn't hear you sneak up on me.'

'I was hardly sneaking,' her mother said drily, standing beside her at the balustrade. 'What's got you so enraptured?'

'Nothing. Just looking to see if I recognise any of the yachts heading this way.'

'And?'

'Too far away to tell. Looks like we'll be the third party to arrive.' There were two superyachts already anchored, and they sailed past them, the crew scurrying around preparing to dock at the small harbour that could accommodate only two vessels. Lydia's brother refused to dredge the shoreline of his precious island to accommodate more.

'Are any of *them* here yet?'

Them. Meaning the Tsalikis.

Lydia's fingers tightened but her voice remained steady. 'No.'

'Good. I couldn't face seeing any of them before my breakfast has been digested. Have you eaten?'

'I'll get something later.' Her stomach was so tightly knotted she'd struggled to get water into it.

'You need to eat.'

'Don't fuss. I'm fine.'

'None of us are fine, *baba*, but we all need to eat. It's going to be a long couple of days and we need to keep our strength up.'

Lydia nodded automatically. Since their lives had

imploded her mother had gone into self-preservation mode with a steely smile and a steelier determination that whatever happened to the family business and fortune, the family itself would survive. Part of this survival came in the form of food. Her mother had always been a feeder but in recent months, Lydia had been unable to walk through the front door without having food thrust in her face. What they had travelled to Sephone for, though, was going to push her mother's steely smile to the limit: a marriage between Lydia's brother Thanasis and Lucie Burton, the stepdaughter of their enemy Georgios Tsaliki. For the next three days, with the world's press acting as witnesses, they were going to break bread, smile, dance and laugh with their heinous sworn enemy and his equally heinous family. This wedding was the Antoniadises' last chance to save their business and save themselves from destitution.

Soon, their yacht was moored beside Thanasis's and it was time to disembark and play their parts in the performance of the century. With her father striding along the jetty as if he'd spent his whole lifetime waiting impatiently for this wedding and her mother striding purposefully with her steely smile fixed firmly in place, Lydia followed behind them, attempting her own steely smile and trying her hardest not to think that the one thing that could actually break her mother lay nestled in her stomach.

Alexis Tsaliki read the message Thanasis Antoniadis had sent him for a third time, spat a curse, and pressed the intercom. 'Get the jet ski out for me. Now.'

Jumping out of bed, he threw shorts, a T-shirt and a

pair of running shoes on, then raced out of his yacht's master cabin and banged on his father's door. His stomach curdled when his stepmother opened it but there was no time for unpleasantries. 'Where is he?'

'Showering. What's wrong?'

He pushed past her without answering and banged on the bathroom door. 'Dad, get out of there. We need to talk.'

'What's wrong?' his stepmother asked again.

Not bothering to hide the loathing he usually masked for the sake of family harmony, he said tightly, 'Your daughter.' Then he banged even louder on the bathroom door.

'Lucie? What's happened?'

'Dad!' he shouted. 'We need to talk right now.'

The bathroom door opened and Alexis was engulfed in a cloud of steam and the unedifying sight of his father dripping wet from the shower he'd been enjoying. 'What's wrong?'

'Lucie knows everything. She's gone. The wedding's off.'

His father seemed to deflate before his eyes.

'What do you mean *she's gone*?' Rebecca demanded in a high voice. 'How can she be *gone*?'

One of his siblings—and Alexis had many siblings—having heard the commotion, barged into the cabin, quickly followed by another and another and another until it seemed like every Tsaliki in existence was in the cabin shouting over each other, all throwing panicked questions at him.

'That's all I know!' he roared over the noise. 'Everyone get dressed. We'll be anchoring soon and you can take the tender over, but I'm taking the jet ski there now so I can find out exactly what's going on and see if I can find Lucie and talk some sense into her.'

Not giving them the chance to argue, he elbowed his way out of the cabin.

The jet ski was ready for him. Throwing himself on it, he turned the engine on and, not caring that he wore no life jacket, set off at top speed to Sephone.

Lydia saw the figure speeding to the island on the jet ski before anyone else. No trickery caused by distance could discount what the thumping of her heart was telling her, and she gripped her forearms and swallowed back a swell of nausea that was different from the nausea already rolling in her stomach.

'It will be okay, *baba*,' her father said, noticing the change in her demeanour and wrapping a trembling arm around her. Kissing the top of her head, he whispered, 'I promise, everything will be okay.'

She leaned into him, fighting the threatening tears and fighting the growing urge to open her lungs and vocal cords and just scream; scream until her throat was raw and she had no breath left to give.

'Thanasis will fix it,' her father added, as if Lydia's brother were a god amongst mortals and could bend the world to his whim.

'How?' she whispered dully. 'Lucie will never marry him now. It's over. Everything's over.'

She looked at her mother slumped on the fine white sand, the steely smile wiped off her face, her expression that of utter despair. Looked at her brother sitting on the same rock he'd been propped on when he'd explained the situation to them, her mighty big brother who always had the answer to everything sitting there as if all his stuffing had been knocked out of him. And then she glanced again at the figure on the jet ski closing in on the beach.

Another swell of nausea rose from the pit of her stomach followed by a swell of anguished fury and, without thinking of what she was doing, she wrenched herself out of her father's comforting hold and rounded on her brother.

'What the hell were you thinking, lying to Lucie like that?'

His dull eyes barely focussed on hers. His confession had left him spent.

Nearly two weeks ago, Lucie had been in a car crash that had seen her hospitalised for days with a major head injury. Thanasis had brought her to his private island to recover. It had made sense. Sephone was a tranquil Greek paradise and their wedding was being held there. Unbeknownst to Lydia, her parents and the rest of the world, Lucie's accident had been caused after she'd called the wedding off and fled Thanasis's Athens apartment. Unbeknownst to them all too, Lucie's head injury had caused an amnesia. She'd forgotten everything about the wedding, including the huge row that had seen her flee from Thanasis. Between them, Thanasis, Lucie's mother, stepfather and the oldest of her stepbrothers, Alexis, had conspired to make Lucie believe that, far from hating each other, she and Thanasis had fallen in love for real and not just as a game being played out for the sake of their respective family businesses' survival.

'Lydia, don't,' her mother said tiredly. 'Your brother is suffering enough.'

Usually her mother's warning would be enough to make Lydia shut up, but in that moment too many emotions were crowding in her head and chest, and her heart was thrashing too wildly at the jet ski figure closing in on them for her to listen or think clearly.

'*He's* suffering?' she screamed. 'Well, I'm glad! It serves him right! Lucie did *nothing* to deserve being treated like that.' Her back to the sea, she threw her hands on her hips to stop them lashing out at her zombified brother. 'She gave up her home and career to save our business and you did *that* to her?'

Because the engagement and planned wedding had never been real. Her father's uncivil war with his old friend and former business partner turned enemy, Georgios Tsaliki, had escalated to the degree that Georgios had sabotaged the engines of their cargo fleet and Lydia's father had retaliated by having millions of cockroaches and rats let loose in Georgios's own fleet. What had been treated in the press as an amusing rivalry between two rival shipping magnates had overnight become a scandal that had ballooned as old dirty tricks between them were either brought to light or rehashed with a brand-new slant. The scandal had led to Antoniadis Shipping's main investors threatening to pull their money. If acted on, Antoniadis Shipping would go bankrupt.

Tsaliki Shipping hadn't gone unscathed either. Whilst not fatally wounded like the Antoniadises were close to being, its share prices had plummeted and, with no sign of recovery on the horizon, it was agreed that the only way to manage the situation and prove that the next generation were now in charge and that all the bad blood between the two families was over, was through marriage. Petros Antoniadis's son Thanasis would marry Georgios Tsaliki's beloved stepdaughter Lucie.

Except it had been a match made in hell. Thanasis had been determined to hate Lucie and she in turn had grown to despise him.

Poor Lucie had thought Thanasis's love for her was true and had opened her heart to him.

Lydia didn't have to stretch her imagination very far to imagine how devastated Lucie must have felt to learn the truth and learn that she'd been so cruelly played and her injury weaponised against her.

'He did what he had to do to save us all,' her mother defended.

'Well, he didn't save us, did he?' she cried. 'My honourable brother who never lies…' She shook her head in disgust. 'You men, you're all the same. You lie and you lie and you lie, and now you have the nerve to sit there looking all injured and sorry for yourself? You caused this, Thanasis. *You.* If you'd bothered to take me into your confidence instead of listening to that bastard Alexis, I would have told you not to do it. I would have told you to level with her and now look what we're left with!'

'I will find her and I will bring her back here. She will listen to me.'

The voice had come from behind her, its impact freezing her on the spot.

He'd reached them.

Like synchronised meerkats, her mother, brother and father all looked over her shoulder.

Lydia wasn't sure if time really did stand still or if the roar of blood in her head made it seem that way, but in the time it took her to turn to face him, no one spoke.

She looked at the man she'd last seen in the flesh naked, and came within a breath of vomiting on the spot. Summoning every ounce of her strength, she raised herself as tall as she could draw her short, curvy figure and crossed her arms. Then and only then did she meet the stare that had once melted her bones, and transferred all her anguish and loathing to him. 'You will leave her alone.'

The blue-grey eyes held hers for the beat of a moment before snapping away from her. 'Where is she?'

'Gone,' Thanasis replied in the same dull tone.

'Where? How did she find out? Did her memories come back?'

'I told her.'

'You...' The full, sensuous lips that had kissed Lydia senseless opened and closed as Alexis Tsaliki's handsome face contorted in disbelief. 'You told her? What the...?'

'She needed to know.'

'No, she needed to damn well marry you! Have you lost your mind?'

'Yes.'

'Where is she?'

No one answered. Lydia thought of the supply boat heading towards Kos and the figure she'd seen slip below deck and said, 'Wherever she's gone, it doesn't matter. She doesn't want to marry Thanasis and that's the end of it.'

He didn't even look at her. 'Do you see all those yachts entering your waters, Thanasis? They are your guests. Your wedding guests. The press are on their way here too. If we don't get her back right now it will be too late.'

'It's already too late,' Lydia spat. 'Lucie doesn't want to marry him and I don't blame her.'

It was as if her voice didn't exist to his ears. His attention still on Thanasis, he said, 'I can think of a few places she would go. I'll get people on it. If you can—'

'No.' Thanasis's inertia lifted off him like a blanket as he rose to his feet. 'No. No search parties. We leave her alone. That's all she wants.'

'What's the matter with you? Who cares what she—?'

A roar cut Alexis's words off and then a split-second later he was on his back. Another split-second later and Thanasis was on top of him, his fist raised to land another punch, but this time Alexis was prepared and before Lydia could even blink, he'd flipped Thanasis onto his back, his own fist raised.

It was the scream that stopped Alexis from slamming his fist into Thanasis's face as the bastard deserved.

Breathing heavily, he pulled himself off him, wiped the blood seeping out of his lip with his thumb, and dusted himself down as he cast a disdainful eye over all the Antoniadises…except one. The one whose scream had stopped him giving as good as he'd been given.

'You're all finished. You understand that, yes? Everything you have…' He snapped his fingers together. 'In weeks it will all be gone. The losses my family have suffered will take time for me to recoup but I *will* recoup them, whereas you will have nothing to build back from because it will all be dust, and you will only have yourselves to blame.'

'And you,' said the voice he most hated, the voice whose scream had stopped him in his tracks. 'We will have you to blame too, and every member of your family that chose to lie and deceive a woman when she was at her most vulnerable. I don't know how you sleep at night.'

He tuned out the inflection of tone that suggested the speaker was talking about more than his stepsister. 'My conscience is clear,' he said tightly.

'That's because you don't actually have a conscience... Oh, look, here comes your family. How delightful. Is that really all the Tsaliki spawn squeezed on that tender? You should tell them to be careful—all those egos in one boat could make it capsize.'

Alexis took a long breath through his nose before fixing Lydia with a swift warning stare. 'Unless you want to lose any hope of salvaging something from this mess, I suggest you watch what you say about my family.'

She laughed. 'Or what? You'll bankrupt us? Those wheels will be turning as soon as the news breaks. We're finished, remember?'

'Damage limitation might buy you some time...' There was a tap on his shoulder. He turned to find Elektra Antoniadis's lined face gazing up at him.

He could almost feel sorry for the Antoniadis matriarch. Possibly he would have done if she hadn't been looking at him with such loathing.

'Threaten my daughter again and I will personally see to it that you never father children.'

He gave a bark of laughter. 'I didn't threaten your daughter, I warned her, in the spirit of friendship, not to use that cutting tongue of hers to slander my family. You still have time to prepare for damage limitation and I would have thought you would want me on side when you launch it—after all, you already know to your cost that my family makes a very bad enemy.'

The older woman didn't even blink, turning her long nose in the air and saying, 'More threats. We don't need or want your help or your *friendship*, and if my daughter chooses to use her cutting tongue to speak the truth about a family of degenerates then all I can say to that is that I wholeheartedly support her. Now come, *baba*. We have some damage limitation to be getting on with.'

To Alexis's surprise, Thanasis and his father had already walked away without him even noticing, and then his heart sank when Lydia shook her head and blew out the fringe from her eyes. 'I'll catch up with you— I've got some people I need to practise sharpening my tongue on.'

'Okay. Just don't get cut yourself.' Elektra eyed Alexis as she said that, then gave her daughter a kiss before hurrying after the two Antoniadis men.

Left alone with the one person he'd planned to actively avoid for the whole of his time spent on this damned island, Alexis clenched his jaw and kept his gaze fixed on the tender carrying his family across the sea to the jetty. 'You've obviously got something on your mind so whatever you've got to say to me, get it over with,' he said roughly. 'I've got my own damage limitation to be getting on with.'

'I'm pregnant.'

Her words didn't so much hang in the air as swing on a giant Newton's cradle, the silver balls knocking together to create a sudden deafening roar in his head.

'Say that again,' he dragged out.

'I'm pregnant.'

His chest tightened into an ice-cold ball. The pendulum swung again. Slowly, Alexis turned his head to face the woman standing beside him.

Her stare, what he could see of it beneath her enormous blonde fringe, was fixed ahead at the sea, her chin lifted, a picture of what would be serenity if not for the tremors racking her shoulders.

'You…' He had to swallow to speak. 'You are certain?'

'I had my first scan last week.'

'How…? Why…?' It was like he'd forgotten how to talk. 'Why have you waited all this time to tell me?'

'I wasn't going to tell you until the baby was born but Lucie running away changes everything. My job pays a pittance and my family are on the verge of bankruptcy so there is no way I can support the baby on my own now.'

There was a shout in the distance. He barely heard it, would have tuned it out completely if Lydia's stare hadn't flickered over to the direction it had come from. 'Your family are here. You should go to them. We can talk later. Don't mention the baby to anyone—I think everyone's got enough to be stressed about today. We can tell everyone once we're married.'

He'd barely picked his jaw up when the hazel eyes

he'd never wanted to lock stares with again landed on him. 'I'm sorry, Alexis, but I won't have my child born into poverty. I need you to marry me.'

Her words had barely sunk in when she'd walked away and disappeared into the surrounding trees.

CHAPTER TWO

ONLY WHEN SHE was quite sure that she was hidden amongst the trees did Lydia put a hand to a trunk to steady herself and heave up all the water she'd consumed that morning. Perspiration had broken out all over her skin but she had nothing to blot her face with.

She was shaking, inside and out.

She'd known within a week of her night with Alexis that she'd conceived, known it before her period had failed to arrive. She hadn't told a soul outside the medical profession, had kept it a tightly held secret in her heart. A terrifying and yet miraculous secret. Terrifying because of how her family were going to react when they learned the identity of the father.

In the last six months or so Lydia had watched her parents age before her eyes, watched her father be removed from the company he'd founded and her brother installed in his place, and been subjected to a level of press intrusion she couldn't even bring herself to wish on the Tsalikis. The stress on everyone had been intolerable and she'd had no means to help, could only watch despairingly as her happy family began to disintegrate under the strain of it all.

She'd known the only way their family could rise before the business became ashes had been through forming a truce with the Tsalikis, something her parents had reacted to with fury when she'd suggested it. Her brother though... Thanasis had taken the idea with his usual thoughtful consideration. A seed had been planted. All she'd needed to do, so she'd figured, was plant another seed. The question had been how to plant that seed without her family finding out. The Greek shipping world was a world where nothing stayed secret. There was no way she could waltz into Tsaliki Shipping's headquarters and ask for a meeting without her parents finding out before she'd left the building. Even an innocuous email would be leaked, and so Lydia had dressed up in a nineteen-sixties-style silver mini dress and knee-high heeled boots, and taken herself to Alexis Tsaliki's favourite nightclub, the place he was regularly pictured spending his Friday nights.

Memories were funny things, she thought as she tried to breathe her body back under control. Some events passed and you looked back on them hardly able to remember a thing that had happened. With other events, every minute—*every second*—became etched in the memory...

Lydia had been to Athens' most exclusive nightclub only once before, years ago, for a friend's twenty-first birthday party. As with the first time, she climbed the wide, rounded stairs to the VIP section. This time she climbed them alone, and when she passed through the roped barrier, it was to a booth reserved for one. She'd used half her month's earnings to pay for this booth.

She gave it exactly fifteen minutes before carrying

her champagne onto the dancefloor. Lydia loved dancing, but that night the only thing she had in mind was attracting Alexis Tsaliki's attention, and so she moved to the music keeping her stare fixed on the club's most private booth, the one most hidden in the shadows, where a tall, well-built man with perfectly quiffed hair so dark it was almost black was holding court with a harem of sycophants hanging onto his every word. Lydia would bet every woman at that table's skirt was shorter than her own, and she'd gone as short as she dared without giving both her parents a heart attack. If she wanted to attract his attention, she needed to look the part.

As she'd known would eventually happen, the eyes of the face she only knew from a distance drifted past her and then zoomed back. Their gazes locked. A flicker of recognition flared.

She raised her glass, smiled, and then sashayed off the dancefloor back to her booth.

Barely two minutes later, he slid into the booth beside her.

'Lydia Antoniadis,' he said, spreading out his long arms to rest along the top of the booth, taking a third of the available space. His cologne, a deliciously exotic scent that brought to mind untamed jungles, filled the rest of it.

'Alexis Tsaliki,' she replied with a sweet smile, refusing to be intimidated. But, wow, in person the man was even bigger than he'd looked from a distance, even taller and broader than her brother.

'And to what do I owe this pleasure?'

'Buy me a drink and I'll tell you.'

Blue-grey eyes that made her think of winter skies

and yet weren't in the slightest bit cold narrowed almost imperceptibly before he beckoned a waitress and ordered two glasses of champagne.

'So, Lydia Antoniadis,' he said, settling back again and fixing his stare back on her. 'Tell me why the youngest member of the family at war with my family is here alone in my hunting ground.'

She gave another sweet smile. 'Catching my prey, of course.'

He leaned his face closer to hers, and what a face it was; not a single picture she'd seen of him over the years doing him the slightest bit of justice despite the camera loving him. 'And for what reason do you want to catch me, Lydia Antoniadis?'

'To ask you, Alexis Tsaliki, to consider a truce.'

The beautiful eyes narrowed. 'Now why,' he asked slowly, 'would I want to do that?'

'Because all the negative headlines and publicity mean your company is suffering as much as ours?'

'I think you'll find that your company is in much worse shape than my father's. Or mine as it is now.' Alexis had recently taken control of his father's company. Rumour had it that he'd wrested it from him against his father's wishes.

Their champagne was delivered. Alexis handed Lydia's to her and then raised his own with a smile. 'Your father was too reliant on outside investment, which has made it much more vulnerable to external forces than mine.'

She clinked her glass to his. 'But all the negative publicity means Tsaliki Shipping is suffering a breakdown of consumer confidence as well as plummeting share *prices. I understand you've lost three long-standing contracts in recent months.'*

He had a drink of his champagne. 'I didn't think you were involved in Antoniadis Shipping.'

She swallowed half of her glass and smiled. 'I'm not. But I am an interested party. Obviously.'

'Obviously,' he echoed. 'An interested party close to losing everything.'

'You can stop that happening.'

A smile tugged at his mouth. She couldn't help thinking what divine lips they were, the perfect mouth with a fullness barely a fraction away from being feminine.

But there was nothing feminine about Alexis Tsaliki. He was the most rampantly masculine man she'd ever met in her life and sitting in this booth with him, the full weight of his attention on her, she fully understood why he had such a high success rate with the ladies. He didn't need his wealth to attract them. With his classically chiselled face complete with high cheekbones and strong nose, and bronzed skin the sun adored soaking itself into, all enhanced rather than disguised by his trimmed dark goatee beard, the man was sex on legs.

'So in reality, it isn't a truce you want—in any case, there has been an unspoken truce between us since I replaced my father at the top and the Antoniadis board forced your father to resign—you want my help to stop Antoniadis Shipping from going bust.'

'Do you think you could?'

'I'm sure I could.' His gorgeous blue-grey eyes glimmered. 'The question is, what's in it for me? Since I've taken control of the business, the rot has stopped. Our

share price is rising. Any contracts lost will be either replaced or regained.'

'That could take years.'

'I can play the long game.'

Now Lydia was the one to bring her face close to his. 'The question, though, is can Tsaliki Shipping afford for you to play the long game?'

Their gazes held, challenge firing from both. And then the smile that had been tugging at Alexis's divine lips pulled into a full-blown grin that filled her chest with an inexplicable warmth. 'Do you drink tequila?'

'Only if it's the good stuff.'

His grin widened. The warmth in her chest spread.

'Lydia?' It was her mother's voice, pulling her out of the memory she'd fallen into.

'I'm here,' she called back, wiping away tears she hadn't felt fall.

Her mother emerged through the trees. 'What are you…?' She saw the redness of her daughter's eyes and pulled her into an embrace. 'We'll survive, *baba*. You'll see. So long as we all stick together, we can survive this and start again and come back stronger.' She stepped back and cupped Lydia's cheeks. 'Now dry your eyes—those vile Tsaliki people are on the island and I need you by my side to face them because God knows your father and brother are in no state to deal with them.'

'Thanasis has fallen in love with her, hasn't he?' Lydia sniffed.

Her mother's lips thinned. 'He thinks he has, yes, but that kind of witchcraft is fleeting.'

She hesitated to ask, already guessing the answer. 'Witchcraft?'

'How else could Lucie have tricked him into forgetting that she's a viper like the rest of them?'

'So we are all in agreement, then,' Alexis stated, eyeballing every person around the dining table with the exception of Lydia, who he skimmed past. He'd sent her a message saying to meet him on the beach at midnight. Until that hour struck he could not allow himself to think of the news she'd thrown at him or allow himself to think about her. 'We all keep our mouths shut.' At this, he gave his sister an extra-hard stare.

Athena gave him her most innocent look.

Of all his many siblings, Athena was the one Alexis had always struggled the most to like, and it had nothing to do with her being the only female sibling. He loved her and would protect her with his life, but she had a bitchy streak that rivalled their stepmother's, and it was Athena who was responsible for knocking the first domino that had led to their stepsister, the bride, running away. For all his cool words to the Antoniadises, Alexis did not have confidence that the Tsalikis could get through this unscathed, not after everything that had already happened. They were all at the precipice, closer to falling into the abyss than they'd ever been, and it was down to him to make sure they all knew and understood what was at stake.

'I mean it,' he said grimly, addressing Athena directly. 'You do not breathe a word of what's happened here. We can only hope that Lucie doesn't go running to the press—'

'She won't,' a dull-eyed Thanasis interjected.

'I agree that it's unlikely.' His stepsister had a visceral hatred of the press. 'And so we all play the long game.' For a moment he lost his train of thought, his words pulling him back three months. He blinked the memory away and studiously avoided seeking out the hazel eyes of the woman he'd once delivered those same words to. 'We play the long game,' he reiterated, 'and ride it out. We say nothing because anything we do say can be contradicted if—and I know it's an unlikely if—Lucie speaks out or releases a statement.'

Addressing Athena directly again, he spoke slowly and elucidated every word. 'If you speak about this to anyone outside these walls, I will see that you're cut off. That goes for all of you.'

Outrage came from half a dozen voices, including his usually gregarious father who, like Petros Antoniadis, had spent the entire meeting mute. Both family patriarchs had retreated into themselves.

Alexis slammed his fist on the table. 'Enough! Athena is lucky that she's still allowed to call herself a Tsaliki. The wedding might be off but the peace brokered between myself and Thanasis isn't.' He put a finger lightly to the cut on his lip caused by Thanasis's fist. 'The only thing that's over is the war between our two families.'

Lydia sensed movement and had just enough time to brace herself before the figure appeared from the shadows. It had been the longest day of her life and was only going to get longer. Everything she'd had to cope with so far would be a piece of cake compared to what was coming for her now.

The hulking figure sank heavily onto the sand beside her.

For the longest time, neither of them spoke. The air, though, spoke with a tension thick enough to slice with a spoon.

'So we're going to be parents,' he eventually said.

'Yes.'

'And you want to marry me.'

'No.'

He grunted a laugh. 'I would never allow a child of mine to suffer and that includes suffering with poverty. You don't need me to marry you for that—I will give you everything you need and more.'

Lydia lifted her gaze to the stars, She thought the night sky was why she loved Sephone so much. Here, the lack of light pollutants made the stars shine brighter and in millions times greater numbers than anywhere else on earth. Anywhere that she'd ever been in any case, and it broke her heart for all her family that Thanasis would probably have to sell it.

'I'm sorry, Alexis,' she said in as steady a voice as she could manage, 'but I need the security of marriage.'

'You don't,' he contradicted firmly.

'My parents are going to disown me. They will never accept a grandchild who's half Tsaliki and they will never forgive me for…for…' She swallowed to force her next words out. 'For sleeping with you.'

And they had slept. It hadn't just been all sex. For two beautiful nights they'd turned their phones off and hidden from the world in his bedroom. They'd talked and talked about anything and everything that wasn't their families, watched old films and fallen asleep entwined in each other's arms. It had been the most magical time of her life.

'They won't disown you,' he said tightly. 'You Antoniadises are a close-knit bunch.'

'My mother will see it as a betrayal. She hates you more than my father does. I think he only ever hated your father, but my mother hates all of you and when she finds out she will hate me too.'

'She loves you.'

'That won't stop her from hating me. She didn't speak to her sister for seven years because she found out my aunt had gone to a party hosted by the school bully who'd made Mum's life a misery. She holds onto her grudges and does not forgive. I need security for me and the baby, and I need it now. I need to wake up and know that no matter what happens, we'll have a roof over our heads and food in our bellies.'

'I'll buy you a house and pay for its upkeep.'

'And what if you decide to take it away from me or stop paying the bills towards it? I'd be at your mercy and I can't do that any more. It's only since I found out I'm pregnant that I see how entirely at my family's mercy I am. I live in a cottage on the grounds but it's not mine, it's theirs. I make a living selling my designs to clothing and fabric companies but I've not built a big enough name to sustain myself—I suppose I never really needed to as the company shares my parents assigned me when I was born have always given me a decent income, but that's going to be ripped away with everything else. I've always had a mental safety net around me and it's all being ripped away and when my parents learn about the baby they will cut me off and

I'll be on my own and I will have nothing. Being on my own frightens me enough but being on my own with a baby to feed terrifies me.

'As your wife, you won't be able to just throw me out and leave me with nothing. I'll sign whatever prenuptial agreement you want—marriage won't cost you anything more than it would if you were to just buy me a house.'

In the silence that followed, the beats of Lydia's heavy heart seemed to speed up to a burr, its weight compressing her stomach.

This was a conversation she'd never wanted to have. Never expected to have. The marriage between her brother and Lucie Burton was supposed to save their business and fortune, and even if her parents turned their backs on her, Thanasis never would. She'd longed to confide in him but he'd been under so much stress trying to save the business and convincing the world that his fake engagement was true love that she'd not wanted to add to his burden, not until after the wedding.

All her plans had been ripped away in the same way her future was being, and the only thing that mattered, the only thing she could allow to matter, was the tiny life nestled in her womb.

'Say I go along with this mad idea,' the father of her tiny life said slowly. 'What's in it for me?'

Lydia closed her eyes at the virtual repeat of words spoken all those months ago. 'You'll be able to watch our child grow up and be as involved…or not…as you wish.' She forced a smile to her face so the movements would inject lightness into her voice to deliver what she knew would be the greatest selling point to him. 'And just think what an excellent excuse having a wife in the background of your life will give you when your lovers become too demanding of your time. I won't make any demands on you or your time—you'll be able to live your life exactly as you've always lived it. I won't even have to live with you. I'll be your wife in name only.'

Alexis Tsaliki was a serial seducer. Flirting came as naturally to him as breathing. He didn't even have to try. All he had to do was fix those hypnotic blue-grey eyes on a woman and she was his. Lydia should know. That was how it had been for her. She hadn't gone to that nightclub with the intention to seduce or be seduced—talking to him had been the only thing on her mind—but Alexis had a power about him that turned a level-headed adult female into a creature held hostage by its own desires. She couldn't even blame it on the champagne or tequila. He'd made her heart beat faster from the moment he'd slid into the booth beside her. By the time he'd invited her back to his apartment her body had become such a hot mess of desire for him that if he'd suggested going outside for a quick knee-trembler instead, she'd have given the same answer.

Until she'd met Alexis, she'd never had a fling; never even considered one. In her twenty-seven years she'd had two lovers, both long-term, serious relationships with serious, arty men who wouldn't be seen dead in a boardroom or in a suit. Neither had come within a fraction of thrilling her or rousing the woman in her as Alexis had done.

A man like Alexis Tsaliki was untameable. Only a fool would let themselves believe otherwise and Lydia was no fool. She'd gone to his apartment with her eyes wide open—his sexploits were legendary in Greek society—and what had been a spontaneous magically, passionately glorious one-off for her was just a regular weekend of fun to him. That was why when she'd woken late on the Sunday morning racked with a tsunami of emotions she'd never felt before, including guilt for such a heinous betrayal to her family, she'd made sure to be the one to say their weekend together had been a one-off that no one could ever know about.

While he'd carried on with his life, no doubt not giving her even a passing thought, she'd thought about him practically every second of every minute of every day.

Her weekend with Alexis had been the best worst mistake of her life.

'Okay,' he eventually said in that same slow, thoughtful voice. 'I'll do it.'

Her heart jumped into her throat. 'You'll marry me?'

She hadn't expected it to be that easy. That quick.

'Yes.' She felt his stare land on her skin. 'But I have conditions.'

'Anything.' This was no time for pride. Her family could be bankrupt in weeks and within that timeframe there was a very good chance the pregnancy would start showing. She couldn't keep this a secret much longer. She needed to sort her and her baby's future out now.

'If I'm going to marry you then it's on condition that it's a real marriage.'

CHAPTER THREE

Alexis felt as well as saw the woman sitting on the sand beside him with her arms hugging her knees freeze.

When she responded, it was in a higher voice than the even, reasonable tone she'd carried the conversation with up to that point. 'It isn't necessary to have a real marriage.'

'It is for me.'

'Why?'

'A number of reasons. One—because marriage is not a game to be played, whether it's to gain yourself an advantage or for any other reason. Two—because I will not have the humiliation of the world believing my wife despises me enough that she won't share my bed, and three—because a real marriage between you and me might just do the job Thanasis and Lucie's marriage was supposed to do.'

'Do you seriously think anyone will be fooled by that trick a second time?'

He shrugged. 'Our baby will be all the proof we need.'

'Not neces…'

'That's my condition. A real marriage. Husband, wife, one bed, till death us do part. Take it or leave it.'

A tremor came into her voice. 'When you say one bed...'

'Yes. Sex.' He allowed himself a half-smile, allowed a partial memory of their nights together to infiltrate his mind, of Lydia on top of him, throwing her head back in rapture as she'd climaxed with such force her spasming contractions had pulled him over the edge too. With a snapped blink, he shuttered the vivid memory away and added, 'I figure you should be allowed some enjoyment within it.'

She spluttered with outrage then shook her head vigorously. 'No sex.'

'Then no deal.'

'You don't need to have...'

'You said you'd agree to anything, and that's my price. If I'm going to commit to you and our baby then you can damned well commit to me too. A real marriage, Lydia. All or nothing. Say yes and I will fly you to Agon tomorrow and marry you there on Sunday. In less than forty-eight hours you will be my wife. Say no and take your chances that your worst fears won't be proved right.'

He could feel her turmoil like a wave of tension vibrating off her skin.

Until the night she'd come to his nightclub—and only a select few of his inner circle knew he owned the nightclub as part of his vast portfolio of personal investments—Lydia had been a face he'd known only as a member of the Antoniadis family. A pretty face for sure, but there were plenty of pretty faces in his world and as her pretty face was one he associated with poisonous scorpions, not one he'd had any wish to know.

That she'd appeared in his club seeking him out hadn't been in question, and he'd joined her in her booth fully expecting to be only moments away from calling security to eject her from his premises.

There were many things he hadn't expected when he took that seat beside her: not her reasons for seeking him out, not the open, warm curiosity in her hazel eyes, not the witty playfulness, and definitely not the click of attraction that had sprung almost immediately between them.

He'd invited her to his apartment knowing she would say yes and knowing it had nothing to do with her request for his help, which had been barely spoken about as they'd shared the best part of a bottle of tequila between them and a mountain of chips, and exchanged increasingly more outrageous stories about mutual acquaintances that had them both roaring with laughter. By the time he'd issued his invitation, her legs had been draped over his lap, their hands had been clasped tightly together and their eyes might as well have been glued together because they'd both stopped seeing anyone else.

If one of them had carried a condom, he'd have taken her…or she'd have taken him…before his driver had left the underground car park. *Theos*, he could still remember the thrill of electricity that had coursed through him at the first touch of her tongue against his, still remember the pulsation the first time her fingers had wrapped around his erection, still remember the sound of her first climax cried into his mouth as they'd pleasured each other with their hands.

He'd never known a night like it, a hedonistic, instinctive compatibility that had blown his mind and, instead of sating him, had kept him wanting more; kept them both wanting more. One night had rolled into day and then into another night, time managing to stand still and yet pass in the blink of an eye.

Scorpions had bite but, as he'd discovered that weekend, they tasted divine.

It was on the Sunday that Lydia had unleashed the sting in her tail.

She'd woken him with a quick shake of his shoulder. He'd opened his eyes to find her dressed and the bedroom bathed in daylight.

'I have to go.'

He'd thrown the sheets off to reveal an erection that no man should have been able to produce after the two nights they'd shared. 'Sure about that?'

She'd darted her gaze away. 'Sorry. Things to do.'

He'd sat up and cupped her face before kissing her deeply and then murmuring, 'Dinner tonight?'

She'd pulled away from him and climbed off the bed. Her blonde hair had been all mussed from their lovemaking, her face bare, not a scrap of makeup. He'd never seen a sight so beautiful.

'I can't.'

'Tomorrow night?'

She'd raised her gaze to the ceiling. 'Alexis…what we've shared has been…great, but we can't see each other again.'

His limbs still heavy from all their incredible lovemaking, his loins primed and ready for more, he'd pulled a face. 'Why not?'

Her stare had whipped to him. All the passion and light that had shone from the beautiful hazel eyes had gone. Now all that had rung out from them had been incredulity. 'You have to ask? Seeing each other again is out of the question.'

'If you're worried about our families then don't be—they don't need to know.'

'They must *never* know,' she'd said with such vehemence his hackles had risen. 'No one can ever know and we both need to forget that anything happened.'

It had been his turn to be incredulous. 'How the hell am I supposed to do that?'

'By not thinking about it and not speaking about it. You can't tell anyone, no one, not even your confessor.'

'People saw you leaving the club with me. If you know a way to wipe their memories then I'm all ears.'

'People saw you leaving with one of your interchangeable blondes. No one there would have recognised me—I'm a jeans and baggy T-shirt and ponytail girl, not a mini-dress girl, and the people who know me are more house-party people than nightclub people.'

He'd stared at her with narrowed eyes, a scenario playing out in his head that had driven out the last of the languid contentment and filled his mouth with a bitter taste. 'Did you dress up like that deliberately to seduce me?'

'No! I dressed like that to blend in and capture your attention so we could talk. I didn't think for a minute that *this* was going to happen.' She'd said *this* as if it were a dirty word.

'By *this* do you mean spending the weekend with me, screwing each other's brains out?'

Colour had slashed her cheeks but she hadn't dropped her stare. 'I don't know what you're talking about. I had a few drinks too many at a party on Friday night and slept on my friend's sofa and ended up staying the weekend, and you spent the weekend with one of your legions of lovers.'

'Oh, did I?' he'd queried silkily. Dangerously.

She'd stood tall; determined and unwavering. 'Yes, you did.'

Loathing that had morphed from nothing had crackled between them until Alexis had lain himself back down, hooked an arm over the top of his head and casually said, 'You can see yourself out. If any of the staff see you, introduce yourself by any name you like—you're as interchangeable as all the others who've done the walk of shame from here.'

She'd looked him over one more time, her face now contorted with hatred, and walked out without another word.

Only when she'd closed the door behind her had he clenched his jaw and punched his fist down on the mattress.

The irony that three months later the only woman to have ever walked out on him would be so desperate for help that she wanted marriage should be something to savour, and he had no doubt that when she capitulated to his demands he *would* savour it.

'I need to get back to the yacht, so it's make your mind up time,' he said roughly when she still hadn't answered. 'Do I make arrangements to fly us to Agon tomorrow or do I get one of my people on the job of buying a house for you to live in?'

'You've thrown me,' she whispered.

'I was thrown earlier when a not particularly memorable one-weekend stand told me I'd got her pregnant and wanted me to marry her, so consider us even.'

The brightness of the stars highlighted her features and allowed him to see the flinch his deliberate barb had induced.

Theos, if only that barb had been the truth...

'I'm out of here,' he said, hauling himself up. 'I'll be in touch. Good luck dealing with the fallout with your family.'

He'd taken four steps when she called, 'Okay, I'll do it.'

He stopped walking. 'Do what?'

'Have a real marriage with you.'

He turned around. She was on her feet, gripping her arms. 'But I have conditions too.'

'You're not in a position to make conditions.'

'The wedding has to be secret—I want to hold off telling anyone for as long as possible. My family are under a great deal of stress...'

'As are mine.'

'I appreciate that but my family is very different from yours and my parents are on the brink of losing everything. I don't want to add to the enormous stress they're under until I absolutely have to because I think you and me might be the thing that tips them over the edge. You have no reason to feel sympathy for them but they're my parents and I love them.'

'You cannot protect them for ever,' he pointed out, and allowed his gaze to do what he'd fought it from doing since he'd ridden the jet ski onto the beach, and take in every inch of her. Only now, under the full moon, could he see the subtle changes to her figure that only someone who'd been intimate with her and had committed every inch of her flesh to memory would notice: the pushing of her stomach against the three-quarter-length ripped jeans, the new fullness of breasts that had been perfection itself beneath the baggy white top. Now, she would struggle to squeeze herself into the silver dress that had done its job of capturing his attention so spectacularly well it should win its own special award. 'You will be showing soon.'

The jutting of her chin only proved that she felt every inch of his stare. 'I know.'

'And it's not in my interests to keep it secret.'

'A month. That's all I'm asking for. A month.'

'I will give you a week.'

'But…'

'A week or nothing.' He made to walk away.

'Fine,' she snapped. 'A week. But a week from the wedding.'

'Deal.' He gave a mocking smile. 'Our first compromise.'

'Hardly a compromise.'

'You should be more grateful—I didn't need to compromise. I don't need to compromise on anything. That we're standing here even discussing this is entirely for your benefit.'

'No, for our *baby's* benefit.'

'Once you know me better you will know our baby's security was never in doubt.'

'If it wasn't for our baby I wouldn't want to know you at all.'

'But you, my angel from Hades, do know me, and

intimately.' He had the satisfaction of seeing her beautiful face contort at the reminder. 'Any other conditions?'

'No.'

'No demands that I be faithful?' he said with another mocking smile.

Her loathing was so visible he swore he could taste it. 'I wouldn't waste my breath.'

He laughed. 'In that case, I believe we have a deal.'

'Whoopee,' she said flatly.

'It is usually customary that a deal be sealed with a handshake, but in these circumstances I believe a kiss would be more appropriate.'

She shook her head with a sneering laugh and took a small step back.

'I'm serious, Lydia. We seal the deal and you prove your commitment to us having a real marriage with a kiss, otherwise the deal is non-binding and you have no guarantee I will sign my name on any wedding certificate.'

Her eyes were ablaze with fury. 'You're enjoying this, aren't you? Humiliating me.'

'Very much so, but not as much as I'm going to enjoy feeling your delectable mouth against mine again, so come here and seal the deal.' He pressed a finger to the cut her brother's fist had made on his mouth. 'You can start by kissing this better.'

Lydia tried to hold her ground but the expression on Alexis's face was uncompromising.

This was payback. She knew it. He knew it. Payback for her doing the unthinkable and being the one to walk out on the great Alexis Tsaliki when his ego dictated that he play his lovers like a puppeteer until he bored of them.

If he had any idea that dragging herself out of his bed had been the hardest thing she'd ever had to do... His ego would explode.

She was glad, now, that their circumstances had forced her to go against all her instincts and walk away, because she would have given anything to stay in his bed; given anything to have kissed him back and said yes to dinner with him.

She'd never dreamed making love could feel like that. Be like that. Passionate. Tender. Thrilling. Fun. She'd never believed, either, that she could be like that with someone. Alexis hadn't just stripped her clothes from her but stripped her bare too. He'd peeled away all her layers to reveal the essence of who she was as a woman, a woman who for one gloriously hedonistic weekend had lived only for him. She would love to believe the alcohol they'd consumed and the fact that even talking civilly to each other was a massive taboo had played their part in heightening everything, and maybe they had, to start with, but they hadn't touched a drop of alcohol once at his apartment and she'd been stone-cold sober when she'd had to physically wrench herself away from him...

During their weekend together, she hadn't once forgotten that it was her enemy's bed she'd willingly climbed into, but she had forgotten what kind of man her enemy was. A ruthless man. A man who'd wrested control of his own father's company against his father's wishes and, as she'd learned that day, had had no compunction about serving his stepsister to Lydia's brother on a platter built on a lie.

He was also a man for whom commitment was a dirty word, and why would it not be when he had the looks that would make any passing human take a second look? Combine that with his wealth and you had a man who could have anyone he pleased, and frequently did. If their families' entwined poisonous histories hadn't forced Lydia to drag herself out of his bed and walk away, the most she could have looked forward to would have been a couple of dates before being unceremoniously dumped for the next woman to catch his forever roving eye.

Regardless of their poisonous family histories, she would never have been that woman. Lydia's pride and self-respect were the only things she'd ever earned on her own and she would not compromise them for anyone, not even Mr Sex on Legs.

She'd walked away and so bruised his overinflated ego, and now he was snatching at the opportunity their carelessness—and as hard as she tried, she couldn't pinpoint when, exactly, throughout that long, glorious weekend the passion had made them *that* careless—had provided to make her pay.

He beckoned her with his finger.

This was her last chance. Prove her commitment or he would walk.

But to prove her commitment she had to walk to him. She wouldn't have been surprised if he'd clicked his fingers to lay a path of hot coals for her to tread to reach him.

Heart racing, pulses jumping, she lifted her chin and took the five steps needed to reach him.

His lips tugged into a knowing smile. 'Here first,' he said, lowering his face to nearer her level and lightly tapping the only thing close to a blemish on his face. Not liking the constriction in her chest to be forced to look at that blemish and to remember the blood that had poured from it, she gritted her teeth, and rose onto her toes.

Holding her breath, she pressed her lips swiftly to the side of Alexis's mouth where the cut lay, then stepped back before her lips had the time to register any connection between them.

It didn't stop her heart racing even harder and faster.

His eyes gleamed as he placed his finger to the centre of his mouth. 'And now here.'

She clenched her jaw to rise back onto her toes and press an even more fleeting kiss to the lips that had kissed her in places she hadn't even known were places. Before she could dart back out of his reach and thank years of yoga and Pilates for giving her a core that could lift itself to kiss a man over a foot taller than herself without having to lay a finger on him for support, an arm hooked around her back and pulled her flush to him.

'You call that a kiss?' he whispered huskily. His other hand clasped the back of her head and gently tugged her back, forcing her to meet head-on the blue-grey eyes that had haunted her waking and sleeping dreams for three months. 'Let me show you the kind of kiss I was thinking of...'

His mouth closed in on hers and with her heart now a thrumming burr and her mouth filled with a moisture that had come from nowhere, Lydia closed her eyes. Before she could clench her hands into fists or do any of the other things necessary to keep her senses dulled, there was a gentle, featherlight pressure on her lips and a scent filled her nostrils that made every cell in her body cry.

Determined not to react, she held herself like a statue. Of all the things that had made her recoil from committing to a proper marriage, the strongest had been Alexis's devastating physical effect on her. So powerful had it been that dragging herself out of his bed had been the hardest thing she'd had to do in the whole of her life. She could not imagine what a month of waking in his arms would do to her, never mind a lifetime. Telling herself that this was all a power play and that she'd probably only share his bed for an extremely limited time before he bored of toying with her and bored of *her*—a goldfish had a greater attention span than Alexis Tsaliki had with women—didn't make her feel any better. Somehow it made her feel worse.

She had no choice. Alexis held all the cards and when you made a deal with the devil you had to pay the price. But that didn't mean you had to pay a cent more than he demanded, and if she could make it to the point where he discarded her with her pride and self-respect intact, then she…

The distraction of her thoughts evaporated under the heat of the slow, seductive movements of his mouth and the gentle massaging of his fingers to the back of her head.

With skilful mastery, he coaxed her lips apart and slowly slid his tongue into her mouth.

Her entire system short-circuited.

She swayed, suddenly filled with the dark, exotic

taste that had been part of the whole magical Alexis Tsaliki package, and a flame of raw desire pulsed from the spot between her legs and darted straight into her veins, weakening her legs.

The probing of his tongue deepened, the fingers clasping her head moving up to the band holding her hair in place and then gently sliding it down to the tips and flicking it away. Her hair tumbled down at the same moment her throat betrayed her with a treacherous moan and suddenly Lydia was gripping his strong shoulders and moulding herself to the hardness of his chest, not just responding to the demands of his mouth and tongue but making demands of her own.

With his fingers now threading through the strands of her hair, his other hand clasped her bottom, holding it possessively, the fusion of their bodies as tight as that of their mouths. Arms now wrapped around his neck, she kissed him as if she'd been waiting her whole life for this moment, and when she felt the hard ridge of his arousal against her abdomen she moved restlessly against it, rising onto the tips of her toes in a desperate effort to lift her pelvis closer.

His hand crept up, beneath her cotton top, the heat of his skin burning into her flesh, moving higher to the clasp of her bra. With a practised flick of his fingers and wrist, he undid the clasp, making her a hundred times more aware of the weight of her own breasts crying out for his touch, and when his fingers skimmed her ribcage and then covered one, she cried into his mouth and scraped her nails down the nape of his neck to dip beneath the collar of his polo shirt, a fever inside her, needing to touch him as much as she needed to be touched...

With no warning and no ceremony, he dropped his hands and pulled away from her, mouth and body.

'Wha...?' She tried to snatch a breath, her dazed, unthinking word fading into nothing.

Muscular arms now folded across his broad chest, his face lowered to hers. The lips that had just kissed her senseless smiled cruelly. 'That, my angel from Hades, was a much better effort. Our deal is now sealed. Can you get yourself to Kos tomorrow?'

She nodded dumbly. She could barely stand never mind speak, had to ground her feet in the sand to stop her legs from giving out on her.

'Good. My plane will leave for Agon at four p.m. If you're not there then I will assume you have changed your mind and our deal will be terminated.'

With those parting words, he turned his back and walked away. Lydia was still fighting to find breath when he was swallowed by the darkness.

CHAPTER FOUR

ALEXIS TAPPED HIS long fingers on the armrest and gazed out at the seemingly endless stretch of tarmac. Five minutes until take-off and no sign of Lydia.

He caught the questioning eye of his senior cabin crew member and shook his head. He'd told Lydia four p.m. and he would give her until the clock turned the hour. But not a minute more.

He took a long breath and stretched his legs out. His chest had been tight since he'd got out of bed. He hadn't slept a wink. Too much going on in his head. By rights, he should be hunting down Lucie and gathering all the board members together to drive forward a solid plan to save Tsaliki Shipping from the fate that was coming for Antoniadis Shipping. If Tsaliki Shipping went down then his personal wealth would be safe. Alexis had diversified over the years, building himself a portfolio of assets that had made him a billionaire in his own right before he'd reached thirty. Ultimately, his family would be safe too because he would never let them suffer poverty.

Four minutes.

Alexis had never wanted to take control of his father's company. In truth, he'd never had much interest in the business, but he was the oldest son and it had been expected by his father and, growing up, he'd hero-worshipped the man. It wasn't until he'd become an adult himself that he'd finally admitted to himself that his father's feet were made of clay, and it wasn't until his siblings came of age one by one that he realised none of them had the ability to step into their father's clay business shoes. They were all spoilt; a bunch of useless, work-shy wastrels living off daddy's largesse. Constantine at least tried, but he had no business acumen and zero judgement.

Three minutes.

If Alexis did manage to save Tsaliki Shipping then a hard conversation would need to be had because once all this was done with, he wanted out. So yes, he should be concentrating on the damned business he didn't even want to run and finding a way to save it from a fate that would leave his entire family dependent on *his* largesse, not making covert plans to marry the one woman in the world who despised him. Make that two women. He didn't imagine Lucie's opinion of him was particularly high at that moment, but Lucie wasn't blood and had been too young when her mother had married his father for Alexis to take any interest in her. And she wasn't pregnant with his child.

Theos, he was going to be a father. Since Lydia had bamboozled him with the news, it had sat in him like an extra beat in his heart. Maybe at some point soon he'd have the time to actually think about what that meant. But not yet. Not when he had so much else to think about and contend with.

Two minutes.

He took another deep breath and gave another shake of his head to the stewardess.

Lydia wasn't coming but he would still let the clock count down.

He closed his eyes briefly and allowed himself the luxury of remembering how she'd come apart at the seams on the beach. Only ruthless determination had allowed him to hold onto his own control. He'd had a point to make to them both and he'd damned well made it.

One minute.

He straightened, swallowed the constriction in his throat and opened his mouth to instruct the crew…and then he saw it, a blur in the corner of his eye. A scooter carrying two people speeding towards his plane.

It stopped at the steps that were twenty seconds away from being removed and the passenger jumped off, tugged off her helmet, handed it to the rider and with a quick wave of goodbye raced up the metal steps clutching a small black handbag and virtually threw herself through the door.

Alexis looked at his watch and then looked her up and down. Dressed in tight black trousers, black ankle books and a loose black sheer blouse, all Lydia needed was a black veil and she'd fit in perfectly as chief mourner at a funeral. He was quite sure she'd chosen the outfit for that specific effect and was equally sure, judging by the faint sheen of perspiration on her face and the way her fringe was sticking to her forehead, that she must be roasting in it.

'You look…hot.' In more ways than one, because he was quite sure too that she was oblivious to the fact that the sunlight pouring through the plane's windows had made her blouse transparent and that he could see the pattern of her black lace bra beneath it.

The delectably plump lips tightened, defiance shining from her hazel eyes even as colour rose on her cheeks. 'And you look smug.'

He couldn't argue with that. She was there, throwing herself at his mercy.

Sinking onto the seat across from his, she strapped herself in, aimed the air-conditioning console above her head to her face, and turned her gaze out of the window. 'Are we going or what?'

Or what...?

Throw Lydia to her fate or save her?

Alexis caught the eye of the senior stewardess and nodded.

Minutes later they were in the air.

The skies were so clear and the sun so bright that even at over thirty thousand feet, Lydia could see the white dots of yachts in the blue sea far below them. She wondered if any of those dots were guests at the wedding that had never taken place.

'Did you get cold feet?'

She pulled in a breath before casting a brief glance at the man sitting opposite her whose kisses she could still taste and whose hand she could still feel on the naked skin of her back. It was the first time he'd spoken since they'd taken off.

It wasn't fair that he should look all fresh and rugged and gorgeous while a night of no sleep whatsoever, along with choosing the most impractical clothes to race across Kos in a heatwave with, had left her looking like death warmed up. She wished she could blame her lack of sleep on her family's dire predicament messing with her head but it was all Alexis and the mortifying way she'd melted for him messing with her body and her mind, and it was Alexis's fault, too, that she'd chosen to dress all in black. She'd wanted to send him a message but all she'd done was make herself hot and bothered in the only black clothing she'd packed for Sephone, and while the plane's excellent air conditioning was cooling her skin, it was having no effect whatsoever on her core temperature, and that was all Alexis's fault too.

She hated that he'd spent the short time they'd been in the air concentrating on his laptop as if she weren't right there with him, as if he felt *nothing* to have her right there with him. She hated too that the powerful awareness inside her for him was a living entity she had no control over whereas he could turn any attraction on and off like a tap.

For heaven's sake, he was wearing a white shirt and suit trousers, clothing that had always turned her off men, what with it being the attire her father and brother lived in, and he was *still* sex on legs.

'No,' she answered shortly. Not cold feet in the sense that she'd come close to backing out. Backing out was not an option. The only person capable of saving her family was her brother, and he was falling apart. Marrying Alexis would give Lydia the security she needed for her and her baby and maybe, in time, *she* would have the means to help her family. It made her heart clench to imagine them rejecting that help. Rejecting her. Rejecting her baby.

'Ah, you just thought you'd keep me on my toes by waiting until the last second to arrive, then.'

'I don't know where you get your ego from but not

everything is about you. There was an engine problem with the yacht so we left Sephone later than planned.' Beneath the coolness of her tone, Lydia could still feel the panic that had clawed at her as she'd watched the hours slip by. Thank God for her old friend Maya, who'd made her home on Kos and who'd dropped everything to meet Lydia at the harbour and speed her to the airport, no questions asked.

'What excuse did you come up with to justify not returning to Athens with them?'

'I told them I was going to stay with one of my English friends to get away from everything.'

'You told them you were taking a trip to England and didn't pack any luggage?'

Gritting her teeth at his mocking scepticism, her reply was a short, 'I had to leave it at the harbour.' As much as she'd despaired at leaving her luggage behind—Maya had promised to go back for it and walk it to her apartment for safekeeping—it was impossible to carry suitcases on a scooter. Being late for the flight would have caused a million times more despair. If she'd arrived one minute later, the door into Alexis's private plane would have been closed to her. 'I'll need to go shopping when we get to Agon.'

'I'm afraid that isn't possible. Agon's trading laws forbid retailers to open after five at weekends.'

'Even for hotel boutiques?'

'We're not stopping in a hotel.'

Great. So she was going to be stuck in this awful outfit for the foreseeable future. When life threw crap at you, it *really* threw it at you. 'Fine. I'll marry you in this outfit, then. At least it'll be fitting.'

He laughed softly. 'From your perspective, certainly. Did your family believe your excuse?'

'They had no reason not to—they're used to me flying off to stay with friends.'

'That's good to know.'

There was something in his tone that made her turn her stare to him. 'Why?'

Those gorgeous blue-grey eyes bored into her. 'It's good to know the excuses your wife will use when she lies to you.'

She held his stare with all the contempt she could muster. 'When people lie it's either to stop themselves getting into trouble or to spare the other's feelings. Unless you're planning to beat me to keep me in line, which I don't think even *you* would do, I have no need to lie to you, because I couldn't care less about your feelings.'

There was the slightest flicker in his eye before he gave a half-smile. 'Then I look forward to the day I catch you in a lie.'

And with those unsettling, enigmatic words, he dropped his stare back to his laptop and immersed himself back in his work.

It was movement that woke her. Disorientated, Lydia had to blink a number of times before she remembered where she was. Flying to Agon with Alexis Tsaliki to marry him…

Where was he?

Rubbing the sleep out of her eyes—it must have claimed her quickly as she didn't remember her eyes getting heavy—she looked at her watch. Only forty minutes in the air. She could only have been asleep for minutes.

She straightened, her heart catching in her throat before her eyes registered the figure further down the cabin, in the dining area.

His back to her, Alexis had changed out of his trousers into a pair of faded jeans that perfectly accentuated his perfect buttocks and snake hips, and was leaning over, pulling something out of a carry-on bag, the muscles of his bronzed naked back rippling with the movement.

Her caught heart swelled and she gripped hold of her blouse right above the place it beat the hardest.

He straightened and then more muscles rippled and flexed as he lifted his arms and pulled a white T-shirt over his head.

'Enjoying the show?' he asked before he turned around and flattened the T-shirt over his rock-hard abdomen. Eyes gleaming, he strode towards her. 'I would have showered but time ran away from me.'

She wanted to run away from him. Lydia had never gone so fully from dozing to wide awake in such a short space of time.

'I would suggest you change into something more comfortable too, but with your clothing predicament…' Shaking his head with faux regret, he retook his seat and stretched his long legs out, his foot coming to rest right beside hers. Eyes alive with sensuous amusement, he smiled. 'Unless you would like to borrow something of mine?'

Lydia pulled her feet back. 'I'd rather suffer, thank you.'

'Then you will soon get your wish—we'll be landing in a few minutes.'

***

Stepping out of the plane and onto the private airfield was like stepping into an inferno. From the time it took to walk from the door of the plane to the door of the shining black car waiting for them, a feat that took approximately twenty seconds, Lydia's clothes were clinging to her skin and the hair at the nape of her neck had dampened, which also happened to be Alexis's fault because it had been too dark to find the hairband he'd pulled out on the beach and she didn't have a spare. It was all grossly unfair—she'd seen daisies that would envy his freshness.

Reaching into her handbag, she pulled out her phone. 'Where are we staying?' She would do a quick search to see if there was a hotel with a boutique close by that she could zip into.

'At my villa.'

'I didn't know you had a villa here.'

'I have many properties. This is but one of them.'

'The address?'

He recited it to her. To her immense frustration, it was in an exclusive area with high-end restaurants and boutiques but no hotels.

'We can shop in the morning, before we marry,' he said, reading her thoughts.

'Is it booked?'

'Yes. We marry at the royal chapel at midday.'

It took a moment for that to sink in. 'The royal chapel?' she said in horror. 'Are you being serious? I assumed we were having a civil ceremony?'

'Then you assumed wrong. Prince Talos is an old friend and immensely trustworthy. He's made the arrangements, and is going to act as a witness with his wife. No one will know we've married until we release the news.'

'But a chapel? How am I supposed to make my vows in front of God knowing it's a lie?'

His eyes narrowed a touch before he said in a silkily dangerous voice, 'But it can't be a lie when you're committing to a real marriage with me, until death us do part…unless that in itself is a lie and you're already planning your escape?'

'I don't need to plan anything because if anyone's going to want to escape it, it's *you*.'

The almost imperceptible flicker appeared in his eye. 'And what makes you think that?'

'Because you're a serial seducer who's slept with…' Her stomach turned over. 'I don't want to think about how many women you've been with.'

'Jealous?'

'Don't be ridiculous,' she said before quickly adding, 'It's the reasons behind our marriage that make marrying in a house of God wrong, the vows to love and honour and everything…how can we pledge to love each other when the truth is that we despise each other?' And why did her heart pang to say that?

The strength of his stare in the silence that followed acted like a magnet, forcing her to meet it.

'Why have you never married before?' he surprised her by asking.

'I never wanted to.'

'But if I've been led to believe correctly, you've had two long-term relationships—did you not want to marry those men?'

She turned her stare out of the window. This was her first visit to the island of Agon, a sovereign nation of Greek origin with the same language, currency, myths and legends. The architecture of the pristine town they were driving through reminded her strongly of Crete but with wider roads. She'd holidayed in Crete once, while in her second relationship. The forced proximity she'd assumed they would enjoy together had been the catalyst for their end. She'd been bored out of her mind. 'No.'

'Did you not love them?'

Not enough. 'Of course I loved them.'

'But not enough to marry them,' he observed astutely, correctly reading her thoughts. 'They asked you?'

She sighed. 'Yes.'

'Why say no?'

'That's none of your business.'

'Considering that tomorrow I shall be your husband, it *is* my business.'

'Okay, well I'll answer that if you tell me why you're a serial shagger and commitment-phobe.'

'Hardly a commitment-phobe when I'm marrying you in a matter of hours.'

'Yes, but nothing will change for you. You're not making a commitment to be faithful. You'll still be continuing your serial shagging ways.'

'Your opinion of me never ceases to delight.' Although this was delivered lightly, Lydia detected an edge to his voice, an edge that disappeared when he added, 'But as you're the one who has turned down two marriage proposals, I would say that makes *you* the one afraid of commitment, which is a conversation we shall continue later. We're here.' They'd stopped by the side of the wide road, the driver indicating to turn into a set of high iron gates that were slowly opening. 'For now, I remind you that you have committed yourself to me as my wife, in all ways, and now it is time for you to prove it.'

She whipped her stare back to him. *'How?'*

'Generally people newly in love look at each other with love, so you can start with not looking at me as if you want to bash my brains in when we're in public,' he answered drily.

She jutted her chin mutinously. 'I'm not an actress.'

He gave a nonchalant shrug. 'We made a deal, Lydia. If you're not prepared to stick to it then tell me now and I'll have you driven back to the airport.'

'I'll stick to it.'

'Good, then come here and kiss me.'

'No.'

'Kiss me or go home.'

'I hate you.'

'I know. Now for the last time, come here.'

Jaw clenched, she shuffled across the leather seat to him and twisted to face him properly. The only faint solace she could take at this situation was that this time she was prepared. This time she would keep her composure and wouldn't give an ounce of herself more than necessary.

'How do you want to choreograph it?' she asked tautly. 'Do you want my hands on your shoulders or shall I wrap them around your…?'

Her words were cut off when a large hand cupped the side of her neck and his mouth swooped onto hers, cutting off her breath with her words as the shock of it raced through her, knotting her stomach and bringing every nerve-ending zinging into tingling life.

With skilled precision, he slid his tongue into her mouth, an arm sliding round her waist, pulling her closer and lighting all those nerve-endings like a match against tissue paper. Lydia, her brain cut off with her breath and her words, melted into him.

Leaning into the kiss, leaning into him, she slid an arm around his neck, and kissed him back, each intimate stroke of their duelling tongues adding to the sizzling excitement building low in her pelvis, would have crawled onto his lap to straddle him if he hadn't pulled away from it.

Ready to cry at the withdrawal of his mouth, she gazed at him in bewilderment, barely able to think under the heavy pounding of her heart, and found herself lost in the blue-grey eyes probing her with a look she couldn't begin to decipher.

After what felt like for ever had passed he rubbed his thumb over her cheek and bent his head for one final, gentle kiss. 'There,' he said softly. 'Now you look like you're in love.'

CHAPTER FIVE

LYDIA HAD NO idea how she was able to move from the car into the secluded, whitewashed villa. Alexis's kiss had jellified her legs. That he held her hand jellified the rest of her, and she barely heard the names of the staff she was introduced to. There was a deep, throbbing burn between her thighs and she could only pray she would be able to shower soon to wash away the heat coursing through her veins with cold water. The sun currently melting Agon had nothing on the way Alexis melted her.

She was a tinderbox for his touch, she thought despairingly, despairing even more that a simple holding of hands could feel so thrilling and that she was holding his hand as tightly as he was holding hers. She couldn't even lie to herself that she was holding it so tightly for show like he was. The physical pull Alexis held over her was stronger than her willpower—she had *no* willpower when it came to his touch—and she had to find a way to reverse it, and quickly. Or find a way to dampen it.

So lost in her despairing thoughts was she that when the housekeeper spoke to her, she shook her head to clear her ears because she hadn't heard a word of it. 'I'm sorry, what was that?'

There was avid curiosity on the woman's face…and

on the other staff's too, Lydia realised. 'Do you have any dietary requirements?'

'Umm...' Her mind was so all over the place that she had to think. 'No. No. I'll eat anything.'

'Especially chips,' murmured the deep voice belonging to the hand holdings hers so tightly, and a vivid memory flashed in her mind's eye, of Alexis's seductive eyes gleaming while he'd fed chips into her mouth.

Oh, why, why, why did that fun, gorgeous, sexy man she'd felt such a strong connection to in so many ways have to be her family's worst enemy, the serial philanderer Alexis Tsaliki?

Lydia had never understood the war between their families. Okay, she understood the root causes of it—a business partnership between her father and Georgios Tsaliki that had gone wrong—and understood the enmity her father felt towards his old friend and business partner. And she supposed she understood that marital loyalty meant her mother loathed Georgios too, but Lydia had never understood why this loathing extended to every Tsaliki and why it was expected that she despise them too. She'd tried to despise them for her parents' sake but her heart had never been in it. Maybe if she'd gone to the nightclub with her family's loathing for Alexis in her heart, she wouldn't have been so vulnerable to his seductive power...

And she wouldn't have conceived her child. Her innocent, blameless child, the only innocent in this whole sorry mess, and it was thinking of her innocent child that gave her the resolve needed to climb the wide, winding staircase and cross the mezzanine with her child's father knowing that she couldn't back out now just because she melted for him. If protecting her baby meant losing her family to gain a serial seducer as a husband then that was what she would do. What she *was* doing.

The moment he closed the bedroom door she wrenched her hand from his, then found that same hand itching to slap the knowing smile off his face.

Throwing himself onto the sprawling bed piled with pillows, he lay on his back and hooked his arms above his head. It was a pose that brought back memories of his cruel words in the moments before she'd walked out of his bedroom.

'I hope you're not expecting me to share that bed with you tonight,' she said. 'We're not married yet.'

'But, my angel of Hades, we have already sealed the deal on our commitment and, as I told you when we reached our agreement, I will not have the world—and I include my staff in this—believing my wife hates me so much that she won't share my bed.'

'It's bad luck for the bride and groom to sleep together the night before the wedding.'

'I think you'll find it's considered bad luck for the bride and groom to see anything of each other the day *and* night before the wedding,' he told her cheerfully. 'So we've already broken that taboo.'

'You're actively wishing bad luck on us?'

'My father has been married four times and observed all the rituals in all his weddings, and all four ended in divorce.'

'His fourth one hasn't.'

'Oh, yes. I forgot—sorry, must be wishful thinking on my part.'

Lydia had to bite her cheeks to stop herself sniggering at his droll delivery. Rebecca Tsaliki was the stuff of legends, the ordinary Englishwoman who'd captured the heart—or loins—of the macho billionaire philanderer Georgios Tsaliki and not only managed to get herself installed as wife number four but had him so firmly under her manicured thumb that he didn't dare replace her with wife number five, having to content himself with numerous affairs that she didn't bat an eyelash at instead.

Like father like son, and now Lydia was the one with a lifetime of infidelity to look forward to. Somehow she would have to find a way to channel a little of Rebecca Tsaliki's breezy attitude towards it because she couldn't change the son any more than Rebecca had been able to change the father.

She didn't want to change the son, she reminded herself stubbornly. This whole marriage thing was a sham that would be over in all but name as soon as Alexis found himself a new lover because Lydia sure as hell wasn't going to make any demands on him or demand anything from him, and then they could live in perfect marital harmony far apart from each other.

Sitting himself up, he patted the bed. 'From tonight, we sleep together, no arguments.'

'Fine, but no sex until we're married, and no arguments,' she shot back.

His eyes gleamed. 'Wanting to increase the anticipation, are you? I can get on board with that.'

'No, just delaying the inevitable for as long as I can.'

He swung his legs off the bed, laughing. 'I'm going to take a shower. Want to join me?'

She answered with a scowl.

'Sure about that?' Glimmering eyes locked on hers, he strode like a panther towards her.

Although Lydia's every instinct was to hide before she found herself within Alexis touching distance, she folded her arms over her breasts and clenched every cell in her body. 'Very.'

He stopped before her and dipped his mouth to her ear. 'Just imagine it... I would caress soap over every inch of your delectable body, paying special attention to the parts where you're most receptive...and I remember *all* of them...and then I'd lift you against the wall and take you with the water pouring over us...just like I did last time.'

The only part of him touching her was his breath to her ear but the flame that had taken her was strong enough to induce combustion, and it took everything she had not to falter and to find the strength to drag out, 'I'd rather die.'

He laughed softly. 'You forgot to list another reason people lie...' He lightly covered her breast, feeling its weight and the obvious betraying arousal of her nipple. 'To hide what they're really feeling.' His teeth caught the lobe of her ear and gently pulled before his next murmured words sank straight into her skin. 'And you forget that I know you intimately. I can read your body, Lydia, and it betrays your words.' His tongue licked the tender flesh beneath her lobe as he gently squeezed her breast, sending shivers of arousal through her skin and up her spine. 'Tomorrow you will be mine. *Mine*... For the rest of your life...'

Alexis stood beneath the steaming water and closed his eyes. By rights, he should be exhausted. The hours spent since his talk with Lydia on the beach had been spent fighting fires and getting everything in place for the fires to continue being fought over the coming days. The carefully crafted, ambiguous statement about Thanasis and Lucie's wedding being called off had set off the predictable press feeding frenzy. It didn't help that dozens of the press were already in Greece to cover the wedding.

He wondered if Thanasis now regretted his flat refusal of Alexis's proposal that, to prove they were serious about ending their fathers' war, Alexis marry Lydia. 'Over my dead body,' he'd said, as if he, Alexis, were Caligula reincarnated.

He'd been tempted to casually hand over the lipstick that had fallen out of Lydia's bag when their passion had broken free in the back of his car, and say, 'Can you give this back to your sister for me?' But that would have been his ego talking. For all that Lydia had punched and bruised his ego in the way she'd left him, she didn't deserve the fallout she would have had to deal with.

She would be dealing with the fallout she didn't know he'd protected her from soon enough now. The loathing that had twisted her brother's face at Alexis's suggestion of marriage...

He doubted his own family would be pleased at the turn of events but, as they were currently beholden to his good will, any fallout would be minor ripples compared to the tsunami of opprobrium Lydia could expect from hers. It was one thing to arrange and agree a temporary marriage to cement a truce, quite another to actually be attracted to each other and conceive a child together. He could still feel the hate Lydia's mother had fired at him.

There was still a faint mark on his lip where her brother had punched him. Forgiveness did not come easily to those people. It never had. Alexis's father had screwed Lydia's father over decades before, before Lydia was even born, and still the hate burned.

But the attraction burned brighter and she, the woman who'd walked out on him and whose passion had turned to loathing, would be more beholden to him than even his family were.

She was his now. She was carrying his child and, whether her brother liked it or not, tomorrow Lydia would be his wife, and hell would freeze over before he ever let her go.

Lydia, sitting on the windowsill trying to take in the spectacular view of clear blue seas, turned her head to the opening bathroom door and wasn't quick enough to avert her eyes when Alexis stepped through it with only a towel around his waist. One quick glance was enough to fill her senses with the hard, muscular body she'd spent the last ten minutes studiously refusing to imagine under the shower. Studiously refusing to remember the sculpted perfection of.

Bodies like his should be illegal.

Funny what the memory remembered best though. For Lydia, it hadn't been his sculpted perfection that had stuck so close but the texture of his skin and the taste of his kisses. It was a darkly addictive taste that came from the whole of him, a taste she reacted instinctively and primitively to and that destroyed her willpower with one tiny morsel.

She heard the tread of his footsteps crossing the travertine floor and pressed her hand to her thumping heart.

'Ready for your shower?' he asked in that infuriating cheerful manner he had.

'I've nothing to change into,' she reminded him, refusing to turn her head again.

'I have clothes you can wear.'

'No, thank you,' she said stiffly.

'Afraid that wearing my clothes will feel too much like wearing my skin?'

Unable to think of a retort, she blew out a puff of air.

'We'll be married tomorrow, angel. What is mine becomes yours.'

'No, it doesn't. I already said I'd sign any prenup you demanded.'

'We don't need a prenup.'

That made her turn her head. 'Why not…?' The question had barely left her lips when she made the fatal mistake of dipping her gaze and taking in the unmistakable appendage clearly defined beneath the towel. With a pulse of heat throbbing between her thighs, she shot her gaze back out of the window, but not before she caught the gleam in his eyes.

'You look hot, angel. Sure you don't want to wear my clothes?'

'Oh, shut up,' she muttered. 'And stop calling me "angel".'

'But you are an angel…although I have yet to decide if you come from heaven or only from Hades.'

'Definitely just Hades.'

He laughed lowly, his footsteps treading away. 'What would you prefer I call you? Wife?'

'I'm not your wife.'

'Yet.'

'Why don't you want a prenup?'

'We don't need one. We agreed our marriage would be a commitment for life and I am trusting you to stick to your word.'

'That's a huge risk you're taking.'

'What is life without a little risk?' His voice came closer again. 'Now why don't you take the risk of showering and then change into this shirt? I promise, it will not bite you and I promise you will be a lot more comfortable than you are in those things.'

Wishing she could blame the heat flooding her skin solely on the setting sun's beams penetrating the window, Lydia jumped off the windowsill, snatched the blue garment from Alexis's hand and stomped to the bathroom, all without looking at him. His laughter lingered in her ears long after she'd slammed the bathroom door shut.

Where had this late-onset dose of vanity come from? Lydia wondered with fresh despair. She shouldn't be staring at her reflection wishing for a hairdryer and her makeup bag. She hardly ever wore makeup as it was! And why the hell were her nipples jutting out like that? Alexis would take one look at them and assume she was aroused just from wearing his shirt. Damn him, he'd be right. It really did feel as if she were wearing his skin.

Maybe she should just storm back into the bedroom and push him onto the bed. Get it over with. Use him to get all these hot sticky feelings out of her system and then she'd be able to think more clearly. He wouldn't mind being used in that way. He'd revel in it, his massive ego taking it to mean that she was desperate for him. Damn the bastard, he'd be right, and she would never willingly feed that damned ego or hand any more power to him.

Hanging on the back of the door was a black robe. She yanked it down and shoved her arms into it, then tied it tightly. It fell to her ankles. After rolling the sleeves, she checked her reflection again and expelled a long breath. Visually, that was much better. Now she was fully covered with an extra layer of protection to stop her treacherous body giving her away.

If only the weight of the robe didn't make her feel as though he were embracing her...

To Lydia's relief, the bedroom had been empty of Alexis. Less of a relief had been the expression on his gorgeous face when she'd appeared on the patio to join him for dinner. Amusement. He'd taken one look at the robe and known exactly why she was wearing it. The worst of it was that he didn't have to say a word, and now she was picking at her food and sweltering under the humid air even more than she'd done earlier when the sun had blazed. She would not give him the satisfaction of asking if they could eat inside where the air-conditioning worked like a dream.

'How many properties do you own?' she asked, just for something to say, something to distract from the heat of the sensuous stare she couldn't stop her eyes from seeking.

'Eight for my personal use. As for my business portfolio...' He shrugged and shook his head. 'Do you want me to include business properties like nightclubs and retail units or just the properties I rent out?'

She blinked. 'You own nightclubs?'

'I own many businesses.'

'I know, but I'd never heard of you owning nightclubs.'

'Most of the businesses I own or invest in are done through a company my name is only attached to if a lot of digging is done.'

'Why the secrecy?'

'I don't need my family knowing my net worth. My siblings have bled my father dry over the years. If I fail to save Tsaliki Shipping then I will have to support them—I *am* supporting them—but they need to learn to fend for themselves.'

She took a moment to digest this. 'Did you know our fathers' rivalry was going to lead to their downfall?'

He speared a lemon potato. 'I saw long ago the way things were headed. The world we live in is very different from the one they lived in when their war started. The bottom line is the bottom line, but investors are no longer so willing to risk reputational damage—it matters much more than it did even a decade ago.'

'That goes for clients too,' she pointed out, thinking of the contracts Tsaliki Shipping had lost since the whole toxicity of the rivalry had been exposed.

He bowed his head in agreement.

'You say about your siblings bleeding your father dry…does that mean you see me as a freeloader too?'

His eyebrows rose in surprise. 'Of course not.'

'I still live with my parents…well, on their estate…

and the majority of my income comes from my shares in Antoniadis Shipping.'

'But you still work. You don't rely on your parents' largesse.'

'Of course I do, and from tomorrow I'll be relying on yours, especially when Antoniadis Shipping files for bankruptcy and I lose my income from the shares.'

He fixed her with a stare. 'Have you ever demanded a brand-new penthouse apartment? Or a chalet in Gstaad? Or your own yacht? Or a McLaren fresh off the production line?'

'I wouldn't dream of it, and if I did, I'd be told to buy them myself.'

'And that is my point—my siblings not only dream of those things but see it as their right, and my father never says no. He happily bled money supporting his own lifestyle, Rebecca's, his ex-wives' including my mother's, and all his children.'

'Including Lucie?'

'Lucie's not his daughter.'

'Is that why you thought it was okay to treat her like dirt and trick her into believing she was in love with my brother?'

The dig landed. She saw it, the tightening of his features. 'Lucie agreed to marry your brother. I did not coerce her or bribe her or blackmail her. She agreed of her own volition, and then she let her emotions get the better of her and broke her word—we all knew how things would end if she failed to marry Thanasis; it's what's playing out now. Her amnesia gave us all the chance to play the card again and if your brother hadn't been so damned stupid as to tell her the truth, she wouldn't have run again and your family wouldn't be facing bankruptcy.'

'And I wouldn't be sitting here.'

Now he was the one to consider what had just been said. 'Would you ever have told me about the baby if circumstance hadn't forced you into it?'

'Only out of obligation, but not before the baby was born.'

'What the hell does *out of obligation* mean?'

'I would have told you because you have a right to know and our child has a right to know its father, but I wouldn't have asked for anything from you or wanted or expected anything.'

Incredulity rang from his eyes. 'You think I wouldn't have heard about the pregnancy once you started showing?'

She had a small drink of her water, holding the glass tightly to stop him seeing the tremor in her hand. 'I'd planned to hide myself away after Lucie and Thanasis's wedding. I'm not one for the society social scene so no one would have missed my presence.'

'What about your family?' he asked in disbelief. 'How the hell did you think they were going to react when you told them? Your brother would have hunted me down.'

'I wasn't going to name the father to anyone until after the birth. My hope was that my parents would fall in love with the baby before I told them. I hoped that loving it would make it harder for them to turn their back on it.'

He put his cutlery down and pushed his plate to one side to lean forwards. 'Did you, at any point in all your plotting, consider my feelings and what I would have wanted?'

'Alexis, I was just another notch on your bedpost. If you hadn't taken me back to your apartment that night some other woman would have gone with you, and if you remembered me it would only be because of who I am and the fact that we didn't exactly part on good terms. I thought you'd be relieved to be let off the fatherhood hook.'

'Let off the fatherhood hook?'

For the first time since she'd known him, Lydia saw real anger on his face.

'Oh, come on,' she defended herself, gripping her forearm. 'I can't be the first woman you've had a condom mishap with. For all I know, there could be a dozen mini Alexises stashed away around Europe.'

'No, Lydia, there are no mini Alexises, not in Europe or anywhere. What you and I shared that weekend was *not normal*, do you not understand that?'

'You called me a *not particularly memorable one-weekend stand* only yesterday!' she protested.

His lips twisted. 'They were just words. In my world, what counts is actions and intentions, and your intention until your hand was forced otherwise was to keep me out of my child's life. You didn't even want me to share in the pregnancy with you.'

'Only because that's what I thought you'd want!'

He stared at her for the longest time, long enough for her trembling insides to turn into a guilt-ridden quivering wreck. 'Then you don't know me at all.'

'Alexis...'

He cut her off with the scraping-back of his chair.

'I'm going to bed. I haven't slept for two days and need to sleep. Finish your meal and join me when you're ready—I choose to believe that it's sleep deprivation causing my dinner to taste so bitter.'

He disappeared inside without another word.

Lydia crept into the bedroom. She'd seriously debated finding another room to sleep in but didn't want to make matters worse. She'd angered Alexis enough as it was.

Her heavy heart twisted to see the dim bedside light left on for her. Twisted harder to see the huge form burrowed beneath the sheets and the flash of black hair poking out of the top.

In the bathroom, a toothbrush still in its packaging had been left on the ledge above the sink for her, and she brushed her teeth automatically, her head too full of the man she was about to slide under the sheets beside to even pay attention to the action of rinsing her mouth out.

Was it possible that she'd hurt him?

It had never crossed her mind that Alexis was capable of feeling something as everyday human as hurt, but, hurt or anger or both, it didn't matter, she'd caused it. Hurt or anger or both, she still felt wretched.

The heavy robe hung back on the door, she tiptoed to the bed holding tightly to her thrashing heart and carefully slipped under the covers.

It wasn't until she turned the light off and the only noise to be heard through the darkness was the blood roaring in her ears did she realise Alexis, his back turned to her, was still awake.

'I'm sorry,' she whispered, guilt driving her words. 'I shouldn't have made assumptions. I was...' Terrified.

The positive sign on the pregnancy test had unleashed a swathe of emotions but terror had been the strongest, a future as a single mother without the family who'd always loved and protected her all she could see. Her family who were already having to deal with the prospect of losing everything.

The thought of tracking Alexis down a second time to tell him the news and what she'd believed would be the strong likelihood of him contemptuously offering to pay her off had terrified her too. The bad feelings they'd parted with had still tasted bitter in her mouth but, as hard as she'd tried, she'd been completely unable to stop her mind being consumed by him. Been completely unable, too, to stop her heart skipping and her stomach lurching every time her phone made a noise. Knowing the life growing inside her meant she would be tied to Alexis for the rest of her life…that had been the most terrifying thing of all.

She swallowed to force her next words out. 'I can make all the excuses in the world but I should have told you as soon as I knew.'

His silence spoke louder than any verbal answer could have done.

CHAPTER SIX

THE PALACE GATES opened for her, and in that brief moment Lydia felt like a bona fide princess. She'd seen plenty of pictures of the palace, one of Europe's largest, over the years, but nothing could have prepared her for its magnificence in the flesh. In a country with a strong shared cultural heritage with its Greek neighbour Crete, its palace had a strong Middle Eastern flavour to it, as if it had long ago been built for a great Sultan, its multicoloured turrets and domed roofs gleaming under the midday sun.

Driving slowly through the magnificent grounds, she feared her heart might smash its way out of her chest.

Would Alexis even be there?

She'd been gently woken by a maid with her laundered clothes and a tray of coffee, fruit and pastries. The bed had been empty, not even residual warmth on Alexis's side. But she'd caught the faint trace of his cologne lingering in the air and knew he must have showered and dressed in stealth mode. A kindness to let her sleep a little longer? Did he know that she'd still been wide awake hours after he'd fallen into a deep sleep, her thoughts wretched, longing for him to roll over and press into her, longing to roll over and press herself into him? Or was he still too angry to want to speak to her?

Once she'd finished eating, she'd been given a short brown wig to disguise herself with and a credit card, and then taken to Agon's swankiest hotel by Alexis's driver with strict instructions to be ready for collection in two hours.

Inside, she'd been astounded to find numerous boutiques catering to all tastes.

Lydia could never explain to herself why she hadn't grabbed the first pair of jeans and vaguely reasonable top to wear, nor why she'd bought makeup and perfume, nor why she'd spent so long in the guest shower room that she'd had to run to make it to the car park on time. Nor did she understand why she wrenched the wig off as soon as the driver closed the door and then spent half the journey frantically brushing and fiddling with her hair.

And she would never be able to explain or understand why the fear that had rooted itself so tightly in the knots in her belly was the fear that Alexis had changed his mind, and that no matter how much she rubbed her belly and whispered to the tiny life inside it that its daddy would be there, that he was committing himself to them, she couldn't shake off the even more deeply rooted fear that he would never commit himself solely to *her*.

As far as fears went, it was ludicrous because she'd loftily told him she didn't demand or expect fidelity and he'd never even alluded to it. She shouldn't want it. She shouldn't. She wouldn't.

Somehow she had to find a way to stop herself imagining him with other women. Learn to block her own thoughts, and, if that proved impossible, learn to control the sickness those thoughts always induced.

Be more Rebecca Tsaliki, she chanted to herself. Be more Rebecca Tsaliki.

If the palace itself had a Middle Eastern flavour, the royal chapel, its yellow walls excepted, was pure Greek.

Not a soul witnessed her slip through its doors. Only the prince, a mountain of a man bigger even than Alexis, his beautiful wife, Amelie, and the priest were there to greet her. And Alexis, standing at the altar…

Relief whooshed through every cell of her body. And something else, something that filled her chest and weakened her legs.

He met her at the aisle's halfway point. His face was a mask she couldn't read. 'I thought you might have done a Lucie.'

She had to clear her choked throat. 'I thought you might have done a Lucie too.'

His chest rose before a half-smile played on his lips, and she suddenly found herself overwhelmed with a longing to see the full-blown smile that had so warmed her the first time it had been bestowed on her all that time ago. 'We made a deal, my angel. Now it is time to seal it.'

Alexis recited his vows still expelling relief that Lydia hadn't fled from the hotel and taken the first flight off the island. Even though his driver had messaged when he was en route to the palace, he'd been unable to shake the feeling that the car would arrive empty. But she was here and so ravishingly beautiful that when she'd stepped into the chapel he'd felt her presence like a punch to his heart.

Having expected her to turn up in ripped jeans, and still furious that she'd believed he wouldn't want to be a father, his ego punched all over again at her scathing dismissal of their weekend together, he'd been tempted to wear something similar, only changing into smart navy trousers and a white shirt at the last minute for the sole reason that they were marrying in a house of God and so he should at least make an effort to look respectable.

The last thing he'd expected was for Lydia to make an effort too. She was so naturally beautiful that she didn't need to make an effort but when she did, the effect was breathtaking.

Far from wearing ripped jeans, she stood facing him at the altar in a creamy white floaty dress, the laced long-sleeved top half plunging in a V giving a hint of her growing cleavage, the flowing skirt ruched, the whole thing tied together with a thick brown belt at the waist. She looked like she should be running through a meadow with her long blonde hair trailing behind her.

Their vows made, the time had come to seal their marriage like they'd sealed their commitment to their deal of a real marriage—with a kiss.

Their eyes locked together. He pressed a hand into the small of her back A small hand slid onto his shoulder. His heart thumping a roar in his head, Alexis brought his mouth down to hers as she lifted her mouth to his. He glimpsed a sweep of her lashes before he closed his eyes and their lips fused together in a long, lingering kiss.

Breaking apart, he gazed again into the hazel eyes

now brimming with an emotion he'd never seen in them before.

Euphoria slammed through him.

Lydia was *his*.

She was married. A married woman. Married to Alexis Tsaliki.

God help her.

Prince Talos had arranged a wedding meal for them in a stateroom in the palace, the four of them dining at a table that could comfortably seat fifty.

She was dining with royalty, a thought that was only a dim whisper in a head filled wholly with the man seated next to her, eating, chatting and laughing as if this were all just an ordinary meal. Her husband.

The wedding service itself had passed in a daze but she could still feel the mark of Alexis's mouth from their kiss. Still feel the longing that had ripped through her when he'd made his vows, a swelling of emotion that had filled her so completely she had no memory of reciting her own identical vows in turn.

'I promise you love, honour and respect; to be faithful to you, and not to forsake you until death do us part...'

Why hadn't it occurred to her that marrying in a chapel would mean reciting traditional vows? And why, when the time had come to recite them, had it felt the most natural thing in the world when it was all a lie? As if Alexis were going to be faithful to her! As if he could ever love her! As if she could ever love him!

But it had all felt so natural and, in the moment, right, and now she had an impending sense of doom in the pit of her stomach that she'd just made the greatest mistake of her life.

A hand slid onto her thigh. She trembled as a jolt of electricity shot through her, and tightened her hold on the stem of her glass to stop herself seeking out the hand to hold it.

He was marking his territory, she told herself. Reminding her that *she* was now his territory, reminding her of what was to come when they left the palace, and she didn't know if her growing sickness was nerves, terror or excitement. All she did know was that her heart had forgotten how to beat properly and when his fingers made gentle circles on her thighs, she didn't know if she wanted to grab his hand to shove it off her or move it higher...

As desperately as she wished for time to slow down, it accelerated, their seven courses flashing by at such speed that before she knew it, she was being embraced by the prince and princess with wishes for a long and happy marriage that registered like a distant ringing in her ears. When she climbed into the back of the car she realised she couldn't remember a single thing she'd eaten or a single snippet of conversation.

Nerves hadn't just kicked in, they were doing a full-blown cancan with a vigour that only increased when their car set off.

They were returning to Alexis's apartment to consummate the marriage. To have sex. For Lydia to fulfil her side of their deal as Alexis had just fulfilled his.

A large, warm hand covered the fist she hadn't even realised she'd made. 'How are you feeling, *wife*?'

Terrified.

She tried to conjure a smile. 'Good. You?'

A slow smile curved his cheeks and he leaned his face closer to hers. 'Very good.'

It was the blaze of sensuality in his eyes and the promise contained in it that had her sharply extract her hands from his on the pretext of removing her phone from her bag and checking her messages. She couldn't bear the longing that swelled in her to see it.

Hugely aware of Alexis's silent displeasure at her abrupt turning from him, even more aware that she was close to falling to pieces, Lydia bowed her head and tried to focus on reading the myriad messages she'd received from her mother with updates, along with the myriad messages from friends wanting to know what on earth was going on and why Thanasis and Lucie's wedding had been called off. And she tried harder than ever to block out the hunk of a man whose thigh was pressed against hers, and clear her body and mind of all the feelings and emotions ravaging her.

There was no preamble. They returned to the villa late afternoon and went straight up to the bedroom, Lydia's hand caught in Alexis's possessive hold.

He held the door open for her, then closed it firmly behind them, shutting out the world, narrowing it down to just the two of them.

Blue-grey eyes locked onto hers.

Lydia could no longer feel the individual beats of her heart. All efforts to clear her body and mind had come to nothing. The sickness in her stomach was like no sickness she'd ever felt before.

His stare fixed firmly on her, Alexis removed his

watch and cufflinks and placed them on his dresser, then his fingers pinched the top button of his shirt. Working methodically, he undid the buttons one by one and shrugged his arms free.

She could swear her whole body contracted, and she drank him in, helpless to turn her stare away, helpless to stop her tongue tingling with the remembered taste of that glorious body, her breasts tightening in anticipation of being flattened against it.

There was a buzzing from inside the bag she was holding to her chest as if it were a life raft.

His eyes narrowed. 'Ignore it. You spent long enough on it in the car.'

Call it defiance, stubbornness, fear, anything, but she wrenched her stare from his and pulled her phone out. Before she could swipe to answer it, the phone had been plucked from her hand.

'Give it back, that's my mother calling.'

'No.' He placed it beside his watch on the dresser.

Fear turned to an anger she couldn't begin to understand. 'Give that back!'

'No. I have been more than patient but enough is enough.'

Anger morphing into fury, she charged past him, her stretched fingers about to clasp hold of the phone when an arm hooked around her waist and she was spun around and hauled flush into bare solid torso.

'What are you so afraid of?' he demanded harshly, his features as tight as she'd ever seen them, his stare boring down on her.

Everything.

'*Nothing,*' she spat, raising her arm; would have slapped him away if he hadn't caught her wrist.

'Good, then there is nothing to stop me doing this.' There was no time for her to even breathe let alone brace herself before his mouth came crushing down on hers.

In an instant, the foundations of Lydia's world moved as Alexis's dark taste filled her, his kiss a skilled, ruthless assault of the senses that knocked all the air from her lungs and all the sense from her brain.

His features were still taut when he broke the fusion, but his eyes…his eyes burned with an intensity she'd never seen in them before, trapping her even more tightly to the force of his will.

Nostrils flaring, he clasped her waist and lifted her off her feet, wordlessly carrying her to the bed where he laid her down and pinned her beneath him.

His gorgeous but implacable face loomed down on her. 'I ask you again, what are you so frightened of?'

But she was too choked on the heat his savage kiss had unleashed in her and too overwhelmed with all the other feelings careering through her to answer.

His face contorted although with what she couldn't say, could only feel it, almost like a pain in her heart.

'No more hiding from me, Lydia. No more fighting me. We made our vows and now you are mine, do you understand that?'

The brutality of his words and ferocity in his stare should have made her quail but instead it melted something in her, something deep in her core that made her breathe out a sigh and mutely plead with him to understand that it wasn't him she was fighting but herself because…

Because he was going to break her heart.

The realisation hit her straight in the heart he was going to break.

Staring with equal intensity into the eyes boring into hers brought another truth. She was already in too deep. Even if she hadn't conceived his child she would have struggled to forget him, but she *had* conceived, a part of him combining with a part of her and taking life, and now she carried him everywhere she went. In her womb, in her blood, in her head, in her dreams.

It was all too late. Alexis was already a part of her and he was going to break her heart and there was nothing she could do about it because this was the deal she'd made.

He was giving her everything she'd asked for. He'd married her when he could have said no. He hadn't disputed their child's paternity, hadn't even questioned it. The only thing he'd played hardball over was their marriage being a real one, and she'd agreed to it. She'd agreed to *this* because, deep down inside, it was what she wanted too. She'd just been too frightened to admit it to herself, and now all she could do was her best to protect the parts of her he hadn't yet touched because she couldn't keep fighting against a future that was already written, a future she'd agreed to, sealed with a kiss that had burned her into fondue and which still lingered in her veins.

Her throat still too choked to speak, she raised her hand and cupped his cheek.

He closed his eyes and breathed in deeply. After long, long moments, he recaptured her stare. The hard intensity that had blazed in his eyes softened. 'Our families might be at war, but I am not your enemy. I never have been. I am your husband and you are my wife. It's you and me now, Lydia, and that's how it will always be.'

When his mouth came back down on hers it was with a driven sense of purpose. Fingers dragged through her hair as his tongue parted her lips in an intimate, demanding exploration that sparked electricity into all her senses and opened her up like the petals of a flower blossoming under the sun.

Alexis was her sun, she thought dimly as their kiss deepened and all the passion she'd tried so hard and for so long to contain ignited into an inferno. The sun that breathed life into a body that had never known such pleasure existed.

It was only when Lydia's fingers burrowed into his hair and clasped his skull to fuse their mouths even tighter that the last of the tightness in Alexis's chest breathed free and he allowed himself to let go.

Burrowing his face into the delicate skin of her neck, he breathed Lydia deeply into his lungs, filling himself with the scent and taste he'd been unable to shake since she'd left his bed, and when she gave a soft moan, he drank it through his pores with the same greed.

She was his now, and he was going to make it so damned good for her that she'd never want to leave his bed or his life again.

Lifting himself off her, he straddled her thighs and, without any ceremony, unbuckled her belt. That discarded with, it was easy to slide the sleeves of her dress off her shoulders and then pull it down... *Theos*, she wasn't wearing a bra. Her succulent, perfect breasts with the rosy-red peaks were bare. A deep throb of lust speared him and, unable to resist a taste, he swooped down and captured a breast in his mouth in the way that had driven her so wild before.

Lydia arched her neck and cried out at the tight sensation, and she thrust her chest up and cradled his head, but he was intent on torturing her, moving his mouth down and trailing his tongue over her stomach as he tugged her dress over her hips. With a lift of her bottom, he pulled it down, past her thighs and then roughly dragged it to her feet and threw it to one side before sliding her knickers down and discarding them too.

Making quick work of his remaining clothes, he stretched out on top of her, the tips of her breasts jutting against the hardness of his chest as he cupped her face. 'You will never know what you do to me,' he whispered, and then his hands and mouth were everywhere, touching, kissing, biting, inflaming her skin, inflaming her veins, seeking, searching…and the hot restlessness deep in her core took possession of her until she was nothing but a boneless mass, a creature of pleasure, created for this man and this man alone.

Hands capturing her wrists, his mouth found her breasts again, and all she could do was writhe helplessly as his tongue encircled her peaks, licking and tasting, teasing, teasing, teasing…

'Please,' she gasped. *'Please.'*

Just when she thought she couldn't take the torture any longer, he took a peak into his mouth and released her wrists to slide his hands down the curves of her inflamed body as he suckled, giving her the pleasure she so craved, a pleasure she'd never even known she could feel until she'd fallen hedonistically into Alexis's bed and he'd shown her just how exquisite pleasure could be.

Moving his attention to her other sensitised breast, his fingers trailed over her stomach and then slipped between her legs.

There was a moment of delicious anticipation where she stopped breathing entirely, a faint groan from his throat as he cupped her heat and then he slid a finger inside her and she couldn't hear anything above the roar in her ears.

It was as though she were caught in a fever with his mouth moving relentlessly over her breasts and his fingers sliding in and out of her until, as if he really had been teasing her, he found the centre of where she throbbed unmercifully and, with barely any pressure from his thumb, she erupted, crying out, her hands flailing as her climax took her to the dimension only Alexis could carry her to.

The waves of her climax hadn't even begun to subside when he snaked his way back up her throat to kiss her, reigniting her passion with little more than his taste.

Mouths fused together all over again, she raised her hips and writhed, desperately seeking his full possession, barely felt him capturing her wrists again and pressing them at the side of her head until he broke the fusion of their lips.

Opening her eyes, she found his hooded gaze boring down on her, his breathing heavy.

'Tell me you're mine,' he demanded roughly.

Her throat caught.

He brought his face right to hers so the tips of their noses touched. His arousal was pressing where she most needed it to be but no matter how much she strained her pelvis in a silent plea for him to just *take her*, his stare continued to uncompromisingly drill into her. 'Say it. Say it, Lydia. Tell me you're mine.'

In such a fevered state she'd have said anything, promised anything if he would only just *take her*, she parted her lips. 'I…' And then her words cut away as she found herself trapped in his stare, not just trapped in it but carried into it, like an invisible piece of herself had dislodged and transferred into his possession.

She lifted her head and pressed her mouth to his. Eyes still locked together, she whispered, 'I'm yours, Alexis.'

There was a long moment of stillness before he expelled a long groan into her mouth, and then buried himself deep, deep inside her.

Lydia had carried the sensation of his lovemaking all these long months but time must have diminished it because *this*…

His hot, demanding tongue danced into her mouth and she was lost.

Closing her eyes, she returned his kisses with the same passionate intensity, holding him tightly as she spread her legs even wider and submitted herself to the magic of his lovemaking.

Alexis could hardly hold on. All these months he'd carried their lovemaking in his head but memory had nothing on reality and now he was an electrified coil straining against release, but, *Theos*, the sensation…

She was close to the edge. He could feel it, the delicious tension coiling through her body, the heightened colour on her cheeks when she flung her head back, the tightness of her fingers when they gripped hold of his biceps, the straining sinews of her delicate neck, the growing thickness around his arousal as he drove in and out of her…and then her eyes flew open.

With her lips parted and her hazel stare locked onto his in wonder, the contractions of her release pulled him deeper and deeper until he was thrusting into her with all his frenzied power and his own coil snapped and he came with a load roar of her name.

CHAPTER SEVEN

EVEN THOUGH HE'D propped himself onto an elbow to stop Lydia having to take the full brunt of his weight, a sneaking fear that he could still hurt her and the baby propelled Alexis to move off her. He was still trying to catch his breath. Could still feel the tremors of her body. Hell, he could still feel the tremors of *his* body.

Rolling onto his back, he hooked an arm beneath her and drew her to him.

There was the slightest resistance before she rested her head on his chest and curled into him. Sweat glistened off both their bodies.

He held her tightly and closed his eyes. His thoughts were fragmented, his emotions shot.

'I can hear your heartbeats,' she whispered into the silence.

Cupping her neck, he burrowed his fingers into her hair. 'I can feel yours.' An erratic thud right beneath where her soft breasts were pressing into him, and his loins twitched in response. *Theos*, he could hardly believe fresh arousal was already snaking its way through him... No, he could believe it. Believe it because he'd already lived it, that one hedonistic weekend where unashamed raw desire had ballooned into a passion that had blown his mind.

A need to just *look* at her had him gently manipulating her onto her back and stretching himself over her.

Being careful not to press too much of his weight on her, he soaked in the beautiful face and then pressed a light kiss to the lips swollen from the passion of their lovemaking. 'Are you okay?'

Hazel eyes holding his, she gave the tiniest smile and nodded, and rested her hand at the nape of his neck.

He kissed her again. 'Are you hungry?'

She shook her head and sighed before lifting her head to kiss him. 'Not for food.'

It wasn't possible that he could be hard again so soon but he was, and when she kissed him again, sliding inside her felt the most natural thing in the world.

Lydia opened her eyes to find herself entwined in Alexis's arms and the room bathed in a dusky light that told her the sun would soon be lost to the horizon.

Gently trying to extract herself from his hold without waking him, she was foiled from escaping when he tightened the arm around her waist.

'Where do you think you're going?' he murmured sleepily.

'The bathroom.'

He sighed as if being put upon. 'Okay, I suppose I can allow that.'

'You are too kind.'

'I know.'

Giggling softly, she lifted her head to kiss him, her chaste display of affection morphing into a full-blown passionate kiss when Alexis's fingers speared her hair and his tongue slid into her mouth.

After what felt like a bucketful of kisses, she finally wriggled free and managed to make her liquid legs carry her to the bathroom.

There was a semi-stranger looking back at her in the bathroom mirror. Lydia had met her only once before: the morning after her second night with Alexis. Then, she had gazed at her reflection with sorrow clutching her heart that the most magical time of her life had to end, a little bit like she'd felt as a child when all the lights from the Christmas and New Year celebrations were taken down and all the joy they represented was packed away for what had felt to young Lydia as interminably long months. Quickly, though, that flattening of her spirits would dissipate and life would return to normal.

Life had never returned to normal after her weekend with Alexis. Her spirits had never lifted themselves back to normal levels. She'd carried a flatness in her soul she'd never been able to shake.

Now she looked at the semi-stranger, a woman with glowing eyes and rosy cheeks, and wondered why she'd never met her before Alexis. And couldn't help but wonder when she would disappear and the Lydia who'd always looked back at her would reappear, the Lydia who loved her family dearly but who'd always yearned for something different for herself but had never quite found the courage to go out and get it without detaching the safety nets they provided.

There was nothing safe about Alexis. He came without a safety net. He might dress in suits like her father and brother but he was thrilling and dangerous, everything they weren't, and he was going to break her heart.

She'd made her choice and she wouldn't lie to herself that she'd made it because she had no choice. She'd agreed to this, and she could spend their marriage hating him and fighting him and making them both miserable, or she could take what they did have together and just enjoy it for as long as it lasted. So long as she kept herself clear-sighted about what *this* was then she'd be able to protect the parts of her heart Alexis hadn't yet touched, and then when the time came for her to lie in the bed of her own making she'd be able to lie in it stoically and without complaint. Or at least try.

Back in the bedroom, she crossed to the bed wondering why she didn't feel any shyness about her naked body in front of him. She knew she had an okay figure but she'd never had that body confidence so many other women had and had never been comfortable with parading her nakedness in front of her partners. But then, they'd never looked at her with such naked appreciation and lust as Alexis did, as he was looking at her now. As if she were the biggest present left under the Christmas tree.

She was about to climb back into bed when her phone started buzzing.

She sighed. She'd had a dim awareness of her phone going off numerous times over the last few hours, reality doing its best to intrude.

'Ignore it,' he urged, throwing the sheets back and reaching an arm out to her. 'This is our wedding night.'

Torn, she bit into her bottom lip. 'It might be important.'

Eyes gleaming, he pointed to the huge erection he was sporting. 'More important than this?'

She couldn't help but laugh, even as the spot between her legs throbbed.

The amusement on his face dimmed a little and he expelled a long breath.

'What's wrong?' she asked.

He shook his head. 'Just thinking that's the first time you've laughed since I saw you again.' That flicker in his eyes made a brief return. 'I was starting to fear I'd never hear it again.'

'A man like you?' she said lightly to mask the tendrils of her heart tightening. 'I didn't think you were scared of anything.'

His stare was serious. 'Neither did I.' And then a smile curved his lips and with a speed and agility no man of his size should have, he twisted over and caught her by the waist, lifting her onto the bed and pulling her on top of him. 'Now I've got you.'

Laughing, she tried to wriggle off, might have succeeded if he hadn't captured a breast in his mouth.

'Alexis…' Her protest died in her throat as a surge of electrical desire pulsed straight from her breast into her groin.

His mouth now snaking up her neck, he found her lips and kissed her passionately.

'Let's have this one night,' he murmured huskily, his fingers skimming down her back to grope the cheek of her bum. 'Forget the world and our families and just live for now.'

By the time he drove inside her, she'd forgotten anyone else existed but Alexis.

* * *

Lydia stood on the balcony of Alexis's room gazing out at the peaceful lapping of the sea on his private beach. They could be the only two people in existence.

She sighed. 'Do we really have to go back?'

Arms slid around her waist, a hard body pressing into her back. 'One day of marriage and already you are selfish for me,' he murmured, almost purring like a satisfied cat.

She was glad he couldn't see her expression at his jovial arrogance or he would recognise the truth in his words. 'As amazing a lover as you are, I was thinking more about everything we've got coming for us when we get back to Athens.'

His mouth brushed her ear, a hand cupping her breast. 'You think I'm an amazing lover?'

A delicious shiver ran up her spine. 'With all your experience there would be something wrong if you weren't.'

He playfully pinched her nipple. 'You do love cutting me down to size,' he mused, sliding his hand back down to her stomach and resting his chin on her head. 'I'm not afraid to say that I'm entirely selfish for you and if I could extend our time here then I would, but there are too many fires to put out.'

Lydia's heart should *not* sigh at his admittance of being selfish for her. Alexis was sex mad. The difference between them was that she was only sex mad for him and she would rather dye her hair blue than admit this or admit he was the first man to have ever made her climax. Alexis's ego did not need feeding.

Determined not to let her mood slip, she lightly said, 'Don't you employ staff to put fires out for you?'

'I do, and they've been fighting them since we got here, but it's not fair for me to expect them to do it any longer. I took control of Tsaliki Shipping from my father with the promise that I would turn its future around for the better. Now that things have gone to hell, I can't leave it to others. It's my responsibility to fix things, no one else's.'

Not wanting to think of her brother battling the same fires but with no hope of extinguishing them, Lydia leaned back into Alexis and closed her eyes. It was time to face her immediate future head-on. 'Where will I go?'

'What do you mean?'

'When we're back in Athens. I suppose I should go home—'

'Your home is with me,' he cut in firmly.

'But we're not going to be announcing our news until Sunday. What am I supposed to do until then? Just hide away?' She couldn't be seen around Athens. Her face wasn't well known like Alexis's or her brother's, but all the recent publicity had put her in a spotlight she'd never been under before, and there was always the chance she'd bump into someone or be seen by someone who actually knew her and knew her family. While her parents had been glad of her supposed trip to England and its means of getting her safely out of the media's firing line, how could she justify being back in her home city and not going home to them? Just to imagine the turmoil they were all going through made her feel wretched. Knowing she'd married Alexis to save her own skin made her feel worse, a feeling that didn't change when she reminded herself she'd done it for their baby's sake or when she reminded herself that as soon as she was in a position to help, she'd be there for them.

She still hadn't checked her phone. Barely a whole day had passed since Alexis had swiped it from her hands and now the thought of scrolling through her messages filled her with dread. Her mother would be going out of her mind.

'It's only for six days,' he said. 'Anything you need to entertain you by day will be provided.' He dipped his mouth back to her ear. 'And I'll be home to provide a very different kind of entertainment by night.'

Just to imagine it was enough to fill her with longing and for her legs to weaken. The jut of his arousal poking through his shorts and into the small of her back wasn't helping, and when she clamped her hands to his to stop them wandering back to her breasts, she held them tightly in part to stop herself from dragging his hands back up to them.

'I still need my clothes,' she reminded him. As sensually erotic as it felt to wear Alexis's shirts, she wanted her own stuff.

'I'll have them collected and brought to the apartment. Give me your friend's address and I'll make the arrangements now.'

'Is this always your approach to solving problems? Just get on and sort it?' Not just problems but things he wanted. He'd wanted her and he'd had her. He'd wanted a real marriage and within two days he'd got his wish. When Alexis wanted something to happen, he made it happen.

'What other way is there to approach them?'

'I don't know. Until the war between our fathers hit the news and everything imploded, I lived a charmed life. Everything was easy. I never wanted for anything.'

And, she was starting to suspect, it was fear of actually wanting for something that had stopped her cutting the safety net her family provided. Maybe all this was a punishment for being so complacent about her place in life. 'What gave you your drive? Why were you the only Tsaliki offspring to get out there and make a name and fortune for himself off his own back?'

He exhaled heavily into her hair and when he spoke, it was without the sensual undertone that had been lacing his voice the whole conversation. 'Because I didn't want to be my father.'

That was not an answer she'd been expecting.

'I grew up wanting to be him,' he explained quietly. 'I idolised him. When he divorced my mother and I was told I'd be staying primarily with my father, I was glad.'

'How old were you?'

'Eight, and it took me another twelve years to realise my father is actually a narcissistic arsehole who uses his money as a weapon. He paid my mother and my first two stepmothers off and God knows how many mistresses. I'm one of nine and I'm quite sure there would be more of us if Rebecca hadn't forced him to have a vasectomy after Loukas was born. He likes to keep everyone close, one big happy family all feeding his ego and living off his largesse, but all it does is create a cycle of dependence and allows him to get away with and justify any kind of behaviour.'

'So how were you able to see through him if your siblings haven't?'

'I'm quite sure all my siblings have seen through him too but they're happy to be props in Georgios Tsaliki's tapestry of what a great, generous man he is. I wasn't.'

'But *why*? What made you different?'

'Partly it's to do with being the oldest. I'm thirty-seven and can remember a time when it was just my father, my mother, Constantine, Atticus and me. This was before Dad really made a success of the business and traded my mother in and our lives became a circus.'

'Did you see much of your mother after the divorce?'

'I saw her all the time. My father's a generous man and bought her a house close to ours. She would often join us on holidays too. Our relationship's a good one.'

'I'm glad.'

'See?' he said in a lighter tone. 'I *can* sustain a relationship with a woman.'

Lydia cut through the wave of sadness Alexis's snippet about his early childhood had provoked by forcing a small laugh at a jest that made the sadness heavier. 'You said you're different from your siblings in your drive partly because you're the oldest. Does that mean there was something else at play?'

'Yes, and that something was your father.'

His words hung between them until he said, 'Lydia, I grew up believing the Antoniadis name was synonymous with the devil. You were all vultures who'd built your fortune off the back of my father's work. As my father would tell it, he was the brains in the partnership between himself and your father, and when your father severed it, he took all the best contacts and systems my father had put in place leaving my father to start again from nothing. I still don't know the truth of this and I doubt I ever will because both men tell a different story, but when I was twenty I passed your father in the street and I was curious, mostly because he didn't have devil horns in his head.'

'My father's a good man,' she said quietly.

'He behaved as badly as my father during their war but I believe that fundamentally he's a better man than him. Seeing him sparked something in me and I started asking about him with contacts, just to get an outside perspective, and all I heard were good things. A good man, a good and fair employer. No scandals, no illegitimate children, no largesse... I'm not saying learning about your father made me want to be like him because I was twenty and his life sounded as exciting as magnolia paint, but it was one of those lightbulb moments—that my father wasn't the great man I'd always believed, that he was actually selfish and venal and that I was on the path to becoming a carbon copy of him. It just sparked in me a whole new perspective of my father and myself, and it also made me realise I was completely dependent on him and that if I didn't do something about it, I would be dependent on him for the whole of my life. It lit the fire in me to find my own path and make my own mark on the world.'

Lydia held the hand pressed against her belly, digesting all Alexis had just revealed to her and thinking, too, about how her desire to find her own path outside the family business had extended only as far choosing graphic design over shipping and moving into the cottage at the bottom of the family garden. The Antoniadis Shipping shares assigned to her had been deliberately designed to give her a modest income that would need to be supported by her own endeavours, but, in reality, she'd never really *had* to work. She'd had the same kind of expensive education as Alexis but she'd done little with it. Everything about her was modest, from her income to her home—which wasn't even hers—to her car, to the few boyfriends she'd chosen, nothing to set her alight or put a fire in her belly, her existence entirely forgettable.

How had she never seen that before?

No one could ever forget Alexis. He had a fire in *his* belly, an inner spark that shone brightly and drew people to him like moths to bask in the heat of his flame. Lydia had been drawn to that fire from the first lock of their eyes, and now she couldn't help herself fearing just how badly she would be burned from it.

Not wanting to think about the future she'd chosen to walk into, she said, 'How did you do it?'

'My father refused to give me or my siblings shares in the company because he didn't want to cede any potential control to us, but he paid me a good salary. I started investing it.' He laughed but there was little humour behind it. 'One thing I didn't expect was that he would respect me for it and that in itself spurred me on further. When you get to know my father you'll learn he has a real magnetism. Basking under his approval makes you feel like the king of the world. He's a man full of contradictions and my feelings for him are just as contradictory. For all his selfishness and narcissism, he has a generous heart.'

But in that moment she couldn't have cared less about contradictions or generous hearts. 'You want me to get to know him?' she asked in horror.

'You will get to know all my family,' he said calmly, as if this were nothing at all.

'But…they will hate me.'

His voice hardened. 'Some of them might—Athena is a given, but she hates everyone—but if they want to stay on my good side, they will treat you with courtesy and respect or face the consequences.'

'I can't come between you and your family!'

'*You* are my family now, angel. You are my wife and you are carrying my child. That makes you more important to me than anyone.'

The most important person until the novelty wore off, she thought wretchedly but didn't say.

If there was one trait of his father Alexis had enthusiastically embraced, it was his womanising, and to endure it she was going to have to play the role of Alexis's stepmother, Rebecca Tsaliki. It wouldn't happen just yet, not while the chemistry was so strong, but it would happen, and she really must stop thinking about it otherwise the future with Alexis that had been prewritten would start to eat at her before it had even been lived.

'My family will never accept you or our child and I have nothing to threaten them with to force them,' she said miserably. 'In a week's time I'm going to be lucky if they let me keep the Antoniadis name.'

His hands moved from her stomach and slid up her arms to her shoulders and gently turned her around. Tilting her chin with his fingers, he quietly said, 'Lydia, I'm not going to pretend I don't know what's at stake for you or that things are going to be easy for you, but, whatever happens, you are not alone. Know that. We're in this together.' And then, as if to prove his point, his mouth came down on hers and he proved just how together they were.

CHAPTER EIGHT

THERE WAS REAL apprehension weighing down Lydia's chest when they took the elevator from Alexis's apartment block's underground car park up to his penthouse, and it had nothing to do with being hidden away in it for the best part of a week to look forward to. Her apprehension came from meeting his staff. Three months ago his butler had been on duty when they'd arrived back from the club and had been the one to deliver food to their room, while a maid had directed her to the elevator that took her down to the block's lobby when she'd done the *walk of shame* as Alexis had called it. She didn't know what would be worst—seeing or not seeing a flicker of recognition. If they didn't recognise her then she really had been just another interchangeable face to emerge from Alexis's bedroom, but if they did then she would have to live with them thinking God knew what about her. She knew she shouldn't care what strangers thought of her but she did care, deeply.

'You're sure your staff can be trusted to keep their mouths shut about me?' she whispered, as if the elevator had hidden microphones the staff were listening in on.

If he was annoyed at having to answer the same question for the thousandth time, he hid it well. 'I pay them too well to talk and even if they wanted to, the non-disclosure agreements they've all signed are watertight,' he reassured her for the thousandth time.

'I'm sorry. I just couldn't bear for my family to hear about us from anyone but me.'

He squeezed her hand. 'They won't.'

The elevator door opened and they stepped into the small, unfurnished room she had only the vaguest memory of.

'Tomorrow, I will have your eye-print added and give you all the access codes to the building,' he said, indicating the retinal scanner beside the reinforced steel door. 'It will allow you to come and go as you please.'

'I won't be going anywhere for a week, but thanks.'

'If you find yourself getting cabin fever you can always go out in that brown wig.'

'I'd rather not risk it, but thanks.'

'The option's there if you want it.'

'Thanks.'

Instead of putting his eye to the scanner, he narrowed his gaze. 'What's wrong?'

'Nothing?'

He raised both black eyebrows. 'I can feel your tension. What's wrong? Tell me or else I can't fix it.'

She smiled, the weight lifting a fraction. 'Alexis, you can't fix everything.'

'Want to bet?'

'Some things I have to fix myself. I'm worried about what your staff are going to think about me, which is a me problem not a you or them problem.'

His stare held hers, that flicker in his eyes making a blink-and-you'll-miss-it appearance, and then he smiled and pressed a chaste kiss to her mouth. 'My staff will love you, I promise.'

He put his eye to the scanner. The green light flashed and the door opened, taking them through to the first of the many sprawling reception rooms in his impressive apartment. Not that Lydia had paid much attention to the apartment during her one visit to it before—on the way in they'd been too intent on making it to the bedroom for her to notice anything and on the way out she'd been too intent on just leaving without bursting into tears to take in any of the décor or furnishings.

The weight in her chest lifted a fraction more to find warmth in the eyes of the staff she was introduced to. The maid who'd shown her the way out wasn't there but the butler was, and, though she caught recognition from him, the warmth of his welcome was enough to put her fears in this regard to bed.

'Your cases have been delivered and unpacked for you,' the butler said once the others had disappeared.

'Already?' There wasn't much difference in flight times from Kos to Athens as from Agon to Athens, but she'd only given Maya's details to Alexis a couple of hours ago.

'You should know by now that I only employ the best people,' Alexis murmured. 'Let me show you the rest of the place and then we can shower before dinner.'

It came as no surprise that the two-storey apartment was a strong contender for the Ultimate Bachelor Pad of the Year award, coming complete with games room, cinema room and party room—the disco ball on the ceiling away gave its purpose—that were all interlinked with bars in each of them. The main living areas were all high ceilings, sash windows, dark leather sofas and glass tables. Everywhere they went were splashes of original pop art, from Warhols and Hockneys to colourful, eye-popping work created by more modern, contemporary artists.

'You can study them all tomorrow,' Alexis said, tugging at her hand when Lydia found herself enthralled with an utterly bonkers red apple on a seesaw. 'I've got a surprise for you.'

'What surprise?'

He gave her a stare. 'It wouldn't be a surprise if I told you, would it?'

They took the marble stairs to the top floor where Alexis's bedroom was, but instead of going through its door, they carried on past other doors to the end of the wide, light corridor. He flung the final door open for her with a flourish.

To Lydia's bemusement, she'd been shown to an office. A very nice office, with three huge desktop computers set out on a horseshoe desk, a coffee machine, sofa and six more pieces of pop art on the walls, and with an amazing view of the Acropolis. She assumed it was the view that was the surprise because she could think of nothing less thrilling than an office.

'What do you think?' he asked, staring at her with a tiny bit more intensity than the occasion called for.

She returned his intensity. 'It's the best office in the whole wide world.'

His brow furrowed and then he burst out laughing. 'I'm not showing you this for the sake of it—I'm showing you it because it's yours.'

Now it was Lydia's turn to furrow her brow. 'What do you mean by mine?'

'*Your* office, to work on your designs or play solitaire or whatever you want to do in it. I've had it on good authority that these computers are the best for your line of work but if they don't suit your needs or are not to your taste or liking we can change them…'

'Wait,' she interrupted. 'Are you telling me you've created an office for me?'

'And I thought you were quick on the uptake.'

'Alexis, I only agreed to marry you on Friday.' Although she supposed it would technically have been Saturday. 'Today is Monday.'

'Yes, it gave my staff plenty of time to arrange it all. Once we've broken the news of our marriage to the world we can get an interior designer in to discuss what else you'd like to do with it and colour schemes of how you'd like the rest of the place to look and feel.'

'The rest of the place?' she said faintly.

'This is now your home and it needs to feel like yours too or you will never be comfortable here.'

But there was no time to digest any of this for, without any warning whatsoever, Alexis had scooped her into his arms and was marching her down the corridor.

'What are you doing?'

He grinned. 'What I would have done yesterday if I hadn't thought you'd punch me—carrying you over the threshold.'

It was the brightness of the room that stopped Lydia from planting the intended kiss on his mouth.

In utter disbelief, she turned her head from left to right as far as her neck would extend.

The last time she'd been in this room it had been an unashamed bachelor's bedroom with seduction unashamedly in mind, with luxurious charcoal panelling and black silk sheets on a waterbed so big that if it had burst they'd have had to swim to safety. Other than the layout, nothing remained. Now, the walls were painted a soft eggshell green and cream, the bed of equal size but with a wrought-iron frame and luxurious cream and gold bedding that matched the new drapes hanging on the windows and the new, lighter, hardwood flooring…

This was a different room, she realised with a sinking heart. She'd been so desperate to leave the last time she'd been here that she'd remembered the position of the room wrongly.

'I thought I was going to be sharing your room,' she said, trying not to let her dejection show as he carried her to the bed. Dejection over something that just a day ago had been what she'd wanted. If she hadn't become so lust-struck she'd be celebrating this turn of events.

He laid her down and stretched on top of her. 'You are. This is it. Do you like it?'

'What, this is your room?'

'*Our* room now,' he corrected. 'But formerly my room.'

She wriggled out from under him so she could take it all in again and wrap her head around what she was seeing…

He propped himself on an elbow. 'Anything you don't like, we can change.'

'No, no, it's lovely, it's just…so different.'

Unsure from her expression and tone what she really meant, Alexis stared more closely at her and dubiously asked, 'Did you prefer it as it was?'

She gave a bark of surprised laughter. 'God, no! It was awful!' Colour stained her cheeks and she quickly added, 'I mean, it wasn't particularly to my taste.'

He smiled wryly. 'I didn't imagine it was and that's why I had it all changed.'

'What? All this has changed since Saturday?'

He stroked her soft cheek and said words that told a version of the truth. 'When I knew I would be marrying, I set things in motion.' Putting his mouth to her ear, he seductively whispered, 'How about we christen the bed before we shower?'

She pulled her head back to stare at him wonderingly. 'Do you mean…?'

He smiled at the movement of her throat when she couldn't finish her question. 'No one else has slept in this bed.' He laced his voice with meaning. 'This is our room and our bed and no one else will ever sleep in it but us.' He gave a wider smile and slid his hand down to her belly. 'I suppose we can let our baby share with us on occasion.'

To his incredulity, water filled her eyes and a tear spilled down her cheek. Palming the cheek, he wiped the tear with his thumb. 'I thought this would make you happy.'

Blinking back more tears, she bit into her bottom lip and gave a shaky smile. 'It does. I'm just feeling a bit emotional—probably tiredness and baby hormones.'

He gazed at her intently. 'You are sure that's all it is?'

She nodded and wrapped her arms around him, nestling her cheek into his shoulder. 'I'm sure. What you've done in here is beautiful.'

He held her tightly, breathing in the scent of her hair

and rubbing his hands over her back, and assuring himself that she was here, that Lydia *was* his and that given time she would understand the fullness of what that meant...

And understand that he was hers too.

The weight Lydia had entered Alexis's apartment with had become heavier overnight and now, hugging her knees on the bed and watching him dress for the office, she could swear she felt it all the way down to her toes.

It was time for reality to pierce the bubble they'd made for themselves. It already had. It hadn't occurred to her that in all the time they'd spent together he must have turned his phone off because it was currently leaping around on his dresser like a jumping jack.

'Are you not going to answer it?' she asked, trying not to sound wistful.

He met her stare in the reflection of the mirror he was doing his tie up in front of and shook his head. 'I've seen and heard enough. The rest can wait until I'm in the car.'

'I suppose I should look at my phone too,' she sighed and flopped her head back on the pillow. 'Anything I should be prepared for?'

'Lucie's still in hiding. The press are still stalking your brother.' He grimaced and dipped his fingers into a pot on his dresser and rubbed his hands together before dragging it through his black hair. 'A rumour was published overnight on one of those British gossip sites that Lucie ran away to escape a forced marriage.'

Lydia's heart sank. 'Which site?'

He told her. It was a name that meant nothing to her.

'I've instructed my lawyers to get it taken down

but…' He closed his eyes a moment. 'Once a rumour is out there it can be impossible to stop it taking on a life of its own. I've had my fair share of lies and innuendoes published. Normally I ignore them but this one…' He shook his head. 'This one has the potential to cause real damage.'

She thought of the woman she'd seen on the supply boat early Friday morning, when she'd still been working out how she was going to manage three days on Sephone avoiding all contact with Alexis. She'd dreaded it, had felt sick to the pit of her stomach to imagine even glimpsing him. It had been bad enough seeing his face all over the media on a near daily basis. Worse that in a few moments of weakness she'd searched his name herself. Worse still that the algorithms on the social media sites she used had kicked in, and, along with all the graphic-design-related posts, art, music and book posts curated to her specific tastes, had started infecting her feed with posts about Alexis Tsaliki. It meant that since their night together she'd been subjected to regular pictures of him dining and partying with a variety of beautiful women. If anything, his libido had become even more ravenous. There had been three different women in the last month alone.

And that was why she'd kept her mouth shut about Lucie being on the supply boat. If Lucie had needed to run then let her run free, even if one of the consequences of Lucie's freedom had been Lydia's own entrapment with the man she'd hoped to hide away from for ever. Or at least until their baby was born and all the feelings their night together had brought out in her had had the good sense to disappear.

'You'll be safe though, won't you?' she asked, now trying not to sound anxious.

'On a personal level, yes, but when it comes to Tsaliki Shipping...' He lifted his shoulders and grimaced again. 'You can only fight so many fires at one time. Too many and it becomes impossible to contain.' Striding to the bed, he leaned over and kissed her. 'I'll try not to be late but with everything going on, I can't guarantee it. Call me if you need me, okay?'

'Just go and fight your fires and don't worry about me.'

He smiled wryly. 'When I imagined marrying, I didn't imagine we'd only have a day for the honeymoon period.' Another kiss and then he was off, snatching his suit jacket from the armchair he'd draped it over, leaving Lydia puzzling over words that made no sense. They'd agreed to marry only four days ago and that was to put out Lydia's own fire, so why would he have imagined...?

A needle of ice injected itself into her heart.

Her brain working hard, she climbed off the bed and treaded her toes into the newly laid hardwood floor and thought back to the time she'd had contractors in to lay new flooring in her cottage. It had been a lot more involved than she'd initially envisaged. This bedroom was huge and the intricacy of the flooring design meant a specialist had been employed to lay it, and she just couldn't work out how Alexis's staff had found a specialist floor layer and employed them to remove the old stuff and then prep and lay the new stuff to this specific design in a maximum of three days.

Despite the warm welcome she'd received on her arrival, Lydia was still apprehensive about leaving the bedroom.

Hunger drove her out. Feeling very much like a house guest abandoned by the owner, she headed to the kitchen she'd been given only a cursory tour of and found the chef already busy preparing for the evening dinner.

Once she'd got over her shock at being addressed as *despina*, a term she was used to associating with her mother, who was the lady boss of her household—Lydia absolutely did not feel like a *despina*—she still felt too much like a guest to say she'd find herself something to eat as she always did at home. Her parents employed chefs too but once she'd moved into the cottage, she'd had the urge to learn to cook for herself. While she would never win any culinary prizes, *strapatsada* for breakfast was the one meal she'd mastered to suit her own taste buds, especially since she'd become pregnant.

Hurried footsteps were followed by the flustered appearance in the kitchen of the maid who'd shown Lydia out of the apartment three months earlier.

'My apologies, *despina*,' she said. 'I didn't hear you leave your room. Let me show you to the dining room—the table has been set for you...unless you prefer to eat somewhere else?' she added with a touch of anxiety.

'The dining room works fine for me, thank you.' Her words had barely left her mouth before she was being chivvied to the smaller of the two dining rooms.

Thinking wistfully of her sunny kitchen and the table she'd managed to wedge by the bay window where she ate every morning looking out over her own private patch of the Antoniadises' landscaped gardens, Lydia took her seat and stared at the abundance of food that had been set out for her. It was the kind of spread she'd woken to every morning of her childhood and adolescence when the family had come together for the one meal where it was just the four of them. It was a rare evening meal when it was just them, her parents' open table policy being taken advantage of by extended family, friends, business associates and even employees, the evening meal often feeling like an extended board meeting. Once she'd officially moved out to what was essentially the cottage at the bottom of the garden, Lydia had still joined them most evenings for dinner, and her heart clenched tightly as it suddenly occurred to her that she'd already enjoyed her last evening meal with them.

'Coffee, *despina*?'

She nodded, blinking back the sudden swell of tears and prodding at her eye to make it seem as though she had something caught in it. 'Yes, please. Sorry, what's your name?'

'Maya.'

Another Maya. Lydia's lungs opened a little wider. She'd never known a horrible Maya.

'Can I be of any further assistance?'

'I'm good, but thank you...actually there is one thing.' Before she could talk herself out of asking it, she said, 'The flooring in the bedroom is different from when I was last here.' No point pretending that she hadn't made the walk of shame with this woman. Mercifully, she wasn't feeling any judgy vibes from her. 'How long ago was the new floor laid?'

Maya's forehead furrowed a little. 'I think two, maybe three months ago. I can check.'

'Don't worry about doing that.' She dredged all the brightness into her tone that she could muster. 'I was just curious—it's all so different from how I remember it.'

If the maid's face hadn't turned the colour of the tomatoes the chef would be using to make Lydia's *strapatsada*, there was a slim chance she would have pushed the timing of the new flooring and the other niggling things to the back of her mind, but Maya's bright red cheeks, tight lips and the way she was rubbing at her skirt told a story Lydia valiantly assured herself it was better to know now. The words Alexis had said before he'd distracted her by telling her the bed was brand new and so silently confirming he'd not shared it with any of his other lovers came back to her.

'When I knew I would be marrying, I set things in motion...'

The drastic change in his bedroom hadn't been for her sake. The wheels for the change had started turning weeks, even months before she'd begged him to marry her.

Whoever Alexis had imagined himself marrying, it hadn't been her.

CHAPTER NINE

ALEXIS RODE THE elevator up to his apartment with a mixture of emotions playing in his guts. His legal team's efforts to get the gossip about Lucie removed had been as pointless as he'd suspected. When he'd finally left the office, *#RunLucieRun* had been trending all over social media. When he'd finally left the office he'd had to fight his way through a media scrum.

His hope that Lydia would spring out to greet him with a smile on her face came to nothing too. He found her in the main living room curled up on a sofa doing something on her phone. She lifted her face at the sound of his footsteps and raised a smile but didn't raise her body. 'How did it go?' she asked.

He pulled a face and threw his suit jacket and tie on the nearest chair. 'A contract we were days away from signing off on and which I'd planned to trumpet in the press as a sign that Tsaliki Shipping is still going from strength to strength, has been withdrawn. I've heard on the grapevine that another of our contracts which is up for renewal at the end of the year is in danger—the owners are in secret talks with one of our competitors.'

'That's worrying.'

He nodded. Lydia had grown up steeped in the business and knew how it worked.

After pouring himself a brandy, he slumped on a seat close to her and looked at her more closely. She looked tired and withdrawn, as if she too were carrying the weight of the world on her shoulders. 'You've been in touch with your family?'

She bit into her bottom lip and nodded.

'So you know?'

'About the shareholder meeting?'

He took a slow sip of his drink and inclined his head. Antoniadis Shipping's major investors were demanding a meeting with Thanasis. Antoniadis Shipping were expecting a new fleet of container ships within the next week. Allegedly, billions still needed to be paid. If those investors pulled their money Antoniadis Shipping would be sunk for good.

She opened her mouth to answer but then her phone buzzed in her hand. She looked at the screen and closed her eyes.

'Not going to answer it?'

'I can't speak to him.'

'Your brother?' he guessed.

Her jaw tightened as she took a long breath. 'It was hard enough talking to my mother. Thanasis is in pieces. I saw a paparazzi picture of him earlier.' She laughed morosely. 'He looks a wreck. I used to think he was the best person in the world and the strongest, and now I'm completely torn. A part of me thinks he deserves all this for the unconscionable way he treated Lucie and then I hate myself for thinking that because the fallout is destroying so many lives. I think it must be destroying him the most because he fell in love with her and now he's lost her and is losing everything else. I've already betrayed my family by sleeping with you and now I'm married to you and carrying your child and so he's lost me too and it feels like I'm leaving him all alone. I don't know how I can speak to him or even what I can say that won't make everything worse for him and for myself because every word I do say will be tainted by lies.' Her stare suddenly landed on his, her eyes flashing. 'And God knows there have been enough lies, by *everyone*.'

Alexis absorbed all this, absorbing too Lydia's unspoken but implicit condemnation of himself for his role in all this. Their fathers' war had started decades ago, before any of their children had been born, but it had been left to the children to be the grown-ups in the room and attempt to repair the wreckage. Their attempts had only blown a fresh bomb on what had already been a vast detonation.

'In hindsight, I would do some things differently,' he acknowledged. He would do everything differently. 'In our defence, once Rebecca had planted the seed of the lie, it seemed the most logical thing to play along with it precisely to prevent the destruction everyone is now living through.' Lucie's own mother had started the lie that Lucie and Thanasis had fallen in love.

'Not you though. You're insulated.' Her smile was grim. 'You're the only one of us all who is going to get through this whole mess unscathed.'

'You forget that though I'm the one with the least to lose, I'm the one who fought the hardest to stop this all from happening.' He drained his brandy and fixed her with a hard stare. While he appreciated Lydia was upset at everything that was happening to her family, he did not appreciate her attempts to make him the scapegoat for it. 'Do not forget, marriage between our families was my idea and it was a damn good one—your brother was the one who screwed it up, no one else. He drove Lucie away the first time by behaving like an arsehole to her and then drove her away a second time by discovering his conscience.'

'At least he has one,' she bit out pointedly.

He studied her through narrowed eyes wondering when the Lydia who'd been determined to fight any good feeling towards him had made a return. 'What's wrong?'

'Apart from my whole life being destroyed? Nothing.'

'Your *nothing* feels very personal. Have I done something to upset you?'

She eyeballed him back with a loathing he hadn't seen since they'd become lovers and then all the air seemed to puff out of her as she sagged in her seat and hung her head. 'I'm sorry,' she muttered. 'I'm feeling very guilty and emotional today and I'm taking it out on you.'

'Are you sure that's all it is?'

She rubbed her face and nodded.

Crossing to her, he sank onto his knees and smoothed her hair off her wan face. 'You look tired,' he said softly. 'How about I run you a bath? Have a long soak before dinner.'

Something agonised flashed over her beautiful face before she dragged up a small smile. 'How can you be nice to me when I've just been all bitchy and mean to you?'

'I've had worse thrown at me.' Instead of this bringing a proper smile to her face, the smile she had formed fell and her eyes closed. 'Lydia, you're pregnant, your family is being destroyed and your whole world is changing. It is understandable that you're on edge.'

She opened her eyes.

He traced a thumb over her cheekbone. 'I cannot perform miracles but, whatever happens, I promise I will not let your family fall into poverty.'

A line creased her forehead. 'Why would you promise that?'

'Because whether they like it or not, their daughter is my wife and they are my child's grandparents, and that makes them my family too.'

Lydia stayed in the bath so long her fingers and toes turned into prunes. Two nights of passionate sex had released so many endorphins or whatever the chemical was that she'd basically stopped thinking with her brain and, having tried valiantly not to think too much in Alexis's absence that day, her thoughts about him now refused to stay tucked away and had returned with a vengeance. And her fears.

This was her life now. What she'd agreed to. She couldn't start acting like Queen Bitch just because Alexis had recently taken a lover and fallen hard enough to consider marrying her. Whoever the elusive lady was, he hadn't gone through with it, not only because he'd married Lydia, which he couldn't have done if married to someone else, but because he'd had flings with at least three other women in the last month, and those were just the ones she'd read about. He'd probably been cock-struck, a term she remembered from her university days when one of the biggest campus players had fallen hard for one of her friends. In the short time they were together, Maya—yes, another Maya—could have asked him to shave all his hair off and he would have slavishly obeyed. Two weeks later he'd come out of his stupor and dumped her. Lydia wished she could tell herself that she was suffering from the female equivalent.

Going to bed with Alexis had been madness but it had been a madness she'd fully embraced and refused to regret. He'd fully lived up to his reputation and more, and she'd walked away on her own terms. Now she got to live that exquisite joy every night and she had no right to feel jealousy at some poor woman whose heart he'd inevitably broken or feel something a lot like rage-fuelled sickness to imagine the next woman whose heart he'd break. She needed to be concentrating on keeping her own future heartbreak to a minimum. She was no longer confident that when Alexis did take a lover she would be automatically cast aside, was feeling increasingly certain that she really would have to emulate Rebecca Tsaliki's insouciance and turn a blind eye and pretend every minute that his infidelity didn't hurt.

The next day passed for Lydia much like her first full day. She'd seamlessly imported all her files and apps and contacts from her old computers to the new ones but, again, couldn't find the head space to concentrate on her work, couldn't even find the motivation to pitch for the new contracts that had popped up on the networking site in the last few days. She couldn't shift the sickness in her stomach. If she didn't know it was all being caused by stress she'd think morning sickness had decided to throw itself at her just as the pregnancy progressed beyond the first trimester.

Restless, bored with being cooped up and not wanting to wallow in self-pity when she had nothing to be self-pitying about considering that, whatever happened, her child's future was secure just as she'd so wanted, she wandered out of the office Alexis had had created for her. Soon, she found herself studying the pop art hanging on his walls. Such fresh, fun pieces ranging from comically sexy to comically absurd and all brought a much-needed smile to her face.

Moving downstairs, she continued studying them. They suited the man who'd bought them and it made her heart pang to think of him fighting fires to save a business he didn't even want for the sake of his father and siblings. The businesses he did own and from which he'd made his personal fortune were all in hospitality, an industry that suited him much better than shipping, which to Lydia was the least exciting industry going. He even made suits sexy, which she'd never thought she'd find herself thinking. Suits, she'd always believed, were for serious-minded and dare she say boring men like her father and brother, and it had been this association that had actively seen her choose arty, poetic men as her partners; men who wouldn't know one end of a tie from the other and who considered reciting sonnets as romantic and the creation of pop art as frivolous. In her quest to not wake up married to a version of her father or brother, for whom the business was everything, she'd inadvertently found herself with men for whom themselves was everything.

Alexis was everything those men were not and far removed from her father and brother. He wouldn't know one end of a sonnet from another but he had a sense of humour and a zest for life which, combined with his dropdead gorgeous looks and sexiness, made him irresistible.

But the man who found the shipping industry as exciting as she did was having to delegate the running of his own business to staff so he could concentrate his forensic mind on saving his father's business from the bankruptcy Antoniadis Shipping was headed for. In just two days, Lydia's brother would sit in his boardroom with his main investors knowing it would likely be for the final time.

Shockingly, despite all the bad blood between their two families, Alexis had promised not to let her family fall into poverty. More shockingly, she believed him. What she didn't believe for a second was that her family would accept his help. Her mother, she knew, would rather starve.

On impulse, she pulled her phone out of her back pocket and was a fingerprint away from calling him when she stopped herself. Alexis was working; fighting the fires that he'd never started even if he had stoked the flames…

Damn it, what had she been doing eulogising him? Yes, he had good traits, many of them, but she didn't need to reinforce them to herself in some kind of daydream like some kind of moon-eyed teenager with a crush. At this rate she'd talk herself into falling in love with him!

'You look like you're arguing with yourself.'

A small scream flew from her mouth as she whipped around and found Alexis standing at the doorway of the dining room where she'd been absently studying a wacky painting of an iconic sixties actress with a cigarette holder in her mouth, the limited palette all fluorescent colours. 'What are you doing home?'

'I live here.' His lips quirked at the corners. 'I had a few hours free of meetings and thought I would join my wife who is suffering from cabin fever for lunch.'

'Lunch?' Where had the morning gone?

His lips quirked again. 'You know. Food.'

God, he was gorgeous, she thought. Just look at him in that dark green suit and with his black hair sticking up on end from all the times he must have run his fingers through it. Alexis was a walking stick of testosterone and to look at him was to make her pulses soar.

Barely aware of her legs moving, Lydia crossed the room, grabbed hold of his tie and yanked him into the room. Pointing to a chair, she barked, 'Sit,' and then firmly shut the door.

The one rule she'd learned in her short time living with Alexis was that when a door was closed it meant the staff were not to enter. She would not let herself think why that was... Actually, she *would* let herself think it. Alexis liked his privacy for sex, and at the moment *she* was his willing partner for sex because she was there and he wanted her, and now he was here and goddammit she wanted him and she didn't have to be in love with him for that. She was just as capable of separating sex from emotions as he was.

'Is this position to your liking?' he asked, seductive bemusement lacing his voice. He'd pulled a dining chair out and placed it against the wall.

'Yes. Now, take your jacket and tie off, and sit.'

He obeyed and then, his eyes alive with sensual anticipation, summoned her with a crook of his finger.

Ignoring his directive, she lifted her top off and chucked it on the floor, stepped out of her sandals and then undid her jeans and pulled them down before stepping out of them too. She made no effort at turning her undressing into a strip show for him but from the expression on Alexis's face, the effect would have been the same, and a giddy sense of power flowed into the hot blood rushing through her.

When Alexis had made the impulsive decision to return to his apartment for lunch, something he'd never done before in the whole of his working life, he'd had dreams of seducing Lydia into the bedroom, of working out all his stress by losing himself in his beautiful wife and her beautiful body. Not once had he imagined this kind of reception and damn if it wasn't as sexy as hell. *She* was as sexy as hell, and now she was prowling across the floor to him wearing only her white lace underwear and with a determined, lascivious glow in her eyes, and it was like he'd woken to find himself in the middle of an erotic fantasy.

When she reached him, she sank straight to her knees and deftly unbuttoned his shirt before reaching for the button and zip of his trousers. Without any ceremony whatsoever she undid them and then tugged them down with his underwear to his hips. A quick lift of his buttocks enabled her to pull them down past an erection that had gone from zero to sixty in seconds, and down to his ankles where she pulled them off and threw them to one side.

And then her lascivious stare landed back on him.

Cheeks heightened with colour, her breathing heavy, she parted his thighs without saying a word, then positioned herself between them and made a fist around his arousal.

His eyes widened at the rush of adrenaline that shot through him.

Still not speaking with anything but her bright, lust-filled eyes, she began to masturbate him, her fist moving up and down his length, slapping his hand away when he reached for a breast.

'Lydia...' *Theos*, that thick voice was his.

With one hand now pressed firmly on his chest to keep him still, she bent her head and took him into her hot mouth.

Submitting to her will and the exquisite sensation of what she was doing to him, Alexis groaned loudly and rested his head back against the wall.

Slavishly she made love to him with her mouth and hand, erotic pleasure thrumming through his every cell...

She cupped his balls.

'God, Lydia...' Her name on his lips morphed into another groan.

Tighter the pads of her fingers pressed into his chest, tighter her hold on his arousal, her movements increasing, and when he raised his head and saw her beautiful blonde head bobbing up and down on his lap, the telltale tugging of his loins was almost more than he could control.

As if she sensed he was on the brink of coming, she pulled her lips up his erection one long last time and then she was on her feet, freeing her breasts from her bra and yanking her knickers down her legs and kicking them away...and then she was straddling his lap.

Clasping his cheeks in her hands, she gazed into his eyes with an intensity he'd never seen in the hazel before, and with a loud moan of pleasure sank down on his length.

Theos, she was more than ready for him.

With only a fleeting kiss to his lips, she dragged her fingers to the back of his head and pulled his face down to her breasts. It was the only control she ceded to him and he took complete advantage, sucking one then the other in the way that drove her so wild. She'd barely started riding him when he felt her thicken around him and then she arched her neck and ground herself down, holding his head tightly to keep his mouth at her breast as she convulsed around him.

It was the most beautiful, perfect moment of his life, and he savoured it, letting her take every ounce of her pleasure before grabbing hold of her hips and thrusting himself hard up into her, his own climax coming in quick succession as he spurted his seed deep inside her and their mouths finally fused as the last of their orgasms ripped through them.

Lydia couldn't catch her breath. Couldn't think. No, was *afraid* to think. The beats of her heart weren't just racing from the thrilling power of what they'd just shared but from fear.

Where had that sensual, demanding woman come from? She'd only met her once, her weekend with Alexis, when she'd been completely unafraid and had made love to him with the same intensity that he'd made love to her. The very fact that she'd been so unafraid that night proved she should have been terrified, and now she was afraid to unwrap her arms from around his neck or move her cheek from his, terrified of what he'd find in her eyes. More terrified of what she wouldn't find in his.

Whatever point she'd been trying to make to herself had backfired, and she had to plead with herself to keep it together, to remind herself that when her skin was no longer pressed to Alexis's and the heavy beats of his heart were no longer dancing with the beats of hers and he was no longer inside her, this rush would pass and all these emotions that had sprung up from nowhere would go back to the nowhere from where they came.

She wasn't falling in love with him. She wasn't. It was just a chemical rush.

Mercies came in unexpected places and hers came from the ringing of a phone.

'That's yours,' she said, climbing off his lap and grabbing his discarded suit jacket where the ringing was coming from and passing it to him, then used the excuse of gathering the rest of their discarded clothes to avoid eye contact a little bit longer, using that fragment of time to pull herself together.

Whoever was calling, he didn't answer. Nor did he mention who the caller had been. The tightness of his mouth, though, told her whoever had called had been unwanted.

He'd just finished tucking his shirt in when his phone buzzed with a message.

Lydia, having pulled her top back over her head, saw the fresh tightening of his lips at whatever was on his screen. 'What's wrong?'

'Nothing.' The way he said it made her stomach plummet and when she recognised the phone, it plummeted some more. Alexis had two phones, one that was strictly for business and one that was friends and family. It was his personal phone in his hand.

'I thought that was my stock answer,' she chided lightly. 'Is it something or someone important?'

The blue-grey eyes fixed onto hers with a gravity she couldn't remember seeing in them before. 'If I tell you, it will hurt you.'

Alarm shot through her veins. 'Is it about my family?'

His expression didn't change. 'No.'

Now her blood pressure plummeted too. Or did it rise? She didn't know, knew only that she felt suddenly light-headed, and not in a good way.

With his *no* hanging between them, poisoning the air she breathed, she somehow managed to hold onto the airiness of her tone. 'Shouldn't you reply to it?'

Grimness crept into his voice. 'No.'

'It's bad manners to leave a lover hanging.' She slipped her feet into her sandals and added, 'Not to mention cruel.'

The tightening of his lips and the flickering in his eyes told her she'd hit bullseye. Smiling to show she didn't care, Lydia strode to the door. 'Call and put her out of her misery. I'll order lunch for us.'

The gravity in his expression didn't change. 'It was over long ago.'

She shrugged and gave another bright smile. 'Then deal with it however you see fit. Just remember she's a human with feelings.'

Only after she'd popped into the kitchen to order food for them did Lydia lock herself in a bathroom and throw up what remained of her breakfast.

CHAPTER TEN

ALEXIS STUDIED LYDIA discreetly but thoroughly as they shared their evening meal on the roof terrace. The humidity had lessened a little, the blazing heat of the day now a bearable warmth, and she'd changed out of her faithful jeans to sit out in it, wearing a simple cream skirt and silver scooped top. The silky hair he adored loose had been tied into an elegant knot and she must have trimmed her fringe because she hadn't spent half the evening blowing it out of her eyes.

Watching her gracefully fork succulent slow-cooked lamb into her succulent mouth made his chest tighten.

'You're beautiful,' he murmured, almost without thinking.

She gave a narrow-eyed smile. 'What brought that on?'

He raised a shoulder. 'Just making an observation. Did you speak to your mother?' Lydia had said before he'd returned to the office that she was going to call her.

She nodded 'She's expecting me home on Sunday.'

Sunday. The date they would tell their families and then the world about their marriage.

The small amount of light in her eyes dimmed. 'She thinks I'm coming home. She doesn't know I'm only coming back to stick the boot even harder into them.'

'What are you going to say to them?'

'I don't know.' Gazing into the distance, she said, 'I keep thinking about what I can say that will stop them hating me or at the least stop them hating our child.' Her stare landed back on him. 'Mum already thinks Lucie used witchcraft to cast a spell on Thanasis. It's a long shot but she might just believe you used your Lucifer powers to trick me into your bed and into a marriage.'

'Even though marriage was your idea and you said your vows under your own free will?' he said steadily.

'She doesn't need to know that.'

'Doesn't she?'

'It would be the most unforgivable thing I could do. You know this.'

'Even though I am prepared to lay it straight with my family and tell them to accept you or else?'

'It's different for you.'

'How?'

'You hold the purse strings.'

'I would still demand they accept you and our marriage even if I had no financial hold over them.'

'My family will never accept you and never accept our marriage. If I'm lucky, they'll let me and the baby through their door one day in the future but never you.'

'And you won't fight to make them accept me?'

She laughed morosely. 'There would be no point. In their eyes, you're Lucifer.'

And Lydia would never try to convince them otherwise.

Taking a deep breath to smother the acidic bile rising in his throat, Alexis said, 'You know, there is still a chance your brother can pull a rabbit out of the hat and convince the investors to hold tight. It doesn't have to be over for Antoniadis Shipping.' He gave a tight smile. 'If the miracle does happen then your family might be more amenable to accepting me.'

Her laugh almost sounded convincing. 'Not even Jesus could perform such a miracle.'

'A lot can happen in two days,' he pointed out.

'Two sleeps but only one full day,' she pointed out back before stabbing at some roasted butternut squash and dipping it into the feta and yogurt mousse.

'I'm just saying don't convince yourself it's game over. Your brother has all the skills and acumen to turn it round.'

'I know he does. It's whether he has the will that's in question. But let's not talk about my family any more otherwise I'll cry and this delicious food doesn't need extra seasoning. How are things going for Tsaliki Shipping? Do you think you've stabilised things yet?'

He shook his head and took a drink of his red wine, which did nothing to smother the bitter taste on his tongue. 'No. The story about us forcing Lucie to marry Thanasis refuses to die and I don't see how it will if she doesn't come out of hiding and officially deny it.'

'You wouldn't ask her to do that, would you?'

He took a long breath. If up to him he wouldn't just ask Lucie, he'd force her, but he kept his private thoughts to himself. His wife had proved very protective and defensive of his stepsister and he didn't want to fall into an argument, not when he was already trying to rid himself of the bitterness that had risen in him at her refusal to even consider fighting for her family to accept him. 'No. But I would hope she did it of her own volition.'

She pulled a rueful face. 'I'm afraid that's as likely to happen as my mother not disowning me. Lucie gave up her job and her home to marry Thanasis for your family's sake, and she was repaid with lies. She doesn't owe any of you or any of us anything.'

He eyed her meditatively and swallowed back fresh bitterness. 'You make it sound like we're still in opposing camps.'

'I'm still an Antoniadis and always will be.'

'But married to a Tsaliki and always will be,' he reminded her, and then took another deep inhale to smother the agitation simmering in his guts. 'For all that things are yet to stabilise, I remain confident that I can still turn things round with Tsaliki Shipping. Do you know of Hans Dreyman?'

'The name's familiar but I can't think where from.'

'Dreyman Co, the German food manufacturer, one of the top food manufacturers in the world. Their products are sold all over the world. You'll know many of their brand names. We've been transporting their goods for years.'

'Is this the contract you heard on the grapevine is threatening to look elsewhere?'

He shook his head and grimly said, 'No, that's a different company. Hans, though, has a lot of influence in the corporate world and if I can get him to lend us his support and endorse us, it will go a long way to calming nerves. I learned today that he's travelling into Athens tomorrow and that on Friday night he's going to Theo Nikolaidis's summer party—I too have an invitation to that party.'

'Then you have to go.'

'Yes. The question is do you want to come with me?'

'I don't know Theo but I know his wife, Helena,' she said slowly. 'She's discreet but we have mutual friends. If I come with you then there's a good chance the whole of Athens will know about us before we've finished our first canapé.'

'It will get you out of the apartment and it might work as a distraction to the news that will have come out about the resolution of the meeting between your brother and his investors.'

'As much as I'd love to go, you know I can't do that to my family—it would be too cruel. Friday is going to be intolerable for them. I can't add to it. We need to stick to the agreed timeline, and you'll just have to go to the party without me.'

'As long as I have your blessing.'

Surprise flashed in her eyes. 'You don't need my blessing to do anything.'

'I don't need it but I do want it.'

'Then fine, you have my blessing to go to the party without me.' Before he could breathe a little easier at this—Friday, he knew, was going to be especially hard for her and she'd be spending the majority of it on her own—she drained her grape juice and jauntily added, 'If you don't want to go alone you must have dozens of names stored in your personal phone who would jump at the chance to be your plus one for the night.'

Working hard to stop the edge creeping back into his voice, he said, 'The only name that's ever been in my phone that I would even consider taking in your place is my sister, Athena, but as she's liable to spend the evening flirting with any man with a pulse and decent bank balance and making snide comments about all the other guests, I'll give her a miss and go to the party on my own.'

She stilled, just a fleeting stillness in which a whole host of emotions flashed in her eyes, but he saw it and the edge subsided. He mustn't forget that while they were both navigating their new life together, Lydia didn't just have her family's destruction hanging over her along with the real possibility of losing her family, but was pregnant too. He shouldn't be adding pressure to her or allowing bitterness to set in over things that were yet to happen.

'One party you won't have to miss is the one I'm hosting next Friday at the nightclub. It's for a friend's birthday, and you *will* be coming with me for it.'

Her smile looked forced. 'I'm not a nightclub kind of girl, remember?'

He looked her up and down, the silver of her top reminding him of the dress she'd worn their first night together. 'I don't know,' he murmured. 'You seemed to enjoy yourself at my club the last time you were there.'

Lydia was lying on her side, Alexis spooned against her, his hand making slow circles over her belly. She couldn't settle her brain. When Alexis had come home from work they'd taken a swim in the roof terrace pool together and played three games of backgammon before getting an early night that had turned into a long night of lovemaking, but she was still too jittery over what tomorrow would bring to switch mind or body off.

'You never did tell me why you turned those marriage proposals down,' he said sleepily.

Her eyes opened. 'You already know the answer,' she whispered. 'I didn't love them enough.'

Didn't love them enough because in her yearning for something different, she'd gone for arty men too absorbed with themselves and their artistic creations to fall in love with, men she'd never had to cut the safety nets for. Never even wanted to. She'd refused to entertain even living with them. She'd wanted to escape the 'men in suits' who filled her life, wanted something different for herself than the life her mother had made, but had never found the courage to fully go out there and get it.

'But you did love them?'

Her heart swelled and then tightened, and she had to swallow a compression in her throat to answer. 'I don't know. I thought I did…or maybe I just told myself I did. Maybe you were right when you said I'm a commitment-phobe like you.'

'No,' he corrected quietly. 'I said you were the one afraid of commitment, not me.'

'Alexis, I'm twenty-seven years old and you're only the third man I've been with, whereas you've been with…' She swallowed, unable to voice a number that didn't make her stomach twist.

'I've been with a lot of women,' he supplied into the silence.

'And how many of those women have been more than a fling?' For all that she'd valiantly tried to block her thoughts from returning to the call and message that had come through on Alexis's personal phone after they'd made love in the dining room, Lydia's mind now filled with the myriad women she'd seen pictured on his arm. Nausea filled her twisted stomach. Which one of those women had been the one to try to reach him that day? Had she been the woman he'd wanted to marry?

'Not many,' he confessed.

It took a long beat before she could force herself to ask, 'And of those, how many have you even contemplated a proper relationship with?'

He took a deep, long inhale as if bracing himself before saying, his voice heavy, 'Just one.'

A sharper, hotter twist in her stomach and a deeper roll of nausea stopped her probing any further.

He tightened his hold around her and kissed the top of her head. 'I made my vows to *you*, my angel. Never forget that.'

Friday morning arrived and with it a sickness in Lydia's stomach far worse than any other.

In a few short hours the shareholders' meeting would commence. Unless a miracle occurred then in a few short hours Antoniadis Shipping would cease to exist.

She waited until Alexis left for another day of fighting fires in his office before getting out of bed.

She'd been cooped up for long enough. She needed to get out into the fresh air, proper fresh air, now, before the sun rose higher and the temperatures soared.

All too aware of the press and members of the public with nothing better to do than stalk Alexis's apartment block with the cameras of their phones primed, she threw her running clothes and trainers on, shoved her hair under the brown wig, filled her bottle with fresh water, donned her running shades, and sneaked out through the apartment block's car park.

Minutes later she was entering the metro, only one

stop away from the one she took from her family home, with early-bird tourists and the day's workers, emerging back into the morning light a short while later at the Acropolis stop. She didn't receive a second glance from anyone. Instead of turning right with the tourists, she turned left and joined the Dionysiou Areopagitou walkway. Just past the church of St Demetrius she disappeared through the trees onto a wonderfully shaded and cool running route, pounding the familiar path to the old quarry, paying no attention as she passed it nor any attention to the solo rock climber already scaling the crag further along, no attention to anything at all, not even when she took the landscaped walk up to the top of the hill.

Only when she reached the marble Philopappos Monument did she stop to drink some water and take a breath. A couple of tourists of around her parents' age had already reached the hill's summit and, though she couldn't understand the language they were speaking, she knew they were raving at the spectacular view of the Acropolis. Just as she was wondering if they'd yet found the wooden observatory from where it felt like you could reach out and touch the Parthenon, the woman held her phone out to Lydia and made the universal sign of taking a photo.

Sticking her thumb up to show she understood, she took the phone and as she lifted it to get them and the Acropolis into frame, the couple put their arms around each other and pressed their cheeks together, beaming grins alive on their faces. A pang of melancholy tightened her chest at their obvious happiness, a pang that grew when they headed off on the path she'd just run with their hands clasped together. Her parents were still like that with each other.

Theirs was a future she would never have. Not with Alexis.

Wiping away a tear that had fallen from nowhere, she drank some more water and set back off to finish the trail.

For all the good the run had done her physically, emotionally Lydia felt worse. The tenterhooks she was hanging on were bleeding her heart. She couldn't stop checking her phone for updates of the meeting, and by the time lunch had passed, the only news to have come out was that the investors had left soon after they'd arrived. No press release was, as yet, expected.

As for her brother, there had been no word. Neither of her parents had heard from him.

Selfishly—and Lydia hated herself for the selfishness of her thoughts and emotions—it was the evening's party making her feel so sick. This was a society event that would be packed with the rich and beautiful. There would be women there who'd shared Alexis's bed. What if one of those women was the one he'd thought about marrying, the one woman he'd contemplated a real relationship with? As hard as she tried, Lydia just could not stop herself thinking about her, couldn't stop herself trawling the Internet for all the women he'd been linked with since their night together. Which one was she? And then she'd wondered if maybe the woman had come before her and that Alexis had cheated on her with Lydia. And then she'd wondered why she was doing this, why she couldn't just do as she'd promised herself and make the most of what she had with Alexis while she had it because, while she had him, Alexis was everything a woman could dream of in a man and in a husband.

She thought back to the night they'd agreed their terms of marriage and his mocking smile as he'd said, *'No demands that I be faithful?'*

'I wouldn't waste my breath.'

What if she *had* wasted it? Would she still be facing a future that sat in her chest like the weight of doom? And what if…?

What if she were to ask it of him now? What if she were to lay her heart on the line and admit the thought of him with another woman made her feel physically sick? He wouldn't laugh at her, that much she knew. He would take her seriously, but that didn't mean he would give her the answer she craved. For heaven's sake, she shouldn't even be craving it! She'd known what she was agreeing to when she'd agreed to this marriage, and torturing herself like this was only going to make her ill and she couldn't allow that to happen, especially not with her precious baby to think of.

Her next call to her mother went to voicemail.

Needing to be alone, she went up to the bedroom and curled into one of the sofas, hugging the phone to her chest. For the first time since she'd gone to her first childhood sleepover, she felt a keening ache for her fierce, determined, loving mother, but the one thing she felt so in desperate need of comfort for was the one thing she couldn't yet tell her about and would be the thing that drove them apart.

Maybe she should go to the house and sit with them while they waited for news…but how to explain that she was magically back in Athens? She'd been so grateful that with everything going on her parents had been too distracted to question her about what she'd been getting up to. She hadn't had to lie to them since the initial lie that she was going to England.

How was she going to cope without her family? She didn't know how she could, but she had no choice. Would have no choice. Could only pray their anger with her didn't last for ever because certainty was growing that she was going to need them.

By the time Alexis came home it felt like she was close to breaking. How could there be no news? How was she going to endure Alexis spending the evening in the presence of ex-lovers and probable future lovers? Who was to say he'd even come home to her after the party?

The bedroom door opened.

She jumped to her feet. 'Have you heard anything?'

'Only rumours,' he said heavily as he threw his suit jacket and tie onto the nearest surface, one of his habits she was already becoming accustomed to. Crossing the room to her, he wrapped her in his arms and rested his chin on the top of her head.

Neither of them spoke for the longest time, and as the seconds passed and Lydia's lungs filled with his divine scent and the beat of his heart thrummed steadily against her, a little of her angst loosened. Alexis would never know how comforting his embrace was to her and how safe it made her feel, even if that comfort and safety were dangerous wishful thinking delusions of her own mind.

'I don't know what happened in the meeting,' he eventually said, 'but the one solid piece of news I received from a reliable source is that Lucie was seen entering the Antoniadis building shortly after the meeting started.'

Lydia reared her head back so she could look up at him. 'She's back?'

'Yes, but whether it's for good or ill, I don't know. Nothing has been seen of her or your brother since.'

Closing her eyes, she rested her face back into the crook of his neck.

He massaged the back of her neck. 'I don't have to go tonight. I can stay here with you.'

'You have to go.'

'I don't.'

'You do.' Touched beyond belief that he would even consider missing the party for her sake when it was so important that he go, she looked back up at him and smiled wanly. 'Antoniadis Shipping is probably over but you can still save Tsaliki Shipping from the same fate. Both of our fathers' legacies don't have to be destroyed.'

'Lydia...'

Her heart skipped at his tone and the intensity in his blue-grey eyes pierced straight into her veins, and then whatever he'd been about to say to her was forgotten as his hungry mouth found hers. In moments he had her against the wall, all their restrictive items of clothing ripped off, and he was inside her, her arms tight around his neck and their mouths fused together as, for a few heady minutes, they both forgot everything except each other.

After making love again for a much, much longer time, Alexis went for his shower. Alone in the bed, Lydia checked her phone and sighed. Nothing.

She felt better in herself though. How could she fear Alexis would already be looking for a lover when the chemistry between them blazed so strong?

She must have dozed off for the next time she opened her eyes, he was leaning over her, fully dressed in an embroidered blue suit with matching waistcoat but no tie, and smelling so fresh and divine that she grabbed the back of his neck to haul him closer, just so she could bury her nose into his neck and inhale him.

Laughing, he buried his nose into her neck before his mouth found hers and he kissed her with a savage possessiveness that left her breathless with longing.

Eyes gleaming, he gave her one more kiss before moving away and then pointed down to his crotch. 'Look what you've done.'

She grinned and sat up, deliberately letting the sheets fall down to expose her breasts. And then, to tease him some more, deliberately cupped one breast while dipping her other hand between her legs.

He was back on the bed before she had time to blink.

CHAPTER ELEVEN

AFTER TAKING A shower and having something to eat, Lydia sat in bed stalking her phone. When Alexis had finally left for the party it was with a promise not to be too late and with the order that she be waiting in bed naked for him, an order she was more than happy to obey. It was also with the promise that if he heard anything about her brother, he would call her, a promise she'd made in turn.

Putting her phone to one side, she gazed up at the ceiling. She had to stop worrying about the future. It would happen when it happened. For now, Alexis was hers and she was his...

Her phone rang.

She snatched it up. It was her mother.

Once the call ended she sat for a long time in a fugue trying to process everything. She needed to call Alexis but as she put her thumb back to her phone, a massive burst of euphoria wrenched through her and suddenly she didn't want to speak to him, she wanted to see him, *needed* to see him, right now.

Leaning over to the bedside table, she pressed the intercom.

'Can you arrange for a car for me, please?' she said quickly. 'I'll be ready to leave in ten minutes.'

Call done, she bounced off the bed and raced into her dressing room. Throwing on underwear first, she chose a taupe dress she'd bought on a whim because she liked the colour but had never worn. Mid-thigh-length, it wrapped around the neck halter-fashion but draped so cleverly over the breasts and belly that no one who knew her would suspect she was pregnant. A vigorous brush of her hair, a sweep of mascara, blush and lip gloss and she was good to go...until she was halfway down the stairs and realised she was barefoot. Luckily she still had the sparkling silver sandals she'd bought for the wedding, and she slipped her feet into them, enjoying the elevated height they gave her.

Feeling like she could fly, she climbed into the back of the waiting car and told the driver to take her the short drive to Alexis.

The Nikolaidises' home was classical Greek architecture at its finest, and when Lydia got out of the car she imagined senators from ancient times passing through the marble pillars flanking the entrance.

Helena Nikolaidis was at the door to greet her—without an official invitation Lydia had given her name to the security guards at the bottom of the drive who'd only taken her seriously because she was an Antoniadis and the fact she was being driven in a chauffeured car.

'Forgive me for gatecrashing,' Lydia said after they'd exchanged kisses, 'but I'm here to see Alexis Tsaliki.'

Helena arched an eyebrow in surprise then quickly composed herself. 'You are more than welcome,' she assured her, although she was clearly itching to ask why Lydia would be seeking her family's enemy. 'Let me show you around and see if we can find Alexis—I can't remember where I last saw him.'

Inside, the home was of a free-flowing semi-open-plan design with wide sliding doors separating the plentiful rooms, central to it all a stunning white marble circular staircase. There was a real buzz in the air, champagne and canapés flowing, the music playing loud enough to dance to but low enough to still make conversation. People, hundreds of them all clothed in beautiful dresses and tailored suits, were mingling all over the place, some in small huddles where it looked like they were exchanging state secrets and others in larger groups where they were clearly just enjoying each other's company.

One of the waiting staff approached Helena and whispered something in her ear.

'Excuse me,' Helena said to Lydia. 'There's something I need to attend to. I won't be long.'

'Don't worry about me,' Lydia assured her. 'I'll find him.'

Alexis was so tall he should have been easy to spot, but after scanning all the faces on the ground floor, trying to blend in and be unobtrusive so as not to catch the attention of anyone who knew her, she'd seen no sight of him. A small group of guests, though, were climbing the wide stairs from the basement, and, seeing another guest descend them, she decided to follow suit.

The basement was a vast, open space that covered the whole footprint of the house with artfully decorated pillars structurally supporting it running across its centre. She saw two snooker tables in one section, gambling tables, a large fully stocked bar manned by three staff, comfortable sofas, caught a peek of a home cinema behind velvet curtains, but no Alexis. Ready to cut back across the basement and go up and explore the gardens, she suddenly glimpsed a couple leaning against one of the pillars. Or, rather, the man wearing the navy embroidered suit and holding a glass of champagne was leaning back against it. The woman, taller, blonder and more beautiful than Lydia, was leaning into him, their torsos a feather away from touching, coquettish delight alive on her face. Laughing, she put her hands around his neck, pressed her breasts into his chest and leaned in for a kiss.

Lydia's chest turned to ice.

How the hell had he allowed himself to become trapped? Alexis wondered. He still hadn't spoken to Hans, and now Angeliki Poulis, an old flame, had made a beeline for him and was under the impression that he wanted to hear every last detail about her recent trip to Marrakech and that he would find every last detail as scintillating as she believed it to be.

Refusing to respond in kind to her flirtatious smiles and giggles, he simply waited with barely concealed impatience for her to stop talking so he could extract himself without having to cause a scene. Angeliki was a spoilt daddy's girl who thrived on drama. Alexis didn't want any drama, wanted only to find Hans, have a good talk with him, and then go home to Lydia. But, of course, he couldn't tell Angeliki that. Angeliki had the biggest mouth in Athens.

When she put her hands around his neck and leaned her face closer for a kiss, his patience snapped. Clasping the hands, he was about to pull them off him when the hairs on the nape of his neck lifted.

Turning his head, he saw the small, curvy figure in the taupe dress some distance away, her gaze fixed on him with an expression that could only be described as agonised horror.

The drumming of blood in Alexis's head and disbelief at the apparition before him froze him into place and froze his reactions, and now he was the one watching in horror as Lydia's open mouth closed into a tight line and her beautiful face contorted.

She'd already reached the stairs when he pulled himself out of his stupor.

Disentangling himself from Angeliki like he'd been scalded, he hurried after his wife, taking the stairs three at a time and then taking the quickest, longest strides of his life to catch her as she stepped into the central reception room, overtaking her and then spinning around to block her path.

If it were possible for fire and brimstone to be fired from eyes then he was a damned man.

'That was not what it looked like,' he said immediately and firmly.

She folded her arms across her chest and gave a shrug of contemptuous nonchalance. With a smile so brittle the slightest knock would shatter it, she said, 'It really doesn't matter. I just came here to tell you that Lucie did come back to save Antoniadis Shipping—it appears she's as madly in love with my brother as he is with her. The investors believe she's spent the last week in hospital with a relapse of her head injury. A statement will be issued in the morning about the new date for the wedding. Antoniadis Shipping has been saved and I imagine the knock-on effect will benefit Tsaliki Shipping too. I just thought you'd want to know all that.' Her smile widened. 'Looking at all the guests here, you're going to be spoilt for choice over who to celebrate the hardest with. Enjoy the rest of your night.'

Lydia had barely taken three steps past him when Alexis caught her wrist and spun her back round.

'What the hell, Lydia?' he said tightly, his face dark with anger.

Drawing herself as tall as she could get, knowing the entire fabric of her being was a thread away from unravelling, she hissed, 'Take your hand off me.' And then she snatched her wrist away with such force that she stumbled, would have gone sprawling if he hadn't caught her with one deft hook of his arm.

Before she could pull herself away a second time, he was frogmarching her through the reception room whilst simultaneously using the hand not trapping her to him to call his driver.

Once outside and away from the prying eyes of the other guests, Lydia pulled herself out of his hold and held tightly to her belly, as if she could protect the growing life from the cauldron of nausea bubbling and broiling inside her, the euphoria of her mother's call all gone.

'What the hell is wrong with you?' he demanded. 'Nothing happened. Nothing was going to happen. I was about to extricate myself from the situation when I saw you standing there.'

'I don't care! I'm not your keeper!'

'If you don't care then why are you shouting and why the hell did you run away?'

'Because it was humiliating!'

Because after the coldness of shock had come the heat...red-hot jealous heat.

She, the woman who'd never experienced an ounce of jealousy in her life, had wanted to fly at that woman with her arms around Alexis and physically drag her off him, and then batter her fists into his chest and scream in his face until he swore he would never look at another woman again.

'*Humiliating?* Angeliki didn't know I was married—no one knew because you insisted we keep it a secret, but do you seriously think I was encouraging her?'

'I don't know!' All Lydia knew was how she'd felt in the moment when all the fears she'd tried so hard to bury had been realised and the future she'd been dreading had revealed itself more sharply and painfully than she'd ever allowed herself to imagine.

Oh, God, tears were burning the backs of her eyes, her heart thumping so hard the beats pounded like drums between her ears. She wasn't just close to unravelling, she was close to disintegrating and she needed to get a grip on herself right now.

Large hands clasped her shoulders, his stare boring so hard into her that it compelled her to lift her gaze to the tight fury etched on his handsome face. 'Do you seriously think I would try to hook up with someone else the first minute your back's turned? When we've only been married five minutes?'

'But that's just it, isn't it?' she cried. 'Five minutes or five weeks or five months, we both know it's going to happen, especially when the baby comes!' When she was sore and tired and needing her bed for sleep and only sleep.

If she'd thought his face was etched with fury before, it was nothing on what blazed on it now. Releasing her shoulders to fold his arms around his chest, he said tightly, 'You never fail to assume the worst of me.'

'I'm just being realistic! I do believe you that nothing happed with that woman but I can't help how I feel and we both know it will happen in the future—you're Alexis Tsaliki!' She *did* believe him—Alexis was no liar—but the jealousy and pain that had burned through her...she could still feel its scald in her veins, and it came to her that one day soon, she would feel this pain and it would be for real, and if it hurt like this now then she couldn't even imagine what it would feel like then, when he was burrowed even further into her heart. 'I thought I knew what I was agreeing to and thought I could handle it but I *can't*. I should never have agreed to your terms and I wish like hell that I hadn't. I can't pretend to be like your stepmother, I *can't*!'

It was like the whole of his enormous body flexed. 'What are you saying? Spell it out to me, Lydia.'

'That I want to go home!' she screamed. 'My real home!'

For the longest time he simply stared at her before his features contorted into something almost inhuman. 'Oh, you do, do you?'

She shivered, suddenly frightened, not of him but of something about him, the inhuman contortion that managed to be human enough to make her pounding heart twist.

The car that had so recently dropped her off pulled up before them.

Alexis opened the door, and in a tone cold enough to freeze the sun, said, 'Get in.'

Wishing she could run away, run until her muscles screamed in protest, Lydia got into the car and compressed herself into the door at the far side.

Not a word or look was exchanged between them during the drive back. For the first time ever, Alexis angled away from her... No, that wasn't right. He'd turned away from her the night before they'd married when she'd confessed her reasons for not wanting to tell him about their baby until it had been born.

In silence, they got into the elevator. Powerfully aware of his tightly controlled posture and of the tension emanating from him, Lydia squeezed her eyes shut and concentrated on breathing. She was trembling, every part of her turned to jelly.

He held the door open for her and then strode ahead, removing his suit jacket as he walked and throwing it onto the closest armchair in the living room. 'Take the rest of the night off,' he said curtly to the butler.

When Alexis was growing up, whenever a member of the family had an upset stomach, his father would order a port and brandy to be concocted for them, a medicinal trick he'd picked up on an English business trip. Always as healthy as a horse, Alexis had never needed this concoction but the tight, nauseous feeling in his guts was worsening by the minute and he poured himself a healthy measure of both and drank it in one large swallow. Pouring another, he restrained himself by only drinking half of it.

Only then could he bring himself to look at her.

Leaning against the bar, cradling his glass, he breathed in deeply and contemplated her with an evenness that was at complete odds with the heavy, erratic beats of his heart. He'd never felt the vibrations of his heart through his skin before.

Lydia had perched herself on an armchair. Her face, he noted cynically, was etched with misery.

'So, my angel from Hades, you have decided that you don't want to be married to me after all.'

She flinched. She would never know how fitting his name for her was. His beautiful angel sent from Hades to destroy him.

'Just tell me one thing—was this your plan from the start?'

Her eyes widened, eyebrows drawing together in confusion. Her voice was barely audible. 'Was what my plan?'

'To hope for a miracle with Antoniadis Shipping.'

The throat he'd fooled himself into believing would be his to kiss for ever moved. 'I hoped but I didn't dare believe it would happen.'

'But you did hope for it, and did you plan from the start to leave me if your hope was realised and the company saved?'

'No, of course not.'

He gave a sardonic laugh. 'So you're an opportunist then. I should have known.'

'What are you talking about?'

'Don't treat me like a fool. You only agreed to my terms because you didn't trust that I would always provide for you and the baby without a ring on your finger. The company being saved means your income from the shares is safe and you no longer need me, even if your family do throw you out and disown you.' He gave a tight smile. 'And I am sure you know me well enough by now to know that I will still be a father to our child and provide for it.'

'I have never thought that, not once.'

'Maybe not consciously but your wish to return your *real home* tells its own story. Tonight was the perfect storm for you. You have never trusted me and seeing me with Angeliki gave you the out you've wanted from the start—you saw what you wanted to see and jumped at the escape route it opened for you.'

'That's not true!' she protested shakily. 'Not in the way you're making it out to be. I told you already, I do believe you that nothing happened or was going to happen between you, but—'

'But you still saw what you wanted to see—what you *expected* to see—and jumped to the easiest conclusion because all you see me as is a sex-mad Lothario who would cheat on his pregnant wife at the first opportunity.'

'No!'

'*Yes*. In your eyes I'm just Alexis Tsaliki, the commitment-shy Lucifer who can't be trusted to keep his trousers on when a beautiful woman catches his eye.'

'You never promised to be faithful to me.'

'Yes, I did.'

'You did *not*! When I said I wouldn't waste my breath in asking it of you, you *laughed*.'

'"I promise you love, honour and respect; to be *faithful to you*, and not to forsake you until death do us part",' he ground out. 'To be *faithful* to you. I made that promise to you in front of witnesses and God.'

'But you didn't mean it!' she cried. 'You never once said you were going to take our vows seriously.'

'Because I knew you wouldn't believe me—in my world, actions speak louder than words, and I'd hoped, by proving myself a true and faithful husband to you, that you'd learn to trust me and believe in me, but as I've learned with you, I'm damned whatever I do. You don't want to believe in me.'

'I do, of course I do, you're the father of my child, and it's all well and good saying that actions speak louder than words but your track record... You don't *have* a track record! You've never sustained a relationship with a woman in the whole of your adult life! For heaven's sake, Alexis, you were only in a position to marry me in the first place because either you or the woman you came close to committing to got cold feet within weeks.'

'What the hell are you talking about?'

'The woman you were going to marry! The one you made the changes in your bedroom for! That happened weeks and weeks before we married and can only have lasted five minutes because I lost count of the number of women you were pictured with after I left your bed.'

The laughter that followed this landed like nails on a chalkboard to Lydia's ears. Shaking his head, his face twisted in something that could be either a smile or a grimace, he swirled the liquid in his glass before throwing it down his throat, and then he reached for the bottle of brandy, refilled the glass and took another large drink of it.

The smiling grimace was still alive on his face when his eyes next locked onto hers. 'It was you.'

'What was?'

'The woman I was planning to marry. It was you, Lydia. It was always you.'

CHAPTER TWELVE

THE ROOM WAS SPINNING, Alexis's face a sudden blur, the noise in Lydia's head deafening.

'You're drunk,' she whispered uncertainly.

'Not yet, but by the end of this night I hope to be.' He winked, raised his glass to her, and drank half of what remained in it. Wiping his mouth with the back of his hand, he gave another of those awful laughs. 'Did you not listen to me when I said I didn't want to be like my father? Or when I told you on the night we agreed to marry that marriage is not a game to be played with? I've seen too much pain and hurt caused by marriage vows taken in vain to ever play that game. I always knew I would settle down when the woman I could see myself growing old with came into my life, but I wasn't prepared to string women along and ruin lives until I found her.' The ugly smile faded into starkness. 'I found her three months ago.'

Her thumping heart jumped into her throat.

'Something happened between us that weekend, Lydia, and I know you felt it too, and I don't just mean the sex.'

She shrank into herself, remembering the way they'd parted. Remembering, too, how much it had hurt to walk away. 'But…that can't be true…you were horrible and dismissive to me.'

He held her stare. 'Have you never heard of pride?'

Blood was whooshing through her head, a roar of noise that made it impossible to think coherently, impossible to take in what he was saying.

'When you left…' He swore and drained his glass. 'I couldn't get you out of my mind.' He tapped his temple. 'You were in here. Everywhere I went. It was like you'd possessed me. I kept hearing your laughter and smelling your perfume and I knew there was no way I could spend the rest of my life without you in it. That's why I proposed a marriage between our families—the truce was just a smokescreen. I didn't even need it. Tsaliki Shipping had already weathered the worst of the storm of bad publicity.'

'But if you…'

'I proposed a marriage between you and me.'

She shook her head, not in disagreement but in disbelief. 'No. That can't be true.' It had always been Thanasis and Lucie…hadn't it?

'Ask your brother.' That awful, awful laugh rang through her ears again. 'He turned me down flat. Looked at me as if I were the devil reincarnate for even suggesting I marry you. I think that was the point when I really understood why you'd had to walk away from me. That war between our fathers…it poisoned everything but it poisoned your family most of all.'

'But…if he said no to you marrying me and if you didn't need a marriage to seal the truce, then why let Thanasis and Lucie marry?'

'I didn't need the marriage but your family did. *You*

did. I knew I couldn't press my wish to marry you without exposing our weekend together and causing you pain, but I couldn't walk away from the negotiating table without making sure you were protected. When my father refused to let Athena marry Thanasis, I nearly gave up, but I was able to turn him round to the idea of Lucie marrying him.' His laughter was a little less awful this time. 'I couldn't have predicted that encouraging their marriage would lead to such near-disastrous consequences for Tsaliki Shipping too, but it wasn't the business I was thinking of when I was so angry with your brother for confessing the truth to Lucie—it was you. It's always you. Everything I've done since that weekend has been for you.'

Turning his back to her, he poured himself another large drink. 'I prepared myself for the wedding. I knew I would have to avoid you. At that point I thought there was no future for me with you. You would never choose me over your family, I knew that, and I was trying to forget about you, but just hearing your voice...' His shoulders rose sharply. 'You called me a bastard. The first words I heard you say in three months was a rant to your brother about listening to *"that bastard Alexis"*.'

He took another large drink then turned back to face her. 'And then you told me you were pregnant.' He shook his head and closed his eyes. 'I couldn't even process it. Not to start with. And your demand that I marry you? And you were so matter-of-fact and cold about it. The passionate, warm, affectionate woman who'd lodged herself in my heart had gone and you were treating me with the same contempt as your brother, and I was so angry with you for that. So fucking angry and wounded you would not believe. But you know what the worst thing is?'

She shook her head dumbly.

'When I demanded a real marriage, I was bluffing. I would have still married you if you'd refused it and given you the terms you wanted because there is nothing I wouldn't do for you. Even when I've been furious with you and hated you I would have still walked on broken glass for you.' The laughter that came from his throat this time was bitter and yet made her want to cover her ears and howl more than the awful nails-on-chalkboard laugh. 'I could walk on that broken glass and you'd still believe I was walking to someone else because you're too damned scared to trust me.'

She shook her head. 'I do trust you, Alexis, I do. You said that nothing happened with Angeliki and I believe that because you're not a liar.'

His voice hardened into granite. 'Your instinct is to distrust me. Your whole life has been spent hearing poison about my very name. You see what you want to see and believe what you want to believe. I know you have feelings for me. You're as jealous and selfish for me as I am for you but unlike you, my angel from Hades, I've not been running away from commitment, I've been running to it but my running stops now because I no longer trust you. You clearly want out of this marriage... consider your wish granted.'

'What?'

'Don't look so shocked. This is what you want, and have I not made it clear enough that I would do anything you want? It just so happens that this is what I want too. When you told me you were mine, you didn't mean it.'

'I *did* mean it. When I married you I believed I was committing myself to you for life.'

'But you never really wanted it and you never believed I was doing the same.'

'Can you blame me? If you'd told me all this before then—'

'Then what?' he demanded roughly. 'Can you really put your hand on your heart and say you would have believed me?'

'We'll never know now because you never gave me a chance with the truth!'

'The truth about my love for you didn't need spelling out. It was there the whole time—you just refused to see it. You were never prepared to give the whole of yourself to me because of who I am, and you still won't. When you tell your parents about us, I don't want you making excuses for being with me and begging their forgiveness, I want you to stand proud beside me and tell them, *This is my husband, the father of my child, and I choose him of my own free will because I love him and nothing you can do or say will ever stop me loving him*. Can you do that, Lydia? Can you stand up to your family and be honest about your feelings for me?'

She shook her head in bewilderment. 'You know I can't do that. They would never forgive me.'

'And I know I will never forgive you if you don't. It seems I have my limits too. I don't want half-measures, Lydia, I want everything from you, your love, your faith and your trust, and I no longer trust I will have any of it, so I will settle for nothing because I never want to hate you.' The flicker of a smile played on his lips. 'As they say, it's the hope that kills you. Well, I'm out of hope.

I will buy you a house like I originally suggested and put it in your name. Tell me what you want for maintenance and I will pay it. If you choose not to tell your family about our marriage then I will respect that but I will not—and let me be very clear about this—I will not be denied my role as our child's father. Once our child is born you will tell your parents that I am the father and I will be involved in his or her life and neither you nor your family, if they stand by you, will stop me.'

'I would *never* do that,' she said vehemently.

'Good. Then we won't have a problem.' He finished his drink, put the glass on the bar without looking at what he was doing, stretched his neck and strode to the door. 'I'm going out.'

'You're what? You're going out *now*?'

'I cannot be here when you leave so I'm going to check into a hotel with a fully stocked bar and get very, very drunk. I'll get my team onto finding a temporary place you can move into first thing in the morning, just until you find a home you're happy with.'

He really did want her gone, Lydia thought dimly, the coldness in her chest she'd barely felt until then spreading. None of this felt real, like she'd fallen into a waking dream.

He turned to face her with twisted lips. 'However, my advice to you is to return to your family. I would imagine that with the business saved they'll be in a frame of mind where they just might forgive you for sleeping with the enemy.' Now his whole face contorted. 'It's just a shame that you will never have the courage to fight to make them believe that I'm no enemy to them and that I have never been an enemy to you—but then, to have that courage you'd need to believe it yourself, and we both know you don't have any belief in me or courage in yourself.'

He closed the door softly behind him but the sound had the same impact on her as if he'd slammed it.

All the lights in the Antoniadis house were on, shadows flickering in the windows. The taxi driver one of the maids had called for Lydia drove past the dozens of cars parked outside and followed the driveway as far as it would go until he reached the small white cottage where the only illumination came from the outdoor sensor light.

Dressed in her usual slouchy top and jeans, the top button of which had refused to do up, she treaded heavily to her front door and let herself in. Once she'd paid the driver, who'd kindly brought her suitcases in, she gazed around at the walls that felt so much smaller than they had eight days ago.

Was that really all the time that had passed since she'd last been in her cottage? Only eight days? It didn't seem possible.

In her bedroom, she looked in the mirror and then, unable to bear the dullness in her eyes and the strange ashen colour of her skin, looked away, brushing her hair and tying it back without looking again at her reflection.

The noise coming from the main house filtered into the night air when she was halfway through a walk that felt twice as long as it ever had before, and suddenly it came to her that she was free. Free from Alexis. Free from a marriage she'd never wanted. Free from all those overwhelming emotions being with him made her feel:

the jealousy, the possessive need, the tortured thoughts. Her family was saved and she was saved too. The plan she'd originally made to get through the pregnancy and then tell her family about her baby's father was viable again…

Her heart sank a little as she thought of the party she'd gatecrashed earlier. If they'd been seen arguing outside the house, then her brother would be bound to hear about it. What had *possessed* her to take such a risk?

She would cross that bridge when she came to it, she decided, and then smiled to know that within just two hours of her newfound freedom, she was feeling like her old self again. Alexis hadn't burrowed into her heart as deeply as she'd feared or as deeply as his arrogance had let him believe. Love? Oh, she'd come close to falling in love with him but she hadn't crossed the line from lust into love and now there was no danger that she ever would because she was free, and it felt fantastic, like the heaviest weight in the world had been lifted from her.

With a beaming smile on her face, she opened the kitchen door and stepped into the most raucous party she'd ever known her parents to throw. Fighting her way through the throng in search of them, a search that seemed to take for ever as all the partying guests knew her and enthusiastically embraced her, she thought every member of her family, her grandparents, aunts, uncles and cousins, and all her parents' friends and every senior employee of Antoniadis Shipping were crammed into the house celebrating the miracle.

'*Baba!*' She turned her head to find her mother elbowing her way to her from the dining room. 'You're back!' she cried, throwing her arms around her. After smothering Lydia's face with kisses she stepped back a little and cupped her daughter's cheeks. 'Let me look at you...*baba*, you look tired! Oh, this is such a lovely surprise—we weren't expecting you home until Sunday. Come on, let's find your father, and get you a drink and get some colour on those cheeks.'

Hands clasped together, Lydia let her mother drag her through the crowd to the kitchen where her father—she must have walked straight past him—was supervising one of the caterers in the making of a vat of punch by pouring liberal amounts of vodka into it.

'Baba!' he cried when he spotted them, and then Lydia was pulled into another tight embrace and her face smothered with a dozen more kisses. A glass of punch thrust into her hand, her parents raised their glasses and she followed suit, and when they both drank liberally, she kept her lips tight around the glass rim to stop any of the potent liquid seeping into her mouth. They were both too high on the euphoria of their business being saved to notice, too euphoric to notice too when Lydia discreetly switched her punch for an alcohol-free one.

'Is Thanasis not here?' she shouted over the noise.

'No, he's gone away with Lucie. They want some "time alone together".' Her mother rolled her eyes gleefully at this.

Lydia hardly dared to ask. 'Does this mean you are okay now about Thanasis loving her?'

Her mother threw an arm around Lydia's shoulder and kissed her temple. 'How could I not be? She has saved us and your brother loves her and she must love him too to have forgiven him for what he did to her.'

Hope opened its wings in her heart. 'Even though she's a Tsaliki?'

The glee on her mother's face deepened. 'But she isn't, is she? She was never properly one of those devil's spawns, and now she has turned her back on all of them to join the Antoniadis camp and hates them as much as we do, if not more!'

'If that doesn't call for another drink then I don't know what does!' her father interjected, his glee as evident as her mother's, and the wings of hope closed back up again.

Her fingers tightening around the glass, Lydia joined her parents in raising a toast to Antoniadis prosperity, and wondered why she'd even felt that hope. This was where she belonged. Here. With the people she loved and who loved her. Her family. She should be counting her blessings that Alexis had set her free. She *was* counting her blessings! Except…even in the haze of her euphoria, sickness roiled deep in her belly, and she didn't understand why she'd had to tighten her hold on the glass to stop herself from throwing the liquid in her mother's face or why she felt so strung out beneath her skin that there was every danger that one wrong word addressed to her would see her dissolve into a puddle of tears.

Alexis lay fully dressed on his hotel bed watching the early morning light filter through the curtains. Or trying to. The room was spinning. A whole bottle of the hotel's finest Scotch had finally kicked in.

Good. Let oblivion take him. Let him have this one night to wallow in misery and drink himself into a stupor. One more night of making terrible choices.

Lydia had gone. The message from his staff had come before he'd even settled into his hotel room. He'd laughed to read it. Of course she'd gone. The path of least resistance, that was Lydia's way. The only thing she'd ever fought for was their baby and he was the fool who'd let himself believe she would ever fight for him. It had never been about him. If her family's business hadn't been so close to destruction he still wouldn't know she was expecting their child. She would have kept it a tightly wrapped secret because she was a coward. A coward who loved her family and was terrified of losing them.

She loved him too even if she couldn't—wouldn't—see it. But, as with the two fools who'd come before him, she didn't love him enough, and he was the arrogant fool to have let himself believe what she felt for him was different. If it was different then it wasn't a difference that was enough. Not for her.

He tried to drag air into lungs that no longer knew how to breathe for themselves. Better they end it now. He didn't want to hate her. Okay, he did want to hate her. He wanted to convince himself that his father had been right and that she was all the things he'd said the Antoniadises were the whole of his life. A scorpion.

He'd always known Lydia had a sting in her tail. She'd stung him the morning after their glorious passionate weekend together. He'd just never appreciated how deeply the sting would penetrate the second time it hit him, embedding so deep that he didn't know how to begin ridding himself of its pain. If half a bottle of brandy and a whole bottle of Scotch couldn't touch it then what hope was there for him?

Somehow, he needed to learn to navigate the rest of his life without her.

The darkness he craved was getting closer, his heavy eyes closing.

A solitary tear rolled down his cheek and then oblivion.

CHAPTER THIRTEEN

CLOUDS WERE GATHERING above Athens that early morning, the first break from the unremitting sunshine in over three months. Lydia took her seat amongst the extremely early-bird tourists and the first of the commuters and tried to shake the clouds gathering in the unremittingly sunny mood she'd determinedly retained for the past week.

The train set off. Moments later it stopped. Her heart clenched. A week ago, this was the stop she'd embarked at. It had taken her the full week to pluck up the courage to take it again and prove to herself that she really was over him; that there had never actually been anything to get over, that the madness of lust she'd found with Alexis was gone.

Don't think about him.

She'd been too busy to think about him other than in the abstract. Lydia had found a new energy. She'd thrown herself into her work, pitching for more contracts in a few days than she'd done in a year. No more picking and choosing the most exciting ones to catch her eye, now she was approaching her work like she always should have done, like a business and not like a hobby for a spoilt rich kid. If she'd approached it like this from the start then she would never have had to go crawling to Alexis when bankruptcy had loomed. She would already have been self-sufficient from her own endeavours.

Her parents had been too busy riding the wave of euphoria at the saving of the business to ask any questions about her time in London so she'd been spared from having to tell more lies. She never wanted to tell another lie. A few more days and she would tell them about the baby.

If anyone other than Helena realised she'd been the woman to leave the party with Alexis then they were being remarkably discreet. It looked like she'd got away with that moment of madness. She should be relieved but she was too numb to feel anything, and she still didn't know what she would say to her parents. Before, she'd planned to simply refuse to reveal the identity of the father until the baby was born and they'd fallen in love with their grandchild, yet whenever she tried to envisage the scene now, the sickness that had become a permanent part of her welled up and stopped her.

She couldn't leave it much longer. If they weren't so wrapped up in their euphoria they would notice her waistline had thickened. That morning, she'd caught sight of her naked figure and seen a small but detectable curve in her belly. Not quite a bump but definitely a precursor to one.

She'd come within a breath of calling Alexis to tell him.

There had been no contact between them. Not a call, not a message. Nothing. Radio silence.

She continued not thinking about him all the way to the Acropolis stop, all along her route on the Dionysiou Areopagitou walkway and past the church of St Demetrius, still not thinking about him when she disappeared through the trees onto the running route. The thickening clouds meant she didn't need to seek solace from the heat of the rising sun. But this was her route, the safe, comforting, familiar path she always took, and she pounded along it to the old quarry, still not thinking about him as she passed the crag and took the landscaped path to the top of the hill.

When she reached the marble Philopappos Monument, she took a long drink of her water and, before she could stop herself, she turned her gaze in the direction of the district where Alexis lived, easily seeking out his apartment block. She'd looked out at it from this very spot an average of five times a week since their weekend together. This was the first time she'd looked at it with dark clouds looming over it.

Was he there or had he already left for work?

Don't think about him.

Was he choosing which of his many, many, many snazzy suits to wear for the day?

Don't think about him.

Still unable to wrench her gaze from the direction of his apartment, she absently rubbed at her belly and the weird bubbling sensation that had just started in it...

Like flutters. Bubbling flutters...

Her eyes widened and she pressed harder. That was her baby. She could feel her baby. She could feel her baby!

Still pressing into her fluttering belly, she excitedly unzipped her side pocket and pulled out her phone. She needed to call Alexis. He needed to know this momentous milestone...

A fat raindrop fell on her nose. Another landed with a splat on her chin. In moments, the heavens opened with a load roar and seconds later Lydia was soaked to her skin, still holding her belly, water pouring off her phone.

Cursing, she wiped the phone on her soaked T-shirt and tried to unlock it but her fingers were too wet for her fingerprint to work and the deluge too heavy for facial recognition to work either. Excitement turned into panic. She couldn't remember the pin code she hadn't used since she'd first set the phone up. Hardly able to see at all through the waterfall of water, she tried every pin code she'd ever had, her need to speak to Alexis and share the news and hear his voice, right now, growing stronger with each failed attempt…

Her screen locked itself at the exact same moment the fluttering bubbles stopped.

'Please,' she sobbed to her baby, rubbing vigorously with one hand as she manically shook her phone in a futile attempt to bring it magically back to life. 'Please, do it again. Please. Please…'

Oh, God, she was crying, and no sooner had she realised her face wasn't just wet with the rain but with her tears, a keening wrench sliced through her chest, the greatest pain of her life ripping her heart in two and bringing her to her knees with a howl.

Call him? *Call* him?

Lydia didn't need to hear his voice. She needed *him*. Alexis.

She shouldn't be calling him to share the news. She should be there with him, living the experience with him, in his apartment, in the bedroom he'd turned into a beautiful sanctuary for her because he loved her. Alexis *loved* her. He loved her and she'd closed her eyes and ears to it.

She couldn't close her eyes and ears to it now. Each

and every heavy raindrop fell on her like a mark of condemnation: condemning her for walking—running—away from him like a frightened child instead of fighting for them, and all because she couldn't handle what she felt for him and had never believed that she was enough for him; condemning her, too, for burying her head in the sand ever since, and all because the truth was too terrifying to contemplate, that to admit her real feelings for him meant admitting that she'd thrown away the best person in the whole wide world because she was a coward.

Another long, interminable day had bled into another long, interminable night, and now, with another long, interminable day to look forward to, Alexis stared out of his bedroom window at the torrent of rain lashing the streets. Finally, the weather matched his mood. Good. Why should he be the only one to suffer? The darkness of the rainclouds was nothing on the cloud that had lived in his heart since he'd returned to an apartment empty of Lydia.

She'd taken everything of hers. His cleaning crew worked such magic that not even a strand of her hair remained. The only item of hers he still possessed was the lipstick that had fallen in the back of his car that first night. He'd taken to carrying it around with him.

Time, they said, was a healer. *They* were liars. All time did was rip the gaping wound in his heart wider. He'd never imagined missing someone could be a physical pain.

How the hell was he supposed to move on when Lydia's ghost lived within the walls he slept in and in the very air he breathed? Somehow he had to find a way because this pain was beyond endurance.

* * *

The rain poured harder than ever but Lydia no longer cared. She lifted her face to it and accepted the drenching she deserved.

The safe, comforting, familiar path she'd taken on this run was the path she'd been taking all her life because she was too much of a coward to divert from it. Too much of a coward to forge a life, a real life, for herself. Too much of a coward to fight for the man she loved because she'd never had to fight for anything before, not even for herself. Yes, everything Alexis had said had been the truth, all except for one thing. She *did* believe in him. It was herself she'd never believed in. The great Alexis Tsaliki, a force of nature who burned brighter than the sun and who could have any woman he so desired, loved her. He wanted *her*. Just her. She was enough for him.

How could she have walked away after everything he'd done for her and everything he'd said? How could she have left him knowing that to leave him would be to destroy him? And destroy herself too.

She loved him.

The rain had stopped.

Lydia opened her eyes to the sun burning through the clouds. Its warmth bathed her skin.

She laughed and lifted her chin even higher. She loved Alexis. She loved him. She was his and he was hers, and she would do whatever it took, fight any fight needed, to make him understand and believe that she was his for ever.

Lydia let herself into her parents' house. Her running clothes were still damp from the rain but she didn't want to go back to her cottage and change, not until she'd done what needed to be done, now, before her father left for work.

They were both in the dining room finishing their breakfast, her father dressed in his suit, her mother still in her dressing gown.

'I need to talk to you,' she said without any preamble.

Her mother's lined face…the last year had seen those lines turn into grooves…furrowed. 'What's wrong, *baba*?'

'Before I tell you, I want you to know that I love you.'

'You're scaring me. Are you ill? Come and sit down. Petros, pour her a coffee.'

'No, no coffee for me, and I'm not ill, it's nothing like that, although I think you might prefer it if I was. I'm fourteen weeks pregnant with Alexis Tsaliki's child.'

Stunned silence.

Lydia opened her mouth and launched into the whole sorry story right up to the night she'd left Alexis, the only omissions the details no parent needed to hear about their child.

When she'd finished speaking, more stunned silence bounced loudly between the dining room walls.

After for ever seemed to pass, her mother rose unsteadily to her feet. 'Get out.'

Lydia closed her eyes, sucked in some air and ground her feet to the floor. Only when she was steady in mind and body did she open her eyes. 'I'm sorry. I know this is your worst nightmare come to life but Alexis isn't who you think he is—he isn't his father and he doesn't deserve to be blamed for his father's sins. If you want to thank anyone for saving the business, then it should be him. He's a wonderful man and he loves me and I love him, and he's going to be a wonderful father.'

'Get out and never come back.'

'I'll be out of the cottage by the end of the night.'

She'd reached the front door when a hand gripped her arm. 'He might not take you back,' her mother said with a viciousness that's sting was lessened by the tears in her eyes. 'And what will you be left with?'

Lydia smiled sadly. 'The knowledge that I fought for him just as he's spent the last three months fighting for me.' And then she kissed her mother's cheek and walked out of the door.

Alexis approached the booth he'd slid into the first time he'd spoken to her.

Voices echoed.

'So, Lydia Antoniadis. Tell me why the youngest member of the family at war with my family is here alone in my hunting ground.'

'Catching my prey, of course.'

He could never have guessed in that moment how deeply and entirely she would catch him.

A hostess passed carrying a large bucket of chips. Just to see them and remember Lydia's love of them was another punch to his guts, and he made a sharp turn to the bar, unwilling to wait until he'd taken his seat at his personal booth.

He glanced at the tequila on the top shelf…

Only the good stuff.

'Get me a large Scotch,' he told the barman, and indicated for him to keep pouring until the liquid was a fraction from the rim. He drank half of it, looked at the remainder and then thought, to hell with it, and downed the rest before pushing the empty glass back to the barman and telling him to refill it. He hadn't touched a drop of alcohol since that first night he'd drunk himself into oblivion, though God knew he'd wanted to. It didn't numb the pain but, if he was lucky, it might numb his senses enough to get through a few hours of partying before he could make his excuses and leave, and return to a life now empty of all meaning.

Lydia climbed the wide, rounded stairs to the VIP section. The bouncer guarding the roped barrier checked her name off the list she'd maxed out her credit card to get on and let her through.

'Is Alexis Tsaliki here yet?' she asked with a brightness she had to dredge from the pit of her stomach to achieve. The Alexis she knew would never let a friend down—she doubted he had ever let anyone down in his life. He'd promised his friend he would host a party for him that night, and so he would be there to host it. Despite her knowing this, it still came as a relief when the bouncer nodded in answer.

This wasn't going to backfire, she told herself staunchly as she walked past the booth she'd hired all those months ago. Alexis *did* love her. If she had to have faith in only one thing then it would be that. The purest, most unconditional love in the world.

The dancefloor was packed and she had to elbow her way through it to reach the DJ.

Catching his attention, she rose onto her toes to tell him what she wanted.

He reared back and looked hard at her, as if satisfying himself that she hadn't just been released from an asylum, then turned his gaze to the direction of the most private of private booths before looking back at her.

She held the stare unwaveringly.

He inclined his head in dubious agreement.

She expelled a breath and smiled her thanks, then elbowed her way back through the dancefloor until she reached the exact same spot she'd danced at all those months ago and fixed her gaze at the club's most private of private booths, the one most hidden in the shadows, where a tall, well-built man with perfectly quiffed hair so dark it was almost black was holding court with his sycophants. Except, if it was a court he was holding, it was a court he didn't want to be at. His gaze was fixed in the distance. He didn't look bored. He looked vacant.

Her heart ballooned.

Why had he bothered to come? Alexis asked himself moodily. He should have stayed at home. The club's vibe was doing nothing for him, the incessant chatter and laughter of his friends and various hangers-on like sharp needles in his head. He couldn't even be bothered to drink himself into oblivion as he'd intended, his second full glass of Scotch mostly untouched.

He slumped back in the booth, lifted his face to the ceiling and closed his eyes.

'Anyway, Anastasia said…'

He tuned the voice out, would have inched away but was penned in. He didn't care what Anastasia had said. He didn't care about anything. Only Lydia. He should have been honest about his feelings from the start instead of expecting her to be a mind reader when he'd always known that she didn't believe him capable of being faithful and had known how much the thought of losing her family was hurting her. Where his feelings for Lydia were straightforward and uncomplicated, Lydia was not him, and he'd driven her away, punished her for not having the same faith in her feelings and in him as he had…

'I have a special request for Alexis Tsaliki.'

His eyes snapped open at the DJ's words echoing loudly through the speakers.

'Your wife asks that you join her on the dancefloor.'

A loud roaring noise filled his head, louder than the music, louder even than the sudden booming of his heart.

Hardly daring to believe what he'd just heard, Alexis slowly lowered his gaze.

A small curvy figure in a mid-thigh-length silver mini dress was standing directly in his line of sight on the dancefloor. Her blonde hair was loose around her shoulders, wisps of her fringe falling into her eyes.

Their stares locked.

Her chest and shoulders rose.

Slowly, she raised her arm and held her hand out to him.

Unable to tear his stare from her, not at all certain he wasn't dreaming this, barely aware that the people penning him into the booth had all fallen into stunned silence, Alexis rose to his feet and took the most direct route to the woman shining brighter than any strobe light by climbing over the table.

Lydia fought to keep her feet grounded, and keep her trembling hand held out to him.

Time slowed to a crawl.

There was not a flicker of emotion on his face and yet each slow step he took to her added to the emotions filling her so completely she could hardly breathe for them.

He stopped a foot away from her.

Her extended arm fell to her side.

The blue-grey eyes that had seduced her so completely from that first look bored into hers. The longing making her heart cry reflected back at her.

She took the final step to him.

With a tremulous smile, she palmed his cheek.

His lids closed in silent reverence before his stare locked back onto hers.

Bringing her face to his, she looked deep into his eyes. 'I have told my parents everything. They know I'm yours. Because I *am* yours. I'm yours, Alexis Tsaliki. Now and for ever.'

His jaw tightened. Long fingers caught the hand palming his cheeks. His breathing had become heavy.

She slipped her other hand around his neck and threaded her fingers through his hair. She could feel the tremors in his powerful body and dimly marvelled that this man, this titan of a man, loved her. Her.

'I love you,' she said, willing with every fibre of her being for him to feel her words and not just hear them. 'I love you, and there is nothing anyone can do or say that will ever stop me loving you, and there is nothing I wouldn't do for you. I would walk on broken glass for you, and I give my heart into your keeping of my own free will and I trust and have faith that you will keep it safe for ever because I am yours and you are mine and I can't go on without you.'

Alexis's fingers tightened around the dainty hand holding his cheek, his heart thumping so hard it threatened to burst through his ribs.

The hazel eyes gazing so intently into his filled with tears and then her voice broke. 'Please forgive me.'

Air expelled from his lungs in one long exhalation and for the first time in so, so long, Alexis found he could breathe. Bringing his mouth down to hers, he kissed her, closing his eyes and letting his senses fill with the softness of her lips and beauty of her scent.

'My angel,' he groaned before cupping her cheeks to stare into the eyes that were finally shining openly with love for him. 'You will never know how much I have longed to hear those words.'

Her arms slid around his neck, but the smile she gave still contained fear. 'Can you forgive me?'

With another groan, he brushed his lips to hers. 'There is nothing to forgive. You are my heart, Lydia, and I should have had more faith that you would feel the truth of it.' He rubbed his nose to hers. 'And more patience. My pride...my stupid pride pushed you away from me again. If you hadn't come to me tonight I would have come to you and got down on my hands and knees to beg you to come back to me. Forgive me?'

She sighed, and it was like she was expelling all the air from her own lungs in one long exhalation. 'There is nothing to forgive. Your impatience and pride are a part of you and you wouldn't be you without them.' And then she smiled, and it was with such dreaminess that the last of his own fear turned to smoke and vanished. 'I love you.'

'And I love you.'

Her smile shone straight into his heart. 'Can we go home now?'

'As long as you're with me, I will go anywhere.'

Her lips fused to his in a kiss full of all the same passion and tenderness brimming in his heart. 'Then take me home and love me for ever.'

If the intercom hadn't been buzzing so incessantly, Alexis wouldn't have been woken from the best sleep of his entire life. Holding firmly to his wife, who was curled into him, he reached over to the bedside table and lifted the receiver. 'This had better be important.'

Once his butler had relayed the news, he muttered a curse and said, 'Let him in.'

Lydia lifted her head and sleepily asked, 'What's wrong?'

'Your brother's here.'

She blinked. 'What? Now?'

'Yes. He's refusing to leave until he speaks to me. You stay here. I'll—'

He never got to finish saying that he'd deal with Thanasis, for Lydia had shot off the bed as if she were turbo boosted, snatched her robe off the floor where she'd dropped it, and was shrugging her arms into as she stormed out of the bedroom.

Half laughing at this newly found terrier side to his wife, Alexis pulled his discarded trousers on and followed her. He was halfway down the stairs when he saw her steaming over to her brother, who was standing by the apartment's main entrance.

'If you lay a hand on him then you and I are through,' she blazed, not letting him even open his mouth. 'So if that's what you've come here to do, then turn around and go. I love Alexis and he loves me. We come as a package now, so deal with it.'

Alexis stood behind her and wrapped his arms protectively around her waist while Thanasis folded his arms around his chest and arched an eyebrow. 'Have you finished?' her brother asked.

That nonplussed her. Folding her arms in turn, she nodded primly. 'Yes.'

'Good. Because I'm not here for a fight.' His eyes fixed on Alexis. 'My parents told me everything and while I will never forgive you for the way you treated Lucie, I love my sister and I want her to be happy.' His lip curled. 'Apparently she loves you and thinks you're going to be faithful to her, so if you can look me in the eye and promise that you *will* be true to her and that you'll always love her and take care of her then I will give you both my blessing.'

Alexis actually felt his wife go rigid in shock.

'Is this some kind of joke?' she asked.

Thanasis flashed a brief smile at her. 'No joke. I have no wish to lose you over this bastard and I'd very much like to be a part of my niece or nephew's life, and I know our parents want the same too.' His smile dropped. 'They love you. Just give them time. It won't be long, I promise.' His gaze fell back on Alexis. 'Well?'

'I love her,' Alexis told him, not wavering. 'And I meant every word of the vows I made before God.'

For the longest time, Lydia held her breath as she watched her brother eyeball her husband. Whatever he saw in Alexis's stare must have convinced him of the truth for the hardness in his eyes softened a touch and he extended a hand to him. 'Welcome to the family.'

Hardly able to believe her eyes, Lydia watched her husband and brother shake hands, and then a moment later she was being pulled into her brother's embrace. 'Be happy,' he whispered fiercely.

'I am.' And knowing she had her brother's blessing and that her parents still loved her completed it for her.

He kissed the top of her head and then turned to leave. 'I'll be in touch.'

'Thanasis,' Alexis called as he was closing the door.

Her brother looked back.

'Tell Lucie I'm sorry.'

The ghost of a smile played on Thanasis's lips. 'You can tell her yourself at our wedding.'

With the door closed, Lydia looked at Alexis. He met her stare and cupped her cheeks, disbelief apparent on his handsome face. 'Did that just happen?'

She couldn't hold back the beam a moment longer and then, just when she thought her happiness couldn't be more complete, fluttering bubbles thickened in her belly...

'Our baby!' Tugging Alexis's hand down to her abdomen, she pressed it tight to the place where the flutters were happening. 'Can you feel it?'

His gorgeous eyes lit up with wonder. 'That's our baby?'

'It is!'

He shook his head in awe. 'God, I love you.' And then he kissed her and carried her up to their bedroom to show her exactly how much he loved her.

EPILOGUE

Lydia spied on her father, making sure he didn't put the whole bottle of vodka into the vat of punch. Noticing her, he winked, tipped a little more in and then screwed the lid back on. Standing behind him, egging him on, was her father-in-law.

Grinning, she weaved her way through all the guests into the huge kitchen, where her mother was supervising the caterers unloading all the party food. The plentiful surfaces were practically groaning under the weight of it all.

'Come on,' she said, sliding her arm into her mother's elbow. 'This is a party. You're supposed to be enjoying yourself, not working.'

'But I don't want you having to do anything, *baba*— it's your celebration.'

'That's why we have the caterers here, and, as Alexis owns the company, they're going to do an extra specially good job for us, so please, let them get on with it and come and enjoy yourself.'

'It really is a beautiful house,' her mother said as they wandered through to the main reception room.

'You're just saying that because we're only two minutes away from you now,' Lydia laughed. When she'd been in hospital giving birth to their second son, their oldest son, Matthaios, had stayed with her parents. When they'd collected him the next morning and found him playing football with his grandfather and uncle in the sprawling garden, they'd both known the time had come for them to buy a family home with a garden for their children to play in. Six months later, they were finally settled in and throwing their housewarming party for it, both families coming together in another celebration.

It had been amazing how magically babies worked at dissolving family feuds, and while Lydia's mother would never make a friend of any Tsaliki apart from her son-in-law, she politely tolerated the others and pretended not to notice the rekindling of her husband's friendship with Georgios. Lucie, too, who had more reason than anyone to hate her stepfamily, had found motherhood softening her attitude to them and had recently rekindled her relationship with her own mother.

This all made Lydia very happy. Family was everything to her and as far as she was concerned, the more in it, the merrier.

Once all her guests were settled in and enjoying themselves freely, she went back into the kitchen and helped herself to an enormous plate of chips, then sneaked out through the back door into the garden and into the balmy summer air. There, she followed the path to the tree to the left of the swimming pool. Waiting for her beneath it was the person who made her the happiest of everyone.

Alexis saw her and grinned, and raised the bottle of tequila he'd sneaked out and the two shot glasses.

Let their guests entertain themselves. They were going to have their favourite kind of party—a private party for two.

* * * * *

Did His Pregnant Enemy Bride
sweep you off your feet?
Then don't miss the first instalment in the
Greek Rivals duet
Forgotten Greek Proposal

And why not explore these other stories by Michelle Smart?

Cinderella's One-Night Baby
The Forbidden Greek
Heir Ultimatum
Resisting the Bossy Billionaire
Spaniard's Shock Heirs

Available now!

UNWRAPPING HIS FORBIDDEN ASSISTANT

LORRAINE HALL

MILLS & BOON

For all my Christmas angels

CHAPTER ONE

AMELIA BARESI WASN'T afraid of a good cry. In fact, she rather welcomed it. Especially when it pertained to her late father. Crying was an expression of grief, grief an expression of love and time lost. She held these things close to her heart.

Discovering her father's old journals from before she had come to live with him had caused a lot of tears, a lot of grief, but also a wonderful sort of connection to the father she'd lost in a terrible plane crash two years ago.

His journals began when he started his work with the Follieros as a young man, and she'd been following his journey, from scrabbling his way out of poverty with a mix of luck, timing and tenacity to revered personal assistant to the Folliero heir, Diego.

Every night, she curled up in bed and read a few entries about her father's life, carefully doling out pages so each night felt like some part of Bartolo Baresi was still with her.

She liked the symmetry of it, even if it was based on tragedy. Every day, she worked as Diego Folliero's assistant, living in the Folliero Castello di Natale, and every night she read about her father having done the same.

Amelia was not a stranger to tragedy. She had been raised by her mother in London for eleven years, before her mother became sick and finally admitted to Amelia that her father did not know she existed. In the final months of her mother's life, Alice had made strides and amends to track down her father.

Bartolo had been shocked, and no doubt there had been anger and bitterness there toward her mother for keeping Amelia a secret, but he had accepted his daughter with open arms. When her mother died, he'd brought Amelia to the Italian Alps and Castello di Natale, and raised a twelve-year-old girl as best he could. He'd even made his home base the castello, doing his work for the world-gallivanting Diego in one place as often as he could.

Then, ten years after her mother passed, he too had died, leaving Amelia an adult orphan, with absolutely no idea how she would move through the world on her own.

She had had her first real conversation with Diego at the funeral, since he almost never spent any time at the castello, no matter how often his parents tried to get him to.

Even at twenty-two, and mired in her grief and aloneness, Amelia had known he didn't want to be there.

But he'd come, expressed his regrets and offered her a job.

She'd taken it, a lifeline. She didn't need the job, per se. Her father had been frugal with his money and—with the Follieros' advisement no doubt—made sure the money was in places that passed directly to her without much interference.

But the job offer had been a chance to hold on to her father a little longer. It was the only thing she knew for sure she could do in that moment. Step into his shoes. Do what he would want her to do.

Two years later, she thought she'd done an excellent job, even if she knew Diego mainly kept employing her because of guilt...or whatever it was he felt. Still, she'd been able to stay at the castello—since closed to all and sundry except staff—and build herself into Diego's formidable public face, since he'd become a recluse high on his mountain.

It was her curiosity about that, she supposed, that kept her reading her father's journals through Bartolo finding out about her existence, then trying to raise a teenage girl while doing his job, because he also often wrote about Diego.

Father had been Diego's assistant, but Amelia could tell from his writings that he'd viewed Diego as something like a ward, though he'd only been about ten years older than Diego himself.

Amelia liked to believe that Diego offering her the assistant position meant he'd viewed her father in a similarly positive light.

That was the kind of man her father was. A caretaker. And that was the kind of woman he had wanted her to be— thoughtful and caring. He'd raised her to be aware of all the ways she was fortunate and help those who were less so. And he'd never just meant monetarily.

Though she'd never dreamed of being someone's personal assistant, she'd found she enjoyed the role, knowing each day she was doing something that would make her father proud.

But she'd enjoy it more if she could understand her hermit boss. She'd given Diego his space at first because he'd been mired in grief as well—he'd lost both parents and his sister in one fell, unfair swoop in the same plane crash. But it had been two years now, and still he lived in his horrible little cabin far away from civilization, only communicating via email and very occasionally a phone call, expecting Amelia to handle whatever needed to be done face-to-face.

She wondered what her father would have done in her position. She tried to consider that in all things, but this one especially. She searched for answers in his journals.

Then, one cold late-November night, curled in bed in the castello, fire crackling in her bedroom's fireplace, Amelia finally read the entry that gave her an idea.

Diego is a troubled soul, but there is a good man under there. If only he'd find the humility to develop it. In some ways, he reminds me of myself. In some ways, it has healed me to watch his parents misunderstand him as mine understood me, spoil him as mine did not.

He will be a good man someday. I wish I could convince him of that.

A good man. She dealt with a stern, taciturn, grumpy man—via email and texts mostly. She had never considered Diego good or evil. Honestly, he was more of a robot overlord to her than anything else.

But her father had thought he would be a good man someday. Her father had wished this.

And suddenly, Amelia knew what she would accomplish this holiday season. Another way to keep her father right here with her.

She would find a way to fulfill her father's wish.

Diego Folliero couldn't say he liked living as sparsely as a monk, but that was the point. Not liking it.

He had studied the idea of penance deeply over these past two years. In his understanding, pain was the price of survival. Neither guilt nor self-flagellation could bring his family back, but the cold water he had to haul from the icy alpine lake, the fire he had to start to cook anything, the trials and tribulations of life on a tiny, remote mountaintop where Castello di Natale could be seen below was the price.

He had been selfish. He had survived. Now he suffered.

It was right.

He awoke to a frigid morning. The pain of cold sank into his joints, and he thanked the universe for it.

His pain was his price.

He got out of bed and pulled on the warm, serviceable clothes he would need to survive the day, then went about his morning routine: build up the fire in the lone fireplace, boil water for bitter coffee. He buttered a piece of rustic bread—both food items he'd had delivered from a scrabbling farm not far away.

It was not any pain to eat so humbly when the items were made so well, but he overpaid for the privilege.

After breakfast, his next task was to deal with work. There was one modern amenity he allowed himself—internet, and the power required for it. He would have cut this off as well, but in order to continue the Folliero legacy, he had to be somewhat reachable. Still, he did not allow himself to use electricity, communication or this connection with the outside world for pleasure. It was for work and work alone.

He settled into the chair at his desk, both hardscrabble items not meant for any comfort. His assistant vetted all his emails, so only the most important ones made its way to him. Every morning, he read them, dealt with them and then went back to his life of penance.

But today, an email from his assistant caught him off guard.

Mr. Folliero,

Your presence is required at Castello di Natale this Christmas season. I have handled your travel arrangements, attached below. We look forward to seeing you.

Warm regards,

Amelia

It was such a nonsensical email to receive, he stared at it, read it at least five times, trying to understand what on earth had happened for him to receive such a missive. His *presence* wasn't required *anywhere* anymore because he refused.

His cheerful assistant had clearly gotten some kind of wire crossed.

He scowled at the email. It was addressed to him, signed by her. Where could the confusion be? She had been his assistant for the last two years now—efficient and excellent, which he hadn't expected since it had been a guilt hire after all—but Amelia Baresi had never pushed his refusal to attend any meetings or event in person or even via video call. She'd accepted it, dealt with it.

She was his proxy, and she understood that. Or *had* until this moment.

Well, he would clear up any confusion. Without even opening her attachment, he hit reply. His response was simple, no greeting or salutation. Just:

No.

He walked away from his computer, found himself pacing the small room that made up the living area. He stopped, scowled. Work had not agitated him in some time. *Feelings* aside from the acceptable guilt had not stabbed through the fog of nothingness in years.

He didn't like it.

The computer dinged, signaling another email. A strange feeling, something he might have once called anticipation, settled in his chest. He crossed back to the computer, opened the email with another scowl.

Mr. Folliero,

So sorry for the confusion! I'm afraid no is not an answer, as it was not a request. A car will be there soon.

Regards,

Amelia

He didn't miss the fact she'd dropped the *warm* from her *regards*, or that the apology and exclamation point were passive-aggressive at best.

The fact this his *assistant*—in other words, the woman who worked *for* him—thought she could order him about with *not* requests was...

Infuriating? Maybe. The past two years had dulled all his emotion to a gray sort of numb. So the spark of something like irritation was almost fascinating.

He typed out his next response with that strange feeling sizzling inside him. When he hit send, he didn't even go through the pretense of standing. He sat at his chair and waited for the response to his I will not be getting in any car.

It came in less than two minutes. This time, she had copied his informal style—no greeting, no send-off.

We can discuss it when I arrive.

When she...*arrived*? Diego looked up at the door. *Arrive*. Amelia Baresi had never once darkened the door of this place. No one had except the occasional messenger or delivery man. All items left at his doorstep, no interaction required.

This was done quite on purpose and for a wide variety of reasons.

Arrive.

He got to his feet and strode over to the lone window. He looked out over the world outside his cabin. It wasn't actively snowing, but the entire yard, such as it was, was covered in the snow that packed down month after month way up at this elevation. It would be almost impossible for a vehicle to make it up here.

Did she know that? What could she possibly be after? For two years, she'd been exactly what he'd wanted—needed. Hands off and efficient.

What had changed?

It didn't matter, he decided, moving away from the window. Nothing mattered except his penance. So no matter what she was after, what she thought she was doing, it wouldn't matter.

Diego Folliero was exactly where he was meant to be, and nothing would change his mind about that.

CHAPTER TWO

AMELIA SAT IN the back seat of the car watching the icy, mountainous terrain go by. She hadn't been sure her presence would be necessary, but after Diego's last email, she was glad she'd decided to come.

She had not expected him to jump on her request that was not a request, but she'd hoped that maybe curiosity might lure him down to the castello without too much back-and-forth.

She should have known better. Nothing in the past two years had given her any indication that Diego was *biddable* any more than her father's journal entries did.

Luckily she'd come armed with a few reasons why he should want to reinstate the Christmas celebrations at Castello di Natale, which obscured her real reason for trying to bring him back to, well, real life she supposed.

Perhaps it was none of her business that he'd turned himself into a hermit, but if her father were here, she was sure he would do the same. And since she had nothing else left of her father, this seemed like a way to…feel connected to him again. Something far more tangible to honor his legacy of caring for people than just *work*.

So, she would turn Diego Folliero into a good man. Or unearth the good man underneath whatever he'd turned himself into.

Whether it was overstepping or ridiculous or she was met with continued resistance, she would simply keep moving forward. Until she reached her goal. No matter what. Maybe Father was gone, but she'd never stop hoping to earn his approval.

The car pulled to a stop in front of a small cabin. It was well tended but incredibly rustic. She studied it in shock and concern. Surely… Surely this wasn't right. She knew he'd been isolated, but this was beyond isolation.

It was smaller than the garden shed at the castello. There was only one window, and it was barely larger than her hand. Little puffs of smoke wisped up from the chimney, giving the impression that the cabin was warmed solely by…fire.

She met the driver's gaze in the rearview mirror. His expression was sheepish, a kind of acknowledgment that things were this…dire.

She had never in a million years imagined this. The man had *internet* but no evidence of running water.

Before she could decide what to do about it, the door opened and a man appeared. Not just any man. Diego. His form took up the entire expanse of the doorway. He was dressed in very plain clothes, but it did not take away from the sheer impact of him.

It was no surprise that he was handsome. Perhaps she hadn't had the presence of mind to catalog all the details of that kind of handsome at her father's funeral, but she knew it existed. She'd seen pictures of him. She'd heard all the stories of how women had thrown themselves at him before the plane crash.

She'd known it, understood it, but still hadn't expected it to be quite so jolting in person. Because it *was* a jolt, like a shot of electricity along her nerve endings. Not at all pleasant, but interesting. Different.

Alarming, certainly. It shouldn't feel like this, like a blast to the solar plexus, to simply look at him. Not when he wasn't dressed as befitted his station or bank account. Not when he'd clearly been buzzing his own hair short. Not when…

Get yourself together, Amelia.

She inhaled deeply, let out a shaky exhale. She was simply having a physical reaction to the moment. She had gotten through the last two years with clear goals. Funny they all centered on Diego, a man she barely knew. A man she barely saw or truly communicated with.

Now here she was, dealing with him on a personal level, determined to find that good man her father had seen, and she wasn't about to be flustered or lose sight of her goals because he was *attractive*.

"Take the car out of sight," she told the driver. "I'll text you when we're ready to leave, and you can return." She had the sneaking suspicion she would not be welcomed, so she needed to have all tools at her disposal.

She got out of the car, marched through the icy cold to the doorway. She fixed a pleasant smile on her face. "Mr. Folliero," she greeted, making sure she sounded businesslike. "It's good to see you again."

His expression was stony and stoic. He looked her up and down in a quick dismissal. "I cannot say the same," he said, his voice a low rasp, as if he were not used to speaking.

She blinked once at the unexpected rudeness, tried to keep her smile from faltering. "Well." She couldn't think of anything else to say, even as she listened to the sound of the car's engine disappear.

"I did not invite you," he said to her stunned silence. "I do not intend to return to Castello di Natale *ever*, let alone this holiday season. So there is absolutely no reason for you to be here. Uninvited. Unwanted."

Ouch. She could handle uninvited, but *unwanted* was a little pointed considering her life situation.

No. There wasn't really anyone out there living who *wanted* her.

But her father had, and that's why she was here. "I apologize. I'm sure you're very…" She trailed off, attempting to look beyond him into his cabin, or hermitage or whatever word befitted the sad little shack. "Busy. In some fashion or another. But your presence is needed, and I'm afraid that cannot be disputed."

"*I* dispute it."

Amelia narrowly resisted rolling her eyes. In a way, she was used to his lack of manners, but she usually got to roll her eyes from behind a computer screen. Now she had to manage her face and her tone.

"We can stand here in the freezing cold, trying to enact some sort of power struggle," she said, making sure her voice revealed only a reasonable suggestion, even though it clearly wasn't. "Or you can acknowledge we're on the same team, have the same goals, and let me in so we can discuss how to move forward."

"I do not wish to move forward."

She sighed, packing as much condescending disdain into the sound as she could. "Honestly. After two years, do you think I would simply arrive on your doorstep demanding your appearance for fun? No. You are needed."

"And I am telling you, my *assistant*, that I am not and will not be."

Stubborn did not do the man justice—but she'd come

prepared for stubborn, hadn't she? "I was under the impression that you cared for my father, as I know he cared deeply for you."

"What does that have to do with anything?" Diego demanded.

"You would let his daughter freeze on your doorstep after all he did for you?"

There was a moment, maybe more than one, when she thought the guilt trip wouldn't work. That having the car leave wouldn't aid her any. That he'd step inside, slam the door and happily leave her to freeze, refusing to ever come down the mountain.

But then, on a disgusted noise, Diego moved out of the doorway and allowed her entry.

It wasn't *much* warmer inside. The cabin was mostly just one big room with next to nothing in it. A fireplace, the fire in it small and crackling. She moved toward it now to find warmth. A table and chair stood in a far corner, with his computer and a view of a crude kitchen-like area.

"This is…actually shocking." She had assumed his isolation was about just that. Keeping the grief and condolences away from him. Maybe she'd assumed he'd wanted to remove himself from things that reminded him of his family.

She had lived at the castello for ten years before the Follieros' deaths and could count on one hand the times she'd seen Diego. His relationship with his family had been… complicated. Amelia hadn't needed to know the specifics to know that.

The Follieros spoiled their children, but they didn't… spend a lot of time with them. They did not seek to understand them. Amelia had always inferred that Diego stayed away because distance was better than arguments.

Which didn't negate grief—she'd never thought it did.

But she hadn't for one second thought he'd be living like… a pauper. Like some kind of monk suffering for his religion. She had simply thought, much like when her father was alive, that he stayed away from the complicated. But this was…something more than that.

She wrung her hands by the fire but didn't feel the warmth. She felt chilled through.

She had sorely miscalculated a few things.

"I should have brought a therapist," she muttered, then winced a little. She almost apologized for the unfeeling remark, but Diego was scowling very unwelcomingly at her. Impressive arms crossed over his chest, glaring at her like she was a vermin he'd like to eradicate.

She might have altered her plan, let him stay, acknowledging that a simple trip down the mountain would not solve his problems, but it was clear this man needed to find his way back to civilization again. This couldn't be a healthy expression of grief. Hiding. Isolating. Living this… rustically when he didn't need to at all.

Perhaps if it looked like he *enjoyed* it. If he smiled, if he seemed comfortable or at ease. But the only thing he reminded Amelia of was a throbbing, raw, open wound, prowling around a cage.

Her father would be appalled. And that was enough to push her into action.

"Well. This has gone on long enough. Far too long, in fact. If you have anything of import, I suggest you pack it. We need to get back down the mountain before the weather turns."

"I do not know how much clearer I can be. I will not be leaving. I will never step foot in the castello again. These are simple, clear-cut terms. If you cannot take them on board, perhaps you should start looking for a new position."

A trickle of fear moved down her spine, but she firmed herself against it. She didn't want a new position. That's why she'd ensured she was indispensable at this one. So he could not get rid of her. So she would be cut off and alone, just as she'd been when each of her parents died.

Diego and the castello were her last connections to her father, and she had lost all connections to her mother, so she would not lose these.

But ensuring she was indispensable over the past two years meant she had *some* security, because this was a man who prized his privacy above all else, and while she might be invading it right now, anyone who took her place would have to be trained all over again—without the intimate knowledge of the Folliero family.

If he fired her, he would have to find someone to take her place. Something he clearly did not have the capability of doing way up here.

So, one way or another, he'd have to leave this place.

She met his hard, dark gaze. Empty and intimidating. She would *not* be intimidated. Not by a man her father thought was good.

"You think you can replace me?" she asked in the blandest, most casual tone she could muster.

His gaze moved over her, a slow, dark tour that made her want to fidget, that caused a strange warmth to creep over her skin.

He said nothing, but she held on to the fact that he did not immediately jump to *yes* as a good sign.

"You could try to replace me, of course," she continued when he didn't speak. "But considering the sheer amount of work I've taken on, you wouldn't be able to train anyone to do what I do, because I'm not sure you *know* all that I do. Sacking me would not be the efficient choice."

"I'm not going down there," he ground out.

Stubborn. Her father had written at length about the Folliero stubbornness. And the way Bartolo had dealt with it was simply to be immovable in return. So that's what she'd be.

"Very well." She aimed a pleasant smile at him. Just because they hadn't dealt with each other much in person didn't mean she didn't know he was stubborn to a fault. Didn't mean she didn't deal with all the arrogant, unbending men of his companies.

She knew how to handle thar particular brand of rigidity. With her own pleasant refusal to break.

She lowered herself onto the lone chair, hard and uncomfortable. "I'll stay."

Diego did not like the feeling of being speechless. He did not like the feeling of being maneuvered. He did not like *feeling*, and she was causing many of those to rumble around inside him like unwieldly ghosts.

She was beautiful. Her blond hair was pulled back in a little twist suitable for an office. She had an angular face that might have been too sharp if her coloring wasn't so warm. Her eyes were a fascinating shade of blue that leaned into gray. Like a changeable winter sky. She wore trim pants and a sweater the color of plums underneath a fashionably and suitably long coat.

She had the kind of beauty that stirred old impulses he'd long since thought he'd beaten out of himself.

He'd enjoyed women once, and women had quite enjoyed him. Those memories felt like they belonged to someone else. Or had, until Amelia had met his gaze with that unfazed determination. For a moment, the reaction was visceral enough that he almost recognized the man he'd once been.

Almost.

"I do not know what happened for you to think that you are somehow in charge of me, Ms...." He trailed off. Calling her Baresi reminded him of her father, another death that sat on his shoulders...perhaps even heavier than the rest.

Bartolo Baresi was the best man Diego had ever known. Diego had loved his parents, but they had been children of privilege and acted as such. They had believed, and led him and his sister to believe, they could have anything and everything they wanted the moment they wanted it. They had loved their family, but he did not know that they'd had much selflessness in them. Much...care. If he or Aurora had not behaved the way his parents expected, they had been...difficult. So difficult, Diego had learned that the best course of action was to stay away.

But Bartolo had always been a link back to them, back to the Folliero legacy, back to some potential better version of himself. Bartolo Baresi had embodied both care *and* selflessness.

And it was the lack of everything in Diego that had caused a good man to die. Diego's family to die. They had all waited for him on that increasingly icy tarmac. They had believed he would come. He had *told* them he could come.

He'd been drunk and careless in Madrid.

They'd taken off too late.

His fault.

He did not like to think of that day, but he forced himself to. If his adolescence and early adulthood had been a study in ignoring everything difficult, he'd learned in his guilt and his penance that he must absorb everything difficult. That he must be the opposite of the man who'd caused such tragedy.

So he met the gaze of Bartolo's beautiful daughter, who watched him with gray eyes that gave the off-putting feeling she saw too much, too easily. "You have crossed a line," he said firmly.

She shook her head as if she could simply disagree with his lines, even though *he* was *her* boss.

"You put me in charge of your affairs. We have a problem that now requires your presence. The fact of the matter is, we have let two Christmases pass without holding the annual Folliero Christmas ball. And the profits at Castello di Natale have suffered."

He waved this away. It was inconsequential. "I have other businesses."

"You do, but the Christmas business was the one your father was most proud of."

"What do you know of my father?"

"Aside from living under his roof for ten years, you mean?" she asked, a kind of sweetness in her tone that didn't match her words. She was very good at that.

He looked at this woman. He knew next to nothing about her, except the sad circumstances that had brought her to Castello di Natale and required Bartolo to stay at the castello rather than continue to travel with Diego.

Diego had resented her existence at times but never thought much of her beyond that. Never considered that she'd lived in the castello with his parents, his sister. He knew nothing about her or how she'd moved through the Folliero world, because he had been off enjoying his twenties. His lack of responsibility. His wealth and freedom and all the many pleasures that came with it.

Pleasure. Avoidance. Enough alcohol and women to numb it all. So he'd rarely thought of anything more complex than which club to go to that night.

Now this woman was in his space. Now she was...demanding things of him.

He would have dismissed her outright, even if he owed her father's memory more than that. After all, what was more guilt? But she'd made too good of a point... The amount of work and effort it would take to replace her would require him to return to the world at least for a little while anyway, and it would mean...too much connection.

He could let it all crumble. The business. The legacy. But continuing it was too wrapped up in his penance.

"I miss my father like a limb," she said very quietly, sitting there on his only chair, a beautiful, discordant note to the bland, unwelcoming room. "But I miss them too, you know. They were not my family, but they were part of the fabric of my life, and they were never anything but kind to me."

Grief, guilt and a thread of bitterness spread through him. He held on to the bitterness. "How novel."

Her mouth curved ever so slightly, a kind of wistfulness that snagged his attention, his interest, against his will.

"Your sister would have said the exact same thing if I'd suggested your parents were kind," she said softly.

"Because they were not." But they hadn't deserved to die because of him. Perhaps people like them did not have the capacity for kindness. Perhaps, like him, they had been nothing but spoiled and self-centered.

Still, he lived. They had died.

"People are complicated," Amelia said, one hand resting over the other in her lap, her legs crossed at the ankle. All prim, easy grace.

"As is the situation we find ourselves in," she continued. "You do not wish to return to the castello, or a life...around people, I suppose? Whatever it is that keeps you up here, alone and isolated and..." She trailed off, her gaze taking in the kitchen, the fireplace, the lone window. Then her gaze pinned him. "Is this some sort of...self-punishment?"

He refused to answer that question. He refused...*this*.

Except she was still here, and he did not know how to fix that just yet.

She shook her head when the silence stretched out into long minutes. "I'm afraid whatever it is you've attempted to accomplish up here, hidden away from the world, it must come to an end. Regardless of whether you want to or not, you must return to the castello."

"I certainly do not. I do not know what has come over you, but you are *my* assistant."

"Yes, that is the job title." She studied him, a little dent appearing between her eyebrows as if she was deep in thought. "I did not take you for a coward."

"I am neither coward nor brave. I am nothing."

Her face softened. "That isn't true."

"It is."

"My father didn't think it was true. Are you calling him wrong? A liar?"

If he thought that of me, he was wrong.

He could not vocalize that, though. Not to her. Not when he could see his own grief reflected in her fascinating eyes.

Eyes that suddenly got very hard looking. "If you do not do this, I will be forced to cancel the ball this year."

"You should not have planned a ball this year."

"And furthermore," she continued, as if he hadn't spoken at all, "I will be forced to close Castello di Natale. Permanently. And offer it to the highest bidder."

The words were harsh. Final. *Impossible.* "You cannot... do that. Close *or* sell. These are not your choices to make."

She stood from the chair, fixed him with a stern look.

Triumph lit her eyes, making them look closer to silver than anything so ordinary as gray. "I think you'll find that in the very documents you signed of my contract, you gave me just enough power to do exactly that. If you do not return with me *today*, I will move forward with plans to close and sell. Forever."

CHAPTER THREE

AMELIA DID NOT allow herself to grin, though she desperately wanted to. Watching shock chase across Diego's face felt like the thrill of a lifetime.

She *did* have the upper hand. Because he had afforded her a lot of power in order to keep himself isolated. She had not planned to use it quite so forcefully, but…

She didn't like being here. She didn't like thinking about *him* living here for two whole years, and her allowing it. It was a tragedy. She'd known he felt grief, maybe even some guilt, but she hadn't known it was *this* bad. She really hadn't thought much about him at all, which felt like something that would have disappointed her father.

She wouldn't disappoint his memory. She wouldn't close or sell the castello, even though she technically *could*. She didn't need to, nor did the business require it.

But she could threaten it, and Diego could believe her capable of doing so. She could get him down the mountain. She could…show him what life was like. She had to.

For her father.

"Do you need to pack anything?" she asked pleasantly enough.

He stood there, no doubt inwardly fuming. He said nothing, but fury all but waved off him. Danger seemed to fill the entire room, but it didn't fill *her*. Not with fear or anything as sensible as all that.

No, whatever fizzled around inside her felt nothing like fear. She didn't want to come up with words for what it might be, because then she would have to ask herself why *danger* felt like…*excitement*.

Without a word, he turned on his heel. He stalked away, through a door she could only assume led to a bedroom. For a moment, she stood where she was and breathed very carefully around the strange things crashing inside her.

Then she followed.

His bedroom was another shock, another little dagger of pain. It was basically a closet. The bed was little more than a pallet. There were no windows. No fireplace. She heard herself whisper his name in abject horror without really meaning to.

He whipped his head around to face her, giving the impression of a wounded animal lashing out. She wanted to reach over and soothe him, even knowing that, just like that wounded animal, it would not be welcomed.

"I will go down to the castello," he bit out. She could see now that he had a leather tote opened on the pallet bed. "Only to have a face-to-face meeting with everyone necessary to ensure that you never have the power to shut it down."

"We could have that meeting now, if you'd like. After all, I'm the only one with power to ensure I *don't* have the power. Unless you terminate me, I have full control over the castello."

"Very well, I will meet with the attorney required to terminate *you*."

Worry settled into her chest, but she didn't let her smile falter. "If that's really what you want." She motioned at the bag. "Would you like me to pack for you? I'm still your assistant until you see things through with the lawyer."

He stared at her as if she were a madwoman. Maybe she was. She didn't need to push this. She didn't need to make threats to get him off the mountain. She could return to the castello and let everything continue as it had.

But he lived like…like a prisoner. And she could see the words her father had written in her mind's eye.

He will be a good man someday. I wish I could convince him of that.

Amelia would use whatever means necessary to convince him. To make her father's wish came true. Because if she was doing what he would have wanted, enacting the things he would have done—if perhaps a year or two too late—then it was like he was still here. Making the memory of him proud kept him alive inside her heart, she liked to think.

So she would do so. Before a new year dawned.

"There is nothing to pack," Diego said darkly. He lifted the bag to his shoulder. He'd put *something* in there, but not clothes or toiletries. She couldn't even hazard a guess as to what it might hold. In two strides, he stood in front of her, glowering down at her. "You will regret interrupting my peace."

He smelled like woodfire. His eyes blazed with fury. He was so much larger than her. Physically intimidating, and yet she did not feel any kind of self-preserving impulse.

Quite the opposite. She had to curl her hand into a fist to fight off the impulse to reach out and *touch*.

She took a step back, afraid of her *reaction* to him more than she was of *him*. "Alternatively," she said, seeking a calm and reasonable approach to his fiery response, "we could handle this in a rational manner. I could remain in your employ. You could allow me to open up the castello for its traditional Christmas events, thus helping that arm of your businesses. You could make a small handful of appearances, and when all is said and done, and the clock strikes midnight on a brand-new year, if you still feel as you do now, you may return to…" She made a show of looking around. "This. And I will close the castello to the public forever. I won't bother you ever again, except to do your express bidding. Unless you'd like to fire me, that is."

His gaze moved over her, and she had no idea what he was cataloging when he did that. What he saw. What it meant to him. But he seemed to keep doing it, taking her in as a whole.

"Such promises," he muttered darkly, then pushed past her and out of the cabin.

It would be twenty-four hours—at most, Diego decided. He would have her contract altered, her power stripped. A simple meeting with his lawyers should make it so.

He would not get rid of her, though it was tempting. But he needed her for the day-to-day. Once she had no power over the castello, she could go back to doing what he'd hired her to do. She would understand that random acts of greed would not go unpunished.

Because what else could trying to sell the castello out from under him be?

She would stay in his employ because she was good at the jobs she was supposed to do, but she would not have the power to sell *anything*. Surely his lawyers could see to that. He could have called them, but he knew his presence would ensure they took this seriously. And it would ensure Amelia Baresi could not corrupt his plans.

What had changed in two years to have her suddenly crossing every boundary he'd so piously planted?

It did not matter. She did not matter. What mattered was arranging everything the way he chose, the way that suited his punishment.

The idea of returning to the castello was a physical, blinding pain.

Pain is the price.

So maybe this too was part of his penance. He didn't *enjoy* that thought, but he reminded himself that his choices required him to move *toward* the pain now, embrace it.

He left the cabin without a backward glance, following Amelia out to where a car was pulling up in the snow. He found himself stopping short, already stabbed clean through by the identity of the driver.

He recognized the man, or thought he did. "Armondo…"

"That is Mondo, Armondo's son," Amelia said, the correction quiet and gentle. "Armondo still does some driving for the castello staff, but not these treacherous roads. They're just a little too challenging for him these days."

Diego looked at the driver through the glass—a picture-perfect replica of Armondo, if he hadn't aged at all since Diego's childhood. Diego remembered his father sneaking off to smoke a cigarette with Armondo when he would drive them into Bolzano for business. Mother did not approve of smoking, so those trips were the only times Father had indulged.

For all their faults, they had been devoted to each other. For all their faults…

"Shall we?" Amelia asked, her voice soft as she gestured to where the car waited.

Diego moved forward stiffly, some of his motivating

fury dulled by the sight of someone he kind of recognized. Armondo—no, his son.

Mondo opened the door for them. *"Buon pomeriggio, signor."*

Diego could not find his voice to respond, so he nodded and slid into the car. Amelia entered on the opposite side. They left a large gap between them on the expensive leather seats.

They drove in a heavy silence. Diego didn't miss that when Mondo had a straightaway and could take his focus off the curving, narrow road for a moment, his gaze lifted to the rearview mirror, as if he were studying Diego and not sure what to make of him.

Amelia had her phone out, occasionally typing some sort of quick missive into the machine. She paid almost no attention to him at all.

Diego realized he had not been in a car for almost the entire time he'd been up at the cabin. He had walked everywhere he needed to, or had deliveries made when necessary. Being in a moving vehicle going *down* the mountain was disarming.

Everything about this day was like an earthquake, scrambling up the foundations he'd built. Out of guilt. For his penance.

They wound down from the part of the mountain where his isolated cabin was situated to the broader valley in which the castello was nestled. It was amazing what a mind could remember, what instinctual memory the landscape created. Because he knew the moment he'd see the first spire of Castello di Natale around the curve. He could count the seconds to when the first tower would come into view, then the second, then the third. Almost as if the entire castle was mapped into his bones.

If the feeling hanging around the center of his chest did not feel *singularly* like dread, he would not admit it to himself. Dread was the only feeling he allowed.

When the car drove from paved road to cobbled drive, Diego had to focus on breathing in and out carefully so he would not have a physical reaction Amelia might take as weakness.

He had heard so many people throughout his childhood go on and on and on about the beauty of Castello di Natale. The perfect Christmas castle. Opulence and luxury mixed with tradition, and a coziness that allowed each guest to feel every inch the wealthy class they were, while reminding them of something simpler.

Even when he had been a different person, he had never understood why the generations held on to this tradition. Opening one of their homes to other wealthy families, throwing grand Christmas balls, as his great-great-grandparents had once done in order to save their riches. His parents had enjoyed such revelry, he supposed, and showing off for their friends.

While Diego had once enjoyed a party, he'd never enjoyed the feeling of his parents wanting him and Aurora to *perform* for their friends, as if they'd had children only to make them behave like trained monkeys.

But the tradition had continued. Until death. Until tragedy. He had considered selling off the *castello*, and all the Folliero holdings, in those first grief-stricken days. Get rid of everything. Be nothing and no one since he'd killed them all.

But when he'd met with the lawyers and his father's assistants and staff to arrange just that, he hadn't been able to verbalize the desire. In that moment, selling it had felt like murdering them once again.

So he'd shut up the castello but held on, keeping the same staff in place. And now, even two years later, he could not fathom selling *or* opening the castello.

"How long has it been?" Amelia asked, her voice gentle and kind.

How she could sound either when she had taken this evil turn of forcing him from his solitude and penance was a mystery to him, but the question hung there between them.

How long had it been? He'd not been home to the castello in quite a few years. Even when attending Bartolo's funeral in the valley, he had not darkened this door. He had kept his distance.

"You were likely still in diapers."

"Don't be ridiculous." She gave an injured sniff. "I was twelve when I came to live here. I remember a few of your visits quite clearly."

He eyed her. "Do tell."

"Well, Aurora loved to complain bitterly about your presence. And I was her favorite ear for complaining."

"I did not realize you and my sister were close." He could not bear to say her name aloud. It brought up too many images of a brazen young woman, spoiled in her own way but bright and vibrant. Someone who could have made something of herself, if her life hadn't been cut so tragically short.

Because of him.

"Close? No. She did not consider me the same *class* as her, but despite that snobbery, she was an odd sort of kind to me, and she liked to have a rapt audience. I was young and lonely and happy to be anyone's audience, particularly if they were under the age of thirty."

He regarded her then. Her regal profile. The straight, elegant way she held herself. She had come to Italy at the age of twelve because her mother had died... Diego could not remember how. Only the sudden shock that Bartolo would be bringing a child into the castello and would no longer be Diego's right-hand man in the same way he had been since he'd started university.

"Why did you come to an isolated castello? Why did your father not raise you in Milan? Or leave you in London?"

Amelia lifted a shoulder. "I couldn't say. I never really thought of it. My mother was dead. I didn't really care where I was, as long as I was with someone who loved me."

She didn't say it in any kind of pointed way, but it felt a bit sharp all the same. A reminder that she, too, had lost her parents, and he wasn't special.

But she didn't know that her father's demise was partly Diego's fault. No one did. Except him. She might have grief, but she did not live with guilt.

The car rolled to a stop behind the castello. Amelia moved to get out herself, then looked back at him with something akin to mischief in her steely eyes. "The other thing I remember quite clearly was you loving to make a drunken scene when you came home. Perhaps we can avoid that this time around, hmm?"

Then she was out of the car, striding toward the castello—*his* Castello di Natale—as if she were in charge. Of this place, of his family's legacy. Of everything he had pushed away, determined it was his *penance*.

But he was beginning to wonder if that penance would have been staying here all along and living with the ghosts of those he'd killed.

CHAPTER FOUR

AMELIA HAD MADE certain the castello would be decorated for Christmas before they arrived. Not just decorated, in fact, but decorated in the exact way it would have been when Diego's family was alive.

She'd done much of it herself before she decided to head up the mountain to fetch him, but she had left the last few details to the staff. She'd made sure they had pictures of the balls from when Diego was a child so they could make it a picture-perfect copy of all those years ago.

She was proud of her foresight, because while she'd thought that would simply be good practice, now she thought it might actually...get through to him, and this wall he'd built between himself and the real world.

She had known he was grieving. She had known he felt guilty for not being on that plane like he was supposed to have been. She had even had an inkling that these were the things that had prompted his extreme isolation. But she had *known* this in a far-off, inconsequential sort of way. Assuming that said isolation was comfortable, easy—perhaps not fully *healthy*, but not...extreme.

Now that she'd seen just how extreme his self-punishment was, she was determined to show him there was life on the other side of grief and guilt and pain.

A good man existed under all those things. Her father

had thought so, so it must be true, and the only way to honor her father was to prove it to Diego himself.

Her first attempt would be to use the ghosts of his Christmas pasts to open him up to that. She couldn't help but think it would have to work at least a *little*. Because remembering her parents and her past with them always caused her to ache now that they were gone, but it was a comforting ache. Remembering them meant remembering love, and, in doing so, reminded her that while her parents might have died, that love did not simply evaporate. It lived on inside her for as long as she did the things that would make them happy. Proud.

Diego had hidden himself away, sunk into the hard grieving part of loss rather than keep moving through life. So now she would require it in her father's stead. So that Diego felt the love that must still exist there, even if he'd had a complicated relationship with his family.

She walked across the paved walkway to the back door, nodding in approval at the greenery and red bows adorning the windows even at the back of the *castello*. No detail had been missed. In the darkness, every inch of this place—inside and out—would glitter with Christmas lights.

There wasn't much snow this far down the mountain, but hopefully some would fall before the ball to add to the overall effect. She'd already decided to hold it whether Diego approved or not, whether he came or not, but she was still holding out hope she could convince him to attend.

She *would* convince him. She *would* get through to him.

She supposed she should be more concerned she wouldn't have a job and he'd hire someone to cancel all her plans. A life without this job would be…terrifying.

But something about that realization was concerning.

In a strange way, it made her see that she too had been in a holding pattern the past two years. Running around acting as his assistant, doing his bidding—as was her job—and little else.

She did not have friends. She did not socialize outside of work, outside of the castello. She'd hidden herself away and let working take the place of…living.

She hadn't been terribly unhappy, and grief filled in all the lonely spots in a way that was oddly comforting. This had made it easy to not realize she wasn't happy. She wasn't living. She wasn't doing what she'd promised her parents' memory: that she would do her best because it was what they would have wanted.

This realization shrouded everything with a new sense of tension, worry. What if she messed everything up? What if she pushed him too hard, and he fired her, and she ruined everything?

What if, in all that ruin, she became truly untethered and fully alone?

She breathed carefully through the anxiety. Her father had always urged her to make a plan when she was worried. To take it step by step. A wrong plan could be fixed, but inaction left you in the same place.

It was better to be afraid, to be forced into a new situation, than to stay wallowing in the old. Diego could fire her. He could cancel the ball. But he could not take her goals away from her.

She would prove to him he was the man her father had thought he was. And if it required living an entirely different life from the one she'd comfortably settled into over the past two years, then so be it.

Because that would make her father happy and proud.

"So be it," she whispered to herself firmly. She stopped

at the door, turned to find Diego had not followed. He was still by the car, his gaze on the castello in front of him.

He stood there, expressionless. She knew he had some reaction to being here, though. He would not stand as still as he was if he didn't have *some* feeling about it, but the feeling was hidden deep under a sheet of stoic rock.

It was her job to find a way to break that rock apart. "I suppose you have not celebrated Christmas up there in your isolation," she offered across the expanse of the walkway. Then she crossed back to him, linked her arm with his in a friendly move that caused him to stiffen even further.

She kept her voice light and cheerful. "Well, no worries. We will celebrate big enough for these lost years. Just as your family would have wanted."

He looked down at her, said nothing. The moment extended, tight like a rubber band that would either break completely from the pressure or snap back into place with a painful *whack*.

But neither happened. After moments of the tension building, he simply took his arm out from hers, looked away and walked inside.

Amelia didn't immediately follow. She let out a slow breath, trying to find a calm center in the midst of all the strange sensations his dark gaze affected inside her.

As though he were in charge, when she was the one who'd gotten him down here. She was the one with the power, even if it was his name on all the businesses. *She* had handled everything for too long for him to be fully in charge.

Or so she told herself. But actually dealing with him, butting heads with him in person rather than through email, made her realize her position was far more precarious than she'd initially thought. Part of her wanted to give in to that pressure. To step back, do as he said.

But a bigger part of her could see her father's careful handwriting.

He will be a good man someday. I wish I could convince him of that.

"I will convince him of that," she whispered into the quiet night around her. "I promise." Then she waited, not going inside just yet. She watched the sky turn dark, searching for that first star to appear. When it did, in perfect harmony with the timed lights, she smiled.

Not all wishes came true, but she wouldn't say no to a little celestial luck.

Diego thought he might crack into two and crumble. Perhaps the pressure of all this would simply cause him to die, just as the blunt force of a plane hitting a mountain had killed his family.

And hers.

There was something about acknowledging that she was Bartolo's daughter. That she'd known his family. Been this very tangential part of his world—far more connected to the pieces he knew than to him, but here. Part of the castello. Part of the Folliero world.

Which meant she had her own grief.

But nothing to feel guilty about.

It was not the comfort he thought it would be. Who could be comforted in this nightmare?

They'd entered through the back, which had never been a part of the home he'd been in much. Still, there was something about the smells here—yeast and cinnamon and pine—that brought old memories back.

An old life back. He thought he could simply ice it away.

Ignore it. Focus on the injustice of her ruining his perfectly organized penance.

Then he'd moved into the first living room.

Everything came to another halting, painful stop. There was a strange ringing in his ears, loud enough to be Christmas bells. For a moment, he thought maybe he was hallucinating. He could all but see the ghosts of his childhood in every corner. Dressed in their Christmas finest. Drinking. Laughing. Sparkling.

It looked exactly as it used to. Was it memory or reality? It was all so disorienting that he wasn't sure.

He blinked once, tried to swallow the hard weight in his throat. The room came into focus, decorated just as it was in his memories. Greenery in boughs across the fireplace. Unlit candles in red, green and white scattered across everything. Angels that seemed to peer at him from their mantels, finding him unfit.

The tree in the corner was huge, and white lights glowed from the scented branches. Red bows, gold bells, silver angels. He recognized all the ornaments—not individually, but as the aesthetic his mother had preferred.

Mother had insisted they all handle the trees in different rooms. Aurora had been in charge of the tree in the library. Father, his den. Diego, the sunroom. Because Mother and Father liked classic Christmas decor, Aurora's tree had always been a brightly colored rebellion, but she'd still partaken.

As a child, Diego had enjoyed the tradition, what felt like autonomy. As a teen, he'd resented it more and more and more. This insistence he be involved in a family performance that, to him—though he wasn't able to articulate it then—showed just how separate they all were rather than demonstrate any familial connection.

Because the four of them had never understood one another. Never tried to. They were connected by a name, by a legacy, but that was all.

Diego turned away from the tree, strode out of the room. This was temporary. This was simply to meet with the lawyers tomorrow. It was nothing else. So he did not need to engage with these pointless memories.

Everyone was dead, essentially by his own hand. Everyone except Amelia.

He refused to look back to see if she'd followed him inside or into the main room. He would not engage with her anymore. Whatever she was up to, whatever her goals, he had no interest.

Diego moved through the house feeling as though a noose was fastened around his neck. Every step in the castello was like a splint being shoved under his fingernails. Painful memories he wanted to push away, ignore. Run from.

So once he finally made it to his old room—even though that too was pain—he elected to stay there. He did not respond to Amelia's summons to dinner. He didn't touch any of the food brought up to him on a tray.

He sent a missive to his lawyers that he expected them at the castello first thing in the morning, then stripped and took the coldest shower he could manage, reminding himself pain was the price. Pain was good. Pain was what he deserved.

In that icy shower, the hard band around his lungs eased. Yes, pain was what he deserved.

He got out of the shower, dried himself off and then stood at the foot of the bed, staring down at the carefully made-up monstrosity. A huge mattress that would be like sleeping on a cloud. Soft bedding that would keep him warm even as he shivered, naked and with hair dripping, in the still air of the room.

One night. He needed only one night to solve this complication. Tomorrow night he would be back in his cabin. Back in his...

It was his punishment, his imprisonment, but it was confronting and confusing that he'd prefer *that* pain over *this* pain, as if it hadn't been a sort of selfless penance at all but hiding from the truth that his family was gone.

He ripped back the covers on a growl. This was *her* fault. She had jumbled things up. He would not be fooled into thinking soft beds and warm rooms were what he was really afraid of, because that was ludicrous.

One night—to handle *her*—and then he would go back to what was *right*. He would not be lulled into falsehoods that there were things to face here in the lap of luxury.

He settled into the bed, convinced it would be a miserable night of sleep. Instead, to his surprise, the exhaustion won. He slept hard, but not restfully. Dreams seemed to hunt him through the dark, snatches and flashes of people and places he'd known.

And the screams of everyone he'd loved who'd died because of his selfish choices.

He awoke to the dark, or partial dark. A bright swath of light was widening across the bed as his door opened.

He expected staff. Maybe someone with a breakfast tray or someone to tell him his lawyers had arrived. He did not expect Amelia to sweep in carrying a tray. He did not expect daylight to be creeping through the edges of the drapes. He did not expect *any* of this.

"Good morning," she greeted cheerfully, marching over to his desk and depositing the tray of food and coffee on it. "I would have let you sleep later, but your lawyers are set to arrive in less than an hour, and I thought you'd want the opportunity to eat and dress before they do."

Diego simply lay there, trying to take in this onslaught of information. Two years without much in the way of human interaction seemed to have dulled his ability to deal with... any people. He wouldn't have cared, except it was starting to make it feel like Amelia had the upper hand.

Impossible.

She turned to face him, that sunny smile in place, those gray eyes alert and taking in the room around her. She was dressed in a trim kind of dress suitable for any office, sensible heels, her honeyed hair pulled back yet again in some fussy clip that seemed to have a candy cane theme to it.

He pushed himself into a sitting position, trying to shake away the dregs of sleep and dreams. He raked a hand through his hair. If he were at his cabin, he would have buzzed it. It was getting to be too long, too close to the old Diego and his perfectly coiffed style.

He pushed any memories of that old life away. The lawyers. They would be here soon. And once he dealt with them—and they dealt with *her*—he could...leave this horrible old nightmare.

But when he looked at her again, she was standing in a strange position. Almost like she'd been in the middle of doing something but had been frozen in time. She looked... shocked.

It was only then that he realized he was naked under the blankets pooled at his waist. Whether she knew that or not, he could not tell, but she was getting a full view of everything above—getting and *taking* that full view.

For a moment, eyes wide and mouth hanging open just a shade, she took in the sight of him. A pink flush appeared on her cheeks before she blinked and seemed to pull herself together to look away. She fussed with the tray. She said nothing.

But she had looked. Blushed. *Enjoyed.*

It was almost as if something in his brain short-circuited then. Thrust him back into a former life, a former body. Sensations, impulses, behaviors not foreign so much as… memory. From a long time ago, a whole different person ago. And yet the desire to reach and touch that person, *be* that person again, was something he hadn't felt in so long that he reacted without fully thinking it through. Without remembering himself *now*.

He tossed the covers off and slid out of bed. Amelia turned, her mouth opened as if to say something, but the words never came out. She made a squeaking sound and then whipped around, putting her back to him.

"What are you doing?" she finally said, her words little more than a screech.

"Getting dressed," he replied casually. He walked over to the closet. Inside were all his old clothes, exactly as he'd left them whenever he was last here. He kept full sets of clothes at all the places his parents liked to jump to and fro. Would they fit him now, different person that he was?

He did not feel embarrassed in his naked state. She did not have to look if she did not want to.

He took a pair of boxers, soft even after years of no use. Far more comfortable than the clothes he allowed himself on the mountain. He glanced over his shoulder.

Amelia was looking. Her gray eyes met his, a mix of so many things in their depths that he was very nearly winded.

Questions. Crackling heat. A dangerous need. Hope. Fear. Desire. So much damn desire.

It had been years, *years*, since he'd touched a woman— been touched at all.

And it was beyond ridiculous to even entertain for half a second that Bartolo's young daughter, his *assistant*, would enter into any *touching* equations, even if she did like what she saw.

As much as he liked what he saw of her.

He turned back, grabbed a pair of pants and hitched them on. He didn't bother with a shirt. Perhaps it skirted a few lines, was something the *old* Diego might have done, but she'd conned him down the mountain, so maybe she deserved to deal with his old self, his old ego, his old selfish desires.

Desire. He could practically taste it. Her. Her hair would feel soft and smell of something delicate. Her skin would be warm velvet. Her mouth...

Pain is the price.

A sharp reminder, the stab of guilt that no one who had loved him, counted on him, believed in him was here to have any of these sensations, feelings, *likes*. They were dead.

His life was meant to be a penance, his own death, not an enjoyment.

She would be quite the enjoyment.

He gritted his teeth against the traitorous voice of his former self and kept a safe distance between them. "Am I meant to eat with an audience?"

Her cheeks were flame red, but she didn't scurry away. She moved carefully, as though she felt fragile. She took a few steps away from the desk, giving him access to the tray of food. Too decadent. It all smelled like heaven.

Or she did.

"I thought we could go over my plans before you met with the lawyers to have me sacked." Her voice was not quite itself, but it didn't shake.

"I do not plan on having you sacked," he muttered, pouring himself coffee. It wasn't the bitter, weak brew he allowed himself on the mountain. It was rich, deep, delicious. He wanted to spit it out.

But it moved down his throat, warm and decadent. It eased through his body with treasonous delight.

"Then perhaps we could go over your plans," she said.

The devil on his shoulder was straining at its leash. He could not stop himself from a slow, sensual smile. Full of promise. Full of intent. One that made her pupils dilate and her breath catch in her throat.

"Oh, I have quite a few plans for you, *tesoro*."

CHAPTER FIVE

Amelia felt like she was on fire. She felt like she'd run a marathon. She felt a million physical things she could not name, all pulsing through her like...like...

She didn't know. And still she understood that it would be *dangerous* to know. For the both of them.

So she could not stay here, in this moment of physical reactions short-circuiting all her faculties. She had to move forward. She had to...to deal with business. *Business.*

She cleared her throat, then had to clear it once more to speak. "I am happy to discuss whatever plans you wish." She'd meant to say this as professionally and formally as possible.

Instead, her cheeks heated even more, because she knew it sounded more like an *offer* than a business proposition. Like *plans* had nothing to do with the castello or Christmas or his soul.

She was not offering anything. Why she needed to remind *herself* of that, she wasn't quite certain.

Perhaps if she had some experience, she might understand. But she'd never had much of a life outside the castello. Never thought much about pursuing one. Even when her father had been alive, the thought of leaving hadn't crossed her mind. The castello had become home, her father

her lone constant. She hadn't been eager to leave, to chart a course, and her father had never pushed her to.

Only now did she realize that meant she'd missed out on the normal things a woman of twenty-four might have experienced. Flirtation.

Lust.

Perhaps if she had some experience, what she'd said to him *might* be an offer.

And that was a terrifying thought, all things considered. Especially when that sharp smile didn't change, when that gaze that felt as hot and heavy as a brand only became more so.

When her entire body reacted, like she'd simply been a match waiting for friction to come alight. If she were someone else, would that be the kind of thrill she jumped into headfirst?

You are not someone else.

She needed to get a hold of herself. She needed to get *out* of here, because he wasn't pulling on a shirt. So he stood there, barefoot and naked from the waist up, the fascinating grooves and dips of his chest and abdomen a picture she wanted to sear into her memory.

Didn't want to. *Couldn't.*

He was her *boss*, and perhaps she had friendly feelings toward allowing him to see the good inside himself for her *father*—a man he was closer in age to than *her*—Diego would not view her in such a way.

Would he?

Get a grip, Amelia.

"But for now," she said, her voice a high squeak that she sought to tame with the rest of her words, "I will leave you to get ready for your meeting." She forced her mouth to curve upward, but it felt nothing like a smile. Perhaps a grimace, at best. She turned on her heel and warned herself to walk slowly and gracefully out of his room.

She was almost certain she accomplished little better than a scurry.

She had things to do, but she made a beeline for her own room. Five minutes. Five minutes to find her center. To... process what had just happened.

She slid into her room, closed the door behind her, then simply leaned back against it. Her hands were shaking. She curled them into fists. She closed her eyes and tried to rationalize...everything.

She had seen him naked. He had clearly held absolutely no embarrassment about that.

And why should he when he looks like that?

Well, that was not at all a productive thought. Any more than having his naked form emblazoned on her brain now was productive.

Why *had* he done it? She shook her head. It didn't mean anything. He'd simply become unused to the normal rules of society by isolating himself up on that mountain. Or he could not even see her as a person, simply an object to do his bidding, and therefore it had not occurred to him how she might react to...nakedness.

That she might look. That she might...*really* look.

Either way, it hadn't *meant* anything. She'd woken him up. He'd needed to get dressed. So he'd gotten out of bed.

Naked. A tall, broad, muscular specimen of a man. Dark hair smattered in interesting places, and the most interesting thing of all...the hard, shocking length of him.

And she'd been lanced through with fire. With a distressing bolt of what could only be described as *need*.

But she did not *need* it or him. Her body had reacted, probably mostly to all the things she did not know about...

the male body. But her mind was in charge *now*, and she could chalk it all up to surprise and...well, science.

It happened, these types of reactions. Maybe not to her, but she'd read about it in books. Intense physical reactions to chemistry. He was certainly too old for her, and he was her boss. These were all *intellectual* reasons not to have a reaction to him, but she was smart enough to know that intellect did not always have control over feeling.

So she would have to accept that she was attracted to him. That this, of course, meant nothing. It would just require a certain kind of...bracing herself. She would not waltz into his bedroom thinking that would be a smart move. Not if he felt comfortable simply being naked.

Whatever he was doing on that mountain wasn't simply twiddling his thumbs. He was doing *something* to carve out all that impressive muscle. He was clearly very, *very* strong. And very, *very*...big.

She closed her eyes against another wave of intense physical response. Something was wrong with her. Perhaps she needed some kind of therapy. She'd seek it out.

After Christmas. After she showed Diego that he was more than his grief or guilt or whatever it was that had stopped him from thinking he was a good man even before his family's deaths.

She inhaled carefully, gave herself a reassuring nod and then pushed off the door. She had work to do.

Diego had been gone so long from "real life" that he'd forgotten how much he detested lawyers. This *business*. He'd spent so much time hating himself for his selfishness that he'd forgotten at least *part* of the impetus to waste away his twenties had been prompted by how much he hated all the things his father had wanted to pass along to him.

"You were the one who set up this in the first place," the first lawyer said, disdain dripping from every word.

Diego found himself retreating to old patterns. Impulses he'd thought had died with his family. Sarcasm, for starters. "Was I?" he drawled. "A shocking revelation."

The lawyer's face got very pinched looking.

"*Signor*, this is not so simple as a quick meeting," the second lawyer said.

She was much more reasonable, far less stuffy. And still her words were firm and not what he wanted to hear.

"You signed over an incredible amount of responsibility to Ms. Baresi. We can untangle that responsibility, but it begs the question of who then takes it? If you are planning on staying within reach—"

"I am not." He needed his mountain, his solace, his *penance*.

"Then you'll need someone to replace her. Living by proxy requires *having* a proxy."

"I simply want to block her from being able to sell my own property out from under me." He ground this out, wondering when in the last two years simple directives had come to be *arguments* instead of *his* staff jumping to do *his* bidding. How he suddenly was forced to deal with all he had eschewed.

"You need someone reachable who can handle the day-to-day needs of the castello. If it is to be you making those decisions—"

"Enough." He'd fire the whole lot of them. He'd have Amelia make certain…

Damn Amelia. He was only in this meeting, this house, this fiasco because of *her*, and they were telling him it would be *complicated* to pluck her from the carefully woven fabric of the castello business.

She'd no doubt done it on purpose. Maybe she didn't *seem* like the scheming type, but he'd only trusted her because he'd trusted Bartolo. Perhaps it had been a mistake.

But these lawyers made it seem like a mistake he did not wish to deal with correcting. Perhaps he *should* let her sell the castello out from under him. He got the money either way. It wasn't like she could do it for her own gain. She could only act in *his* interests.

So why is she threatening to sell?

He glared at the lawyers across the table from him, then waved them away. "You are useless, and you may go back to the holes you crawled out of."

The man's face got very red. The woman rolled her eyes. But without argument, they both got up, collected their things and left him to brood in the formal office his father had once presided over.

Diego stared at the huge painting that hung on the wall across from him. A family portrait that had required interminable hours of sitting when he'd been an antsy young man.

His mother, painted much younger than she'd actually been at the time. His father, painted taller. The frown his sister had sported any time they'd had to sit for the painter had been turned into a serene smile she'd never once been capable of accomplishing. And he…

He looked at a version of himself that was so certain of his place in the world, so certain of all he was entitled to. Brash and arrogant and…listless. Purposeless. He felt like the only one who was honestly portrayed in the painting, but perhaps that's because he could only look on the young man he'd been with disgust.

But sitting here, facing himself, he was confronted with a question he had not expected. A question he did not want.

How was he any different from that young man? How was his *penance* doing any good? Or was that too simple selfishness? Was that all he was? His chest got tight, and it was hard to inhale around this confrontation of thought.

A quick knock sounded at the door, and before he could decide on how to deal with an interloper on his current internal crisis, it opened. Amelia walked in with the same purpose she'd walked in with at his cabin in the mountains, and then again this morning in his bedchamber.

But he was dressed this time around, and he watched as her eyes darted away from him, like she was remembering the last time she'd entered a room with little warning.

Because her cheeks grew pink as she stood there, though whatever was going on in her imagination did not leak into her voice. "If you are done with your lawyers and I am still employed, we have an appointment."

He could address that—her employment—but he didn't want to. "What kind of appointment?"

Her smile was…soft. Sweet, almost.

He hated it.

"Come, Diego. Where is your sense of adventure?"

"Dead."

She tsked, not at all cowed by his harsh response. "You breathe, *caro*. You are alive. This cannot be changed in this moment any more than death can be changed in any moment."

Her words shook him, though they shouldn't. Of course he was alive. Of course he *breathed*. He knew this.

And yet…the way she said it, with a cheerful gentleness, as though she understood the depths of despair that went into knowing you were alive when you should not be. Others were dead and they should not be.

She did not know, could not know, the weight that he strove to make right with his punishment.

"Come," she said, a warm, gentle order. "Breathe. Live. If only for a moment."

He wanted none of it. Still…he found himself following in spite of it all.

CHAPTER SIX

AMELIA KNEW IT had been a Folliero tradition to visit the Christmas markets in the towns surrounding Castello di Natale in the weeks leading up to Christmas Day, so she would force Diego into reliving such traditions for as long as she could force him to do anything.

She was a little surprised he hadn't put up more of a fight, especially as furious as he'd looked after the meeting with his lawyers.

He'd no doubt found out what she already knew—though he *could* get rid of her or strip certain powers from her, because he had instilled so much responsibility and power to act in his stead, it would take time to untangle her completely. Especially if he didn't want to do the work she'd have to leave behind if he fired her.

This gave her *some* satisfaction, and it was something she tried to hold on to as she found her gaze drifting to him. To places she should not look. To things she should not remember existed under the fabric of his clothes.

She carefully folded her hands in her lap and chastised herself to keep her eyes there. She hoped that his meeting had not gone well this morning, and it meant she could stay in this position, well, forever, but at the very least with enough time to get through to him.

So she had to use her time wisely. Today, they would

spend the afternoon at the Christmas market. Tonight, they would have a pleasant, homey meal. Together.

Whether he liked it or not.

This entire endeavor was about life. About Christmas, which was about togetherness. Since he had no family to speak of, no friends since the accident, she was about all he had left. So she would be there and do everything she could to help a good if misguided, man find himself and wade out of his debilitating and self-harming grief.

For a brief moment, it dawned on her that she was in the same position. *He* was about all she had left. If he did not spend Christmas with her, she would be…alone.

But *she* was happy, for the most part. She talked to people. She did not self-punish. So it was *not* the same. *She* had celebrated the last two Christmases—with tears, yes, but she hadn't hidden away from her grief.

The car came to a stop, and Amelia lifted her gaze to the window. The entrance to the market was a grand wrought-iron archway decorated with greenery, bright red bows, golden bells and a dusting of snow that hadn't accumulated on the ground.

Beyond that, stalls stretched out, decorated in bright colors. Greenery and red bows littered every available decorative space while people moved together, shopping and taking it all in. The mountains loomed, beautiful and awe inspiring, in the distance.

Amelia couldn't stop a smile. It was stunning. It was perfect. She pushed her door open and stepped out into the cold, the sounds of carolers somewhere in the crowd immediately wafting through the air.

She waved off the driver and skirted the vehicle to open Diego's door for him. He got out of the car like an old man, careful of any move that might break a brittle bone. His scowl was as dangerous as any blade as he took in the festive scene around them.

Stalls of crafts and homemade treats. Scents of cinnamon and vanilla and roasting nuts filled the air. Christmas music flitted around them—from string quartets, carolers and even speakers at some of the stations. It was a beautiful cacophony of color and noise and *life*.

"What are you attempting to accomplish with this?" he demanded—and it was a demand, all sharp and angry, but she heard something under all that. Saw something under all his fury.

Hurt. Pain. So much damn pain.

Yes, sometimes one had to hurt in order to find healing. He would, no doubt, shy away from some of that. Fight it. This would not be easy.

And she would not give up. For her father's caregiving legacy.

Despite an internal hesitation, she reached out and tucked her arm into his. His heat enveloped her, and she could smell something piney and fresh coming from *him*, not the scene around them. All too clearly she could remember what he looked like completely naked, moving across his room.

She pushed the memory away and pulled him forward into the melee. And she told him the truth, in as much effort to remind herself why she was here and shouldn't be thinking about him *naked* as it was to have him possibly understand.

"My father thought you were a good man but that you struggled to see that in yourself. I think remembering who you are might allow you to see the punishment you've doled out to yourself is pointless."

"You're wrong on just about every level," he replied.

"And I cannot fathom why some tacky market would change my perception of anything."

"Then there is no danger in walking around the market, Diego," she returned brightly, still pulling him forward. "No need to fear it."

He stopped dead in his tracks, causing the people behind to bump into the both of them. They expressed outrage, until Diego whipped his furious gaze toward them. They lowered their eyes, mumbled apologies and skittered off.

His dark gaze moved to her. She shivered underneath her coat, and definitely not because of the cold air. He was angry, and it didn't scare her. It *excited* her, and she did not know what to do with that at *all*.

"Fear?" he repeated, very carefully.

She had to swallow to speak, but she certainly wasn't going to let this *awareness* of him as a man stop her from speaking her mind. Stop her from her goal. "Yes, I think you're afraid of anything that might remind you that you're alive."

She led him to a stall that sold Christmas treats, trying to cast back to think if she'd ever known what Diego might favor in terms of dessert.

"Alive," he repeated in the same stunned, offended kind of manner, but he allowed himself to be tugged along. "You do realize *your* father is *also* dead because of me?"

So many things about that sentence caused her pain. The finality of the word *dead*. A reminder that she would not return to the castello and find her father waiting for her. But as big as all that hurt was, she also felt a deep, sharp edge of sympathy for what must be going on in Diego's mind to blame himself so fully, so simply. "Diego, fault is complicated."

"You'll find in this case it is not. There is no arguing it

away. They waited for me. I let them. I had no intention of coming. The wait was pointless and allowed the weather to turn, thus causing the plane to crash."

He delivered this all dispassionately, but underneath that layer of stoicism, of distance, was the pain that caused this self-recrimination. Amelia's heart ached for him, but she knew that would be rejected, so she sought to deal in facts and reality over feelings.

"Who's to say they would have survived if you had been there and on time?"

He looked at her as if she'd taken full leave of her senses. As if suggesting he might not be the sole fault of the *accident* was a personal attack. "Every report on the matter."

"Reports aren't reality. They're supposition." She said this with an easy shrug, because it was all tied up in a fact she'd had to learn at a young age. "*Life* is supposition. You can choose this one—the one that absolves you from living, but I will not absolve you of anything while you hide away in your own self-pity."

"Pity?" Again his tone was all offended fury.

But he wouldn't be offended if some part of him didn't know it was true. "Yes, pity." She gestured to the man behind the counter, handed him the correct change in exchange for a slice of *pandoro*. She held it out to Diego, powdered sugar dusting off the paper that held the slice and onto her coat sleeve. She paid it no mind.

"Eat," she instructed.

When he did nothing—not take the offered cake, not refuse, simply stood there staring at her as if he couldn't find the words to suitably mark his anger—she shook the cake at him again and adopted her best scolding tone.

"Don't be petulant. Take a bite."

Something in his expression changed at the word *bite*.

Some of that stiffness left his shoulders. His sharp gaze seemed to…smolder. Like it had this morning, reminding her of what she'd witnessed. Against her own will, her eyes drifted down before she shook herself into maintaining eye contact with him.

But this wasn't better. He leaned forward then, slowly, his gaze never leaving hers. Even as he bent closer, and closer, until his mouth closed over the edge of the cake and he took a bite while she held it.

She felt as if she'd been struck by lightning. How was that sensual? How did that have an effect on her? She did not know. Only that it was far too easy to now imagine his mouth closing over some part of her.

Electricity. It shot from the top of her head to the tips of her toes, until she felt as though she vibrated from some inner power she could not name. She throbbed, everywhere. Deep, deep in her core, at her neck, between her legs.

"Be careful, *tesoro*." She could feel his warm breath against her cheek. She could feel her own breath struggle to inhale, exhale. "Should you bring me back to life, you might not like what I would like a bite out of."

The problem was, she thought she'd like it very much.

Nothing in this whole ordeal was what Diego might have anticipated. That Amelia would somehow be able to lure him off the mountain, that his lawyers would be wholly unhelpful, that he would find himself in the throes of desire when it came to Bartolo's daughter.

His *assistant*.

He thought all these things would have been easy enough to handle if *she* behaved sensibly, but she was affected by him, and she did not seem to have the sophistication required to hide it.

Her reaction to him, and how much it roared through him, was a temptation he had never thought he'd feel again. He had thought about sex up there on his mountain over the past two years. There had been days he'd awoken hard and wanting, some lurid dream in the recesses of his mind and his past. But this was rare, and easily dealt with.

There was nothing easy about the increasing tightwire desire toward Amelia. He had no defenses for this. Before his isolation, he had given in to whatever desires ruled him. After the accident, he had rejected all his desires and had thought easily enough.

But temptation had never been so tantalizingly close up in that stark cabin.

Amelia had dragged him through the market, buying treats and trinkets, chattering incessantly and pretending the moment over the *pandoro* had not happened. She acted as if there was nothing but a pleasant kind of amiable friendliness between them. Slightly warmer than colleagues, but only slightly.

He wanted the same ability. To shove it and his reaction to her out of this moment. Out of all moments. This was… disorienting. And worse, it was like suddenly there was too much being shoved at him. He could not input it all. He wanted nothing more than to return to his isolation, where everything made *sense*.

But it was that *want* that had him going along with the trip through the market. That had him eating dinner with her back at the castello rather than hiding in his room. It was the *want* of solitude that had him forcing himself to do the opposite.

Now it required him to ignore the way candlelight played over her face at dinner, the way her gray eyes changed depending on the topic she regaled him with, the thorny push and pull of want and refusal. Bitter and painful, reminders that he *lived*, as she had said to him, but with the punishment of refusal he was so used to.

He'd planned to return to the mountain. Let her sell whatever she wished, even if it would produce his father's ghost. Perhaps that was the right choice.

He would have left the castello, then and there, and never seen her again. He *would*.

Tomorrow... Tomorrow he would return to his penance.

When he informed her of this as they stood from the dinner table, she studied him with those damnable eyes. Then she nodded slowly.

"I suppose it will be easier to return," she offered. Gently.

He blinked at her, wholly taken aback by the word *easy*. She was constantly saying these words not delivered as accusations even though they *were* accusations. Offensive ones at that.

There was nothing easy about the life he'd built up there. That was the entire point. It was a challenge. It was pain. It was *sacrifice*.

Then she *laughed*. "Oh, you look so grumpy with me." She reached across the space between them, gave his shoulder a friendly kind of shove. Which only stoked the flames of his insult higher.

Friendliness. As if they were...siblings or some such. As if she had not watched him walk across the room, naked, with avid eyes and heat in her cheeks.

"I guess easier isn't the right word," she amended, attempting to look both contrite and like she was putting that repentance on.

"I should like to see you do half the manual labor required of living the way I do," he said stiffly, unable to let the insult just *sit*.

She made a kind of face then, as if she was trying not to laugh.

Laugh.

At *him*.

He could only stare at her. How dare she.

But she nodded, looking almost solemn. *Almost.* "You're very right. I'm sure it's physically challenging, and perhaps mentally as well. Not the kind of thing I'd choose to do, for certain."

Perhaps. "Yet you call it easy," he reminded her, not sure why he needed her to agree that what he'd done was far harder than *staying*, but he wanted to see her realize she was wrong. He needed her to admit that she did not understand in the slightest.

"Well..." She gave a little shrug, then met his gaze straight on. "It allows you to ignore all this." She made a gesture toward the tree, the house, who knew what all that gesture encompassed. "You claim these...challenges up on the mountain are your punishment for being responsible for the deaths of your family and my father, but it seems to me it's just made it very easy for you to forget about all you've lost. I mean, the physical labor alone must take a toll that makes it *very* easy to sleep at night."

He had no words. Shock muted him. Paralyzed him.

She'd called him responsible for the deaths, hadn't even tried to argue with him this time. No *supposition is life* and whatever rot she'd said at the Christmas market. Just *responsible for the deaths* this time around.

She was *right*, of course, but he'd expected her continued absolution. Not *admittance* of his crimes.

She was accusing him of *sleeping easy* despite this. Of taking the *easy* way out.

"You see, *I* chose to live with what I lost," she continued, and this time her solemnness did not seem so put on. "It did not require carrying water from a stream or cosplaying the nineteenth century, no. But it did require a different kind of fortitude. Perhaps fortitude is not what you're looking for, and that's fine enough."

She shrugged again. "It is your choice, of course, what punishments you see fit. My feelings on the matter are rather inconsequential, don't you think?"

She didn't wait for him to find an answer. She wafted out of the room, leaving only her scent and infuriating words behind.

And he stood there…seething. Furious. Because…he could not find a way to argue against what she'd accused. He had considered his sacrifice to give up the monetary luxuries his position, his family name, had brought him to be pain, suffering, *punishment*.

But he had not faced the pain of what he'd lost by being *away* from all these reminders. He took a slow look around the dining room, where he'd eaten many a holiday dinner with his family in his youth. He had pushed *this* away.

He did not want to come out and say she was *right*, but there was a part of what she was accusing that was not *wrong*.

If facing this room, Christmas, his memories was pain, and it *was* pain, then it was what he should do.

He would stay, let her shove Christmas and memories down his throat until he drowned. Only when the comfort of his luxurious surroundings outweighed the emotional pain of memory would he leave.

She was right. It would have to be this way.

Pain. Pain. *Pain*.

His due.

CHAPTER SEVEN

AMELIA WAS QUITE pleased with herself when Diego made no plans to leave the castello the next day. Reverse psychology had worked wonders. She had been afraid it would not work on him, but he was so deep in his complicated grief, guilt and denials that it was clear he hadn't seen through her.

What a triumph.

She didn't know that he was avoiding her on purpose all morning, but she suspected he was. What else would he be doing in this big house alone? She considered bringing the lunch tray to him herself, but the last time she'd brought him a meal hung heavy in her mind.

Part of her wanted to anyway, to prove she could. To prove that it hadn't affected her at all. But it *had* affected her, and it did not leave her feeling any of the ways she thought she might or should.

She should be afraid. Offended. Disdainful. Wholly and utterly uninterested.

Instead, even the memory left her feeling jittery with excitement. Just thinking about going up to his bedroom had her imagination running wild. He did something to her, and she wanted to dive deep into what that something was and could be.

Why don't you?

No. That would be… Well, for starters, it would be selfish. It would be about what she wanted, or thought she might want, or at least her body wanted even if her mind had its doubts. It would not be about *him*, even if he had some of the same…*wants*.

Did he?

She stilled at this internal question. Since the market, she'd been grappling with herself. Her interior thoughts, feelings and reactions. But she hadn't considered his. Not when it came to the physical reactions he may or may not be having.

He was experienced. He knew what he was doing—stirring up feelings. Maybe he'd isolated himself from the world for two years, and that meant he probably hadn't had any women up at his little cabin, but he'd spent *years* being an adult male moving through the world with extreme wealth, privilege and attractiveness.

He knew what he was doing. He probably knew what *she* was feeling. She, on the other hand, inexperienced and slowly realizing just how sheltered she'd kept herself despite a life of loss, had *no* idea how to navigate these waters.

What did a person do when desire seemed to cloud their usually extraordinarily rational train of thought? What did a person do when being in the same room with a man made them feel like they were a live wire, crackling and exposed? Dangerous.

In all the best ways.

It was moving through her now, that heat, that excitement, and he wasn't even *here*. And even if he were… He might create these feelings inside her, but did he reciprocate any of them?

If he had any reaction to her, it could simply be that he was a certain kind of desperate born of two years of isolation. He might have this reaction to any woman who crossed his path right now.

Well, that was a depressing thought.

"It should be a reassuring thought," she muttered to herself aloud. Because no matter how curious she might be about the physical reactions in *her* body, it did not mean anything would come of that curiosity.

He was her boss, and she had a singular goal when it came to him.

Her goal was simply to show Diego that his guilt was wrong. There was a natural impulse to blame oneself. Even she had gone through that phase briefly after their deaths. But though she understood too easily how cruel life could be, she'd never been able to sink into that guilt the way he did.

She would have to show him that what he thought of himself was not true or conducive to the life he *should* be living. Not just because he *was* a good person, but because he owed it to the people he'd lost to truly live—the way they could not.

Amelia moved about the kitchen gathering her supplies, feeling wound up and frustrated, which was a common enough occurrence around *him*, but it was even more annoying when he wasn't even *here*. She was letting just the thought of him make her crazy.

With a scowl on her face, she measured out flour. Making cookies would soothe her. Would remind her of who she was. Not a sexual being. A practical one who cared about the needs of *others*, not herself. That was the Baresi legacy she was striving to uphold.

She had given the kitchen staff the day off so she could have the kitchen to herself for her annual holiday-cookie baking. She would have invited Diego down, but making cookies was something she doubted Diego had any old memories about. His mother had not been known for her time in the kitchen, or too many maternal instincts at all, but making and decorating Christmas cookies reminded Amelia of *her* childhood Christmases, so she set about to do it for herself. This season might be about bringing Diego back to life, but that didn't mean she couldn't also enjoy her usual Christmas traditions.

And if he was distracted by cookies, perhaps she could talk to him about the ball. She was getting more confident she could assure his attendance, but she wanted to get a sense of what he remembered about the old Christmas balls, what she could recreate to get through to him.

But she did not think of the ball as she got everything out to make the dough. She did not think of what she would do to convince Diego to attend.

She thought of his mouth. His gaze. His body. And what he could do with all those things if she convinced him to.

Diego had planned to stay far away from Amelia. After all, whatever her role in all this was, it had nothing to do with why he'd decided to stay.

He was here for pain.

But eventually, as the day wore on, he realized that avoiding her was cowardly. That all this *avoidance* was not quite the penalty he had been trying to achieve. Pain meant facing things.

Every second should be a challenging misery. Every moment should be a reminder of all he was that was wrong, that had caused horrible things to happen. Hiding in his comfortable bedchamber was not exactly *fun*, haunted by memories of Christmas seasons from his childhood.

But it was not the kind of pain he felt in Amelia's presence. A kind of sandpaper-under-the-skin feeling. He found himself conflicted over what he should be seeking out. What was the most fitting punishment.

Painful memories. Painful resistance to temptation.

He thought memories made the most sense, especially considering his two-year isolation from exactly that, drowning memories of his family and his loss in physical labor. But it was not the same kind of active pain that being around Amelia —and from keeping his hands to himself.

He deserved that pain, that suffering. The active kind. The kind that reminded him exactly what kind of man he was. How little he deserved to be alive. He should be seeking out real punishment because she had not been fully wrong. Some of his punishments had been weakness hidden under the guise of pain.

So he moved through the house, ghosts of every Christmas season he'd ever spent here as a child in every nook and cranny, and then found her in the kitchen.

She was at the oven, her back to him. She wore a silky skirt that clung to the curve of her ass, flirting there at her knees. Her sweater was the color of the Christmas bows that seemed to be everywhere in this damn house. Christmas music swelled softly from somewhere, but his eyes were transfixed on *her*.

She moved gracefully, humming, her honeyed-blond hair pulled back and swaying with every move. And then he watched as she bent over, carefully placing a pan inside the oven, the skirt stretching over the sweet shape of her, filling him up with a sharp and potent and *instant* bolt of lust. Lurid and *wrong*.

But he could picture it so easily. Having her. It would only take moving over to her. Whispering a few words meant to entice, a few well-placed caresses. He had already seen her reaction to him, perhaps as effortless and violently organic as his own. It would take no time at all to seduce her, lifting up her skirt, finding her wet and willing, and sliding home. He would have her writhing in pleasure, begging him for release in seconds.

He stood at the entrance to the kitchen, hard and pulsing, trying to get a handle on some center point of himself that knew this was wrong.

His body was simply reacting to a lack. For *years* he'd glutted himself whenever he'd wished. Then he'd cut it off completely. For two years. Swearing off pleasure was simple enough, or close to it, when you removed all temptation. But refusing temptation was the true punishment.

He should thank her for this opportunity, because little up in that cabin had been as physically torturous as *this*.

She turned then, and clearly could not read the electricity in the room or the pained denial in him.

"Oh, you've finally appeared. Fantastic." She smiled at him with a kind of cheerful welcome that wound around all the sharp edges of sexual need inside him and warmed. Making all those feelings far more complex than they had any right to be.

"We are baking cookies," she announced.

We.

He took in the kitchen. Pans and bowls and little jars full of colorful things. Baking cookies? What on earth was she on about? "No. It appears *you* are baking cookies."

"Well, then you could watch me do it. Would you like to help decorate them? Maybe you'd like to be the official taste tester."

Nothing she was saying or doing made sense. She was all but infantilizing him. Suggesting he decorate and taste cookies? It left him with only automatic rejections, even if he'd meant to be more open to all the different types of pain she could inflict.

"No, I would not. If this is some strange show-me-my-childhood attempt, you'll find my mother did not *bake*, nor did anyone expect us to be in the kitchen fiddling with sugar."

"Well, that is a shame. Because my mother always had me make Christmas cookies with her, and it's one of my fondest Christmas memories."

"Yet neither are here, are they?" It was a cold kind of statement. The type he was used to making in his own mind to remind himself of what damage he was responsible for.

Amelia did not deserve the same, but it was such habit that it had simply fallen out of his mouth. Hung there between them like a wound that needed tending.

But men like him deserved no tending.

And Amelia didn't look hurt or harmed. She studied him, head cocked, as if he were a strange specimen. As if, should she look deep and hard enough, she'd unearth all those wounds inside of him and tend them against his will.

"My mother is dead, yes," Amelia agreed. The words were simple and matter-of-fact, but tinged with a kind of empathetic warmth he had yet to figure out what to do with.

"As is yours. We've dealt with our grief in opposite ways, I think. I have no wish to forget my mother, punish myself for her absence. Instead, I wish to remember her and honor what she was to me. So when I do the things we did together, she feels near. That is both sad, I suppose, but more a great comfort. Because I cannot bring her back from death, of course. It's the closest I can come though."

The idea of comfort made him recoil. This idea that grief could have two sides to it. Pain and comfort. Happiness and sadness.

That was a luxury for the guilt-free, he supposed. "You make no sense."

"Do I not make sense, or do you simply refuse to see the sense I make?" She shrugged as if the answer made no difference to her. "Guilt is quite the crutch you've built for yourself. I have no such crutches."

For a moment, he could not form a word or a thought. It was now the second day in a row she'd cut him straight through with some kind of accusation that didn't feel like one. Her accusations felt like observations.

Observations that twisted everything he thought he'd been doing into a question. When he knew…he knew what he was doing was right. Maybe sometimes he faltered at choosing the best punishment, sometimes he fell into habits that were no longer painful enough, but punishment was what he deserved.

"You consider my guilt a crutch?" he demanded. Suffering and penance…a *crutch*?

A timer went off and she held up a hand before bending over the oven once more and then pulling out a large pan full of delicious-smelling cookies.

Cookies. That smelled and looked like Christmas. While she called his guilt a crutch.

And looked so dangerously appealing, even reeling from her words he watched the move of fabric against her legs. Imagined the feel of her no doubt soft skin under his palms.

"Have a seat, Diego," she instructed, reminding of some long-ago nanny who had thought she had the right to boss him around. She'd learned soon enough that Diego was not the recipient of *bossing*. She'd been sacked before he'd learned her name.

Because that had been the story of his life. If he had not liked something, someone else had solved the problem for him. And then he'd turned eighteen, and his parents flipped a switch. Suddenly expected him to handle everything, like it was age and not experience that mattered.

He had not handled a damn thing, except wasting his life away and keeping as much distance from them as he could and keep his inheritance.

A habit you've continued, have you not?

Amelia had never said such things to him, and yet it was her voice in his head, pointing out all the ways he'd been shirking responsibility and letting Amelia handle the business side of things while he punished himself.

He deserved to be punished though. That had been important. Keeping all his father's businesses going had been only important in so much as they existed, not that he had to have any part in them.

Amelia sighed, moving over to him. She reached out, even as he flinched, and put her hands on his forearms. She had small, graceful hands, warm against the fabric of his shirt.

"Diego. Take it from someone who has suffered loss as well, we all have crutches to get us through. Grief is not… science. It is emotion. We all must try to handle it in our own ways. But some ways are not healthy, and sometimes it takes someone else to point that out. There is nothing wrong with realizing you've…fooled yourself, I suppose, into thinking this pain you subject yourself to makes the grief irrelevant. Or that the choices you made make *you* irrelevant."

She gave his arms a squeeze. Her gaze was soft. Everything about her was so damn soft. It was why every sling seemed to land so deep. She was…deceptive. Yes, that was it. She was deceiving him with soft eyes and soft deliverance of harsh words.

She needed to be shown her place.

"It is the strangest thing," he drawled, taking a step forward...which caused her to take an uncertain step back. She didn't drop her hands though. They remained curled around his arms like an anchor. "I don't recall hearing about you becoming some kind of therapist, *tesoro*."

Her gaze sharpened, but she took another step back to his step forward. Still not letting him go.

"I've simply been through a similar loss, Diego. And come out on the other side, *twice*, with healthy coping mechanisms for these losses. I'd like to help you find the same."

He looked around the kitchen pointedly. Because it was *his* kitchen, all in all. Because she was making cookies for *him*, after being at his beck and call for two years, presumably building no real life out of the castello or his business holdings.

"Have you come out the other side?"

She blinked once. Yes, he had his own arrows to launch. And it felt *good* when they landed. Almost as good as being this close, as watching her expressive eyes darken into a slate gray with frustration.

"It seems your life is very...narrow," he observed, adopting the same light tone she often did when cutting him in half. "Have you any friends? Any...life outside these castello walls?"

He moved closer, surely driven by his own insult and making certain she felt the same. Until she was caged against the counter by his arms, and only his arms. She could have ducked under them. She could have ordered him back. But she held his gaze, chin raised. Then she did the damnedest thing.

She closed that bit of space between them, pressing her

body to his. She moved her hands up his arms to link behind his neck. "Is this what you want?" she asked, sounding innocent when the way she pressed her soft, pliant body to his was anything but. "You needn't pick a fight to be this close to me, Diego."

She was testing him. Maybe even testing herself. He could not give in to such tests. He would not.

But for a moment, he wavered.

And she took advantage of that waver.

CHAPTER EIGHT

AMELIA HADN'T PLANNED to do it. In fact, she'd told herself not to. To step away. There would be no getting through to him on a basic level if everything they did was clouded by...*this*.

But he was so close, and he was looking at her mouth. There was a hunger in his eyes that she wanted to experience. It echoed deeply inside her, an alarming and alluring pulse.

So she'd gotten closer. And then closer. Until she could feel his body heat, smell the soap on his skin. Until everything they'd been arguing about seemed to fade away and all she could think about was how much she'd like to know.

Because he was right. She'd built no life outside the castello. Had it been grief? Had it been fear? Simply a habit she hadn't known how to break when everything else was breaking apart around her?

She wasn't certain. But she was hardly going to bow down to his challenge. She hadn't *punished* herself, even if she'd made some isolating decisions. She certainly wasn't going to be so afraid of what she might have been doing to not reach out and try something new.

He'd challenged her, and that had tipped that tightwire between fear and excitement to ignoring fear if it meant meeting that challenge.

So she did the only thing that seemed to make sense in this stretched-out moment of touching each other, looking at each other, *testing* each other. She pushed onto her toes and pressed her mouth to his.

Lightly. Perhaps the things raging through her were nowhere close to *light*, but she thought he felt…fragile. Oh, he was a strong, impressive specimen of muscle and power, but under all that was something…delicate.

Perhaps the tiniest flicker of the humanity he was so determined to ignore. She wanted to fan it to life as much as she wanted to know what existed on the other side of all this physical want.

The kiss remained gentle, but she could feel the hard, dangerous outline of him against her abdomen. All that power chained back. It was intriguing, and there was a part of her that was curious what it would feel like unchained. What she was missing.

But a bigger part of her was afraid of the dangerous lines she was walking. She could admit that perhaps she, too, had hidden herself away in her grief, but she didn't think that meant she needed to destroy *everything* just because she wanted to meet a challenge.

Feel a tempting fire.

She eased back and forced herself to meet his gaze. She'd meet the challenge, even if she wasn't quite ready to dive headfirst into the fire.

He looked down at her, ice in his eyes. But there was no ice in *him*. Still, his words cut. "What the hell are you doing?"

Humiliation and hurt warred with insult. She did not look away. She refused to. If he didn't know what she was doing, he hadn't needed to kiss her back. *He* was the one caging her against this counter. *He* was the one who'd advanced.

"Do not play games, Diego," she scolded lightly. "Not if you do not wish me to follow along."

"Games," he repeated, utter shock chasing across his face. "You think this is a game?" It was only then he seemed to realize he was still holding on to her. He stepped back, not exactly gracefully. It was more of a stumble, as if she'd stabbed him clean through.

"You are young and naive, colored by your father's overly kind impression of me, I suppose. You have fooled yourself if you think there are…games being played here." He straightened, scowled at her in a way she supposed was meant to be intimidating. "You haven't a clue as to who I am, what I am, Amelia."

It didn't intimidate her at all. Mostly because the way he said it made her wonder if *he* knew who he was.

She moved closer to him once again, reached out and fitted her hand to his cheek. "You could show me."

For a moment, he was perfectly still. She didn't even think he breathed. But she saw a fire leaping in his eyes that echoed in the pit of her stomach. Though hers remained while his was quickly banked.

"Oh, I could show you quite a bit," he said darkly, moving away from her hand. "You have no idea the things I could show you."

"Is that a promise?"

"It is a warning, *tesoro*. I would have expected your father to have taught you to heed a warning."

With that, he turned on his heel and marched out of the kitchen, leaving her twisted up in a million knots. Shame and desire. Concern and a wistful yearning for recklessness. So many conflicting emotions, and part of her wanted to hide away from that. In all her life, her parents had always tried to protect her from that.

They had not argued in front of her, though her father had no doubt been angry about not knowing she existed for so many years. They'd treated each other with kindness, but Amelia had *sensed* their bitterness toward each other, toward her mother's illness, toward everything.

But she had been shielded. Just like in the Folliero home. She had been treated a bit like a…pet. Her father had kept her as hidden away as possible, unless Mrs. Folliero wanted to dress her up in Aurora's hand-me-downs and insist she perform piano pieces for the family—which was only ever a jab at Aurora's refusal to play. Meanwhile, Aurora had used Amelia's company as somewhere to lodge all her complaints and make all her contempt for the family and its treatment of her known. And heard.

And Diego, much like his father, had never really acknowledged her at all.

All these people were gone now, except Diego. And Amelia was now the adult in the situation, not a child. She was the one in charge.

Now there was no one to shield her, and she had two choices. Continue to shield herself, hide away from life's complexities. Just as her life had always been.

Or be the kind of woman who handled complex, and since the people who'd shielded her from so much had *died*, it left the second the only true option.

What that meant for her and Diego, she did not yet know for sure. But she wasn't about to be *warned away*.

Diego was disgusted with himself. He had resisted, but not enough. He had endured pain, but it seemed to have no satisfaction.

Which was the point, he supposed. He stormed back to

his bedchamber, his body a maze of different kinds of pains and thwarted desires.

She'd put her mouth on him. He could not fully come to grips with this turn of events. His assistant. Bartolo's young daughter. A woman who didn't even *know* him—not really.

She'd pressed her mouth to his, and he would never be able to erase the hint-of-sugar-and-vanilla taste of Bartolo's daughter.

Bartolo, who was supposed to have worked *for* Diego but had set expectations for him instead. Who had pointed out his extravagances and the way he lashed out to hurt. Who had calmly, steadily insisted there was a better way to be than the way Diego chose.

Without ever turning away from him. Without ever despairing of him. For years, Diego had *hated* Bartolo, this "assistant" who had felt more like a nanny or prison warden. Who could not be swayed by threats or bad behavior.

And then it had slowly shifted, until Diego craved those behavioral guardrails. He'd still enjoyed his excess, his irresponsibility, but with a guiding point of *right*, he'd felt less self-loathing. Less self-destructive.

Still quite a bit of loathing for his family. Still plenty of selfish desires he wasn't about to resist. But there'd been a sense that once he *had* to, he could make himself into a more respectable person.

And then all those selfish desires he hadn't curbed caused them all to *die*. While he lived.

Lived long enough to kiss Amelia Baresi. Not as monstrous as murder, but at the moment, with the desire for her still roiling through him, it felt similar. It all felt dire, like the weight of it should bury him alive.

Instead, he lived. He moved. He…

You breathe, caro. *You are alive. This cannot be changed in this moment any more than death.*

She had said those words to him, with a gentleness he could not grasp, could not understand. Bartolo had been steadfast. Diego had known that, for whatever reason, the man had cared for him, wanted him to be better. But it had not been centered in the warmth his daughter now extended him.

As if Amelia understood some piece of what went on in his mind. But she *didn't*, because she thought it was a self-punishment he did not deserve.

He pushed through his room and then out the French doors onto the terrace outside his room. He had brooded out here many a winter night, frustrated that his parents insisted on this isolated mountain retreat for the *entire* Christmas season.

He'd felt like a prisoner then. Because it had all been a performance. They hadn't wanted to spend quality time together; they'd wanted to show off their picture-perfect family to… Diego didn't even know. Who had they been trying to impress? And for *what*?

Even now, it filled him with an impotent anger to go along with all the other jagged edges cutting around inside.

He sucked in a breath out here in the dark. The air was frigid, the mountains grim shadows all around him. Lights dotted the landscape—from the castello, from the village beyond.

He was no longer a teen simply angry he was stuck here, though there was some irony to be found. His body raged like a teenage boy who'd never touched a woman. His frustration blazed in much the same way as it had back then.

Except everyone from *back then* was dead.

And the woman causing him to feel like a thwarted,

hormonal teen was his punishment. Yes, he deserved this. That kiss. Her interest. He deserved having to resist it all.

And there was the answer. This was pain, and so this was right.

Every day, he would force himself into her orbit. Every day, he would resist whatever she offered. Every damn day, until something broke. Until it felt like enough, or she sent him back to his seclusion.

He sucked in the icy air and began the process of settling. Yes, that was the answer. Throw himself into all she wanted, into her, but resist this magnetic physical pull. Day after day after day. The more it hurt, the better punishment it was.

Christmas markets, Christmas cookies. The whole thing. Down to the Christmas ball. This was what she was insisting on having. This was what she'd collected him for. The damn ball.

He wanted nothing to do with it. He never had—and now that it was nothing but a memory of everything he'd killed with his carelessness, he wanted it even less.

So he would involve himself in every last detail. He would throw himself into the planning and execution and spend every last hour of the ball weekend *socializing* with the people who had once attended his parents' parties.

This time, with Amelia at his side.

Pain was the price, and he would finally be paying it in full.

CHAPTER NINE

AMELIA HAD NOT slept well. Fueled by too much sugar because, yes, she'd mainlined a *lot* of those Christmas cookies. But also fueled by too much internal flummox. She kept replaying that kiss in her mind, even when she tried not to. She tried to think about plans for the ball, Christmas events she could take Diego to. She even stayed up later than usual reading through her father's journal, thinking the sadness over his absence might penetrate this strange haze around her body.

But too many entries were about Diego, his self-destructive tendencies and how little the elder Follieros seemed to know what to do about it. How they enabled his refusal or inability to look within and what her father had done to try and rectify it.

And when she thought of the boy her father had worried about, she thought about the man who'd sequestered himself on an isolated mountain thinking he was somehow... punishing himself.

Self-destructive, yes. But it wasn't the guilt she thought that was causing it. It was the grief. Grief and pain that were clear as day in his dark eyes.

Dark eyes that drank her in like she was something delicious. He'd caged her against that counter, and a selfish man, at least to Amelia's way of thinking, would have taken whatever he wanted, damn the consequences.

But he had not pushed her, had not initiated the taste. She had, and he had let her. Maybe he had kissed her back, but she knew something more lurked under the surface. He'd let her set the tone.

What would it be like if he broke through said surface and took what he so clearly wanted?

And so, on went the thought cycle, always coming back to *what if*, and the incessant, needy throb of her body that hadn't stopped since he'd loomed over her.

She was well aware there were ways she could handle the edgy thwarted desire herself. But she couldn't bring herself to do so as long as *he* was there, when she might have to face him knowing why she'd done it.

Had he handled his own thwarted desire, down the hall in his bedroom?

Which brought images of that first morning, and his naked body. Would he have taken the long, hard length of himself in his own hand and—

She rolled over and gave a frustrated scream into her pillow.

She had gone into this knowing she couldn't *plan* anything. People were unpredictable, and she hadn't known how Diego would respond or react to anything—except knowing he'd be reticent to return to normal life, to let his guilt go.

She'd known he'd be perhaps even more than reticent to see himself as a good man, as her father had so genuinely wished for him.

But she had not, under any realm of possibility, counted on finding this sort of all-encompassing attraction she'd only previously read about. Never experienced. She had not expected it to swamp her, distract her and otherwise make everything she'd set out to do seem as though it was on a shaky foundation.

She supposed why it was so frustrating was that she didn't quite know how to handle the attraction side of things, no matter how many different tactics she tried. Throwing herself into it hadn't gone well—he'd left her feeling needy and alone. Keeping herself apart didn't do much either—she was still obsessing over him.

So what was the answer?

She didn't know, and that was obnoxious. She was a careful, determined person. She made plans and accomplished them. She didn't wander around not knowing what to do. Her parents had both raised her with the expectation that if you noticed a problem, you endeavored to solve it.

Maybe this wasn't solvable in all those easy ways, but it didn't mean she could shirk her *other* responsibilities. So she forced herself to set it aside, set *Diego* aside. She went through a quick—cold—shower, then went down to breakfast and her to-do list for the day.

This morning, she would work on ball preparations. In the afternoon, she would convince Diego to accompany her down to a nearby village for a nice stroll. The nearest village put out elaborate nativity scenes made by local artists every year—something she wasn't sure he'd attended in his youth but knew his parents had donated money to the artists in years past, so he had to have *some* awareness of them.

And they would be outside, so she would not have to deal with what happened in the kitchen.

No, she wasn't going to *hide* from it. She just needed some time to…sort through it. And being alone didn't seem to be the best way to do that. Not…just yet, anyway.

Satisfied with this plan, she went downstairs and poured

herself some coffee before settling into her small office. It had once been Aurora's "music room," and Amelia kept the small antique piano in the corner. Sometimes when she felt lonely, she'd go play a tune and imagine the house was still full and no one had died.

She wondered what Diego would think of that story. Would he commiserate? Or would that be too close to *feeling* for him to take on board?

She shook her head, irritated with herself for obsessing over him. Yes, her holiday project was getting through to him by year's end, but that didn't mean every waking moment had to be about what he thought or felt. Especially not if she was going to make certain this ball was everything she wanted it to be.

"Good morning."

Amelia jolted, sloshing a bit of coffee over the rim of her mug. She blinked up at the intrusion to find Diego standing in the doorway.

Sounding cheerful. Amelia didn't trust it, but she returned his smile anyway. She met his positive attitude with her best approximation of one. "Good morning."

He was dressed for the day in casual attire, and he walked into the room like he owned it.

Because he does, Amelia.

He looked around and seemed to take in the different details. Did he remember his sister playing music—or, more often, refusing to play—here? Did this room mean nothing to him? She couldn't tell. Especially when he said nothing, just walked the perimeter of the room.

The silence gave her too much room to think—about last night, about *her* night. So she blurted out the first question she could think of. "Did you sleep well?"

He paused ever so slightly, studying her as if looking

for a deeper meaning to the question. Which reminded her of what had kept *her* up most of the night and made her cheeks warm.

She thought she recognized amusement in his gaze, but his expression remained neutral enough to pretend like she was imagining things.

"Yes, I suppose I did," he said, approaching her desk, then taking a chair and pulling it up across from her.

Silence stretched out, and Amelia had to swallow because even though she tried not to, she seemed to be reliving that kiss right here. The soft give of his mouth, the hard lines of his body, the way it had fizzled through her like a dangerous liquid she only wanted more of.

"Can I help you this morning?" She tried to keep her smile in place, but it became more of a grimace as she heard the squeak in her own voice.

He leaned back in the chair, folded his arms behind his head. "I have come to do your bidding."

"My..." Her brain short-circuited for a moment. What exactly was her bidding? Playing games? Last night? Something...else?

"You did want me here for the Christmas ball, did you not?" he asked, just a little *too* pointedly.

"Yes, the ball. Yes." She forced another smile at him that she hoped looked in control and as if she were humoring him with just a *dash* of condescension. "I'm hoping you'll attend of course."

"That is the plan, as it stands. But it is not for some time yet. Surely there is much to do to prepare. I seem to recall my mother running about, pulling out her hair, the weeks before."

"Yes, she did often get...overwhelmed." Amelia had always felt Mrs. Folliero simply enjoyed any reason to be dramatic, to yell at the people who worked for her, while having a simple excuse like the ball so she didn't need to *really* apologize.

Father had explained to her, in his gentle way, that sometimes Mrs. Folliero needed some attention, and that was the only way she knew how to go about getting it.

Amelia studied Diego. She wondered how many of his issues were simply from not *knowing*. How to get the attention he wanted, or the care, or whatever it was.

Surely growing up pampered had left some lessons fully unlearned. Just as Mrs. Folliero hadn't known how to behave when she wanted attention. She hadn't known to just *ask*. She'd had to create drama.

So Diego didn't know how to be good, or heal, or feel his guilt. He needed her to teach him.

"So put me to work," Diego said, spreading his big hands wide on the desk between them.

"To…work," Amelia echoed, her thoughts scattering as she took in how *big* his hands were. That there were calluses and scars because he had been physically punishing himself for two years.

What would it feel like to have rough, scarred hands on her bare skin?

He leaned forward, that same amusement sparkling in his eyes while his face showed none of it. "Is your hearing all right this morning?"

Amelia did not understand what had changed. She did not know how to *accept* this change. Was it some kind of trick? It certainly couldn't be a genuine change of heart already.

Could it?

No. He was…playing a game. And she could certainly play back. She ignored his question about her hearing, swallowed her hammering heart and clasped her hands over her notebook. "Yes, there is much already in place, but much to do to ensure it all goes smoothly. We have a kind of theme this year." She looked from her notebook to him, making sure to meet his gaze and hold it.

"As it's the first Christmas ball since we've lost them, I wanted to honor Christmases past. Both nostalgic, but also a kind of…memorial. To what we lost." She watched him carefully. His expression betrayed no feeling on the matter.

"I'm sure that will appeal to many guests," he said genially. "My parents had many friends."

"And you want…to have a role in that?" she asked, not bothering to hide her suspicion. "Creating an homage to the past?"

"*Want* is not the word I would use, Amelia, but yes. I will have a role in this. I will be here at least until the Christmas ball, as you originally suggested." His smile was polite. His words a clipped kind of disinterested, but not rude. Sort of blank, like it mattered not at all to him, no matter what they did.

But it had to matter. Somewhere deep down, she was sure it *had* to matter. They were talking about honoring his parents, his sister. Perhaps they had not had the best relationship, but surely memorializing them would mean something to him.

And if he was giving her the opportunity to reach that place inside him where the past mattered, she had to grab it with both hands. For his own good and healing.

"I've based the menu and decor on what I remember and what records I've been able to find, but we could go through my plans and see if they match your memories."

"What about my mother's records?"

"Records?"

"Oh, yes, she kept meticulous records of all the balls. Well, her assistant did. You don't have those?"

"It was necessary to go through your father's office and records for the business side of things, but Mrs. Moretti handles the day-to-day of the castello. I suppose she would have your mother's records." Amelia frowned a little. Mrs. Moretti had never mentioned any records about the ball while Amelia had been prepping and planning, but Amelia had never asked outright.

Diego pushed to his feet. "Then let us go fetch those."

Amelia didn't immediately get up. She stared at him, maybe a little open-mouthed, for a few seconds before she managed to get her wits about her. "Have you had some sort of personality switch, Diego? Shall I call a doctor?"

His mouth curved on one side ever so slightly, reminding Amelia too clearly of the kiss last night. She knew what those lips felt like against hers now, and every time she looked at them, she could all but relive the sensation.

"You can believe whatever you wish, *tesoro*."

Diego's amusement at baffling Amelia faded the moment they walked down the hall to Mrs. Moretti's office. She had a small room off the kitchens to keep the castello in running order. She had been in that position for as long as Diego could remember.

What Diego could not remember was the last time he might have seen Mrs. Moretti. As an adult, he had not often interacted with the staff. Still, when they walked into the room, Diego recognized her immediately.

Time had stamped heavy lines across her face. She looked the same and yet not at all. An elder version of Mrs. Moretti. Except she *was* older. She *was* Mrs. Moretti because time had passed.

It was weirdly disorienting, not because she should not look old, but because it reminded him that his parents would not ever have the privilege. All those years his mother had opined about the possibility of *wrinkles*, and then she'd barely had the chance to develop any.

Both his parents, really, had been so concerned with their looks, their aging. And then, because of that selfishness Bartolo had tried to scold him out of, they'd never been given the opportunity.

"Diego," Mrs. Moretti said with some surprise. Her gaze darted from Amelia and back to him. "Mr. Folliero," she corrected, as if realizing he was no longer a boy but now the master of the house. "It is good to have you back at the castello."

The polite thing would have been to say it was good to be back. He could not get his mouth to say the words.

"Mrs. Moretti, Diego is helping with some of the Christmas-ball plans now. He thought there might be some records of his mother's that could help us." Amelia's smile was polite but remote.

Probably because Mrs. Moretti was more or less ignoring the fact she was there, keeping her gaze and attention solely on Diego.

"I do indeed have many of your mother's records. Straightforward things like menus and plans, like I've shared with Ms. Baresi." She did not so much as look at Amelia, which was odd. "But there is more. The photo albums, of course." She beamed at him. "I had them set away for you. I always knew you'd return."

Diego could think of nothing to say to that. Even when his parents had been alive, there'd been no plans to return. He'd enjoyed a life far away from his family, Italy and this damn, suffocating falsehood.

"I'll go collect them, shall I?" She gave Diego a fond pat as she passed him, scurrying out the door, clearly eager to impart these past items he wanted nothing to do with.

And once he fully absorbed that, he carefully turned to Amelia. She was expressly not looking at him. Because she would have used these albums, if she'd been able to. Because Mrs. Moretti had not once addressed Amelia in any way. She hadn't even looked in her direction.

"Why does she ignore you?"

Amelia shot him a kind of baffled look that softened into sympathy, which he didn't know what to do with. "Some were offended by the choices you made."

"Choices?"

"You gave a young woman with no experience the power to make almost all decisions in your stead. No matter how well Mrs. Moretti liked me or my father, she resented that I was allowed to have the final say, even when it was sweeping approval of everything she wanted."

"Why should that be something to be mad at *you* about? I did it, gave you that power. Unless you wielded the power irresponsibly." He could not believe she would. Not just because he'd hired her, but because he'd seen her now these past few days. How she held herself. She had certainly internalized her father's lessons on how to behave.

Bartolo had always been concerned with *goodness* and the *right thing*. That you took care of those who needed taking care of. That *other's* needs were bigger than your own. He had done his level best to impart some of that on Diego, but Diego had more often rejected than accepted it. When Bartolo had been alive, he was like the good angel on his shoulder, whispering what Diego should do.

On occasion, Diego had listened, but more often than not, he was too aware there were no consequences for him, and the devil on his shoulder was far easier and less complicated than doing the right thing.

And then there'd finally been consequences for his actions, and they hadn't hurt him. They'd killed his family.

"I gave her as much power as I should, but it wasn't about the *power*—not really," Amelia continued. She didn't sound frustrated by this, more...weary. As though she'd given up any hope of changing things. "It was about the insult. It's far easier for her to take that out on me than it is for her to take that out on you. You're the poor boy who lost his parents."

He could only stare at her. He had never considered himself a man over worried about fairness, but... "You lost yours."

Amelia shrugged. "I cannot pretend to know Mrs. Moretti's inner thoughts, but the impression I always got is that I had experience losing a parent, that I should have known how to deal and grieve my father's death. That I had a job to do, regardless of grief. You...did not."

"But..." Diego could only stare at Amelia, and the casual way she'd delivered this patently unfair information. She too had been left an orphan, experience or not, and she was younger. She might have secured a well-paying position, but she wasn't wealthy like he was. Perhaps he'd lost more people in one fell swoop, but that did not make her pain somehow less worthy of support than his own.

This was a very strange realization, and one he could not settle into because Mrs. Moretti had reappeared, hefting a large box.

"The *signora* always had little photo albums made to send out to guests, but these were for her and her alone." She set the box on the desk. "Not just of the balls but of every holiday season she spent in the castello. There are some notes here and there as well. Anything you could want to recreate the ball just as she did it." She smiled at Diego.

Diego could not force himself to smile back. Both because of the heft of what was in the box and the fact Mrs. Moretti had purposefully kept this from Amelia. And had no compunction about making that known now.

Still, he found himself frozen and speechless, not wanting what was in that box, not wanting to wade into what issues he might have left for Amelia without ever thinking it through.

She'd never complained. Not once.

"We'll take these back to Diego's rooms so he can go through them at his own pace," Amelia said, stepping forward. She grabbed the box.

This earned her a disapproving scowl, but Mrs. Moretti did not *say* anything or try to stop her, so Diego did not. Not yet. There was too much to sort through.

"Thank you, Mrs. Moretti. You've been beyond helpful, as usual." Amelia said this with a warmth that was hard to disbelieve. Yet surely… Surely she felt bitter?

She didn't act it though. She exited the office, Diego trailing after her—before it dawned on him that the box was heavy, and she was struggling a bit to carry it.

He scooped it out of her grasp. She made a little sound of protest but didn't *actually* protest.

"We needn't go to my rooms," he announced, marching in front of her. "Let us look through this nonsense in your office. That way you can use whatever you wish."

"We can do that if you want," she said in that diplomatic way that hid whatever she really felt. "But you can also take some time. Go through this with some privacy. I can give you some space, Diego."

He should want that. To be alone and isolated while

he tortured himself with a glimpse into the past, into his mother. He should accept that as yet another punishment.

He stalked into her office, let the box fall onto her desk. "No," he said firmly. "You will stay. We will do this together."

CHAPTER TEN

AMELIA FELT LIKE she was walking on very thin ice. She was shocked he'd asked her to stay—okay, demanded her to stay—and be a part of this.

If she thought he was doing it because she would offer comfort, she would warmly agree and jump right in, but he was too big on punishing himself. He hadn't flipped any switches that quickly. Her presence felt more like...an exercise in masochism? Making her watch his pain.

She watched him stare at the box. She didn't think he realized he was breathing a little heavily. That he was looking at the box like it might come to life and bite.

So maybe it wasn't punishment. Perhaps it was wishful thinking, but he seemed so...lost. He hadn't known what to say to Mrs. Moretti. He hadn't known what to say to *her*.

So now he was pretending to know what to do by insisting this be just business. Just Christmas-ball prep. She could tell him she saw right through him. Gamble that her intuition was correct.

She decided against it, though. There was no reason to point it out to him. He'd just double down on pretending it was business and meant nothing.

So she walked over to stand next to him and said nothing as he pulled the box top off with perhaps more force than necessary. He reached in with no finesse and jerked out a large, overstuffed album that must have been on top. His mouth twisted in something like disgust.

"Do you recognize it?" she asked him gently.

"No," he said flatly.

"Then let's sit." She nudged him toward the chair he'd pulled up to her desk earlier, then pulled hers around to this side. He put the book down on the desk in front of them and flipped open the cover without sitting down.

She wanted to admonish him to be more careful, as they didn't know what they were dealing with or how old and delicate what was inside would be, but she bit her tongue.

The first page was a snapshot of two young people. It took Amelia a few moments to place them. "Your parents." They were in casual clothes in front of a fancy-looking chalet.

"Yes." He sounded winded, and he finally lowered himself into his chair like his legs couldn't hold him up anymore. Amelia took a seat as well, moving her gaze from the picture to his face.

"They met skiing. Their fathers had gone to university together, lost touch, then happened upon each other when my parents were teenagers at this chalet." He delivered this information as if by rote, pointing at the building behind the young, smiling couple.

Amelia was a bit surprised he knew how his parents had met, but she didn't press the matter. Not when he was busy already turning the page.

There were more snapshots. Mr. and Mrs. Folliero as young adults in various scenes and poses. "I do not know what this has to do with any ball," he muttered, but he did not close the book or move away.

Amelia leaned forward and pointed to a snapshot in the bottom corner. "Look. That is Dolcina. At Christmas." She could see a nativity in the background, clearly in the nearby village, based on the surroundings. "And look." She pointed at Mrs. Folliero's left hand carefully and, Amelia thought, purposefully displayed on Mr. Folliero's shoulder, so that even in this casual snapshot, the huge diamond was the focal point. "They got engaged."

Diego grunted and turned the page without comment on that. There were more formal pictures here. Of the wedding.

"A Christmas wedding." Amelia smiled in spite of herself. "They did love Christmas, didn't they?"

"Yes. It was a Folliero tradition." He turned the page, clearly not as interested in the beautiful wedding dress or intricate gold-and-green cake as Amelia was.

On this page, there was a family photo. It did not look as if it had been taken by a professional photographer like the other pictures that were displayed around the house, hung by the Follieros before their deaths. This picture was more of a snapshot. Mr. and Mrs. Folliero, young and smiling, with a very large baby on Mrs. Folliero's lap.

Since this baby was the only child in the picture, and he was dressed in blue, Amelia had to assume it was Diego. She laughed, couldn't help the reaction. "Look at that pudgy face."

He scowled at her, but it wasn't anger in his eyes. There was *some* amusement, even as he only grunted and turned the page away from himself as a small, pudgy baby.

There were more shots of Mr. and Mrs. Folliero together than there were family photos that included Diego or Aurora, but these photos were all more casual shots than anything professional or posed, as if they hadn't been too, *too* worried about how they looked.

Amelia glanced at Diego. He was frowning at a page of pictures in which his parents had clearly taken some sort of trip. Sunny blue skies and tranquil blue waters, while the happy couple smiled for the camera in every frame. There were no children to be seen, so Amelia assumed it was a trip they'd taken without Diego or Aurora.

Maybe an anniversary trip. Amelia knew pictures could be deceiving, showing only the happiest moments of a person's life, but she'd also known the Follieros. For all their faults, they had truly seemed to care for one another.

"They look happy, do they not?" he said, still frowning down at them, as if their happiness was some kind of puzzle to figure out.

"They do," Amelia agreed. "They were happy, I think." She didn't know that it was comfort, but she did think it was true.

"It was Aurora and I who were not."

She could not argue that. She'd known Aurora much more closely than Diego, and she had gotten mostly frustration and bitterness from the younger Folliero. She had never imagined Diego was much different, especially since he had not been around often once Amelia had arrived.

"I always thought…" She thought better of her *thoughts*, when he whipped his gaze to hers, stark and angry, a sudden change from the stunned sort of detachment he'd been sporting.

She swallowed, then managed a wobbly smile. "Well, this hasn't quite given us a look into the Christmas-ball past, has it?"

"No, tell me. Tell me what you always thought." He said it like an order, and Amelia felt compelled to obey it like one.

Still, she paused, considering her words and what they might mean to him. In the end, she thought…understanding was the thing he was missing. It was the thing that kept him stuck, seeking punishment over healing.

He did not know how to grieve or heal or seek to understand, so she had to offer it to him, so that he might learn.

"Your parents loved each other, and they knew what to do with that," Amelia said carefully, trying to put the way her father had explained things in his journals into her own words, her own observations of the Follieros. "They loved the both of you, but they did not know what to do with... children. They only knew how to spoil or neglect or demand exactly what they wanted from you. They did not know how to...look at you as people. And because you were children, and your own individual people, you did not know how to tell them. Or show them what *you* needed."

His eyes narrowed. "That's very astute."

"It was more my father's feeling than my own," she admitted. "But I did see evidence of it. Particularly with Aurora. She was so determined to be the *opposite* of what they wanted, and they simply...let her drift away. I suppose they did the same with you. I just wasn't there for it."

Diego was silent for some time, just staring at her. She didn't know what else to do but sit there and wait for him to break the silence or look away or *something*.

When he finally spoke, he ignored the *content* of her words. "Your father discussed my parents' inability to be parents with you?"

"No, no. Not exactly, no. After his death, I found...his collection of journals. Over the past two years, I've been reading through them. It helps me feel like...he's still here, or that I'm getting to know him better, or something. Just a few entries a day so I can spread it out. So I'm still learning new things about him even though he isn't here."

She didn't know why she'd felt the need to confess all that. The details of the how and why. She could have left it at she'd read it in his journals, but instead she'd offered a piece of her heart, her grief.

How she kept holding on to her father, even though he wasn't here. And hearing it out loud sounded...wrong, somehow. Like she, too, was holding on to an illusion that didn't really serve her. Like he had been right when he'd accused her of having no life outside of *this*.

She found the strength to look up at Diego then. His gaze on hers was one of pain and confusion, matching what she was feeling right now.

The past hurt, the future confused, but the present was just a series of days to get through, and wasn't *that* depressing? Why was her present so depressing? And what would her future ever be if she stayed stuck right here?

His gaze was back on the book as he turned more pages. "I'm sure there will be pictures of the ball if we keep looking," he said, sounding uninterested and in control.

While her heart was soft and bruised in her chest, uncertainty shaking all her foundations.

Diego finally moved past his parents as a happy, wealthy couple who loved pictures of themselves—far more pictures of the two of them than their children—and found a few pages that depicted some of the Christmas balls in his early childhood.

Amelia took careful notes about the decor, what she could make out of the pictures. Sometimes she talked about a plan that would be adjusted or something she'd already had just right.

She didn't mention her father again.

He didn't mind pushing daggers into his own pain and grief and guilt, but seeing it reflected in her changeable eyes as a deep, abiding *sadness*, that held nothing bitter in it...

He was the reason Bartolo Baresi was dead. And his daughter sat next to Diego now, trying to accomplish... something by bringing him back here.

He wanted to believe there was something deceitful in it, in her, but he just didn't think it was underhanded at all. She didn't seem to have *underhand* in her. Which made her feel...

Dangerous. Like she had all the power and he had nothing. She pulled every string, and he would simply dance. Because she was good and right.

Which was *nonsense*, but he felt...unsteady all of a sudden. As if her innocent nature, trying to do something out of kindness, was a weapon.

He closed the album, not sure how it could leave him feeling bruised. He'd seen no happy memories of his own in there. Only his parents' smiling faces.

And the haunting explanation Amelia had offered, that they had loved each other but simply hadn't known how to be parents. Likely they'd never been taught. What he remembered of his grandparents wasn't warm in the least. They'd all been cold and removed. They hadn't liked the *noise* of children, so he and Aurora had not often been around them except to perform.

Diego didn't even think he'd gone to their funerals. Had his parents? Had they grieved?

What a strange thing to wonder. He tried to shake the thoughts away. The past was gone. He should be punished for his, but not for whatever had gone on with his grandparents. They had been a nonentity in his life.

Amelia carefully set the album aside, then pulled out another one of similar size and heft.

Diego did not reach for it. He could not make himself. "Perhaps that is enough for one morning."

She gave him one of those warm, sympathetic looks and nodded. "Of course. I thought this afternoon we could go into Dolcina and take in the nativities." She smiled a little ruefully. "I wasn't aware this was where your parents got engaged, but nonetheless. It's a good Christmas tradition."

He could see the picture of his mother grinning with her giant engagement ring perfectly in his mind's eye. A woman whom only adulthood and loss had taught him he hadn't really known.

Hadn't tried to know, because to him she had been one-dimensional, impossible to impress or make happy, so he'd given up. Stayed away.

Because Amelia's, or Bartolo's, supposition was correct. For whatever reasons, his mother—in fact, both his parents—had not known how to get to know *him*. He and Aurora had existed only in the context of doing what was expected or not.

They had mostly not.

He hated that he had reasons for it. That Amelia had somehow forced him into looking deeper into a past he did not need to see clearly. It changed nothing. Because of him, everyone involved was dead, and there was no rectifying any of it. Understanding was a waste. A bigger loss.

And it was all her fault.

"And what exactly do you think comes from this?"

She frowned quizzically and looked over at him. "From what?"

"From shoving Christmas and memories down my throat? What do you get from this? What do you want to accomplish?" If he knew, he could fight it.

Fight her.

She studied him. If she was afraid or irritated by the snap in his tone, she didn't show it. She kept her gaze and her tone even and calm.

"I suppose... I'd like to see you step back into yourself, Diego."

He recoiled. He knew it was a metaphor, but he didn't want to take that on. "And what on earth does *that* mean?"

She didn't say anything for a long time. She stood there, eyebrows drawn together, expression serious. When she spoke, it was soft, but the words landed like daggers.

"My father wrote of you. In his journals. He saw a lot of himself in you."

Diego didn't realize he was shaking his head at first. When he realized it, he stopped.

"He had a similar relationship with his parents, except they were poor, so I think it was far more contentious and dangerous. But he saw a lot of the same wounds in you and wanted to help you heal them."

"And you think forcing Christmas into my life will somehow heal me?"

"No. You have to want to heal yourself. Though I'm not sure I fully realized that until now. I did not realize how much you'd let the guilt poison you from the inside out."

"Guilt is not a poison, Amelia. It is a fact."

It was her turn to shake her head. "No. It is a feeling. Facts are that you did not *cause* that plane crash. You can feel as though your actions did, but that isn't a fact by any stretch of the imagination."

He stood, some force of fury propelling him. "I would be careful how you characterize my guilt, *tesoro*. It is what got you a job and keeps you employed."

She didn't flinch or blanch or react in any of the ways he'd expected. Wanted. *Needed*. Lashing out was supposed to create a wedge. Supposed to ease this pressure inside his chest.

It always had, no matter how often Bartolo had warned

him that someday it would backfire. That *someday* he would meet someone who made that lash a source of guilt.

Little had Bartolo known what Diego could do with *guilt*.

Amelia very carefully got to her feet, calm and collected. "I have handled all the details of your life, your business, for these two years," she said with the kind of quiet gravity he did not know how to interrupt. It held weight and heft, each word.

"I have thrown myself into it. When you threatened to fire me back at your cabin, I was terrified." She shook her head. "Now I'm starting to think I should quit. Or allow you to fire me. Whichever should come first."

He stared at her in utter shock for at what felt like a full minute before he found himself. "You cannot *quit*."

"I could. I should." She sighed, looking around the office. "Will I? I don't know. I'm beginning to think this place, this life, is my own crutch. If I want you to give yours up, I suppose I have to give mine up."

Before he could think of a thing to say, she crossed to him, gave his shoulder a friendly little pat. "We needn't worry about it now. I'll see the Christmas ball through. We can discuss it in the new year."

He watched her go. *Flee*, essentially, like she couldn't stand to be in this room with him for another second.

Like she got to decide. Like *she* alone knew all the secrets to the universe. And he was a fool for not following along. For not jumping to *heal* exactly the way she wanted him to.

Except she'd run away. *Run.* After days of accusing him of only running and hiding. Now she was.

No. Not today.

CHAPTER ELEVEN

Running away wasn't the answer, but Amelia had needed to get out of that room before she started crying.

She *refused* to cry in front of him. Because he wouldn't understand the real reason for her tears. It wasn't him being harsh, or even threatening to fire her. It was nothing about *him*, but he would assume it was. Survivor's guilt and self-absorption was all he had in him.

She knew this wasn't true. The depth of his guilt hid something more than self-absorption. But for right now she wanted it to be that simple. Needed it to be that simple.

He was the problem, and she should wash her hands of him. She *should* quit. She should start making plans for getting him out of her life so he could not casually threaten her employment.

But first, she needed a good cry. Not because of *him*, but because of…a combination of things.

First, that album. All the smiling faces of people who were gone. People who'd never had the opportunity to fix their mistakes, if they would have taken the opportunity. Even though she hadn't loved the Follieros as she'd loved her father, she still missed them. They had been kind to her. Aurora had been a friend of sorts. And Amelia did not know how to ignore that the injustice of the loss weighed heavy on her heart.

And then there was Diego's reaction to it all. He'd tried to be so stoic, but there'd been a war of emotions under the surface as he'd flipped through those pages. She hadn't been able to recognize them all, but she knew pain when she saw it. No matter how hard someone tried to hide it.

Then he'd turned that pain around and launched it at her. She should be used to it by now, but in the softness of the moment, it had caught her off guard. And every time they had an argument like that, she came away with a new understanding of him *and* herself.

It was the *herself* that lodged like a weight in her chest. It was the *herself* that was making things complicated. She had known it wouldn't be easy, but part of her had assumed she would sweep in and solve all his problems. Absolve all his guilt. It might take time and work, but it was possible and it would be done.

It had never occurred to her that by reaching out to him, insisting he return to the world he'd left behind, she might twist some things inside herself. She might realize that she had her own unresolved issues she'd been hiding from.

They were both leaning heavily on these crutches that weren't helping them live any. She had tried to rid him of his, but she could not seem to do it. He *was* hers, so what did she do now?

Perhaps the real way to accomplish her father's goal was to push Diego away. To quit today. Leave him to his cabin and forget the Follieros ever existed.

He'd either figure his issues out or he wouldn't. He would find his goodness or he wouldn't. The end.

Or was that just abandoning him to his worst devices, as his parents had essentially done? Wasn't running the easy way out? Hadn't she accused him of doing just that?

She stalked into her room, closing the bedroom door behind her. She breathed heavily, but the tears didn't fall as she stood in the middle of her pretty, cozy room that she loved so much.

Crying would have been a nice release, but tears seemed stuck in her throat. She couldn't *breathe*, but she couldn't cry. She couldn't move past the twisting, twirling thing inside her that whispered she needed to deal with *herself*.

"He's a grown man," she muttered aloud to the empty room. "At some point he has to make his own decisions, Amelia. And that is *not* your responsibility."

But what *was* her responsibility?

Her father hadn't tasked *her* with getting through to Diego. It was simply a wish he'd written down in his journal years ago. Not knowing he would die. Not knowing Amelia would read the entries, trying to feel comforted by his words since he was no longer here.

She squeezed her eyes shut, desperate for some moisture to spill over, but it wouldn't. She slammed her fist against her dresser, a rare display of absolute frustration that was not soothed at all when the pain that jolted through her arm didn't dislodge the tears either.

All pain was quickly forgotten when her door burst open and Diego stepped over the threshold of her room. For a moment she just stood frozen, staring at him. She could think of nothing to say. Nothing to do.

Why had he followed her?

"We are going to Dolcina," he announced. Ordered?

For a moment, she only stared, not trying to find words or tears or her breath. She just took in this large, wild man standing in her bedroom, demanding…

Storming into her room and demanding she go take in nativities? "Have you absolutely lost your mind?"

"No. We will go see your nativities." He took a step toward her. "We will plan this ball." Another step with each demand. "We will do all your little plots and plans, and at the end of this you will see: You were wrong."

Wrong. She couldn't believe he'd followed her all the way up here to stomp and carry on about her being *wrong*. After... this afternoon. Looking at his parents as they'd been. Discussing how they'd failed him, even if they hadn't meant to.

That he could stand there and demand she be *wrong* was... as heartbreaking as it was infuriating. "Is that all that album meant to you? All those memories and realizations, and all you care about is that I was wrong about how you might feel about it?" Maybe her father had been wrong all along. About Diego. About the Follieros. About *everything*. Maybe...

But no. *No*. She understood Diego. All too well. Or had, until this moment.

Right now she didn't understand him at all because he wasn't running, but he wasn't feeling either. She'd thought he'd lashed out to get her to leave, and so she had. To get a handle on herself before she lashed right back.

But he'd followed? Demanding that she be wrong when she was *right*, damn it. Damn *him*.

She advanced on him now, stalking right up to him, her hands balled into fists as though she might strike him. Not that it would do any good. Not that any of this was for any good.

She didn't know what it was for, just that something needed to explode. Something needed to...*something*.

He was the one who'd followed her to her room, so she would not temper her response to him. If he didn't like it, he could go. Back to that damn mountain of his.

"You act as though guilt is all there is," she shot at him. "The only valid response to everything you've lost. You act as if the guilt is the only thing in you—like nothing exists before it. Do you feel *anything* else?" She clutched his shirt. She couldn't seem to stop herself. She tried to shake him, but he was too solid, too strong. "Do you feel anything at all?" she demanded. Because maybe that was the real problem. She was assigning him feelings that weren't there.

That would never be there.

He stood there, eyes wide, breathing uneven but otherwise unmoved.

And there was no getting through to him. Not with Christmas. Not with memories. Not with kindness or acceptance or any of the things she'd employed so far. He did not want to be reached.

Why couldn't she accept that?

She shook her head, forcing herself to loosen her fingers, relinquish his shirt and him. She had to stop this, give up on him and what she'd hoped to accomplish in her father's memory. It wasn't healing *him*. And all it seemed to do was unravel *her*.

What would be left if she allowed herself to be unraveled? She was *alone*.

Alone.

Maybe that was really the source of all this. She'd reached out to him without fully realizing that what she'd actually been doing was hoping to avoid the horrible realization that she had no one.

Nothing.

Except this ridiculous job. And if he didn't care about anything, what was the damn point of this job anyway? The Folliero name could crumble, he could live his fake life off the grid and she could…

She could…

Something. She would find something. She had to. First, she had to leave. But before she could drop her hands from his chest, his closed over her wrists and held her there.

* * *

Too many feelings roared through Diego. He should have let her drop her hands. He should walk away now. He should *run* in the opposite direction. He knew this. Always, forever, he had done this. When emotions engulfed him, the only safety was retreat.

But her challenge anchored him in place. The tears in her eyes that did not fall, the demand of a question if he felt anything, like there was something more inside him.

Like only she could pull it out.

Except she was giving up on him, as everyone did. He should relish and celebrate this. It was what he wanted. What he always wanted.

And still he did not, could not, let her go.

Do you feel anything at all?

Hadn't that been the problem? Feeling too much? So much that he had to do something to block it all out? He had felt the weight of his parents' disappointment that he did not have his father's head for numbers, so he had gotten as far away from it as he could.

He had used his wealth and privilege to insulate himself from having to care about anything. If there was no hope, he could not disappoint.

And somehow, in his most pointless, useless moments, he had managed not to disappoint them, but to kill them.

What else could there be but guilt? What else should there be? All that existed before had died with them and the choices he'd made to end their lives.

"Are you going to let me go?" she said very quietly, laying down her challenges as only she seemed to be able to do. With quiet, precise cuts.

Without demands. Without disappointment. Without malice, even now.

She seemed to tie him up in knots but make those knots *his* rather than some expectation she'd placed upon him that he could fail.

"Or are you going to hold me here as prisoner?" she continued. "I seem to recall you threatening to toss me out not that long ago, and now you won't let me go."

He should do it. Let her quit. Fire her. Something. He should be the one making the choice. But he said nothing, and he did not let her go. He could see fury there in her placid gray eyes, but she kept it out of her voice. Even as every statement got a little more scathing.

"If you're waiting for me to kiss you again so you can issue warnings and storm away, I don't think I'm in the mood to play those games this afternoon. Perhaps another time."

He did not let her go. He could not look away. He just kept thinking about all the walls he'd built—willingly and unwillingly—to keep these swirling feelings at bay. To keep the emotions and the temper and the *needs* somewhere deep down under a surface that did not care.

And then even that lack of care he had punished with more walls and isolation and pain. Pain was penance. Pain was the price.

And there was pain in him now, but he did not recognize it. Because it *hurt*, but it was wrapped up in a warming want. In the floral scent of this room and her, the way she did not struggle against his hold or look away, like she, too, was snared in this net she did not understand.

Her cheeks slowly shaded pink, like she felt it too. She claimed she wasn't in the mood, but when he loosened the hands on her wrists, danced fingertips across the soft inner skin of her arm, she didn't dart away.

She let out a shuddering sigh and swayed toward him.

"It seems to me you are in the mood, *tesoro*," he said, his voice pained gravel. "Perhaps you are always in the mood when it comes to me, no matter how you *feel* about me."

He watched her face in fascination, in crackling, divided hope—that she might finally step away and leave him to this pain that he had chased down by coming to her room. Pain that was his due and the only thing he knew how to deal with.

And the other feeling one of hope, just as sharp and disastrous, that she might lean forward and dive into this chemistry he should not allow to exist. He should never allow himself to hope for.

But if he allowed it, if he fanned this flame and saw it to its completion, he would have ruined everything, and wasn't that the punishment he really wanted?

He lowered his head. She didn't stop him. She held his gaze as her breath caught in her throat, but she did not pull or push away. She did not turn her head.

And when his mouth touched hers, still waiting for her to stop this madness, she only sighed and leaned in. Just as she had the first time their mouths had touched. All gentle, careful exploration, when everything inside him was the opposite.

There was a raging, clawing beast inside his chest. He didn't understand why it didn't burst free, why the kiss remained gentle, why his grip on her was soft as it traveled up her arms to her shoulders to bring her closer.

"This will solve nothing," she murmured, there against his mouth, even as she pressed herself against him.

"Good." Because he didn't want to solve. He wanted to ruin.

Once and for all.

So he changed the angle of the kiss, the weight of his grasp, and threw them into the fire.

CHAPTER TWELVE

AMELIA KNEW SHE could stop this. The thought revolved in the back of her mind. It was too much, and all she had to do was say *no*.

She didn't want to. All the unknown things that lay on the other side were far too alluring.

No, this solved nothing. They could see this physical combustion through to the other side, and all that lay shattered and confused and undetermined would still exist and need dealing with.

But even without solutions, this was something. She could give him something good. He could give her something good. And if all that was left on the other side was wreckage, then at least she would be forced to *act*, to *be*.

To stop hiding here, not as different as his isolation as she'd like to pretend. That was what bringing him back had done. Maybe it hadn't fixed him, but it had made her realize just what *she'd* been doing.

It was a precipice, between hiding and surviving and flying and living. And if she let this moment expand and grow, if she gave over to the powerful chemistry between them, it would be choosing to grow up, to fly, to live.

It was time.

And then his grip tightened, and all thought was gone. She was nothing but a skittering heartbeat and throbbing pulse. She was nothing but a body, desperate to find pleasure in another body.

His low, throaty growl was one of possession, and it rumbled through her like expensive liquor. Smooth and brutal and potent. His hands moved up, fingers tangling in her hair. His tongue moved inside her mouth, tangling with her own, an almost violent fight for...something. She didn't know what, but she wanted to engage in it anyway.

She felt cool air and realized belatedly he was pulling her shirt up. He dragged his mouth away from hers, but only long enough to tug her shirt off and drop it on the ground. His mouth back on hers in seconds, his rough hands now on the bare skin of her back.

This was perhaps too much, too out of control.

And she *loved* it. The way her thoughts scattered and the only thing she could focus on was the jangling reaction of her body, the heat of his. The wild, twirling ride of his hands on her bare skin.

She wanted more. She threw herself into the kiss, into the dark, exotic taste of him, all while her fingers worked blindly to undo the buttons of his shirt. Once she'd succeeded, she pushed the shirt off, reveling in the sheer size of his shoulders, the hard muscle that existed there. Tense and vibrating while his mouth devoured hers, and his hands streaked down her back, cupping the curve of her bottom and pulling her flush with the hard length of him.

She moaned into his mouth, which tightened his grip and had sparks of throbbing, potent desire alighting every nerve ending. She wanted to ask him for something, but she had no words. Only noises.

Every touch was flame and joy. His teeth scraped down her neck, and she felt as though she'd been thrown into another universe, where pain and pleasure were one, and everything she wanted.

Over and over again.

He pushed down her pants and underwear together so that she was suddenly naked in front of him, her clothes a pile at her feet. And he didn't give her a chance to speak, to breathe. His hands cupped the most intimate part of her, turning her into a quivering mass of nothing but need.

He explored with his fingers, unerringly stroking every last nerve ending. Unerringly building her up only to ease away. Soften the touch, the kiss. Pull back until she made desperate noises, and then he would build her right back up again.

A riotous, torturous tease, and she could only stand there and take it, holding on to him while his mouth traced down the curve of her breast, then fixed over one taut nipple.

She cried out, or maybe just opened her mouth in a silent scream. The orgasm ripped through her like an avalanche, blanketing all that destruction with nothing but pure, unadulterated bliss.

Her knees were weak, and even the arms that held on to him tightly started to slip. But before she could simply fall into a spineless heap at his feet, he swept her into his arms and carried her over to her bed as if she weighed nothing.

He laid her out, looked down at her with those potent, hungry eyes. In this moment, the only thing that was true and right was that he wanted her.

And she wanted him.

Everything else had faded away. There was only this and them as his hands, so rough, so hot against her skin, toured a slow and thorough map of her body. His mouth followed. Everything he did stoked a million fires, and she wanted him to stoke them higher. But he still had his pants on.

There was no going back now. How could there be? She nudged him back, got to her knees as he was. She met his gaze, then found the clasp of his pants with her hands. She didn't look away from him, even as she struggled to undo his pants, unzip them.

There was no going back. No, the lines were crossed, and now she wanted everything.

She was perfection and not deserving it or her did not dull the sublime wonder of it all. The softness of her skin, the delicate sweetness of her taste. The way she enveloped him with warmth, with something that felt perilously close to belonging.

Her elegant pale hand wrapping around him, stroking, something like wonder there in her expression, but more than that. A consideration on her face, as though this was a new problem.

No, not a problem. A curiosity. The first warning bell was too faint to pay attention to, not when his body raged with need. His hand enveloped the back of her head, urging her closer and closer, until she opened her mouth for him.

He took his time, watching those pink lips envelop where he was too hard to stand. The sublime pleasure of it all, that she would be on her knees for him, the delicate perfection of her.

But this would not be enough, and it was already too much. He pulled her away, nudged her back and ranged over her in one swift move. Some other faint warning bell sounded, but he pushed it away harder, because she held on to him, arched up for him, her body begging even if she didn't verbalize what she wanted.

He didn't need her to. He positioned himself at her entrance, found her warm and ready, and he tortured himself with the impossible, glorious give of her. Inch by inch. A pleasure he'd denied himself these past two years, and yet it was still brighter and more glorious than even he remembered.

Until she stiffened there under him. This was a confusing response, so he looked down at her, that third warning bell ringing a little bit louder.

Her eyes were squeezed shut and a dawning horror had him pausing. "Amelia…"

But then she opened her eyes, heated silver. She fisted her hand in his hair and pulled him down for a punishing, bruising kiss and moved against him, making him forget…

She moved against him, so he moved with her. The tension melted away, her hand stayed fisted in his hair, as they rocked in the age-old dance.

Her shuddering release brought him too close to his own, and only the sneaking suspicion still lingering from that initial tension gave him the forethought to pull out, to spill across her stomach.

His muscles quivered as he held himself above her, looking down at her. Surely…he was wrong. He had to be wrong.

She wouldn't have done…*that*. She would have stopped this. She…

He had gone into this knowing there was nothing but ruin, but this… This was unconscionable. He could not hold his weight any longer, too many things roaring through him, least of all the spent wanting that didn't seem to have fully dissipated no matter how thoroughly he'd taken her.

Taken. He rolled onto his back, staring at the ceiling, but it lasted only a moment or two before he had to look at her. Had to make sure…

"You were not a virgin," he said, as if to convince himself. As if to make it true, when all evidence pointed...to the opposite.

Amelia said nothing. She lay there, the prettiest, most perfect picture, mussed and used and sated, expressly not looking at him.

"Amelia," he said darkly.

She turned her head toward him, her expression all feigned innocence. "What?"

"I asked you a question."

"No, you didn't," she replied with that same calm and clear gray gaze. "You made a statement."

His ears were still buzzing, his body still throbbing even as it began to cool. She... She... "Tell me, then, that you were not a virgin," he ground out. An order. Because she... couldn't be.

She met his gaze, chin raised, but she said nothing for a long time. Then, eventually, when he did not look away or let the moment go, she sighed. "Would you like me to lie?" she asked in that gentle way she had that made him feel like a fool.

Why was he naked in bed with a woman who made him feel like a *fool*? An innocent woman...innocent no longer. Because of *him*.

Maybe it was more of that punishment he loved so much, but it was hard to convince himself of that when some primal space deep inside *relished it*. No one else had touched her. She was his and his alone.

Except you deserve nothing and no one.

"You know, if you were concerned about it, you could have asked."

"Asked?" he repeated. "It never occurred..." He had to get away from her. He all but threw himself out of the bed, found his discarded pants and jerked them on. "You will not turn this around on me."

She made a move to get out of the bed, but he held out his hand. "Wait."

She stilled immediately, and he knew the satisfaction over that was misplaced, but it was there all the same. He strode over to her little bathroom, grabbed a frilly towel and made sure to wet it with warm water.

He returned, and when she looked at it with a quizzical expression, he scowled. Then did the deed himself, cleaning off her stomach in quick, efficient strokes.

Something soft and completely out of place was in her expression. He hated it.

"It's all right, you know," she said very gently. "I may be new to this, but I am on birth control."

"Fantastic," he ground out. "That certainly excuses taking your virginity. Your father would be so proud."

Her gentle expression sharpened, but she didn't make a move to cover herself or anything that she *should* be doing.

"You didn't *take* it. My virginity is not a cookie in a cookie jar for you to *steal*. This may come as a shock to you, but I was a fully cognizant and willing participant. This will be hard on you, I know, but I simply will not allow you to pretend *guilt* over something *I* chose. Not now. Not later. Not ever."

He hated how practical she was being when he wanted to rage. He wanted to claw the damn castello down.

And worse, so much worse, he wanted to cover her body with his again, and take and take and take, like he had any right to have something so bright and wonderful.

"Why have you upended everything?" he demanded, because he could not find a way to twist this into punishment.

He'd given himself exactly what he wanted.

She inhaled deeply, then let out a long sigh like she despaired of *him*. Then she rolled off the bed in an elegant move that had all his words scattering. He simply watched her move across the room, naked and glorious, before grabbing something from the back of a chair.

A silky green robe that she now shrugged into, her hair tousled, her cheeks a beautiful pink. He wanted to have his hands on her, and he did not fully understand the *why* of it, because he *was* experienced, and good sex and good chemistry were not unique or new.

But she was. Something about all *this* was. He felt as though there was some claw inside him, connecting him to her. He couldn't separate the physical from the connections they had, and it made it all so much more complicated and confusing and *weighty*.

When she finally faced him, that stubborn chin-up stance she was so good at, he expected a fight. Recriminations for blaming her for upending everything, when obviously they were both to blame.

There. He had shared blame because he would not take *all* of it. *She* had pushed.

And you are older and experienced and should know better.

So maybe the blame *was* all his. It should be.

"I think because it was time for everything to be upended," she said, with a little nod as if to punctuate how right she was. "You don't have to agree with me, of course. Blame suits you better, I know."

He shook his head. This woman had taken him into her bed, let him be her first, and yet she said things like *that*. Saw through him so easily.

"You think so highly of me, *tesoro*." He thought the sarcasm and bitterness might hide the way it scraped raw across whatever was left of his soul, but he saw that soft expression of hers take over.

"I actually do, in spite of evidence to the contrary," she said softly. "I know...you, even if you find that unfathomable. I have worked for you for two years, I knew your family and how you grew up, and I knew the one man who tried to be someone to you."

There were too many things going on inside him. All those things he'd learned to control with space and icy indifference were trying to find purchase. Or worse, they were trying to eradicate whatever purchase he'd managed all these years.

She stepped forward then, reached out and fitted her hand to his cheek.

"I think you have all the potential to be better than you have been. See, the point is not that I think the worst of you, Diego. You think the worst of yourself. My point is that I don't think you realize that is a choice. You could choose something different, and it's hard because you've never had to. But it doesn't mean it's impossible. Especially if you let someone reach out and help."

What was he doing, standing half naked in this woman's bedroom having a philosophical conversation about *choice*?

After he'd taken her virginity, or whatever the hell verb she'd rather use.

He stepped away from her hand. "I should go back to my cabin," he ground out, because this was becoming something intolerable. He'd crossed all the lines he'd once crossed without caring. He'd taken what he'd wanted rather than maintained his penance. It was wrong and he should go.

"What you *should* do is get dressed and come with me to look at some nativities. What you *should* do is decide why you think wasting your life away isolated from all signs of humanity and warmth is better penance than actually *living* for the people who cannot."

He didn't know what to say to these *should*s. Why should she be the one to know what he *should*? Why did she get to decide anything about what *he* should?

"I'll be in the car at noon," she told him. "You can meet me there or not. It is up to you, Diego. Your life, and only your life, is your choice. Your responsibility. Your consequences. Including the guilt you find so damn comfortable."

She did not storm away, as they had a habit of doing from each other. No, she walked over to her bathroom door, humming something that sounded suspiciously like "Joy to the World."

He watched her go, speechless and frozen in place.

What the hell had just happened?

A mistake. What could only be categorized as a mistake.

And you get to choose how to deal with it, Diego. Your responsibility. Your consequences.

He stalked away from her voice in his head, her room, her scent, and still didn't know what the hell to do with any of it.

CHAPTER THIRTEEN

Amelia didn't expect him to show up, not after the way they'd left things, but she'd hoped he might.

He did not. She waited, far too long, and Diego did not appear.

The only upside was that he had not left the castello yet. As he hadn't come with more than his little bag, she knew it wouldn't take him long to pack. So…maybe he wouldn't come see the nativities, but maybe he would stay.

And she would keep trying to get through to him. She wouldn't give up on him, no. If anything, this morning had made clear to her it was that…there was a way to get through to him. There were soft spots beneath all that barbed wire.

But she wasn't going to destroy herself to get to them. She would give him the opportunity to take it off.

Maybe Christmases past had been the wrong tactic. Maybe she needed to focus on *future* Christmases. Not for him. But for herself. Maybe… Maybe she had to do a little inner healing along the way to really help him.

She smiled at the thought as she got behind the wheel. It eased some of her frustration and disappointment that he hadn't come down.

Whether he joined her or not, she was going to go look at some nativities and enjoy herself. Because this wasn't just about *him*—his Christmas pasts, his guilt, his grief. It was about her, too, and she was ready to turn the page from past to future.

So she drove to Dolcina. She walked the streets, taking in the nativities. She took pictures of the ones she liked the best, shopped, and even took a break at a little café for *zeppole* and a coffee. She sat there and felt...renewed.

Sex with Diego had been oddly transformative. Not just because he had done things to her body she had never dreamed of doing with another person, never known *to* dream of. No, it was bigger than that.

She had fully engaged in something not for anything other than pleasure. She had thrown herself into something...*dangerous* wasn't the right word. The unknown, perhaps. She had taken a chance instead of hiding away. She had done something for *herself*, without being concerned about serving someone else.

And it had been glorious. It emboldened her to start thinking beyond just sex. Just Diego.

What did *she* want?

The truth was, it had been easy to stay at the castello and in her job because she *liked* both things. She excelled at handling Diego's business ventures and all his other holdings. She had a head for numbers, she knew how to deal with people and organization was something she got great satisfaction out of.

The life she'd been living *did* suit her. She had simply let it take up too much real estate. She had simply let it take over any self-reflection. She had focused on tasks rather than feelings. Even the way she'd been reading her father's journal, in small chunks, as if she could pretend he was still alive, still with her every night. As if, once she reached the end, he'd really be gone, so she avoided that eventuality.

But he was already *really* gone. The rate at which she read his journals changed nothing. It just allowed her to pretend she could put off that final grief, when the truth was that it was always here. Would always be here.

She had to do things in spite of the grief. Find joy and life beyond trying to live out her father's wishes.

She finished off her pastry, watching with a small, satisfied smile as snow began to fall. She gave herself a few minutes to enjoy the soft, picturesque perfection, then decided she should head back before the roads got bad.

She drove with renewed determination. She would go through with the Christmas Ball because it was a fine tradition and good for the castello. Because it would be good for Diego. *And* because she *liked* event planning.

Perhaps, if it was a success, she would focus more on that than meeting Deigo's every beck and call. She would still be happy to work for him, but he was going to have to start working for himself.

In the new year, they would both have to take some new steps, whether he wanted to or not.

Stepping into the future rather than hiding in the past.

She was humming "O Holy Night" as she walked back into the foyer of the castello. She stopped short when Diego surged forward, looking furious.

"Where have you been?" he demanded, a strange, frustrated energy pumping off him.

She unwound her scarf, hung it carefully on the peg. "Well, I went and looked at some nativities. Just as I told you I was going to."

His thunderous expression was almost amusing. She had not been fooling herself. She *knew* this man. Maybe he didn't know or understand her back—not yet—but that did not strip away her understanding of him.

Anger and ice hid all the more complex emotions, and seeing that in the context of what she knew about the Follieros, she suspected he'd developed those coping mechanisms at a young age.

"I came down," he muttered.

"Did you?" she asked, trying not to grin, trying not to be warmed from the inside out, or worse, apologetic. "At what time?"

His scowl was truly a thing of beauty. "I do not recall."

Which meant he'd come down very late expecting her to be waiting for him like a puppy. And she *had* waited for a time. Should she have waited longer? Should she have...

No. That wouldn't be her. That wouldn't be *them*. He was going to have to make some of the choices. He was going to have to start taking responsibility for himself and his own actions. She could give him some grace. He was new to that after all. But she wasn't going to allow him to coast along any longer.

"You have lessons to learn yet, but I am happy to teach them to you." She lifted onto her toes, brushed her mouth across his in a casual show of affection. But she liked it, and she was doing things she liked.

She tried to walk past him, but he grabbed her arm, pulled her back. "What is the meaning of this?"

"The meaning of what?"

"This? The humming? The kissing? The... You are not behaving the way you should."

"The way I should or the way you want me to?" she returned. She didn't try to escape his grasp. She liked his hands on her, in whatever ways he saw fit. And if that was a failing, she'd deal with it at another time.

When he said nothing to that, she didn't fight his grasp

but instead leaned into it, so it was more of an embrace than anything else. "Why did you come down?"

He frowned at her, eyebrows drawing together. "What do you mean?"

"You did not want to come see the nativities. You did not want to be around me. You wanted to sit in a dark room and hate yourself for some archaic feeling about *my* virginity. Yet you came down thinking I would be waiting for you and that you would go anyway. Why?"

He shook his head, and she didn't know if he was denying her interpretation or just answering.

Still, she was getting to know him, understand him. If she stayed here, eventually he would be compelled to answer. Because he was not as cut off or as formidable as he wanted to be. At least when it came to her.

"I was not going to go, but I did not want you waiting for me," he ground out.

Amelia was frozen for a moment. It was so clear now why he'd been angry when she'd walked in the door. What he'd been thinking.

She reached out, framed his face with her hands, her heart breaking for him. "Not everyone who waits for you dies, *caro*."

He jerked away from her grasp, but she did not let him move away from *her*.

"That isn't what I said," he growled.

"But it is what you were thinking." She gave him another light kiss, couldn't seem to help herself. He needed comfort. He needed warmth. He needed so much, and he was so determined to punish himself instead.

Well, the way she saw it, he'd had enough punishment. Maybe if she showed him the opposite, he would start to leave it behind.

Future over past.

And if that didn't work, she would accept it. She would not drown herself in it. No, she had to exist in this world too.

But first she would try. For the both of them. She pressed her mouth to his, not light or quick this time, but a kiss full of promise. A kiss full of all the *more* they'd had this morning, but with less frustration and anger tinging the atmosphere.

She expected him to resist. She expected a lecture, or maybe some more self-recriminations about *her* choices, but instead he sank into the kiss, his shoulders slumping in something like relief.

He'd been worried about her. Oh, he'd likely convinced himself he was just worried he would cause more harm. He would turn it into *him* being a problem, but that all stemmed from worry and care. He just framed it with him at the center because that's all he knew how to do.

Self-centeredness was not the same thing as self-absorption. He could learn to not center himself in everything. And she would teach him.

He wrenched his mouth away from hers, tried to detangle himself, but Amelia held on. There was something here, and she wouldn't make it easy for him to deny that.

She wasn't about to make anything *easy* on him.

"You don't have to stop."

"This is madness," he stated, but his hands were still in her hair. His eyes were fierce, but there was something lost behind all that fierceness. She could reach his lost, help him find his way. She knew she could.

"*You* are madness."

She laughed in spite of herself. He'd said it like an insult, but she'd never caused anyone *madness* before. It felt kind of powerful.

And if she had any power over this man, she would take it. Take it until he saw himself as a man worthy of something more than punishment. Take it until she led him from the dark to the light.

Diego did not know what had come over him. The living room had been one thing. A momentary lapse, relief that she had not died in some snowy wreck because he was cursed. He could have written that off.

But now it was the middle of the night, and he was in her bed, with her sleeping soundly beside him.

Everything had unraveled, been *upended*, and she might think it had needed that, but he did not think so. Upending confused things. His focus, his penance, was complicated now. Confusing. Instead of the one guiding light through a changed life.

He needed to get back to his cabin. To his penance and solace. He needed to find that center of pain instead of the enjoyment he found in her. It had all gone too far, and he needed to stop before he hurt her as badly as he'd hurt everyone he'd loved before he'd known better.

For some, love was a balm. He thought for his parents it had been. Love had likely saved them from being awful people, even if it hadn't helped them be good parents.

But for him, love had only ever meant confusion and pain. Deep emotions that the only way to deal with had been to separate. To isolate. So he didn't disappoint. So he didn't get cut loose.

He was meant to be alone. To stand on his own two feet. To stay far away from people who would be hurt by him.

Amelia would so easily be hurt by him.

And still, he did not return to his cabin in the morning or the next or the next. He spent his days at the castello, helping Amelia prepare for a damned ball he didn't want anything to do with. Yet day after day, he looked at pictures of his parents, of balls past, of the castello as it had looked in his childhood.

Day after day he was reminded of all he had lost, and it was supposed to be pain and punishment and what he deserved.

But something was happening inside him. Something was twisting those memories. Less like bricks and more like soft stones to be brought out and touched, their smooth, shiny exterior meant to comfort instead of weigh down.

Amelia spoke of *next year*. She spoke of future balls. Worst of all, she included him in that *future*. She spoke of how their "partnership" would need to change in the new year. She wanted to focus on events at the castello. He was going to have to take on more responsibility.

She spoke as if he was just going to *stay*. And he did not correct her. Not because he planned on staying, but because he did not know how to articulate how wrong she was about everything.

She had this rosy, happy version of a future in her head. Just as she seemed to have a rosy, happy version of the past there. She seemed determined to look on the positive side of *everything*, and he had never been around someone like that.

Even her father had not been full of *optimism*. Diego thought that was why he'd handled Bartolo as a slightly overbearing "assistant" as well as he had. They'd both had a rather nihilistic view of what the world was.

But Bartolo had thought in the face of that, you had to be the center of good in your life. That the world did not matter. It mattered what you did within the world.

I killed everyone I loved, including you, in that world. Then defiled your daughter. So.

A tiny bell tinkled somewhere, interrupting Diego's thoughts. A prickle went up his neck, a ridiculous feeling of…something. He shook it away. Amelia was standing over by the tree, fastening little bows to the limbs. No doubt there was some bell there in the tree she'd rustled with her work.

Tonight she was dressed in some soft, casual set in the color of holly berries. She buzzed around the castello like a top, as tomorrow the first guests for the ball would arrive. They would host a large holiday dinner. The following night would be the ball.

Her energy wasn't so much nervous as a determined kind of excitement. It did not remind him of his childhood, full of his mother's anxious meltdowns over napkins or RSVPs. Amelia reminded him of a determined bird—she might flit from one branch to another, but it was always with purpose.

But he could not understand her current purpose—there were enough ribbons on the damn tree to cover all of Italy. He poured some wine into a glass and walked over to her, urging her to take it.

She accepted the glass and stepped back to admire her work. "I don't know if that's enough."

"Well, I shall distract anyone who tries to count them."

She smiled up at him, bright and warm. "My hero. Or you will be, if you wear it."

She was the queen of these moments. Where a lancing pain, a horrible black cloud of all the ways he could not be the man she seemed to think he was, like a *hero*, were never quite strong enough to make him step away, because she immediately changed the subject.

No amount of having her dulled this ache. No amount of release seemed to change that she felt different from every sexual conquest who had come before. That something deep had lodged in his chest and he could not eradicate it.

But pain was the currency he lived his life by now, so as long as it hurt, he supposed it was not the worst thing that he stayed. Pain had to be right, didn't it? Even if it was punctuated by a strange feeling, something soft and settled—contentment, he might have called it.

If he was planning on staying longer than the new year. But he was not.

"I will not be wearing a Babbo Natale hat," he said darkly.

Mischief twinkled in her eyes. "Come now. Have some fun."

Fun. Even before the accident, his idea of *fun* had never been this. And what he might have called *fun* was less about happiness or joy and more about drowning all those complexities inside him.

Drowning had always felt far more comfortable than struggling to the surface. A realization that had all his hard-held beliefs about pain crumbling a bit at the edges.

So he shoved it away. He would not change. Changing was weakness.

Only punishment was strength.

So why are you still here?

He stared down at Amelia, beautiful and happy. She was why he was still here, and it was wrong. It would have to change, but…not yet. "Only if you've a La Befana costume in the works for January, *tesoro*."

"I will have my warts and broomstick ready to go."

The laugh rumbled through him, foreign and light, but anything light, warm, joyful was followed by the icy needled barbs of realization that he did not deserve it.

Alone, he could immediately seek more pain, more penance. With her, she seemed to sense it. Anticipate it and find some way to soothe it. A touch, a smile, a kind word. A kiss, a caress, more.

He should have left then. He knew that. He was getting to the point where he'd told himself it would need to end—where good outweighed the bad he deserved.

But he did not leave or push her away. Instead, when she pressed her mouth to his, soft and sweet, he let himself be soothed.

They had come together in many different ways, but gentleness permeated this moment. Something soft and fragile, and though he knew he did not deserve to touch it, he gave himself over to the need to tend it, worship it.

His touch was as soft as her skin, his kisses as gentle as her spirit. He undressed her with a tenderness he had never felt and would have been terrified of if he could think beyond the drugging honey of her mouth.

She unbuttoned his shirt without hurry, pushed it off his shoulders as if they had the rest of their lives to sink into this moment, into each other.

He knew they didn't, couldn't, but for a moment he let himself pretend.

He lowered her onto the rug, the sparkle of Christmas lights danced over her perfect skin. He pressed a delicate kiss to each refraction of light. Her fingers threaded through her hair as she murmured words of encouragement.

When he entered her, it was on a merged sigh that felt like *finally*. The physical pleasure bloomed with something else. Moving together in a slow, sensual dance. No thought to finding that last release, only the slow, unfurling blossom of a pleasure that went behind body to body, desire born of the sweet perfection of her body.

It had all become more, so much more.

She sighed his name, crested on a delicate wave. And still he did not rush or hurry. He tasted her, rolled with her so that she was atop him, taking her own pace and pleasure. A sensual angel, and all his. Only his.

His own release came on a rush of pleasure, of something deeper and alarming. It twined inside him, and when he realized that it was an emotion he could not label, he could not accept, it became pain.

It was a danger to feel this. To allow it. It was pain to have all this, all of *her*, open up something inside him.

Pain was the price.

He would accept it until it was not.

CHAPTER FOURTEEN

AMELIA WAS NERVOUS, though she didn't fully understand why. Even if things didn't go perfectly, she knew how to deal with event hiccups. She was excellent at smoothing them over. She had handled so many things as Diego's assistant over the past two years that this was hardly *new*.

Except he was here. And she could admit that every morning that she woke with him not just still *here* but in her bed, the more she allowed herself to hope.

Hope was what made her nervous. This happy, settled feeling was what had her heart take up residence in her throat more days than not.

She was nervous because she wanted Diego to enjoy himself. Because she wanted to make him proud.

Because she wanted him to see this whole thing as an expression of her love, even if it hadn't started out that way.

And yes, that was what *really* made her nervous, these feelings burgeoning inside her. She had thought by making sure she focused on herself in this endeavor, that whatever was happening with Diego would be secondary. Instead, becoming happy with herself and her life and accepting what she wanted, and taking stock of what she didn't, somehow made it easier to love.

And the hope he might feel in any way the same was a terrible weight in her midsection. She hadn't been able to stomach any food all day because *love* took up all the space. Love and not having a clue what to do about it.

He was not ready for it, she knew. *She* wasn't fully *ready* for it, but this whole thing had reminded her of all the ways life didn't care what you were ready for. She'd never been ready to lose her mother, to move from London to Italy, to meet a father she'd never known.

It didn't make up for losing her mother so young, but the opportunity to have her father in her life had brought joy.

And then tragedy.

Life was like a constant train, over peaks and valleys. She'd been hiding in a valley these past two years, but life was pushing her up the mountain.

She didn't know that she'd be allowed to drag Diego along with her, and that scared her because it would be a valley to lose him. He had become too much a part of her life. A *partner*. The past few weeks had been like living a little play version of what they could be.

Living in the castello, working side by side, sleeping in the same bed. The future spread out before them with so many options, so long as they were together.

"There you are."

Amelia turned to watch the man in question stride into her room. He held a plate in one hand, but he stopped short. His gaze raked over her, hungry and possessive, just the way she liked. Not that they had time for all *that*.

"You look beautiful," he said simply.

She beamed because compliments from him were rare. At least when they were dressed. "And you look very handsome." He was dressed for dinner in a dark suit. "Though it could use some Christmas pizazz."

He narrowed his eyes at the word *pizazz*, as she'd known he would.

"Never mind that. Mrs. Moretti informed me you have not eaten all day." He put the plate on the desk next to her.

"Oh..." She had to blink down at the plate because there was suddenly moisture in her eyes, and she couldn't let him see it. "You didn't have to worry about that. I'll eat at dinner. The guests should be arriving soon."

"You will eat now. We will not have you fainting. In my experience, this weekend brings out the worst in the people planning it. You have done very well, but we will not have that change."

She had to swallow the lump in her throat and work for a smile and light tone. "Your mother did tend to get a bit...unpredictable around the Christmas Ball. But it was just nerves, and your father always calmed her down. He only tended to lose his temper if he'd had too much wine, and your mother always made sure he was cut off at just the right time." Amelia helped herself to a little wedge of cheese and nibbled on it, hoping her stomach would hold.

"They managed each other well," Diego agreed. She didn't think he'd suddenly lost all bitterness toward his parents, but the more they discussed the past, the more at ease he seemed to come with it.

Like she'd been right all along.

"And your father often stepped in to alter their poor management of me," he said, almost offhandedly.

Amelia felt the now-familiar twining double-emotion reaction to Diego voluntarily mentioning her father. Sharing his experiences with Bartolo came in strange little bursts that filled her heart with equal parts grief and joy.

Amelia liked to think it was one of the things that brought them together, like another gift her father had left behind.

"He never lost his temper," she murmured, hoping to keep the conversation going. Any little scrap of information about her father was to be collected like a little jewel, but when they came from Diego, they were even more sparkling.

"Well, that's not altogether true," Diego returned. He picked up an olive and handed it to her.

Amelia regarded him. While she liked to think she knew her father *best*, Diego had full-on experiences with him before she'd even known who he was and vice versa, so she knew that there were parts of Bartolo that Diego would know that she would not. Still…

"I suppose you could drive a man to lose his temper," she said with a teasing smile, but she ate the olive as a kind of peace offering.

"Indeed. Especially in the early days. My parents hired him to take care of things for me while I was in university. I thought I was very worldly and adult, and I resented having no say in who was hired. I resented…much."

His eyebrows drew together. "I had the entire world in the palm of my hands, and I resented *everything*. I had everything, and I was patently unhappy." He shook his head. "I look back and I do not understand myself."

Amelia was afraid to say anything, that it might break the moment. Not just a memory of her father but also Diego engaging in self-reflection.

"But your father learned to deal with me eventually. In the early days, I think I infuriated him. Especially my…lackadaisical approach to university, you could say. He did not approve of my drinking, carousing and very actively *not* taking advantage of the education my parents were paying for."

Amelia swallowed. "He always wanted to go to university. He couldn't afford it, and his parents did not value education. That's why he was so insistent I have a good one, even though it made it necessary for him to mostly stay here rather than follow you about."

Diego frowned, looking a little arrested. She thought maybe she'd stepped wrong, that he'd close up now, but instead he kept talking.

"That puts things into...more context. I suppose if I'd ever thought beyond myself, I might have seen it. Instead, he seemed...overbearing and dull. An unfair punishment from my parents. One day I'd skipped my exams entirely, partied the whole night before, slept through the tests the next day. Your father had had enough of me at that point. He came into my room that afternoon and dumped an entire bucket of ice-cold water on me and lectured me about at least *going* to my exams, even if I was going to be a waste of space and fail them."

Amelia was shocked into a laugh. "You can't be serious."

"I think it's the angriest I've ever seen... I ever *saw* him. Usually he kept his temper very carefully arranged, you are right. But in the early days, when I had just gone off to university and it was his job to keep me in line...well, it was not all good feelings."

"It must have been hard for him, to work for someone who had so many more opportunities than he did."

"And waste them away. Yes, I did not make it easy, that is for sure." Diego handed her a cracker this time, and she would eat anything he handed her if he kept talking about it.

"I flew home immediately, found my parents here in the castello planning the damn Christmas Ball and told them they had to get rid of Bartolo immediately. Anyone who had ever been harsh with me before had immediately been sacked. A nanny, a butler. But when I went to my parents, told them what happened, I expected them to handle it. They had always handled it before, but...they told me I was a grown man now. If I didn't want Bartolo working for me, it was up to me to get rid of him. They were busy. With the ball."

Amelia frowned even though it did not surprise her, exactly. Her father had written of this. The way the Follieros had determined that at eighteen, a man was a man and their responsibility to their son was done, except financially. But she had never conceptualized what that meant until now.

To go from every whim being catered to, to handling everything yourself in no uncertain terms… "That must have been jarring," Amelia murmured as he handed her another wedge of cheese.

Diego laughed. This time there *was* bitterness. "Just months before I'd told them I was adult enough to hire my own assistants. Now I was yelling at them to fire this one." He shook his head. "And you are right. Even though I claimed to want it, them forcing me to handle something was jarring. I didn't realize it would happen, that they would cut me loose. Oh, not in any real way. I had the money I had, the privilege I had, but they were done…managing it, I suppose. I wasn't prepared. It's not an excuse, of course, but it was…alarming."

"Alarming or terrifying?"

He frowned at her. "Does it matter? I was a spoiled child. And I needed to grow up. I didn't then, but I needed to."

Amelia contemplated how much to give. How much would only make him feel badly. How much would help heal. "It is a parent's job to set their children off in the world. My father said that to me more than once. That it was hard, but he wanted me to be able to exist on my own two feet. It is the *job* of parenting."

"Then I suppose my parents did their job."

"Maybe. Sort of. But you see, even when my father was setting me off into the world, he was there as a soft place to land if I made a mistake. He was *there*. He did not simply…stop being a parent."

"And then he died," Diego pointed out. The implied *because of me* hung in the air.

"Yes, he did, but I'd had the soft landing just the same." Before she lost Diego to his guilt, she grabbed on to the past. "So, what happened after your parents told you to handle his insubordination yourself? You didn't sack him, obviously."

"I tried, I suppose. He'd followed me to the castello, waited outside the room where I'd yelled at my parents to fire him. I walked out and there he sat. I was fuming, so I told him that I would no longer need him as my assistant. That I would not tolerate insubordination. Particularly when it came in the form of physical attacks. I was pompous and overwrought, and your father sat there and nodded along like I was right."

Amelia smiled in spite of herself. That was how he'd gone about winning an argument. Agreeing and agreeing until a person began to realize they were being ridiculous, and Bartolo Baresi was right as usual.

"He stood and shook my hand. Told me he hoped that I took away the lesson he'd wanted to impart. That it was my job to take responsibility for things. That no one else could do it for me. That even my privilege and my parents and my money couldn't excuse me from basic self-responsibility. He said he could leave, then and there, and I could hire any replacement I saw fit. Or we could consider it a fresh start."

Amelia wrapped her arm around Diego, squeezed. "You took the fresh start."

Diego shook his head. "I was being lazy. I didn't want to hire someone else to handle things like correspondence and arranging travel and the like. I wanted someone to do it, and I didn't really care who."

She studied him then. He would remember all the bad… "I wonder, Diego, what made you decide you could not take responsibility for anything except the bad."

His frown turned into something like dawning horror, but the doorbell that played "Ave Maria" sounded around them.

"That'll be our first guest." She rose onto her toes, pressed a kiss to his cheek. "But if you must blame yourself for *everything*, I'd consider that this requires blaming yourself for the good too."

And with that, she left her room, blinking back tears, to greet their first guest.

Diego had known the dinner would be an exercise in annoyance, discomfort and pain. He told himself that was why he'd come. Why he was still here. To see through these terribly painful things. His punishment.

He told himself it had nothing to do with Amelia.

It had everything to do with *her*.

The realization creeped up on him over the course of the evening. A terrible, choking thing he had to pretend wasn't there along with all the grief that shrouded every corner like ghosts of Christmases past.

If he wasn't here for *her*, he would have walked out of the room the first time someone came up to him to express their sympathies over the loss of his family. He would have walked away from the castello and the idea of taking credit for anything *good* forever.

Instead, he stayed. Instead, he nodded along to the sympathies, the stories, the memories. Mostly, it could have been worse, he supposed. But it was as if that thought made the *worst* appear.

Luliana Longo had been a staple at this weekend in his youth, and he'd never understood why his mother insisted on inviting her worst enemy to their *home*. But Mother had thought it gave her the upper hand, to never slight Luliana, no matter how mean and grasping she could be.

"It has been *forever*." She airbrushed kisses across his cheek, then rocked back to study him with sharp eyes he remembered.

She'd liked to pinch young children who got "too loud," then feigned ignorance if they tattled. Diego hadn't tattled. He'd gotten even. He and Aurora had gotten back at her by pouring gravy in her purse. No one had ever been able to prove it was them, either, as Luliana had spent the entire weekend making people mad.

The memory brought him joy. And a sarcastic retort. "If only," Diego replied, but he said it with a smile, so Luliana was frozen there, unsure how to respond.

His smile grew wider.

It was almost as if Luliana saw that smile as a personal affront, or a challenge.

"This brings back so many memories of your dear mother." She blinked a few times, as if to give off the impression of tears, though her dark eyes remained dry as dust. "And that sister of yours. She was…a free spirit, wasn't she? I don't know how you stand it. Being here. Remembering them. Their lives cut so short."

"You're here. Remembering them," Diego pointed out. "I suppose that is what we humans must do. *Remember*." It was something Amelia would say, though she would probably mean it.

"Of course," Luliana replied dully, but then she immediately perked up. "You missed so many of these. Off galivanting. Leaving your poor sister to be one of the few youngsters. She never took it well. It was always the talk of the weekend. What temper tantrum would Aurora throw?"

"None, this time around."

Luliana's mouth dropped at the crude reminder, but it brought Diego no joy because it was only the truth.

Sadly it wasn't enough of a truth to dislodge Luliana from doing whatever it was she was hoping to do. Because she kept talking. Determined, clearly, to tell whatever story she'd approached him to tell.

"You weren't here, but I remember the last ball. My! Aurora got into quite the row with your mother." The woman dabbed her eyes, but Diego could not find any true sadness there. The dark gaze darted around to the chandeliers, the expensive crystal, likely totaling it all down to the cent.

She'd wanted to buy the castello from him. Had harassed him, in fact, those first few weeks under the guise of *helping* him.

He'd forced Amelia to handle it as her first job as his assistant. He blinked once, wondering how he'd forgotten such things. But he'd been...

His first instinct was to call it guilt-ridden, but these days, with Amelia's influence, he couldn't seem to pretend it was anything other than grief and depression. And in the depths of that, this woman had poked at him.

He'd have to ask Amelia what she'd done to get her to back off.

"I've never seen a child say such nasty things to their parents," Luliana continued. "Certainly not in *front* of people." She tsked, as if it were a great shame. Instead of the fact that Aurora being *dead* was the shame.

Diego would have felt anger. Maybe it was kindling underneath the heavy swath of darkness. He wasn't sure.

But the last ball, the one he was supposed to have attended but had decided last minute not to put himself through it, had been right before they'd died. And Aurora and Mother had gotten into a public fight.

He could only hope they'd made amends before...

It was a dark pall, or it would have been, one that sat there and festered, if Amelia had not interrupted.

She slid into the seat next to Diego, moving her arm over the back of his neck. "My favorite memory of Aurora was the year she performed an entire ballet recital at the Christmas Ball. Did you ever hear about that, Diego?"

He could only stare at her, a bright little light in all this vicious darkness. He didn't answer, but she went on with the story anyway.

Aurora had meant to perform a piano recital but had never practiced. So she'd made Amelia play while she performed a little ballet routine she'd designed herself. It had impressed everyone, even Mother, who had always wanted Aurora to be a pianist, not a dancer.

The story was bittersweet. Since Aurora was dead and hadn't gotten to live any life she should have been able to, but something about the laughter, about how easy he could picture Aurora eating up the crowd's—and their parents'— reactions made it feel as though she lived on. In that memory that had everyone laughing or smiling *now*.

Amelia had done that—not just here, he realized in a startling kind of wonder as the decadent *struffoli* was presented to the table. But constantly since she'd threatened him down the mountain.

She had taken all his darkest edges and offered them a kinder edge. Every horrible memory softened with a reason or a better memory. Every stab of guilt he tried to carry, she tried to lift up and away from him.

As if this penance wasn't his to carry.

She made that seem possible. Amelia made it all seem like he wasn't deluding himself. He could have a life. One with happiness and joy and people and *her*, and it wouldn't be a degradation of the people he'd lost.

When that could never be true.

He made it through the rest of the dinner, noted how easily Amelia kept Luliana busy and away from him, down to escorting her to her room for the night after Luliana claimed there was something wrong with her accommodations.

Amelia insisted on taking care of it herself. And while she did, and everyone else drifted off to their rooms, happily full and a little drunk, merry and bright, Diego found himself alone in the great ballroom, where the ball would be tomorrow. It was dark except for all the Christmas lights that twinkled on the tree.

And he knew, in this darkness punctuated by light, that he had allowed himself too much. This was no longer pain. It was something bigger, something he did not deserve.

So now it was time to cut it off.

He had never shown up for anyone who needed him. He had only caused pain. So he could not take this chance at something more than darkness.

He would see the ball through. He would not make *this* harder on *Amelia*. But after...

After, they would need to come to an understanding. His first instinct was to run. To disappear.

But she'd reminded him of the lesson Bartolo had been so desperate to impart on him. He had a responsibility. He could not run away any longer. His choices, good and bad, were his. And they had effects on other people.

"I am sorry it took me killing you all to realize it," he muttered—foolishly, he knew. But there was the strangest *heft* to the air, as if four sets of eyes were on him when there was no one in the room. The lights on the tree twinkled in reds, greens and whites, the air around him still and cool.

Tomorrow, people would be crushed into this room. Dancing, drinking, caroling. It would smell like cinnamon and pine and expensive perfume. There would be joy and celebration, and all because Amelia had decided to make joy.

And tried to give it to him when he didn't deserve it. Her heart was too soft. Her forgiveness too easy. She was young and naive. She didn't understand.

So this had to end.

One more night together. A goodbye of sorts. He would stay through the ball because he did not want to ruin it for her, because whether she realized it or not, she had not thrown the ball *only* for him.

She'd thrown it for herself too. A goodbye, and a step in the direction of her future, all at the same time. Amelia was good at that—those dichotomies.

He did not know how to do both. How to constantly live in two worlds—sadness and hope. Love and regret. Grief and joy in memory. They would split him apart.

No, he would never be able to give her that, and that was where she belonged.

Tomorrow night, he would return to where he belonged. It would not be running away. It would be a concrete, careful choice this time.

Because the choice he'd made two years ago had ended too many lives, and he did not deserve a life of happiness in the one place he'd always run away from, with the daughter of the man who'd taught him every important lesson.

She deserved better. So she would have better.

His choice. His consequences.

What about Amelia's?

He stood staring at the tree, a lancing pain in his chest. The voice in his head sounded too much like hers.

Then a bell tinkled somewhere in the tree, sending a shiver down his spine.

So he left the tree and went to find his goodbye.

CHAPTER FIFTEEN

AMELIA SPENT MOST of her day bustling about, making sure guests were happy and the preparations for the ball were taking place behind the closed ballroom doors, where no one could fully see how the magic was made.

She did not know what Diego was up to, but occasionally she would rush to do something only to be told by one of the staff that Diego had handled it.

Making her job easier.

Every time, it left her a little breathless. Like she wasn't delusional to think that something was happening. A great awakening. A healing. That the tiniest seed of hope for a future might have been planted in Diego and this was how he was showing her.

He wanted to be here. With her. Her partner. The two of them taking care of each other and stepping into the *future*, even as they honored the past.

She wanted that seed to grow, so she didn't allow the fear to dull her hopes. That wasn't what Christmas was about, to her mind. This was the season for hope and magic and joy. She would lean into that.

So tonight. She would tell him tonight.

After the ball, curled up together in what had become *their* bed, she would tell him that she was in love with him. And whatever came after that was hers to deal with.

Her decision. Her consequences.

She liked to think it was full circle. To change what the ball might mean to him into something good. To show him change was possible. Healing was possible. *Good* was possible and he wasn't undeserving.

She didn't allow herself to consider his reaction. It wasn't about *his* reaction. It was about what she felt and sharing it with him. He got to choose how he dealt with that. She could not control it.

If he crushed her heart, at least she'd done something for herself rather than be afraid, rather than blindly follow some grief-stricken attempt to bring her father back to life by doing what he wanted.

Her feelings for Diego were hers and hers alone, and every step she'd made with him had brought them closer together. Every time she'd reached out, he'd followed.

That truth propelled her through the day. Through issues that cropped up that she had to problem-solve. Then up to her room to get ready for the ball itself. She half expected to find Diego here, but he wasn't.

Still, she stopped short because laid out on the bed was a dress of dark red, certainly not hers. She moved toward it, wondering if a staff member had somehow gotten confused and put a guest's dress in her room.

But there was a note laid across the dress. In slashing script she recognized as Diego's handwriting, it said: *Merry Christmas*.

She couldn't even imagine how much it had cost. She supposed that wasn't the point. Considering she handled much of Diego's businesses in some capacity, she knew he could afford it.

That he'd *thought* of it was the point. A gesture that showed he paid attention and had considered this night at least long enough ago to have the dress purchased in advance.

She wished he'd had the courage to give it to her himself, be here to handle her appreciation, but she saw this as progress. As a step toward a future where they were both a little stronger.

He'd started at the bottom of a deep pit of self-loathing and survivor's guilt. She could hardly expect him to jump out of it quickly and easily. Healing required time.

But steps were encouraging.

She smiled, trailing a finger over the velvety fabric, then set about getting ready as she listened to Christmas carols. Once finished, she surveyed herself in the mirror, impressed with the results.

Feeling like some kind of joyous Christmas fairy, she went in search of Diego, hoping to find him before she needed to be in the ballroom.

He wasn't in his room, or anywhere in their personal wing of the castello, so she went down the staircase, only to find him waiting at the bottom. He was dressed in a dark suit, dark shirt underneath. He would not have looked at all festive, instead more like an angel of death, but he had worn the tie she'd set out for him.

It had been his father's. It was a deep green that almost looked black when surrounded by so much of it, but there were little sprigs of lighter green and dark red holly embroidered all over it. A little Christmas pizazz.

For a moment, Amelia didn't move down the stairs. She just stood at the top, looking at him. That tie felt like a sign. Just like the dress. Just like last night.

She couldn't fight all the hope inside her. He *was* changing and opening up. How could she think he'd reject love when he had taken all these steps?

He was staying for the ball, and he was wearing his father's Christmas-themed tie. He had smiled at her story about Aurora last night. These were all steps back into the light, and maybe it was conceited to think she was part of it, but he smiled up at her, there at the top of the stairs.

Because there was something *here*, and they only needed the chance to build from it. She took the stairs down to him.

"You are stunning, *tesoro*."

"Thank you for the dress," she said as she reached the bottom. "It's certainly perfect for the occasion."

He took her hand, brushed a kiss across her knuckles. "As are you. The person responsible for such a night should certainly look it."

She beamed at him, then reached out and straightened his tie, which didn't need straightening. She looked up at his face, wondering if he did not remember that it had been his father's. He'd avoided the Christmas Ball for most of his adult life.

He tucked her arm into his, not mentioning anything about the tie. She would bring it up later. First, they had to face their guests.

While some were odious like that Longo woman who had been disparaging Aurora last night—and who would be forever removed from the guest list thereafter—many were kind, enjoyed both the atmosphere and remembering their old friends they'd lost too soon.

As the ballroom filled with these people, she and Diego mingled. They danced, close enough for people to whisper. Amelia didn't concern herself with it. If they were scandalized by the age difference, by Diego being her boss, by *whatever*, she didn't care.

This was right and real. So she enjoyed herself. She didn't worry when a guest spilled red wine on the expensive antique rug. She didn't fuss over a couple getting into an argument, simply escorted the woman away while Diego escorted the man, and calmed them down. She took each hiccup as it came, dealt with it and moved on.

Because she knew how to plan an event, make it sing. And come the new year, that's what she'd do. She'd help Diego find a new assistant—while encouraging him to take back some of his own responsibilities—and she would focus on events. Either at the castello if Diego approved, or somewhere else if he did not.

As for their relationship...that left a pit of nerves and fear in her stomach. If he returned her expression of love, then... Then they could move forward as they had been. She'd liked these past few weeks.

If he didn't... Well, she wasn't ready to consider that. *That* she would deal with as it came.

The guests began to slowly trickle away, calling it a night, thanking Amelia in many different ways. A few brought tears to her eyes when they said she had thrown as good of an event as the former hostess, and how much that had meant to them.

Yes, tonight had been healing for many. Once the last guest had filtered away, Amelia sat herself on the chaise longue, not having the energy to go upstairs just yet. She slipped off her shoes and sighed at the relief from the heels.

The room glittered, and Diego stood over by the bar, nursing a drink. Amelia could not read his expression, but something like a portent fizzled over her skin.

She pushed it away. "Why don't you turn off the lights and come sit next to me?" she suggested.

There was a moment of hesitation that might have concerned her, but he faced her with a sly grin. "With guests in the home? For shame, *tesoro*."

She chuckled and shook her head. "I want to enjoy the tree lights. Turn the overheads off and come."

He did as beckoned, turned off the overhead lighting so now it was only the twinkling red, green and white of the tree. Amelia knew all the work that had gone into that tree. She knew it was simply some electricity and bits of shiny things placed carefully, but it felt like magic all the same.

Diego slid onto the chaise next to her, and she leaned against him, appreciating the strong warmth of his body.

"It was the perfect night." Just perfect. Even the hiccups had been perfect, because they allowed it to feel real. They would look back on tonight with smiles, satisfaction over handling everything that had come their way.

She turned to him in the glow of the Christmas tree she'd decorated for him. So that he could return to the castello and remember. Feel. Come back to life.

She wanted to look back on this moment, this night, and remember it for being the perfect start to something beautiful and lasting.

His face lit by the twinkling lights, the shadows around them like a cocoon rather than any darkness. But life was both.

And she wanted both with him.

Perhaps she should ease into it, warn him a bit before the words escaped, but in the end, Amelia only had the simplicity of the feeling.

"I love you, Diego."

Amelia had not let herself imagine the moment after. She'd simply told herself she'd handle whatever came her way. Even if he rejected her. This wasn't about *him*. It was about how *she* felt.

But the way he froze, his eyes going flat and blank, was like being stabbed through the heart.

And she hadn't prepared for that at all.

* * *

Diego did not panic. Not outwardly. Not just yet. He had not considered... Not yet...

Perhaps he should have. And because, perhaps, he'd seen it there in her eyes even if he'd pretended he hadn't, he didn't panic. He wasn't ready, but a part of him was.

Because he'd already decided what he'd do, which was why he'd given himself leave to enjoy tonight. A goodbye for *her*.

But now she was talking about the opposite of goodbye, and he would have to ruin everything.

Yes, he supposed it was the punishment he deserved.

Carefully, he took her arm from around him, slid out from the weight of her and her *love*, and got to his feet.

When that was not quite enough to allow him a careful breath, he took a few steps away from the chaise. He had to look away from her, picture perfect in the warm glow of Christmas tree lights, in the dress he'd bought knowing she would look like some kind of Christmas angel.

Which had made it clear, *again*, how little he deserved this respite. How completely he belonged on his mountain, paying his penance. She wasn't going to understand that, but she couldn't. She did not have blood on her hands like he did. She had only grief, not blame.

He'd never convince her, so he didn't set out to. He simply set out to make this as little of a wound on her as possible.

He considered his words, weighed them. Then made sure to deliver them with an authority she would not be able to argue. "Amelia, you are mistaken."

For a moment, a tense silence settled over the room like a lead weight. When she spoke, her tone was cool and cutting. "There's no need to be an idiot about it."

He blinked once, opened his mouth, but no words came. An *idiot*. She'd called him...

She got to her feet now. Without the heels, she barely came up to his chin, but she had the stance of a fighter ready to brawl.

"I know how I feel, Diego. Now, you do not have to feel the same, but you will do me the courtesy of acknowledging that I am a grown woman in charge of my own feelings. I do not say what I do not mean."

"Very well," he said carefully, a negotiator trying to avoid the explosion. "You are not mistaken." He should leave it at that, but... "But you are wrong."

The noise she made was one of such outrage he was surprised it wasn't followed by a blow.

"You are young. You are...inexperienced. And you do not know me."

"Not...*know* you? I have handled every ounce of your business while you've hidden away for *two years*. I was raised by the man who tried to instill every good virtue into you because he saw something in you. *I* see something in you, Diego. Why do you refuse to see it in yourself?"

He hated her question, the way it created storms in his chest, the way it made it hard to breathe. All the ways emotion upended. All the ways thinking too deeply about who he was, who he could be, *hurt*.

So he did not answer her question. He focused on the statements. On the facts. On things that were not at all complicated, but straightforward and sure.

"You are right. I did hide. These past two years I have been hiding. These few weeks have been...informative. But it does not change the basic fact that I deserve this punishment. Now I simply have a better understanding of the *how*s and *why*s of it. I will return to my cabin with a clearer picture of exactly what I deserve. Less about hiding. More about...accepting."

She shook her head. Her eyes were a bright quicksilver, shiny with moisture, but no tears fell. He assumed the color high on her cheeks was temper, because she seemed far more angry than hurt, though he knew she was both.

"I thought you..." She sucked in a breath, seemed to reconsider whatever she'd been about to say. "Do you really think you're unique?"

This question didn't create storms, because it made no sense. "I beg your pardon?"

"You don't think I could look at that day and pick apart a million things I could have done differently that would have kept them from getting on that plane?"

It never failed to amaze him how totally she could silence him. The question was a sharp, burning lance, even when he didn't understand it. Like his heart could absorb her words, but his mind could not.

"Aurora begged me to lie to your parents and tell them she was sick. She thought if *I* lied to them, they might actually believe it. Might actually let her stay behind. She didn't want to go off to Spain for the new year. She wanted to stay here. I could have tried to help her, and she would be alive."

"Amelia..." The thought of Aurora alive because of something Amelia had chosen was...insanity. She couldn't possibly...

"Do you think I'm making it up?" she demanded, enough high-pitched near hysteria tinging her tone that he knew better than to say *yes*.

"Let's take my father, then, shall we? They would be gone over his birthday, and I was irritated that he had not tried to take the day off. That he worked remotely with you all the time, so why did he need to go to Spain with you on his birthday? *I* wanted to spend the day with him. I didn't tell him that, though, because I was hurt he did not want to spend the day with me. I could have told him, asked him to stay. He would have. He would have done anything for you, Diego, but I trumped you. If I asked. Instead, I gave him a chilly goodbye and let him go."

These were not the same. She couldn't make them into the same thing. He had chosen what he'd chosen out of selfishness, and a need to punish his parents for things even to this day he could not fully articulate.

She had simply been herself.

But she kept *talking*.

"You think I didn't go over those events those first few weeks? Pick apart every instance, every instinct that might have changed the outcome of that plane ride? You think that these feelings, these questions, these horrible things, are unique to *you*?"

"It is not the same as—"

"It is *exactly* the same as. Do you think the world revolves around you? That you control all its outcomes? Still? We have no control over the damn world around us, Diego. It will do what it wants. No matter what choices you make. Guilt is just a phase of grief, a misguided belief we have some control, but we have *no* control. Not about the end."

He did not disagree with her. The world was mean and cruel, but so had he been. Self-absorbed and uninterested in anyone else's feelings. Maybe sometimes he'd listened to Bartolo; maybe sometimes there'd been a glimmer of thinking he could be a better man.

The kind who handled his own life and problems. Who didn't let the tides of temper and rejection sway him into deeper holes he dug himself into.

Who loved.

He stared at Amelia now. One tear had fallen, and it trailed down her perfect cheek. Maybe if she wasn't so perfect, he could believe in this.

But he could never be good enough for her.

If he stayed, he would be tempted to listen, to absorb. She would absolve him, and he'd always known that couldn't happen. He couldn't *let* that happen.

He didn't deserve it.

So he did the only thing he could think of.

He turned on his heel and left. He ran away. Not just from the room. He went to the back part of the house that led out to where the cars were parked, took Amelia's keys and drove away.

Forever.

CHAPTER SIXTEEN

It was pitch-black, and Amelia's car did not handle as well as Diego had expected it to as he reached the elevation where snow began to fall much harder than picturesque flurries. Diego clutched the wheel and navigated the treacherous turns with his muscles tensed and his jaw clenched tight.

The headlights did little to cut through the blinding white of blustering snow and the darkened world around it. Occasionally, he thought of turning around. It almost felt as if something was pushing him down the mountain. Almost as if Amelia was pulling him back.

Because that was tempting, and what he wanted, he fought that push and pull and doubled down on his own will.

His tires spun for a moment before finding the traction to lurch forward at a speed Diego wasn't prepared for. The dangerous curve ahead suddenly came too quickly. He slammed on the brakes, which threw the car into a dangerous skid.

He course-corrected, managed to stay on the road rather than crash into the rocky wall to the left or off the treacherous cliff to the right. His heart hammered against his ribs, but he'd avoided disaster. At least so far.

He sucked in a breath and carefully let it out, squinting

into the white world around him. It took a few minutes to fully realize he wasn't stopped, though. The car was…sliding backward.

No amount of brake or accelerator was stopping his movement. He gripped the wheel harder, as if he could will the entire car to do what he wanted by sheer force.

But the car just kept inching back. He jerked on the emergency brake. For a moment, he thought it would hold.

But it only did for that moment, and then he was skidding backward, down the road the wrong way, with another dangerous curve right behind him.

He had two choices. Allow it to, or try to guide the steering wheel so he did not go off the side.

For a moment, he faltered over the choice. Falling off the cliff would be certain death, and didn't he deserve that? Perhaps in exactly this way. Maybe this would be his final penance.

Death would be a reprieve.

Just like love would be.

That strange thought had him turning the wheel, eyes on the rearview, wondering if he could really navigate his way down the road backward in a snowstorm. Even if he tried his hardest, was it possible to do this until even ground stopped his momentum?

Or should he give up? Maybe it was all poetic justice. To die on this mountain. To die, just like they had.

He might have stopped fighting. He could feel that thought crossing his mind, but Amelia crossed his mind too.

She had felt guilt about the plane crash. She had wondered if everything would have changed if she'd done something different. The idea of it still curdled in his gut. How could she possibly have blamed herself? How could she have carried any guilt, even if only for a short time?

When the guilt was all his.

But if she'd felt guilt *then*, would she blame herself over this when he'd been the one to make the decision to leave? To drive into a snowstorm?

Would she feel grief and guilt if he died even though he'd been the one taking his life into his hands?

Couldn't you say the same of your parents and the pilot who decided to take off in increasingly bad weather?

Amelia's voice in his head again. The plane had waited for him because he was supposed to be there. If he had gone and been on time, no one would have had to make that choice. His choice started theirs.

Was it your choice that they would not take your no for an answer? That you did not want to travel with them?

He shook his head and pumped the brake once more, hoping to slow the skid. Hoping to do something.

Instead, it sent him into a spin he could not control this time. Momentum gained and he could not keep the wheel in the direction it needed to be, no matter how hard he fought. With a howl of wind, the side of the car crashed into the side of the mountain.

Glass shattered, pain erupted in his head as the car jerked, crumpled. He felt fire and ice. Pain, pain, nothing but pain.

He was thrust into darkness, and he did not know how to find light.

Amelia cried herself to sleep, what little there was to be had of sleep. The crying wasn't all about Diego, either, though he was the catalyst.

In some ways, it felt like reliving those first few weeks after the crash. The guilt, the pain, the knowledge that nothing would ever be the same. That Diego would never be free of those things, and somehow she was caught up in that because she couldn't get through to him.

She'd told him about her own guilt, thinking it would matter. And it hadn't.

She hated thinking about all the things that felt changeable about that day. She didn't know how Diego had sunk into such awful feelings. They did nothing but weigh her down, make everything seem hopeless and impossible.

How was this any way to live?

But she supposed that was why she understood him, grieved for him, couldn't bring herself to hate him. She'd felt those things herself. It had taken experience and the way her father had guided her through her mother's death to handle them in a way that was healthy.

Diego had none of that. Only the guilt, and for whatever many reasons, he'd gone through life only trusting the bad feelings. Perhaps those had been the only ones that had ever earned him attention from his parents, and so he'd doubled down.

But it only made all the rifts worse.

"And you cannot fix that, Amelia. You were utterly foolish to think you might have." With those firm words spoken aloud to herself, she got out of bed, got dressed and went to deal with her *job*.

It was well before dawn, but she would have to deal with making sure the guests got off safely and soundly, so she wanted to be up and moving.

But the moment she stepped out of her room, she found Mondo and Mrs. Moretti. They were whispering urgently to each other at the end of the hall but stopped when she stepped into the hallway.

They didn't say anything at first, just stared at her with wide eyes.

"Is something amiss?" she asked carefully, fear prickling her skin into goose bumps.

Mrs. Moretti pushed Mondo forward. He looked over his shoulder at her, reminding Amelia of a child pleading to not have to confess to something. Mrs. Moretti was obviously having none of it.

Mondo looked at Amelia sheepishly, apologetically. "Ms. Baresi..." He nervously clutched his hands together, but after a moment or two of her waiting, he straightened his shoulders and dropped his hands. It was like watching a boy mature right in front of her.

"Ms. Baresi, your car is missing."

For a moment, Amelia could think of nothing to say. Her car... Why would anyone take her car?

But then it dawned on her. Diego hadn't just left her presence last night. He'd left the castello.

And stolen her damn car. The *gall*.

"We checked the security footage and—"

"Mr. Folliero took it," Amelia said flatly. It didn't take a rocket scientist to put that together.

"Yes, ma'am," he said apologetically, like any of this was his fault. "We didn't know if... We weren't sure how to...proceed."

Amelia looked from Mondo to Mrs. Moretti. How to proceed. She wanted to laugh. She wanted to go back to bed and just *cry*.

But that solved nothing, and she was in charge here. Because the man in question refused to be.

"For right now, we'll leave it be," she said, trying to sound unbothered. "It's more important we get the guests where they need to be. Use whatever cars you have access to. You have my permission."

"Yes, ma'am." But he didn't leave to do her bidding. He

hesitated, stepping a little closer, lowering his voice as if it might stop Mrs. Moretti from hearing. "I can go get him. It wouldn't take me any time at all."

That sat there between them, like they both knew where Diego had gone. Because where else would he go besides that damn cabin?

"No need, Mondo." Tears filled her eyes, but she blinked them back, coughed the roughness out of her voice and plastered an insincere smile on her face. "We'll handle getting the car back after Christmas." She put extra emphasis on the word *car*. So there was no confusion here.

They would not be going to fetch Diego. He was making his own decision, and she would not change it even if she could.

He had to choose life. She couldn't choose it for him. But she *could* choose it for herself, and that meant not going after him.

"Yes, ma'am." This time he did leave, Mrs. Moretti following without offering any words. But she gave Amelia a little nod that *almost* felt like approval.

Amelia would hold on to that as some kind of confirmation she was doing the right thing by not chasing after him.

Something she, sadly, *did* want to do. She knew it was the wrong impulse, but it existed within her nonetheless. So much so that when she passed his bedroom door on her way to handle their guests, she stopped.

Then stepped inside. She looked around, those tears filling her eyes again. She would cry over him again. She wouldn't promise herself not to. But she would not do it this morning when she had work to do.

Before she turned to leave, she noted that his bag sat on the chair in the corner. He hadn't taken it with him, but he had taken her car.

Perhaps he wanted her to chase after him.

"He'll be sorely disappointed," she announced firmly to the empty room.

And still, she did not leave. She stared at the bag. The bag that clearly had next to nothing in it. What had he brought with him?

It was none of her business, of course. But what did she care about his privacy right now? He'd run away from her love. Why couldn't she poke through his things?

Okay, she was reaching, but she didn't care. Her choice. Her consequences. She marched over to the chair, pulled the zipper with more force than necessary. Inside was something wrapped in a soft cloth. Heavy and square. She hesitated, then leaned in to the anger that had led her here.

She jerked it out of the bag, then unwrapped it.

It was a picture frame. Inside, was a Christmas-themed portrait of the Follieros. Aurora couldn't have been more than four, Diego a tall and handsome teen. She flipped over the picture, surprised to see her father's handwriting on a little note taped to the back.

May they always be with you.
Bartolo

Because this was his family. His castello. His responsibility.

Not hers.

And even though her heart broke for him and all he was turning away from, she knew she had to do what she'd claimed she was going to.

She made her choice. She'd deal with her consequences. She was done with the Follieros. She had stayed on as some kind of keeper of Diego for her father, not herself. If she stayed now, it would be for Diego.

Not for Amelia.

So it was her turn to leave. His employ. The castello. She would not wait for him to come around. She would not keep playing house thinking he might.

No, she was going to go live her life.

And Diego Folliero could go to the hell he'd chosen.

CHAPTER SEVENTEEN

"You must wake up, Diego."

Diego did not open his eyes, even as the voice got more insistent.

He was too used to ignoring his mother's proclamations. They were never what he wanted to hear, and she always—

His mother.

His eyes flew open, then crashed closed again at the painful, searing light causing untold agony throughout his body. He threw his arm over his eyes, but the pain the movement caused nearly sent him hurtling back into the blackness.

He was freezing, shivering. Everything hurt, ached, throbbed. He was wet and cold and…outside? What had happened? Where was he? Why had he thought he'd heard…

He blinked his eyes open more carefully this time. It was still blinding because there was nothing but blue sky above him and white snow around him. He managed to turn his head a little to the right.

No, the snow wasn't all white. Next to him, it was rather red.

That couldn't be good.

He looked beyond the stomach-turning stained snow to his car. Amelia's car. Crumpled against the rock face of the mountain. Glass was shattered across the snow, metal twisted, a grisly scene.

And he was alone and bloody in said snow. But...how had he gotten here? He didn't remember anything besides the initial skid of the crash.

He must have...done something to get over here. Even though it was the driver's side that was crushed against the rock.

He had the strangest mist-tinted memory of being... pulled? By light? But there was no one here. Nothing but the mangled car, and his bruised and bloody and potentially broken body.

Well, he must have crawled across to the passenger side, climbed out and then walked a ways before...collapsing here in the snow.

He remembered none of it. Only the crash itself. A strange light and warmth, which didn't make sense. None of this made *sense*.

Certainly not the marks in the snow that were not footprints, but just a long divot, making it look like he'd been dragged from the car. But there were no footprints of whoever had done the dragging, so...

He tried to move into a sitting position, get a better view of everything around him to make sense of things, but that only caused another wave of excruciating torment, so he didn't try to move again.

But you must.

He looked around wildly, wondering why he kept hearing a voice that sounded alarmingly like his mother's. Even as pain throbbed through him, he searched. The world was bright and peaceful now. No heavy snow, no howling winds, no incessant dark.

There was no one around him though. No evidence of anyone. He was just...alone. And likely dying. Completely and utterly alone.

Just as he deserved, he supposed, though that thought felt incredibly wrong instead of right or peaceful. Amelia would be upset. Even if she hated him, this would hurt her, and he'd already caused her so much pain.

So what was a little more?

Now you must find your phone.

It was a male voice this time.

His heart thundered in his chest, making him feel shakier than even the cold was doing. He looked around again, ignoring the way pain was seared into every second of every movement, but he saw nothing but endless white and the evidence of his car crash. How was he hearing voices? His mother's voice.

His father's voice.

I found it.

Aurora's voice.

He was having some sort of psychotic episode. Hearing the voices of the dead all around him. Or maybe he was already dead. Maybe this *was* the end.

Well, what are we supposed to do about it? Aurora's voice demanded. *He's all the way over there.*

Diego had the errant thought to roll over onto his stomach, crawl toward the voices. But they weren't real voices. He was just…delusional from loss of blood. In the throes of death and hallucinating the dead before him.

A soft wind that almost felt warm, a direct contrast to the icy cold enveloping him, drifted over his face. And in that warmth were words.

You have more strength than you give yourself credit for. You always did.

"Bartolo?" his raspy, barely there voice sounded loud in the quiet all around him. What was happening to him?

Well, he was dying. Bleeding out.

He wanted to laugh, but no sound would come out of his body.

You will not leave my daughter alone as I did.

It was a sharp order that made him open his eyes once again. It wasn't real, but he could *feel* the words. The guilt. Guilt and ghost voices. Proof enough it was just some sort of dark, twisted fantasy.

Because why should Bartolo feel guilty for dying when he'd had no say in it? He hadn't crashed that plane. He'd simply gotten on it and waited for Diego. Just as his family had.

For some reason, he remembered Amelia asking him why he hadn't blamed the pilot, when he'd had a choice not to take off. He remembered what she'd said earlier—last night? "Guilt is just a phase of grief, a misguided belief we have some control, but we have *no* control. Not about the end."

It seemed to hit him harder now. The idea that guilt was only grief. Only an attempt at controlling the uncontrollable. He'd rejected it when she'd said it, not because she was wrong, but because…

It hurt. It hurt to have lost them for no damn reason. It felt better for him to be the reason. It felt better to punish himself than grieve that which he could not change. *Ever.*

Come now.

The voices were insistent, some combination of his parents and Bartolo, a clear enough delusion. But insistent.

Diego didn't want to move, but it seemed wrong to ignore the voices that couldn't possibly be around him. He managed to roll over onto his stomach. He tried to push up, but his arms shook with the effort and his vision swam with agony.

Crawl if you must, Bartolo's voice insisted.

Still, Diego saw nothing, but it felt as though… It felt as though someone was there, pushing him.

He managed to get onto his hands and knees, and as the voice that couldn't possibly be an actual voice suggested, he crawled. Toward the sound of an argument that reminded him of the last time he'd seen his family.

Mother and Father chastising Aurora, while she glibly retorted barbs designed to make them madder.

It wasn't his family. It couldn't be. He didn't believe in ghosts or angels, and they were most assuredly dead. He was simply going insane, but that didn't make him stop his crawl. Because if he could find his phone…

And there it was. He could see it a ways off, lying on top of a large piece of shattered car window. Still so far away.

He's never going to make it.

Aurora's harsh words spurred him on, but a few sad attempts to crawl later, he had to admit to himself she was right. He couldn't seem to make his body move forward anymore. His arms shook so hard and eventually just gave out, earning him a face full of snow.

I'm going to do it.

He didn't know what Aurora thought she was going to do—considering she was dead, just a vocal hallucination. He heard voices calling his name insistently even as he sank into the snow.

Mother. Father. Aurora. Bartolo. All insisting he move. But he couldn't. He was fading again. Dimness crept around his vision. The pain was numbing into something else. Was it death?

Maybe. Maybe he'd join the voices all around him. Maybe it was all there was to be done.

All because he'd sought to get away from Amelia's love. It seemed so foolish now, with all this pain swamping him.

Why had he been so determined to run away from what she offered? How had he fooled himself into believing he was saving her, when all he'd done was hurt her?

You always hurt the people you love.

But if he'd stayed, he wouldn't have. He wouldn't be here. If he'd stayed, worked through his fear, found some courage, he wouldn't have hurt her like this. What a waste to realize this now, as he was dying.

Except he realized he hadn't heard any voices in a while.

And he wasn't dead just yet, because what he *did* hear was sirens in the distance.

Amelia had considered calling for a cab since Mondo and his father were busy using the castello cars to get guests to the airport. She had considered having Mondo drive her up to the cabin—where she would *not* go see Diego at all. She'd simply get in her car and *go*.

It was *her* car after all.

But rushing through her decision to leave for good made her feel like she was running away rather than making a careful, informed decision. So she took her time. Made arrangements for the staff. Wrote her letter of resignation, which she would leave with Mondo to deliver to Diego once she was gone.

She waited for the guests to filter out, wished them happy holidays and wonderful New Years with a smile frozen to her face. While Mondo was driving the last couple to the airport, she packed.

When he returned, she'd ask him to take *her* to the airport.

She had not packed everything. Just enough to get her through the first week or two if she stretched things. Once she figured out where she was going, what exactly she was choosing, she would send for her things.

London felt like the best option for a first stop. She had spent her early childhood there with her mother. Maybe there would be bittersweet memories, but she was hardly going to be afraid of that like *some* people were.

She would need to secure a position, but she was a frugal sort and had been carefully tucking away her salary the past two years. Plus she hadn't touched what her father had left her.

She would now. She would finish his journals, use his money, say goodbye. She would not be afraid to say goodbye.

He would always be with her, regardless of what she did or didn't do with the things he'd left behind.

Amelia hefted her bags downstairs and put them by the door so she would be ready when Mondo returned, but before she could decide what to do next, she heard the shout. Concerned, she raced into the kitchen to find the source. Had someone fallen? Was there a fire?

She found Mrs. Moretti in the kitchen, the house's landline phone at her feet. Apparently the sound Amelia had heard was it clattering onto the ground.

Mrs. Moretti looked as white as a ghost.

"Mrs. Moretti. What is it?"

She picked up the phone she'd dropped and put it back in its cradle. "That was a police officer. Mr. Folliero is in the hospital."

For a moment, Amelia could not react. The words would not penetrate in a way that made any sense. Luckily, Mrs. Moretti kept talking.

"There was a car accident. The ambulance brought him in this morning, but they could not identify him right away. They finally did and… And you must go." Mrs. Moretti crossed to her, grabbed her hands and squeezed hard enough to break through the fog of shock. "You must go at once," she insisted.

Go. Go. She was supposed to *go*, not run back to him.

Car accident. Hospital.

"Is he... Will he..."

Mrs. Moretti shook her head, eyes filling with tears. "They will not give me his prognosis. They were looking for next of kin, and he has none. But you... You'll know what to do, Amelia. Won't you?"

Amelia felt like her mind was a scramble, but she'd done this before.

Oh God. The thought of Diego ending up like the rest of the Follieros curdled her stomach.

She pushed the end result of the past out of her mind. She'd been the one to contact Diego, to handle things, back then. She could handle this. She would have to handle this.

There was no one else.

"Yes. Yes, I'll know what to do." But she didn't move, because... "How will I get there?"

Mrs. Moretti threw her hands in the air, hustled over to a closet and then pulled out a purse. She pawed through it before retrieving keys. "Here. You will take my car."

Amelia looked down at the keys Mrs. Moretti shoved into her hand. She knew where the hospital was. And his being at a hospital was a good sign. A positive sign.

Her father and the Follieros had never made it there. So there had to be some semblance of a living body to try to save. Diego had to be alive. He had to...survive.

She didn't have to go be there by his side while he did it, though. Even if he had no one, that was his own choice.

She couldn't accept that though, even if part of her wanted to. Maybe he'd chosen his pain and his guilt and his punishment, but it would be her choice to abandon him now.

A choice made in direct opposition to what *she* wanted. A choice that would remind her too much of the way she hadn't spoken up to her father when he'd left the last time.

She wouldn't beg Diego to love her. She would go on with her plans to leave.

But first, she had to be certain he was alive.

CHAPTER EIGHTEEN

DIEGO FELT HIMSELF swim through a strange, cloudy mist. He did not hear any voices, and that was both pain and comfort. He wasn't hallucinating anymore, but for a brief few moments, it had felt as though his family had returned.

"I suppose it is lucky you have such a hard head."

He almost winced, thinking the ghost voices were gone but now they were back and he'd have to have a psychiatric evaluation to go along with whatever it took to recover from his injuries.

But after a second or two, he realized it was Amelia's voice.

He forced his eyes open, though they were slow to obey. The room was bright, but not as bright as it had been when he was on the side of the road, bleeding and...hallucinating.

Slowly, things focused, and his gaze settled on Amelia. She stood by his bed, dressed in a drab black. But her hair glowed like a halo, and her silver eyes regarded him.

Perfect Amelia. His angel. His hope.

Because her voice was connected with a living, breathing body. She was real and...he had pushed her away. Pushed her love away. And she was still here.

He still did not believe in the voices, but maybe...maybe he was being given some second chance. A chance to see past the grief, release the crutch of guilt and make things right.

He could make things right.

He opened his mouth, but he couldn't seem to make words come out. Not her name. Not *Forgive me*. Not *I love you*. Not *I swear to God, I heard our families' voices*.

"Shh," she said, moving closer to the bed. "There will be time to talk yet. The doctors are feeling positive about your chance for recovery," she said, pulling a chair next to the bed.

He yearned for her to reach out and touch him, but her hands were carefully folded in her lap. It hurt deep in his chest, while his physical injuries seemed like a dull ache underneath the mists—some kind of painkiller, no doubt. But this pain could not be dulled by any medication.

It was the pain of failure and fear and everything she'd ever accused him of. It was the pain of losing her, when he could have reached out and held her instead.

But there was still time. He had been given time. Somehow.

"I will not scold you for driving into a snowstorm and nearly getting yourself killed," she said primly. "You made your choices, and now you will deal with your consequences." She said this very firmly, but he got the feeling she was speaking more to herself than him. Reminding herself she would not baby him when this was his own fault.

And it was his fault. To run away. To hide away. These were the choices he'd made, and they were *his* fault. But they were not irreversible mistakes. He could learn a damn lesson. He would.

For her.

Because he had been given a second chance. A second chance not allowed his family. Which meant he owed it to them to use it *wisely* instead of wasting it in grief and self-punishment.

This time when he opened his mouth, he managed to rasp out words. Because he had to tell her... "I... I had the strangest dream or hallucination out there. All of them. Their voices."

Her eyebrows beetled together, and she glanced back at the door. He realized his words were garbled, didn't make much sense, and she was worried, likely, he'd suffered some debilitating head injury.

Of course, the words wouldn't make much sense even if he could speak clearly. Hearing voices. But he knew, in this moment, he needed Amelia's take. He had to know what she thought.

He tried again, this time working to make sure he enunciated each word. It was still raspy, but at least she seemed to make it out this time.

"Whose voices?" she asked, still sounding quite concerned.

He should probably not try to explain it to her. It was insanity. But...she had to know, didn't she? She had to assure him it had been a hallucination, or he might actually start to believe it.

Ghosts. Angels. Love from some great beyond.

"My family. Your father. They...spoke to me. Told me to get to my phone. Told me I could not...leave you." He shook his head, but it left him feeling dizzy and nauseous. "A dream. Something pulled me out of the car, but it was just a dream. I had to have done it, of course."

Her eyes got very wide, and she leaned forward. He yearned for her to put her elegant hand on his face, but she didn't. She did speak though.

"The police... I talked to them outside. They cannot reconstruct how you managed to get yourself out of the car. They're looking for whoever might have helped you, but they haven't found them yet."

"I... I had to have crawled out. It was nothing but light that pulled me out, but that was a dream. It doesn't make sense. The voices, they were just...hallucinations to get me through."

"Diego, they also haven't been able to track down who made the emergency call..."

"Ghosts cannot make phone calls, Amelia," he said, sounding very certain...even though he felt not at all certain. "Someone saw it from far away. That's the only reasonable explanation."

But he looked at her gray eyes and knew she did not chalk it up to anything reasonable. To Amelia, some afterlife interference had saved him. A guardian angel. Or angels.

He didn't know if he would ever be able to fully believe that, but what he did believe in this moment was that he had been given a second chance.

One not afforded to his parents, his sister, Bartolo. And he could blame himself for that—it would be so *easy* to blame himself for that—but instead he let it go.

Whatever selfish acts he had done that might have caused damage, he had not been the reason for their deaths.

"Amelia, you must let me... There is so much to discuss."

She looked down at her lap. "Diego, I am not here for any discussion."

"Amelia."

"I'm going to handle the logistics of getting you home, hiring you a nurse, of course, until you are well enough to go to your cabin. I won't leave you in the lurch laid up in a hospital bed, but you should know, I plan to quit the moment I have secured all you need to get by."

"Amelia."

She did not look up. She kept her eyes decidedly downcast. "We both have made our choices. So now we must live with the consequences."

"Am I not allowed to change my choices?"

She so badly wanted to cry. Bury her head in his chest and feel the rise and fall of it and *sob*. He was so injured, but alive.

Alive. That was all that mattered. He had survived. He would survive.

Am I not allowed to change my choices?

Was it weakness to say yes? Weakness to say no?

A tear tripped over and onto her cheek, though she tried desperately to keep them in check. It fell from her cheek onto her hands, clasped in her lap.

"Amelia." His voice was a pained rasp. "Look at me, *tesoro*."

She did not want to. Partly because she hated seeing his face. Swollen and bandaged. There was so much damage to him. He could have so easily lost his life, and *then what*? What would she have done or felt?

It didn't do to deal in *what if*s, though. She knew that all too well.

She blinked back the tears still in her eyes, lifted her face to look at him.

"I know it was a dream," he said, his voice that horrible rasp, but his eyes were luminous and dark. Determined. "A hallucination. It could only have been. But your father's voice… He said I could not leave you like he did."

Anger sparked inside of all this *pain*. "Well, by all means, change your mind over a hallucination." She nearly got up and left right then, but he continued to speak.

"No, *tesoro*, you misunderstand me," he said, a laugh to his voice. A *laugh*. "This voice that sounded as though your father was talking to me was full of guilt, and why should he be guilty? I caused his crash."

"I am done with your guilt, Diego." She got to her feet this time. If she stayed, she might be swayed by him, and she could not let herself be. He'd had some sort of near-death experience, but he still didn't understand.

"Let me finish, Amelia." He reached out, and somehow, even with the hospital bed and machines and *grave* injury, his hand grasped her arm.

"Please. Please stay. Listen. Perhaps I do not deserve it. Perhaps I was always right and there was never any good meant for me—but *please*, let me finish."

He was so desperate, and he was injured.

Am I not allowed to change my choices?

It didn't matter if he changed them, did it? Didn't she have to make her own?

Of course, making her own didn't mean she *had* to leave. She could hear him out. It would be best to hear him out so she'd have no regrets.

So this could be a clean break. So she could have a clean future.

Without him. Your future is without him.

Slowly, she lowered herself back into her chair, holding on to this little mantra. His grip on her arm didn't loosen, and she had to lean forward to make sure he wasn't hurting himself by holding on to her.

"I thought I was dying. Perhaps I was. But these voices were just…just like when they'd been alive. My parents and Aurora bickering. Your father giving me orders I didn't know how to follow. I knew it wasn't real, but it felt so real. I could...*feel* them." He shook his head, pain etched across his bruised features.

Amelia's heart felt bruised too. She desperately wanted to reach out, touch him, skin to skin, some reassurance, but she did not. "Perhaps you were saved by the ghosts of Christmas past." She suggested this both because she couldn't help but believe there'd been *some* kind of otherworldly help he'd received, but also because she expected him to scoff.

Instead, he shook his head, but then it changed into a kind of nod. "Hell, none of it makes sense, so why not?" He closed his eyes for a moment, as if the pain was too much. But when he opened them, his dark eyes were intent and sure. "But the past is gone. And I have not lived in the present. I have lived in guilt because it was easier. I have always taken the easy way, Amelia."

She opened her mouth to defend him, then snapped it shut. She would not defend him to himself. No, he had to make some strides on his own.

"Somewhere along the line, I learned that it hurt less to retreat, to not try, to believe the worst in myself rather than someone else believe the worst in me. Somewhere along the line, hurting *less* became my only goal. And then after they all died, and it felt like my fault, I thought it only made sense to make myself hurt more. And more and more. I never questioned it. I have only understood all or nothing."

Though she'd known this, it was something else to hear him say it, admit it. In a raspy voice, his body in a hospital bed. It made it impossible to deny that this horrible event might have finally gotten through to him.

"You showed me something else," he continued. "Both pain and joy. Forgiveness and responsibility for my own decisions. You showed me there could be all these different things, and they are hard, yes. Which is why I felt as if I could not... I did not think I could handle this dichotomy. I did not want to try."

She had known all this. Had known that his inability to try things stemmed from his own issues. She had tried to tell him all this, but he hadn't listened.

Except, if he was saying it now, he *had* listened. It had just taken time—and maybe a horrible car accident—to get through to him.

"I woke up to their voices. I thought I was going to die. Which I thought may be my due, but I did not want to leave you. Not just because I did not want you to be hurt, but because we had never had a chance. And this was my fault, all my fault, but instead of guilt and pain, I want to *change*. To work."

Her breath caught in her throat. Unable to stop the tears that fell now as he said the rest, his gaze intense and direct, his hand still clutching her wrist.

"None of it matters. The voices, being saved, if you cannot forgive me and bear with me as I try to...heal. I want to...live again. In love this time. Not in penance."

Amelia's chest felt as though it had been cleaved in two, but inside that pain was a warm, beating heart that loved him. And that hadn't changed with rejection. She could not erase the fact she loved him.

"I love you, Amelia. I do not deserve you, but I will work to. I cannot change my past, my choices, my consequences, but you have showed me I can make new choices. I would like to. With you. If you'd let me."

Amelia could not find words at first. Her eyes were full of tears, her throat tight with them.

Now it was her turn to make a choice, and the only one she wanted to make was him. *Them.*

But what if...

She frowned at the sound of a bell, which sounded like the one on the tree at the castello that sometimes tinkled when she didn't think it should. She looked around the room but saw no evidence of any bell.

Her gaze fell back to Diego. There was a knowing in his eyes, and a warmth around the both of them.

Was it a ghost? A sign? Just a trick of sound and light?

She supposed it didn't matter.

She had lost her mother and her father far too young, with no second chances. How could she deny a second chance with love when she had it?

"We both have some work to do, *caro*, but I love you, Diego. A good Christmas present foundation to build our Christmas future on."

His mouth curved ever so slightly, his eyes fluttering closed, clearly exhausted. "I suppose we shall have the ghosts for each."

EPILOGUE

AT THE NEXT Christmas Ball, guests were in for a treat. They were invited to a wedding.

Diego had never done a thing in his life to deserve this moment, but he liked to think that the work he'd done over the past year—on himself, to love Amelia—at least meant he had earned some piece of it.

It had not been easy to work through his grief and his guilt, and heal from his physical injuries as well. He and Amelia had gone through their fights, their low points, but love had always brought them back to each other to take the next step forward.

And he would spend the rest of his life earning this happiness, Amelia's love, in the same way. He had promised himself, and his ghosts, that. Now he would promise her.

He stood in the ballroom in his wedding finery, next to the grand Christmas tree they'd decorated together. Their family attended via pictures scattered about the room, and perhaps the warmth that settled there next to him.

Amelia looked like a Christmas angel in her white dress, her bouquet a cascading delight of evergreen and bright red berries and bows. The smile she beamed his way from the end of the aisle was all the Christmas magic he would ever need.

The sound of a bell tinkling drifted over him—as if to

remind him he had been the recipient of *plenty* of Christmas magic, and he could not disagree.

That bell's little song always seemed to offer a little punctuation to a moment. Diego could have written it off, but what was the harm in thinking that the bell was a sign from those he'd lost that they were watching?

Amelia thought none, so he agreed, and he was happier for it. More blessed for the belief that no love was really lost, only rearranged into something else.

Like the marriage he was about to begin.

She met him at the end of the aisle, beautiful and perfect and his. They listened to the priest and repeated their vows to each other.

Diego promised to love, cherish and protect, just as Amelia did the same to him. When they were invited to mark the promise with a kiss, the bell tinkled again from deep inside the tree, impossibly loud, considering nothing had disturbed the area around it.

A rousing punctuation mark to the perfect moment. A promise that love never really died.

And when their first child was born some nine months later, they named her Belle Aurora. Her sister, Noelle Joy. Their boy, Emmanuel Bartolo. They threw a Christmas Ball every year and invited only those who brought joy and warmth to the occasion.

They raised their children in the memory of the family they'd lost, with stories of bells that marked important moments, ghost voices who saved lives, but most of all with the deep, abiding love they'd learned to give each other through loss, penance and finding the belief in joy all over again.

* * * * *

MILLS & BOON®

Coming next month

BUSINESS BETWEEN ENEMIES
Louise Fuller

My heart feels like a dead weight inside my chest.

I stare at the man standing with his back to me beside the window, panic slipping and sliding over my skin like suntan oil.

Only it's not just panic. It's something I can't, won't name, that flickers down my spine and over my skin, pulling everything so tight that it's suddenly hard to catch my breath. And I hate that even now he can do this to me. That he can make me shake, and on the inside too, before I even see his face.

My stomach clenches and unclenches, and my heart starts to pound painfully hard, and I can't stop either happening. This is his doing. Just being near him does things to my body, things I can't control. But I need to control them.

'What's he doing here?' I say hoarsely. Although I don't know why I ask that question, because I know the answer. But I can't accept it until I hear it said out loud.

'Mr. Valetti is the new co-CEO.'

Continue reading

BUSINESS BETWEEN ENEMIES
Louise Fuller

Available next month
millsandboon.co.uk

Copyright ©2025 Louise Fuller

COMING SOON!

We really hope you enjoyed reading this book. If you're looking for more romance be sure to head to the shops when new books are available on

Thursday 23rd October

To see which titles are coming soon, please visit
millsandboon.co.uk/nextmonth

MILLS & BOON

MILLS & BOON TRUE LOVE IS HAVING A MAKEOVER!

Introducing

Love Always

Marrying a Royal
Nina Milne
Suzanne Merchant
2 BOOKS IN ONE

Summer with the Billionaire
Rachael Stewart
Justine Lewis
2 BOOKS IN ONE

Swoon-worthy romances, where love takes centre stage. Same heartwarming stories, stylish new look!

Look out for our brand new look
OUT NOW
MILLS & BOON

FOUR BRAND NEW BOOKS FROM
MILLS & BOON MODERN

Indulge in desire, drama, and breathtaking romance – where passion knows no bounds!

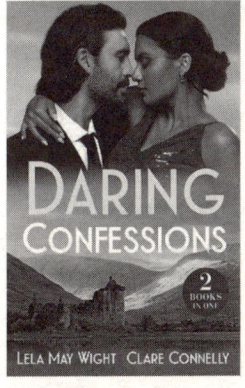

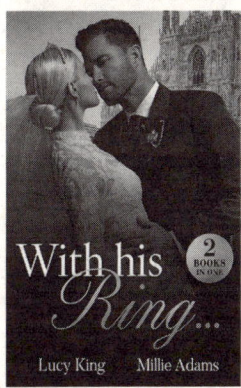

Demand from a Greek — Lynne Graham & Jackie Ashenden

Crave Me — Michelle Smart & Lorraine Hall

Daring Confessions — Lela May Wight & Clare Connelly

With his Ring... — Lucy King & Millie Adams

OUT NOW

Eight Modern stories published every month, find them all at:

millsandboon.co.uk

afterglow BOOKS

Afterglow Books is a trend-led, trope-filled list of books with diverse, authentic and relatable characters, a wide array of voices and representations, plus real world trials and tribulations. Featuring all the tropes you could possibly want (think small-town settings, fake relationships, grumpy vs sunshine, enemies to lovers) and all with a generous dose of spice in every story.

@millsandboonuk
@millsandboonuk
afterglowbooks.co.uk
#AfterglowBooks

For all the latest book news, exclusive content and giveaways scan the QR code below to sign up to the Afterglow newsletter:

SCAN ME

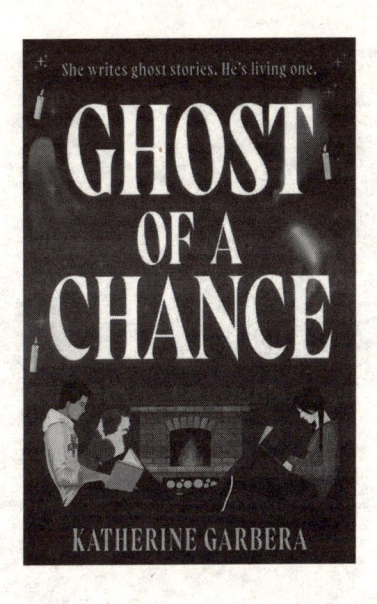

afterglow BOOKS

GHOST OF A CHANCE

She writes ghost stories. He's living one.

KATHERINE GARBERA

- 🛏 One night
- 💕 Second chance
- 🎭 Secret identity

OUT NOW

To discover more visit:
Afterglowbooks.co.uk

OUT NOW!

THE TYCOON'S AFFAIR COLLECTION

BUSINESS WITH PLEASURE

MAYA BLAKE

Available at
millsandboon.co.uk

MILLS & BOON

OUT NOW!

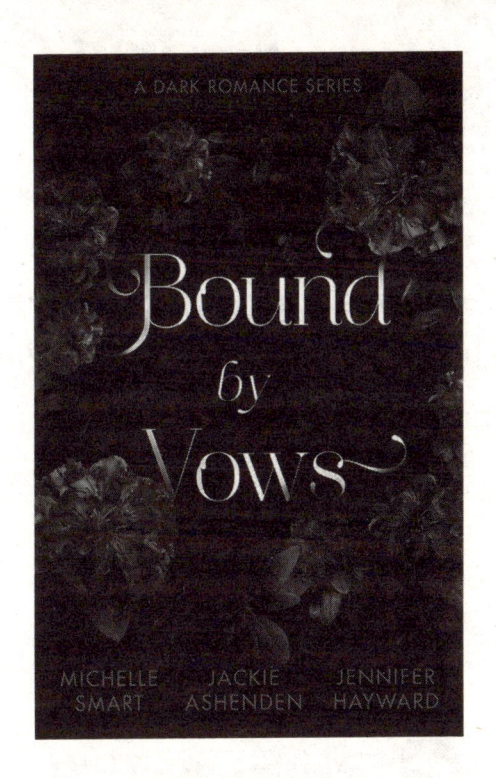

A DARK ROMANCE SERIES

Bound by Vows

MICHELLE SMART   **JACKIE ASHENDEN**   **JENNIFER HAYWARD**

Available at
millsandboon.co.uk

MILLS & BOON

LET'S TALK
Romance

For exclusive extracts, competitions and special offers, find us online:

- **f** MillsandBoon
- **X** @MillsandBoon
- **◉** @MillsandBoonUK
- **♪** @MillsandBoonUK

Get in touch on 01413 063 232

For all the latest titles coming soon, visit
millsandboon.co.uk/nextmonth